James William Mitchell (1926–2002) was born in County Durham into what he described as "cheerful poverty" in the year of the General Strike, the son of a trade union activist father who went on to became Mayor of South Shields. After graduating from Oxford and qualifying as a teacher, he sampled a number of careers before finding his true vocation as a writer. His first novel was published in 1957 and over 30 more followed under his own name and the pen-names James Munro and Patrick O'McGuire. His greatest success though, came as a writer for television. After contributing scripts to series such as The Avengers *and* The Troubleshooters, *he created the legendary anti-hero Callan in the television play* A Magnum for Schneider *and the character went on to feature in the eponymous television series (1967–72) and film, portrayed by Edward Woodward. Mitchell was credited with scriptwriting 30 episodes of the iconic television series, as well as five 'Callan' novels and a long-running series of short stories, first published in the* Sunday Express *between 1973 and 1976, many of which were syndicated to newspapers in Malaysia and Australia. James Mitchell went on to find even more success with the hit BBC drama series* When the Boat Comes In, *set in his native north-east.*

Also available from Ostara Publishing
by James Mitchell

A Magnum for Schneider

Russian Roulette

Death and Bright Water

*

The Innocent Bystanders

Callan Uncovered

by

JAMES MITCHELL

Ostara Publishing

Ostara Publishing 2014

Hardback Edition ISBN 9781909619135
Paperback Edition ISBN 9781909619142

A CIP reference is available from the British Library

Printed and Bound in the United Kingdom

Ostara Publishing
13 King Coel Road
Colchester
CO3 9AG
www.ostarapublishing.co.uk

Contents

Editor's Preface

Uncovering Callan

The *Top Notch Thrillers* imprint of Ostara Publishing is dedicated to reviving and reissuing Great British thrillers which do not deserve to be forgotten, which means that as series editor I get the chance to publish some of the fantastic books I grew up with in the 1960's and 1970's. To my amazement I discovered that the 'Callan' novels of James Mitchell had been out of print for many years, yet surely Callan – that heroic yet tragic character – could not have slipped from memory, could he?

Of course he hadn't – iconic figures don't get forgotten. All the 1967–1972 television episodes of *Callan* – a true television drama phenomenon in its day – and the 1974 film, starring Edward Woodward, had become available on DVD and there was plenty of activity among fans on the internet to convince me that candles were still being held for David Callan. In fact it was through a fan website I learned that author James Mitchell had written a series of Callan short stories for the *Sunday Express* in the 1970's. Some internet sources said there were 9 stories, others that there were 14. In the end, I discovered 24 stories written between 1973 and 1976 plus an earlier one from the *TV Times* in 1967, shortly after Callan made his debut in *A Magnum For Schneider*.

It was while working with James Mitchell's son Peter on the reissue of the first three Callan novels, that the idea of publishing this anthology took shape. It would be the first time the Callan stories had been collected and published in book form and the first time most of them had been seen for forty years. Peter Mitchell mentioned that he had found, in his father's papers, a treatment for an episode of *Callan* and a complete script for an episode – *Goodbye Mary Lee* – which had never been made. The treatment, the script and those 25 stories have, after many months of research, finally coalesced into *Callan Uncovered*.

This could not have been done without the help and support of Peter Mitchell (who came up with the title), Lisa Kenny and all the News Reference Team at the British Library, and those dedicated Callan fans (who really should be honorary members of the 'Section'): Robert Fairclough*, David Rice, Darren Schroeder and, in America, Randall Masteller.

In some of the short stories, portions of text had to be salvaged and reconstituted from far-from-perfect or damaged archive material. Any mistakes are the fault of the editor.

Mike Ripley,
Colchester, August 2014.

{**The Callan File:The Definitive Companion to the Classic Spy Franchise* by Robert Fairclough and Mike Kenwood will be published in 2015 by Miwk Publishing.}

Introduction by Peter Mitchell

I first met David Callan at Nicosia Airport. He was leaning in nonchalant ease against a mock marble pillar but his glinting eyes spotted us as soon as as we had negotiated passport control. The arrivals lounge bustled: smelled of sweat and travel. In contrast, Callan looked cool in floppy hat, washed out T shirt and shorts.

Customs had been tricky. Armed guards had looked on us with suspicion born of experience but nevertheless they let us through with the package – the package that was for him and him alone.Callanadvanceed towards us, eyes fixed; oblivious to the surrounding hubbub. I was new to this: a raw recruit. Maybe that was why I was chosen to be the mule, the patsy. After all being just 13, I was in no position to argue. Nevertheless it was mission accomplished. I'd carried his Lamb and Lady's Finger Madras from Heathrow to Cyprus.

That was 1973 and Mr Callan, or rather Edward Woodward, had kindly invited my Dad and his family for a three-week holiday at his spectacular villa perched high in the hills above Kyrenia. I had a special piece of hand luggage on that trip. Woodward adored hot, spicy curries and as a 'thank you' for his hospitality, my Anglo-Indian Step Mum had cooked him one of her speciality dishes. It had been frozen prior to our departure and was now showing serious signs of wear and tear after the customs officers had stabbed it repeatedly with a bayonet to ensure there was nothing more dangerous than chilli inside.

Woodward was by now a big star in the UK and, in a modest way my Dad had contributed to that celebrity. As the creator and writer of the Thames TV series, *Callan*, he played a part in launching the television career of this extraordinarily talented actor. They became friends and enjoyed working together, talking together and eating my Step Mother Delia's curries together. My father always said that as a writer for television he'd been blessed with his leading actors – James Bolam as the mercurial Jack Ford in *When The Boat Comes In* and Teddy Woodward as Callan. A writer can paint a picture of a character but an actor breathes life into it and gives it that third dimension. The series had been a tremendous success on British television since it first hit the screens for ABC in 1967 and Woodward had become a household name playing the smouldering anti-hero with an exceptional talent for killing people and a deep-seated antipathy towards authority. This was during the Cold War of course, when there were reds under the bed and the threat of nuclear war was neither real nor imagined – always brooding somewhere just south of consciousness. Callan was no James Bond. A simple, working class man, he lived alone in a grubby one-bedroomed flat in West London. His only friend, Lonely, was a petty recidivist with the unfortunate habit of emitting horrendous body odour whenever he was frightened – which was often. So Callan was pretty unfortunate really. His life was sordid, his work was sordid even his cowardly friend was sordid. Nevertheless he was a hit and besides the TV series there was a feature length movie, five novels and a series of short stories that were first published in the *Sunday Express*.Not bad for an insubordinate ex-con whose fictional life contrasted so sharply with that of the man who played him.

The luxury holiday villa was augmented by two cars and a boat moored in the colonially picturesque Kyrenia harbour. Not that the Edward Woodward I knew then was an ostentatious man. He wasn't at all. I remember him as being kind and funny and generous. His soft spot was his boat: a modest craft of 20ft or so with an awning to shield its passengers from the Eastern Mediterranean's summer sun. That boat became the focus of the holiday and now, more than four decades on, I clearly recall the trips offshore to quiet bays where we would drop anchor, swim and snorkel, eat and drink. I suppose if they haven't left me by now, those daily cruises will be forever my abiding memory... along with one other thing. That was Woodward's inability to master my Geordie accent to his own satisfaction. Despite countless efforts to mimic my twang, he invariably drifted off into a Scottish....or a Welsh....or even a rather eccentric West Indian. It was a needless cause of irritation to him but it said a lot about the man as an artiste and as a professional.

It was that meticulous attention to detail that my Dad recognised as his good fortune in his leading man. Callan was such an internalised character with so much felt and so little said – no easy feat for a television actor. Worse still, the small screen had come under close scrutiny from the Mary Whitehouse lobby and Callan was right in the firing line with accusations of gratuitous violence and sliding moral standards. Comparatively tame by contemporary standards, there were countless complaints but the show had its allies too, counting among its millions of fans the Prime Minister of the day, Harold Wilson. You could be forgiven for thinking that this might have said something about its authenticity. I really don't know for sure but as far as the spying game was concerned, I think my Dad was simply taking a shot in the dark.

The series *Callan* began life as a one-off production for Armchair Theatre entitled *A Magnum For Schneider* in 1966. In the orginal treatment for that play my Dad explored the character of his protagonist:

'Espionage is about people. Essentially, it is about one man, and the effect he has on others. He is a man alone: the nature of his trade isolates him from his kind. He can never hope for lasting human contacts: abiding love, enduring friendship. His weapons are treachery, corruption, betrayal, and yet he himself must be immune from these. His weapons are theft, blackmail, murder. The tools of the trade are the knife, the gun and an icy courage no other man possesses. He is the Destroyer. His ordinariness is his protection. He is a highly-skilled cracksman, a master of unarmed combat, a dead-shot with a pistol. He is a killer. But he looks so much like everybody else, he is invisible. It is only when you know him well that you realize his strength, his menace – and his charm.'

So where did James William Mitchell discover the secrets of this murky world and the rather unsavoury traits of those who inhabited it? Looking back on his life there is nothing much to indicate that any of this fictitious world was born out of real-life experience. Like so much else, I think he simply made it up.

Dad was born in the grimy industrial town of South Shields in March 1926 – the year of the General Strike. His father, a shipyard fitter by trade and an active trade unionist, was a leading light in the regional Labour Party and he was an Alderman of the town council. Baby James was something of a surprise, arriving rather late in his parents' marriage – in fact his only sibling, my Auntie Mina, was 15 years older than him. I never met my grandparents on the my father's side – they both passed away before I was born – but family understanding has it that he was more or less brought up by his sister rather than his Mum. They certainly enjoyed a close bond throughout their lives.

People who knew my father as an adult might say he was something of an intellectual and an academic. In fact (and this is something I never knew until after he passed away) he failed his 11-plus and got into grammar school at the second attempt aged 13. He reminisced fondly about his days at Oxford University where he went to study English Literature after the Second World War. That part was certainly true (although I'm told it was relatively easy to get in at that particular time). He did attend St Edmund Hall where he graduated with a rather dubious Third Class degree that in those days apparently you could upgrade to an MA for the princely sum of 10 guineas – a bargain that he readily accepted. A tall, gangly young man with thick-rimmed spectacles, he made his way back home to the North East where he met and married my Mum and began a career as a teacher.

In his spare time he started to write. His favourite authors, he always said, were Dickens and Raymond Chandler. If you want to get an insight into the forebears of David Callan you could do worse than pick up a copy of *Farewell My Lovely*. Take a closer look at Philip Marlowe: morally upright, lover of poetry, devotee of chess. Chandler himself explained that he named his hard-drinking character after Marlowe House to which he belonged during his time at Dulwich College. The house took its name from the Elizabethan writer Christopher Marlowe – another heavy drinker and philosophy student who...secretly worked for the Government. Well, they say there's no such thing as a new idea and if you're going to build on the foundations of others, make sure you choose the best sites. So now compare and contrast with David Callan: hard-drinking lover of books, expert at wargames, troubled by conscience...secretly works for the Government.

All of this, of course, is pure conjecture. The truth is Dad and I never had the conversation. (And anyway, it's irrelevant. David Callan is peculiarly British in design: there's something about the downtrodden and the underdog that we find irresistibly appealing.)

James's writing career started to take-off in the mid-sixties. By then he had a handful of published novels under his belt and he was now turning his attention to television. He wrote an episode of *Z Cars* and a few scripts for *The Avengers* before he decided to take *A Magnum For Schneider* to *Armchair Theatre*. Of course by then my elder brother and I had come along. The writing was going well enough for Dad to give up teaching altogether and he was spending more and more of his time in London meeting with agents, publishers and producers. The old Wolseley car in the garage had been replaced by a red Jaguar and the young Mitchell family were beginning to plan their first foreign holiday. In retrospect these were the first indications that things were about to change.

Just one year before the first of the *Callan* series was transmitted, Dad fired a Magnum charge of his own and left the family home in South Shields and moved in with his new girlfriend in London's Knightsbridge. They'd met at a book launch party and, in keeping with the best bodice-rippers, it was love at first folio.

In South Shields in 1966 not many people drove Jags or enjoyed foreign holidays; even fewer left their wife and kids and moved to London to live over the brush with a woman named Delia (actually, she was christened Ethel but unsurprisingly ditched that at the first available opportunity). So at a stroke my Dad made the decision that was to cement his career as a professional writer and sentence my brother and I to a rather schizophrenic upbringing split between our home and school in Shields and his flat in London punctuated by numerous train journeys from Newcastle to Kings Cross and back again.

My poor Mum, of course, was devastated and what made that worse was my Dad's growing success. As *Callan* became entrenched in the television schedules, James Mitchell became something of a local hero. In the papers, on the radio – even doing the rounds of the small screen chat shows, it seemed as though my absent Dad gained something of an omni-presence – a constant reminder to her that she had lost the man she loved. Not his fault, of course and these days marriage break-ups are a sadly routine occurrence but Norma never did quite get over it and that makes me sad to this day. Why? Because somewhere deep inside, kids always feel somehow responsible – even big 54-year-old kids.

But of course the move south and my Dad's subsequent success offered a rich and fertile formative opportunity for growing bairns. I lived a life of contrasts. In Shields I had dinner between mid-day and 2pm; in London we dined between 7pm and 8.30pm. At home going out in the evening meant playing football with my mates; in London it meant restaurants or the theatre. From a North Eastern perspective,

I had a posh accent whereas my Dad's London friends had trouble making out a word I was saying.There is no doubt in my mind that my adolescence was slightly troubled as a result but I was left in absolutely no doubt that I was loved by both my parents and that was probably enough – just. On the plus side I could navigate my way around a three-volume wine list before I was 18 years old, I was equally at home on the London Underground as I was on the Economic Bus and, having spent a lot of time in the kitchen with my new-found Step Mother, the exotically-named Delia, I learned the Burmese alphabet and the rudiments of good cooking. So all was not lost by any means.

Dad's friends – most of whom were 'in the business' – were regular dinner guests and they included actors, producers and other writers. Teddy Woodward was among them, so too was Derek Horne, the man who went on to produce the *Callan* movie. The London Mitchells were on the up. The tiny rented flat in Knightsbridge had been traded in for a bigger one in Kensington before that gave way to a luxury, three-bedroomed penthouse apartment in (rather aptly) Marloes Road in W8. These were the golden years. The series was a hit, the movie was in the pipeline, offers were coming from Hollywood and even the *Sunday Express* newspaper was running wonderfully-illustrated Callan short stories.

It was a visit to the 'Black Lubjanka' (the *Express* offices) in Fleet Street that first fired my own love of journalism and prompted me to seek a career down that particular road. I had accompanied my Dad to a meeting with the legendary editor John Junor but it wasn't him who turned my head. After that rather brief encounter we had lunch in the famous Cheshire Cheese pub and overheard two slurring hacks exchanging unprintable gossip over their scotch. That, I thought, is a job made in heaven. And so it turned out.

My Dad, of course was only just hitting his stride. He achieved more success and more acclaim with *When The Boat Comes In* for the BBC, an adaptation of *Confessional* for Granada, more books, more films, more stories. Because in essence, that's exactly what he was – a storyteller and his greatest character invention was probably himself but he is hardly unique in that. Hindsight, they say, is 20:20 vision and in adulthood I learnt that many of the stories about himself that he'd shared with my brother and I growing up were completely fictitious. There was the one about his time as an amateur athlete at Oxford when he'd given Roger Bannister a run for his money. (Even as a young man, Dad smoked so heavily he could hardly make it upstairs on a bus.)

Then there was the time when, as a penniless undergraduate, he'd been given a red hot tip for the National by a Scout at his college which had romped home at 100-1 and funded a three month trip to Spain living like a king. (He borrowed the money off his sister.)

A couple of years later when he was teaching back on Tyneside he told us he'd knocked cold a drunken parent who barged into the classroom of 4B. (My mother picked Dad up from accident and emergency with a black eye and a fat lip.)

When he turned his back on South Shields he was the son of a shipyard worker and pillar of the Labour movement. Fifteen years later he had become a staunch Thatcherite who spent month after month offshore to avoid paying super tax. He was a man of contradictions and his view of himself would never sustain prolonged scrutiny but the discrepancies were in the details and the life itself was, by any standard, extraordinary. Writing took him to Los Angeles for prolonged periods (although I don't think actual films were ever made) and to Australia. He bought a second home in Andalucia and took regular therapeutic holidays in Italy where he smeared his, by now not inconsiderable, body with restorative mud. All the while accompanied by Delia, his constant companion.

She was the undoubted love of his life. A beautiful woman with a dazzling smile and a personality to match, she had been the architect of the career, the networker, the deal maker – the Hunter, if you like. Dad was the hired pen; the heavy drinking, chain smoking, charmer who lived in a world of luxurious illusion. She died suddenly at home. (He told us she had suffered a haemorrhage but the death certificate clearly states she died of a heart attack caused by prolonged alcohol abuse.)

From that moment the walls of his castle simply crumbled. The friends had gone, the deals had gone and the money was starting to run out. There was nothing to keep him in London and so he decided to move back to the North East – you could buy wine in Newcastle just as easily by then and we, for our part could keep an eye on him.

I will always value the time I spent with him but I'm especially grateful for the years we enjoyed towards the end of his life. He wasn't well physically – like his leading men, the hard-drinking and high-living had taken its toll. We spent many a happy afternoon watching test cricket on the television and drinking far too much good, red wine. He wrote the last Callan novel during this period. Not his finest hour but what the Hell?

This collection, however, is another matter altogether. Its publication comes about through the suggestion, dogged persistence and astute detective work of Ostara's Mike Ripley. The result of his labours is vintage James Mitchell gathered together in a single volume for the first time. A dozen or so years after his death, it stands as a fitting tribute to the Golden Years of Callan and a life created by James Mitchell.

Peter Mitchell,
Tyneside, September 2014.

Treatment

Editor's Note: An Outline Treatment is the usual first stage of a script for film or television – a brief summary of the plot, action and characters involved – which is submitted by the writer to the producers. *A Funeral Has Been Arranged and Will Shortly Take Place* was probably written in 1970, but was not developed until it was adapted by the author into the script for *That'll Be the Day*, which was chosen as the opening episode of Series 4 of *Callan* and broadcast on 1st March 1972, starring Edward Woodard as Callan, Russell Hunter as Lonely, Ronald Radd and William Squire as Hunters past and present, along with T.P. McKenna, Julian Glover and Patrick Mower. Found among the papers of the late James Mitchell, the outline for *A Funeral Has Been Arranged* is published here exactly as written by the author. As *Callan* was already an established and phenomenally successful television series, Mitchell had no need to explain his main characters or their 'backstories' to his producers but as the professional he was, writing for commercial television, Mitchell made sure his treatment adopted a clear three-act format.

A Funeral Has Been Arranged and Will Shortly Take Place

Outline for a CALLAN episode

It is announced that Callan is dead, and Hunter is making arrangements for his funeral; the last job before he leaves, promoted to higher things. Liz is in tears. Even Cross and Meres – recently returned from the U.S. – mourn their colleague. Callan went to do a job in East Germany and was killed there – so they believe. A down-and-out's body is substituted for his, but Callan (officially described as a Civil Servant) has died and must be seen to be buried. Security demands it. His obituary appears in a newspaper, and his funeral is arranged...

Lonely, eating fish and chips with his aunty, reads the notice in the paper that is keeping his meal warm. The description of Callan – 'honest, law-abiding, a public servant' – baffles him, but he mourns his friend...

Callan in fact is in the Lubyanka. The Russians got him in East Germany, alive. So far they haven't hurt him too much, but they will...

The funeral takes place; the surviving Hunters, Meres, Cross, Liz – they're all there. Even Lonely arrives, with stolen flowers...

In the Lubyanka his interrogator tells Callan that he is beyond hope. 'Even your own side say you're dead'. He hands Callan the newspaper with the obituary.

* * *

Hunter is about to leave his job when he hears that there is a chance of capturing Zhelkov – Callan's Russian equivalent. He decides to stay on a little longer and sends Meres and Cross to pick Zhelkov up...

In the Lubyanka Callan, still stubborn, refuses to talk but the beatings stop. He is to be exchanged for Zhelkov...

Exchanged, but in good condition. Fattened up, healthy, unmarked. A doctor – Nikich, himself a prisoner – is sent to treat him. He tells Callan about the man who betrayed him and so many others to the KGB. A man called Karsky. With Nikich's devoted help, Callan is at last fit to travel – and Nikich too must journey. To Siberia.

* * *

Zhelkov and Callan meet briefly in a Helsinki hotel. Each exchanges one set of guards for another. Zhelkov leaves with the two KGB men who brought Callan: Callan with Meres and Cross. In the hotel lobby he sees a man identified as Karsky enter the lift, alone. Callan remembers Nikich, who selflessly nursed him back to health.

He insists on leaving Meres and Cross and follows Karsky into the lift, saying he's forgotten his wallet. He comes back down alone, and they leave in a hurry...

Callan has broken the rules and he knows it. In killing Karsky he not only put himself but Meres and Cross at risk. The new Hunter will have a lot to say about that...

Callan goes to seek his own grave. Beside it Lonely stands, mourning his friend. When he sees Callan he faints, and Callan catches him and looks at the headstone: 'David Callan. 1934 – 1972. Deeply mourned.'

'Blimey,' says Callan. 'You can say that again.'

The Stories

Merry Christmas from the Section first published in the *TV Times*, Christmas edition 1967.

Stories first published in the *Sunday Express*:

File on a Deadly Deadshot	(11th March 1973)
File on an Angry Artist	(18th March 1973)
File on a Reckless Rider	(25th March 1973)
File on a Weeping Widow	(1st April 1973)
File on an Angry Actor	(26th May 1974)
File on a Lucky Lady	(2nd June 1974)
File on a Dancing Decoy	(9th June 1974)
File on a Deadly Diary	(6th October 1974)
File on a Classy Club	(13th October 1974)
File on a Fearsome Farm	(20th October 1974)
File on a Careful Cowboy	(27th July 1975)
File on a Doomed Defector	(3rd August 1975)
File on a Pining Poet	(10th August 1975)
File on a Powerful Picador	(17th August 1975)
File on a Difficult Don	(24th August 1975)
File on a Darling Daughter	(1st February 1976)
File on an Awesome Amateur	(8th February 1976)
File on a Joyous Juliet	(15th February 1976)
File on a Mourning Mother	(22nd February 1976)
File on an Angry American	(29th February 1976)
File on a Deadly Don	(15th August 1976)
File on a Tired Traitor	(22nd August 1976)
File on a Harassed Hunter	(29th August 1976)
File on a Beautiful Boxer	(5th September 1976)

Merry Christmas from the Section

Lonely said: "He's still there, Mr Callan."

"Good," said Callan.

"Very restless he is," said Lonely. "Walks about all the time."

It was cold in the street, and Lonely was huddled inside his raincoat, his hands deep in his pockets.

"Anything else, Mr Callan?" he asked.

"No," said Callan. "You can scarper."

The wind lifted a piece of paper from the gutter on to Lonely's legs. He bent down and picked it up. It was wrapping paper. White, with the green and red of holly picking out the words Merry Xmas. Lonely looked at his watch. "Another half hour to go," he said. "Merry Christmas, Mr Callan."

"Merry Christmas."

Callan watched him go. In that bitter cold, Lonely's footsteps should have rung like metal, but he made no sound. Callan looked from the doorway to the window opposite. The curtains were drawn tight, but they had been treated by experts. From a certain angle it was possible to see through them. Callan watched, and the blurred outline of a man got up, drew the curtains closer together.

"So you can be frightened," Callan thought. "You ought to be mate." He turned in the doorway and opened the door with the key Hunter had given him, and went inside, flicked on a pencil torch.

A neat house in a neat street. Christmas tree in the hallway, cards on the living room mantel-piece, on the top of the piano, the sideboard, the TV set. "From Edna and John," "With love from Aunty Glad," "From all at No. 64." The house had no right to be empty at eleven thirty on Christmas Eve, but Hunter had said the occupants would go to visit the wife's father in Birmingham, and Hunter was right. A careful hand had disconnected water, gas, electricity, and the house, in spite of its tree, its paper-chains, its brash, bright cards, was cold and dead. The right house for Callan.

He went upstairs, walking as they had taught him, and no board creaked. The bedroom door was where Hunter had said it would be, and Callan went inside, drew the blinds, flicked on the torch again. There were three small beds in the room, a toy train stacked in a corner, a shelf of children's books, and a row of dolls, headed by a gigantic teddy-bear. The bear had lost half an ear, and its stuffing had slipped. It looked as if it had fought one fight too many. "You and me both son," said Callan.

He switched off the torch and pulled back the curtains, opened the window a foot, and sat down on the floor. The light still shone in the window opposite, but the shadowy figure had gone. "Lying down," Callan thought. "Looking at the ceiling. Waiting. Worrying. He's got a right to worry."

He reached inside his overcoat pocket and took out the box, rectangular, seventeen inches long, three pounds in weight. Callan opened it. Inside was the moulded fibreglass stock of a rifle. Recessed in the stock were the rifle's barrel and action. Callan pulled them out and assembled them, and even in the dark, his hands were sure. The Armalite AR-7 Explorer took shape under his fingers, and he loaded it with the same careful skill. Eight shots twenty-two calibre. A twenty-two bullet doesn't do much unless you put it in the right place. But the right man can kill with it, even firing through a curtain. Even at Christmas.

Callan sighted the Armalite, getting used to its weight once more. Even fully loaded, it weighed less than three pounds. You had to be careful, but if you were, the bullet went where you pointed it. Satisfied, he knelt by the window and looked out. The light was still on. Henderson still wasn't visible.

The cold in the unlit room was intense. Callan blew on his fingers, rubbed them together, over and over. When the time came, his hands had to be good. Killing Henderson was the most important thing he had ever had to do, and he had to do it right.

Henderson was a double agent, the only one in Hunter's section who had ever gone double. But one was enough. He had cost the department seven lives: Barber and Roberts in East Berlin; Pollard in Moscow; McKay and Peters in Warsaw; Lipyatt in Prague; Hedges in Leningrad. Callan had trained Hedges, and liked him. From what Hunter had said, Hedges hadn't died easy. The KGB had wanted the answers to many questions, and no doubt Hedges had given them some—before he died. With time and patience any man could be broken, even Hedges . . . Callan felt cold again, and crouched inside his coat. "Come on Henderson, you bastard," he thought. "Come on."

Nothing happened. Maybe Henderson had found out about the curtain. Maybe he was lying safe out of the line of fire, laughing at the man he knew must be waiting for him, shivering in the cold. Maybe he'd told his friends.

Henderson had good friends, the best. KGB executives. They guarded Henderson as if he were Lenin's tomb, even in London. There were three of them with him now.

His friends had given Henderson a Christmas present. A Russian passport. And a one way ticket to Moscow on a Tupolev jet from Paris. They didn't want their wonderboy picked up at London Airport. But first they had to get him to Paris. So they'd moved him out of the embassy in Millionaires' Row, dumped him down here in the suburbs, and waited for the pick-up. They would have got away with it too, if Hunter hadn't wanted Henderson so badly. He'd had every man watching and waiting, at the embassy, at the staging-posts like this one across the street. And in the end, he'd found out where Henderson was going, and sent for Callan, and Callan had sent for Lonely. No one could watch a house like Lonely, and still not be seen.

It had been Meres' job to get rid of the people in the house where Callan was waiting, and he'd done a good job, Callan admitted. Toby could be as smooth as a billiard ball when he had to. He'd gone there representing a TV pro¬gramme, asking them what their Christmas wish was, and they'd wished for a new car to see the in-laws up in Brum. They'd got a Cortina, and a real interview with microphone and camera. The nits would watch for ever to see themselves on the box, though. That interview was for Hunter's files. They'd managed a few shots of the house across the street, and one of the window, with a KGB man watching and worrying. Oh yes, Toby had done very nicely.

And so had Hunter. Now it was up to Callan. He looked again at the window, and still there was nothing. On either side, the lights were going out. Stockings were filled now, parties wrapping up. This was a mum's and dad's street, and the mums and dads were saving their strength for tomorrow's booze-up and indigestion. Callan looked at the luminous dial of his watch. Twelve-seventeen. "Merry Christmas Callan," he said. There was nobody else to wish it for.

He thought about the briefing in Hunter's office. "You'll get him," Hunter had said, and this time he'd neither argued nor pleaded. He knew that Callan wanted Henderson dead as much as he did. Callan had sent Lonely to watch, and practised with the Armalite until he was sure, thinking of nothing but the job, not even of Hedges.

There'd be time for that when Henderson was dead.

The light across the street went out. Callan swore, softly and com¬prehensively. Hunter had been so sure that Henderson wouldn't sleep, not with the pick-up due at two.

Callan faced the fact that he would now have to kill Henderson when the pick-up was made. Inside his mind, fear screamed its hysteria, but his body was motionless, his hands steady. He was afraid. That was fact. That he must kill Henderson was also a fact. One fact did not cancel out the other. He waited . . .

At twelve-thirty the band came down the street. Three cornets, two trombones, a tuba, a bass drum. They were tiring now, but they still marched in step, their rendering of "While Shepherds Watched" uncertain but brave, as the drum nailed them to the beat.

They marched to the corner of the street, where the lights still blazed, formed a circle, and began to play "We Three Kings", "God Rest Ye Merry Gentlemen", "In the Deep Mid-Winter", the music floating softly up the street on the cold air over the sound of voices calling greetings, the rattle of silver in a collection box. Callan thought of his boyhood, and the last Christmas before his parents were killed by a V2, but his eyes never left the window. It was during the last bars of "The Holly and The Ivy" that the light went on. Callan brought the Armalite to his shoulder, and waited as the blurred figure grew larger and larger, then —incredibly—drew back the curtains. The band began to play "Silent Night" to the drum's inescaping 6/8 thumping, and Henderson traitor, betrayer, leaned out of the window to enjoy for the last time the sentimental melancholy of an English Christmas, looking up the street to the lamps winking on gleaming, battered brass. Behind him a KGB man moved into the room, three seconds too late. A lifetime too late.

Callan's first shot went through Henderson's ear, cut through to the brain. The second hit him in the heart. With frantic speed Callan raced to the door, his hands dismantling the Armalite as he went. Barrel out. Action out. Snap them into the butt. Put the butt in the box. And all the time running. Downstairs, to the kitchen, to the back door, while the band still played, having drowned out the crack of the Armalite. Only the KGB knew Henderson was dead.

In the lane behind the house a post office van was waiting. Its driver took Callan home and no¬body noticed. At Christmas time a post office van is the most anonymous vehicle in the world. Callan got out without a word, leaving the Armalite in the van. He walked up to his flat, thinking of Henderson.

Henderson had died because he was sentimental. That was his weakness. Every agent had a weakness, and that weakness was the reason why they died. Callan wondered how much longer he had to live, and Christmas had never seemed further away.

By the door of his flat he took out the Noguchi Magnum from its shoulder holster, held it flat by his side, then opened the door left-handed, switched on the light and went in. There was nobody there. He shut the door, and leaned against it, shaking. He spotted it at once. A parcel on the table. A parcel wrapped in paper decorated with holly. Slowly, carefully, he unwrapped it. Inside the paper was a bottle of whisky. Callan put it down and looked at the paper. It was dirty, as if it had been blown along a gutter. Then he lifted it to his nose, sniffed at it. The paper smelled.

File on a Deadly Deadshot

"Like it?" Hunter asked.

Callan weighed the shotgun in his hands, then swung it to his shoulder. Feel and balance were so perfect that the weapon handled like an extension of his own body. He lowered it then, and looked at the polished wood of the stock, the dull-gleaming barrels.

"It's beautiful," he said.

"I think we can allow the word," Hunter said. "It's a Purdy. One of a matched pair. They were made for my father. Ever fire one?"

"I've fired shotguns,' said Callan. "But not one of these."

"They're the same as any other," Hunter said, "except that they're a bit more accurate than most. Let's see what you can do."

They walked down the track that led to the clay pigeon stand, and Callan looked around for the servant who would operate it. There was none.

"This shooting club is for gentlemen," said Hunter, "and gentlemen very often miss. You don't. I should hate it to be known that I brought a professional here." He climbed into the seat. "When you're ready."

Callan loaded both barrels, and looked up, letting his eyes grow accustomed to the clear, cold autumn light, breathing slowly and evenly, letting his whole body adjust to the rhythm he would need if his shooting were to live up to Hunter's expectations.

"*Pull,*" he said.

The clay pigeon came up low and fast, travelling across the sun. Callan fired, and the gun did precisely what he expected: the clay-pigeon disintegrated.

"*Pull.*"

Another one, climbing this time, moving against the darkness of distant trees; but again the gun obeyed him to the letter, and the disc was shattered. And so it went on; over and over. The speeding, difficult target never quite fast enough to escape the gun's perfection. When at last Hunter called a halt. Callan looked at the shotgun with something like awe.

"It's incredible," he said.

"You both are," said Hunter. "Even my father—" He broke off. His father was dead, and he himself had no sons. That was a bitterness he could not share with Callan.

Callan said: "You want me to use this thing for a job?"

It was hard to believe that Hunter would permit any fragment of his personal life to intrude into his profession.

"I do," said Hunter. "I know you find the fact surprising, but once I've explained the thing to you I think you'll understand why. We'll talk over lunch at my club."

Callan reacted to that one; couldn't help it. Hunter never took operatives to lunch at his club.

"I have to be sure that your manners are as good as your shooting," said Hunter.

Game soup, steak and kidney pie, a peach, then cheese, and to drink, claret that Hunter had insisted Callan choose.

"Not quite as good as your shooting," Hunter said, "but then nothing could be. All the same—I think you'll pass."

"Pass where?" said Callan. "All you've told me so far is that I'll be living with the nobs for a bit."

"Whitmore Hall," said Hunter. "That's Lord Marsden's estate in Northumberland. You're going there to shoot."

"Who?" said Callan.

Hunter grimaced. Callan's forthrightness was as displeasing as his sense of humour. When he combined the two he was insupportable.

"Lord Marsden is something of a marksman," he said. "He is also somewhat impecunious. He has formed the habit of inviting other marksmen to shoot there at this time of year on a competitive basis—"

"Winner take all?"

"Almost all," said Hunter. "Marsden charges an entrance fee to cover hospitality."

"How much?"

"Five hundred pounds."

Callan whistled.

"He must be very hospitable," he said.

"He is," said Hunter. "That's why he so often wins." He sipped at his claret. "Not a bad wine, incidentally. You chose quite well."

Callan waited, as Hunter sipped again. "Baumer will be there," Hunter said. "He's quite a fair shot I believe."

"Baumer?"

"Textiles, clothing, banking, construction," said Hunter. "Forty or fifty million pounds' worth. Jewish — and very pro-Israel. Six months ago he built Israel a series of rocket-launching pads — and refused payment. An Arab terrorist society has sentenced him to death."

"You're sending me to Northumberland to shoot an Arab with a Purdy shotgun?"

"No," said Hunter. "The Arabs have put Baumer out to contract — according to Israeli Intelligence, which is usually very reliable."

"Shin Beth knows what it's doing all right," said Callan.

"I agree," said Hunter.

"So why don't you let them handle it?"

"Nobody handles anything here except me," said Hunter. "Besides — if you save Baumer's life Shin Beth will owe me a favour."

"So will Baumer."

To Hunter, jokes were meaningless: he ignored them.

"He is to die at Whitmore Hall," said Hunter. "A shooting accident."

"Who's going to commit the accident?"

"I don't know," said Hunter. "That's why I'm sending you."

"Look, Hunter," said Callan, "nobody can stop an assassin. You know that."

"This man is a professional," Hunter said. "He has to be—if it's a contract. That gives you rather more scope."

"It also means he'll be a better shot."

"All Marsden's guests are excellent shots," said Hunter. "I told you. Many of them are well-born or well-connected—or both. Be discreet."

Callan said: "I can't make any promises. ... You really don't know who's got the contract?"

"I don't *know*," said Hunter. "I don't even suspect. But now and again I have nightmares."

"About who?"

"My dreams are my own," Hunter said. "Besides I want you to go there with an open mind. I could be wrong, you know, David. The possibility is remote, but it is a possibility."

"When do I go?" Callan asked.

"On Friday," Hunter said. "Take a valet with you."

"A *valet*?"

"It's expected," Hunter said. "You don't wish to appear eccentric."

"No, indeed," said Callan, and smiled. "Is Meres available?"

"Toby has a job at the moment. But several of the others are free."

"I'll see," said Callan.

"In every other respect you have a free hand," said Hunter. "Your cover story's in the file at headquarters."

"How's the file labelled?" Callan asked. "I mean if you don't know who the feller is——"

"It's labelled Deadshot," said Hunter, "appropriately enough."

He lifted the wine-bottle, discovered that it was empty, and sighed.

"I shan't object to an accident," he said, "provided that it happens to the right person."

"Me?" said Lonely, "A valley?"

"You could do it on your head," said Callan.

"It's the only way I bloody could do it," said Lonely, and gulped at his beer. "Mr Callan I can't even talk proper."

"You don't have to," said Callan. "You used to be my batman. You saved my life during the war."

"What war, Mr Callan?"

"Any bloody war," said Callan. "Look—do you want a hundred nicker or don't you?"

"But—but what would I have to do?"

"Press my pants," said Callan.

"I could do that," said Lonely. "I always get laundry duty when I do bird."

"There you are then."

"But—what I mean—what d'you want a valley for?"

"To make me look posh," said Callan. "So mind you polish my shoes properly."

They drove north in a Bentley that Hunter had provided: a new and ostentatious Bentley that proclaimed the newness of its owner's fortune, as did the brand new and too geary clothes in the over-elaborate suitcase. For Callan was not a gentleman. He was a nouveau-riche adventurer who'd made a slightly dodgy fortune in Malaya, got out just in time and devoted his retirement to shooting. Of all the things he took with him only the Purdys held any sense of tradition — and according to his story he'd won them in a poker game in Kuala Lumpur. Callan moved into the outside lane of the motorway, and risked a glance at Lonely, laboriously thumbing his way through a book of household hints.

"I never knew that," said Lonely. "Talcum powder for grease-stains. Handy that is."

"Think you can handle it?"

"Do me best," said Lonely. His voice was uncertain.

"And the other little job?"

"Piece of cake," said Lonely. This time his voice held no doubts at all.

They left the motorway, fretted and fumed through Newcastle, to a wild and desolate sea-coast, before Callan turned the great car west towards empty moorland, mile after mile of it, and Lonely looked out of the car window and shuddered.

"Blimey," he said. "Ain't they never heard of people up here?"

But then the car reached the brow of a hill, and looking down they could see a great house of grey stone set in a formal garden flanked with woodland.

"You never told me we was going to stay in a palace," Lonely said.

"Stick with me kid," said Callan. "Nothing but the best for my mates."

"That's as maybe," said Lonely, "but I'm the one what eats in the servants' hall."

Lord Marsden had five guests for that shoot: Baumer, Endicott, Lorimer, Minns and Callan. Endicott was in plastics, Lorimer was a landowner, and Minns owned garages. They all dressed more quietly than Callan, who had added a ruffled shirt and maroon bow tie to his corded velvet dinner-jacket.

Even Lonely thought he was over-dressed. But the talk that night was of guns and shooting, and when they discovered that Callan knew about these things, and ate with the right knives and forks, they accepted him readily enough. After dinner, when they settled to poker, and Callan lost, they accepted him more readily than ever.

As he played each hand Callan looked at the men around him. Baumer, at 50, was the oldest; the rest he would guess were all under 40 and different as chalk and cheese—Endicott was plump, Lorimer tall, Minns stocky—except for one thing.

Each man had an economy of movement and quickness of reflex

that put them in the marksman class, but only one of them, according to Hunter's information, was willing to use those gifts against another human being.

And it was next door to impossible to guess who that one was. Endicott, who dragged and worried at his cigar whether he won or lost—or Lorimer, who won steadily and yet never relaxed, or Minns who invariably took one look at his cards and then left them face down throughout the rest of the hand? Or Marsden maybe, so solicitous about offering the brandy to his guests, and so forgetful about taking any himself?

They played till midnight, and Callan wrote out cheques to Lorimer and Marsden, and hoped to God that Hunter would allow them on expenses.

"Not too early a start tomorrow, gentlemen," Marsden said. "Breakfast at eight—and after that we'll meet in the gun-room."

"What do we start on?" Callan asked.

"Clay pigeons," Marsden said. "I hope that's agreeable to you?"

"That's fine," Callan said. For clay pigeons they'd be together in a group, so that gave Baumer at least one more day to live.

He went up the staircase to his room to find Lonely yawning over a shooting jacket he was supposed to be brushing.

"Any luck?" Callan asked.

"You're joking," said Lonely. "The other valleys was in and out of their bosses' rooms half the night."

"How about you?"

"I dubbined your boots," said Lonely, "and I pressed your trousers." He brooded for a moment. "Demeaning, that's what it is," he said at last. "Stuck-up gits."

"Who?"

"Them other valleys," Lonely said. "I knew they'd be la-di-da. Still—look on the bright side. They can't, none of them, play brag."

He brought Callan's tea to him next morning, and listened while Callan told him what to do.

"I heard about the clay-pigeons," he said at last. "The valleys all has bets on."

"That'll be your chance to take a look around," said Callan.

"Do me best, Mr Callan."

"Don't let anybody catch you at it."

"What, them gits?" Lonely's scorn was withering. "They couldn't catch cold if they slept in a deep-freeze, that lot."

Callan went down to a breakfast of Edwardian amplitude, then carried his gun-case to where the others were waiting. Every one of them had guns as sleek and elegant as his own, and watched as Callan opened the case and assembled his.

"Purdys I see," said Endicott.

"That's right."

"And quite old by the look of them."

"I think you'll find they still work," said Callan.

"I'd better explain for the newcomers," said Marsden. "We usually shoot for five hundred a gun. That is to say whoever makes the most hits takes the pool. You can enter more than one gun if you like."

One'll do me, thought Callan, but all the others entered two, so two it had to be. Another thousand quid. Hunter must think I'm made of money, he thought.

They shot well, all of them, even better than he'd expected; but one by one they dropped out. First Marsden, made over-anxious by greed, then Minns, who was too cautious, then Endicott who was that little bit that fatal little bit too slow.

Baumer. Lorimer and Callan were left, and now the clay-pigeons were coming up two at a time. A left and a right. And that took care of Lorimer, whose weakness was impatience.

With clay pigeons, to fire too soon is as bad as firing too late. Baumer and Callan went on. The magnate's eyes and co-ordination were wonderful, and Callan began to wonder if he would ever miss. But he tired at last and Callan didn't.

They walked back together to the house, and Baumer looked at Callan; at the too new, too ornate shooting clothes, the worn and elegant gun-case.

"This is the first time I ever lost here," he said. "You're good."

"Thank you," said Callan.

"Better than good," said Baumer. "You're a phenomenon, Mr Callan."

"I hope that's a compliment," Callan said.

"I hope so too," said Baumer.

"I looked all over," Lonely said. "Nobody's got one, Mr Callan."

"You're sure?"

"Positive," said Lonely.

Callan said: "Then we're in shtuck."

"I did find something else though," Lonely said.

When he told him what it was, Callan said: "I'm an idiot."

Lonely thought it seemed a funny reason for Callan to give him another tenner.

Next day was wood pigeons; the wariest and wiliest bird target there is. One gun, a thousand pounds on it, and the winner was the one who shot the most pigeons. No dogs. Every man did his own retrieving. Go into the woods, find your own hide, and the best of British luck. As a way of setting up a shotgun accident it couldn't be bettered.

Callan stayed as close as he dared to Baumer and bagged three pigeons, then Baumer went deeper into the wood. Callan thought this had to be the time, propped the Purdy against a tree, and crawled after him. A Ghurka had taught Callan about tracking years ago in the jungles of Malaya and Callan had never forgotten his lessons. He made no more noise than his own shadow and finished up at last behind a bush ten yards away from Baumer. Waiting. The most nerve-racking part of his trade.

Then Baumer got one, and moved forward to fetch it as a tall figure appeared in the clearing behind him. A .38 Magnum revolver appeared in Callan's hand as the tall figure moved forward and called out, *"Baumer."*

Baumer was already turning as Callan yelled, "Don't move, Mr Baumer," and stood up to face the tall man, who looked at the Magnum revolver as if it couldn't possibly be happening, then his gun hand tensed, and Callan said, "Don't try it. Not with that thing."

Baumer said, "May I turn now?"

"Just be careful," said Callan.

Baumer turned, and looked at the weapon in Lorimer's hand. Two barrels and a handgrip, like an eighteenth-century pistol.

"Who are you supposed to be, Mr Lorimer? Dick Turpin?" Baumer asked.

"That's a sawn-off shotgun," said Callan. "A bit clumsy, but it'll kill you just as well as the big one. Easier to manage, too, if you were faking an accident. Lay it down, Lorimer."

Lorimer made no move.

Baumer said: "How much were they paying you son?"

"Enough," said Lorimer.

"Well, well," Baumer said. "And you a gentleman."

"One thing I've learned," said Lorimer, "is that no-one can be a gentleman without capital. Surely you know that?"

He turned away from them, and Callan raised the Magnum, but before he could use it the sawn-off shotgun roared and Lorimer fell. Callan walked over to him and took away the gun, then looked around for Lorimer's shotgun, eased it into his hands, and tried not to look at what was left of Lorimer's face.

"At least he died like a gentleman," said Baumer. "How did you know, son?"

"We had a tip one of them was after you," said Callan. "A mate of mine looked the guests over—looking for a handgun." He hefted the sawn-off shotgun. "He found this instead."

"Who's 'we'?" said Baumer. "Shin Beth?"

"Sort of," said Callan.

"They told me someone was after me too," Baumer said.

"Perhaps next time you'll listen to them," said Callan, and turned towards the house. "Shalom."

"Lorimer?" Hunter said. "You're quite sure?"

"I saw him try it," said Callan.

"You—arranged things."

"Yeah," said Callan. "He tripped over a stump and his gun went off. Blew half his head away. Very nasty."

"And the sawn-off shotgun?"

Callan put it on his desk.

"Did you happen to notice the shotgun you left by the body?"

"Yeah," said Callan. "It was a Purdy. Looked a lot like yours."

"It was," said Hunter. "His grandfather and my father ordered their guns on the same day."

File on an Angry Artist

"A painter?" said Callan. "You mean art?"
"I do," said Hunter.
"But I don't even know what I like"
"Then this will be an excellent opportunity for you to find out, Hunter said.
He threw the file across the desk to Callan; yellow cover—surveillance only. The name on the cover was Richard Hodge. Callan turned to the first page and looked at the photograph of what seemed to be an angry and very muscular hippy.
"Never heard of him" he said.
"Perhaps you have heard of his brother Brian? Worked in the Foreign Office. . . Middle East Desk. He stole some papers about the Trucial States. What force we'd use to preserve our Interests there. One of the oil sheiks offered him a fortune for them."
"Didn't he commit suicide? Shot himself?"
Hunter looked at his fingernails.
"It appeared so," he said. "Meres was very close to him."
Callan said, "So either way it was suicide."
Hunter said, "Quite so. . . But Meres didn't get the papers back — And Hodge and his brother got on well."
"You want me to find out if he's got them?"
"Yes," said Hunter. "He may not have them of course. That's why his file's surveillance only."
"And if he has got them? "
"I want to talk to him," said Hunter.
He took the file from Callan, looked at Hodge's strong, scowling face.
"Perhaps then he'll merit a red file," he said. "By the look of him it would be a more appropriate colour."

New suit, ready made but expensive, and just a little vulgar; handmade shoes, a tie that didn't quite belong with the shirt—or the suit. Money, credit cards, cheque-book, a gold fountain pen that was very vulgar indeed, but no gun. Not for a surveillance job; not yet.
Callan looked at himself in the mirror and was satisfied. Risen from humble circumstances to affluence, he thought, and doesn't care who knows it. The wearer of this suit doesn't go to an art exhibition to criticise, he thought; he goes to try.

The gallery was a long way from Mayfair, which meant, so the expert had told him, that Richard Hodge hadn't arrived yet. On the other hand he was lucky to be having an exhibition at all with all the competition there was these days. Unless he'd financed it himself.

Such things had been known to happen. . . but not to Richard Hodge, thought Callan. Not unless he'd found a new and wealthy friend. On his file it had said: "Income and Assets: Virtually nil. Occasional recourse to National Assistance."

He parked the rented Mercedes across the street, and looked across at the gallery. "A. J. Meyler," It said. "*Paintings, Sculptures, Objets d'Art.*" A clean shop, and a tidy one by the look of it, but not a prosperous one. He left the car and crossed to the shop window.

It held one painting: a violent explosion of red, yellow, and black; jagged lines across an agonised and writhing background. "*Animus One,*" he read. "*Richard Hodge,*" and beside it a neatly lettered card, "*Richard Hodge Exhibition.*" He went inside.

He didn't know quite what he'd expected: dark drapes, perhaps; easels of expensive wood, and a bunch of trendies sipping champagne.

What he got was an almost empty room, its only asset the very effective lighting that flattered the pictures on the walls. A young man and woman in paint-smeared jeans stood In front of one picture and argued; a girl in a kaftan and beads, sat behind a desk reading *The Kama Sutra*, and that was it.

As Callan walked past her she handed him a catalogue without taking her eye from the page. The illustration she was looking at made more sense than the pictures on the walls at that, thought Callan. At least you could tell what it was supposed to be about.

He began to look at the pictures. "*Animus Two.*" "*Animus Three.*" "*Vietnam Massacre.*" "*Bloody Sunday.*" This geezer had a one-track mind. But it got to you, eventually, all that striving and strength and rage. And in between, sketches, drawings, whatever you call them. Mostly male and mostly nude, and muscled like giants. Callan moved on, and the two paint-smeared figures chanted like a litany "No sense of massing." "But the rhythm's Strong." "Oh certainly. If only the colour—"

"But it isn't, is it?"

Callan looked at yet another furious painting, and a voice behind him said: "Powerful don't you think?"

He turned quickly, to confront a neat and worried-looking man, who was making frantic "Shut-up" signals to the paint-stained ones.

A. J. Meyler, Callan thought. He needs a new suit, but at least he can recognise a customer. He looked again at the picture, which was called "*Holocaust.*"

"Is that what it's supposed to be?" he said.

"My dear sir—that's what it is," the man said. "Observe the use of massing, the urgency of the rhythm, the inexorable use of colour—."

On their way to the door the paint-stained ones sniggered, but the cultured salesman's patter went frantically on till Callan said : "None of this means a thing to me. Not a bloody thing."

"Oh dear," said A. J. Meyler"

"It's the wife, you see." said Callan.

"The wife?"
"My wife," Callan said. "She saw one of these catalogues a friend of hers got. She fancies this stuff."
"But you don't?"
"Can't make head or tail of it," said Callan.
For a moment it seemed as if A. J. Meyler would warm to him. but then the gloom returned.
"Perhaps if your wife were to came here herself—"
"Can't do that," said Callan. "I'm buying her one of these for her birthday. Surprise like. But I'm damned if I know which one."
A. J. Meyler looked at him as at a fellow sufferer. "Perhaps if I may suggest—" he began.
Behind them a voice said, "Don't bother—"
Callan turned more slowly this time. It was Richard Hodge all right, and he must have been moving damn quietly. Callan looked down at Hodge's feet. They were bare.
"You," Hodge said, nodding at Callan, "Out."
"Mr Hodge, really," Meyler said.
Hodge moved in closer. "You heard me," he said. "Out. Before I put you put,"
He's big all right, Callan thought. Six two and a chest like a barrel. I bet he's never lost a fight in his life.
Aloud he said. "You bloody fool. I've come to buy something."
"Not from me you haven't," said Hodge.
"And why the hell not? Don't you think I've got the money to pay for it?"
"Money?" Hodge said. "Of course you've got money. Money's all that bastards like you believe in . . . All you bloody well respect."
The girl behind the desk took her nose out of *The Kama Sutra* to nod approval.
"Well then?"
"These pictures are my work," Hodge said. "My whole life. Do you think I'm going to sell one to somebody who comes in here and says he can't make head or tail of it—just because he's got money?"
Callan said: "It's not for me. It's for my wife."
"If she's stupid enough to marry you," said Hodge, "she's too stupid to appreciate that picture. Now then. Are you going?"
"No," said Callan. "I'm not. You'll have to put me out."
"Gentlemen. Please," said Meyler, and Hodge moved forward. Callan stepped back and took hold of "*Holocaust*" by its frame.
"Suit yourself, son," he said. "If you don't mind your picture getting damaged." Hodge stopped dead.
"You wouldn't dare," he said.
"One way to find out," said Callan,
"I'd kill you for that."
Callan said; "That wouldn't mend the picture."
Hodge looked at him and said. "You mean it, I swear to God you mean it."
Callan gave no answer and suddenly Hodge threw back his shaggy head and bellowed with laughter.

"For God's sake, put the picture down before you drop it," he said. "I like you man. I really do." He turned to Meyler. "Any of that champagne left?"
"A bottle or two," said Meyler.
"Bring it," Hodge said, "Let's all have a drink. This one's got guts and money. I didn't think that was possible."
The champagne was Taittinger, a Blanc de Blancs, but they drank it out of two beer glasses and a tooth mug. The girl behind the desk got hers in a cup. It tasted delicious, but she didn't let it interfere with her reading. Hodge knocked his back in one smacking gulp, topped up his glass, and Callan's, then put an arm round his shoulders.
"Now," he said, "let me give you some art education." He talked, and Callan listened: art was struggle, art was violence, art was—if struggle and violence succeeded—liberation. Half an hour and two bottles later Calian allowed himself to be convinced, and looked rather blearily at the pictures. One of them had a little red stacker affixed to the frame. That, he said, was the one he liked.
"Sorry chum," Hodge said. "The sticker means it's sold."
"But I like it," said Callan, swaying just a little.
"So did the bloke who bought it. Don't you like any of the others?"
"Course I do," Callan said "Like 'em all. But that there—it's liber-li-liberated."
He stopped and shook his head.
"That must have been good champagne," he said.
Hodge laughed. Even his laughter was aggressive.
"I like you," he said. "I really do. What's your name?"
"Matt Jackson."
"Come round to a party tonight, Matt. Maybe we can take another look at my pictures afterwards."
"Suits me," said Callan.
"If I was you I wouldn't bring your wife," said Hodge.
"That suits me an' all"
"I do like you," Hodge said "Tell you what—if I still like you tonight—I'll give you a picture for nothing."
A. J. Meyler winced.

"An artist?" said Lonely.
"That's right," said Callan.
"Does he have any models? "
"What a dirty minded little man you are," said Callan.
"Nothing dirty about it," Lonely said. "Beauty unadorned. It's art, that is."
His eyes had the same look as when they beheld a plate of fish and chips with vinegar on.
"Mostly he draws fellers." Callan said.
"Oh," said Lonely, disappointed. "A poof."
"If he is he takes exercises." said Callan. "You want, to watch him son"
He showed Lonely a photograph of Hodge: at once there came the familiar, terrible smell.

"He'd eat me," said Lonely.

"If he saw you were tailing him—but he won't. You're *good* son."

"I don't know that I'm that good."

"I do," said Callan, "and I'm the judge."

Lonely sighed.

"A hundred nicker," he said. "If he spots me it'll pay for me funeral."

Callan handed over money, and Lonely counted briskly. Suddenly he stopped.

"Suppose there's fighting?" he said.

"Suppose there is," said Callan.

"Well I mean—look at him."

"If there's fighting," Callan said, "I promise you won't be there to see it. You might put me off. Now—tell me again what you have to do."

They met again later at a pub in Notting Hill. Lonely's first pint disappeared in one urgent swallow and Callan ordered another, sipped his tomato juice.

"Thirsty work, tailing," said Lonely, and looked at Callan's drink. "You given it up then, Mr Callan?"

"I'm in training," said Callan. Lonely shuddered, "Don't start," said Callan. "Just tell me about Hodge."

"Left the gallery about six," said Lonely. "Went to a caff."

"What caff?"

"The Oasis," Lonely said. "Marble Arch way. Had some grub with a Paki. Stuff called cous-cous. Looked like semolina to me."

"It is," said Callan.

"Disgusting," said Lonely "They ate meat with it."

"You're sure it was a Pakistani?"

"Looked like one," said Lonely. "Kept going on about his master."

"What about him? "

"Said he'd sent the money and Hodge would get it tomorrow, so it was time he delivered."

"What then?"

"I went to Hodge's place like you told me."

"Find anything?" Lonely shook his head. It was a disappointment, but Callan had been prepared for disappointment.

"All right, old son," Callan said. "You're doing well. Just, one more job and you're finished. You know where to find me?"

"Yes." said Lonely. "You'll be among the models. They can't all be fellers."

Callan watched him go, then went to a phone, and dialled the number he would never forget.

"Yes?" the girl's voice said.

"Let me speak to Charlie please." said Callan; then Hunter came on, and he told him what he wanted.

The party was noisy, drunken, psychedelically lit. Hodge had crammed more than 50 people into his basement flat, and it, bulged. Callan stumbled across couples of indeterminate sex who appeared oblivious to everything: even the record of a pop group that apparently used sledge-hammers and anvils instead of drums. At last he reached Hodge, who stood with a girl on each arm.

"Matt," he said. "Good to see you. Here. Have one of these."

His massive forearm moved, and one of the girls was in Callan's arms. She giggled, and kissed him, and Callan was aware of the acrid smell of pot.

"I'm a good host." said Hodge. "I look after my guests. Find you a place to lie down if you like."

"When I'm ready I'll find my own," Callan said.

"I don't know when I liked anybody so much," Hodge said.

The party went on and on and on. The girl Callan held went to sleep for a while, but revived after she'd drunk Callan's whisky. In one corner a group argued about Zen Buddhism, in another a group passed round a joint as if it were a religious rite, and all the time the music pounded like artillery.

Callan's girl said she was hot and took off her dress. Half-naked, she looked as vulnerable as a child. Callan gave her more whisky, and she went back to sleep.

He was still holding her when Lonely came in. Callan had never seen the little man look so reproachful.

"Fellers," he said.

"Let's have it," said Callan, and Lonely told him.

As he finished, Hodge came up, and glared at Lonely.

"I'm bloody sure I didn't invite you." he said.

Carefully Callan put aside the sleeping girl, and rose.

"It's my foreman." he said. "Hope you don't mind, I told him where I was. One of the machines is acting up."

"Trouble up at mill, eh?" said Hodge.

"Something like that. I'll have to go there—but I'd like to look at them pictures again first. I could be tied up for a bit."

Hodge said, "Meyler's here. I'll get the keys."

He went off, and crossed the room.

Lonely said, "Thanks Mr Callan," then stiffened. "Over there," he said. "By the fireplace. It's the Paki."

Callan looked quickly at him; dark and lean, drinking coke. The room's only loner.

"I thought it might be," he said. "Only he's an Arab. Cover me will you."

Lonely moved in front of him, and Callan's hands were fast and precise. He pulled up one trouser leg and shifted the gun that was taped to his calf to his trousers' waistband.

"Funny place for a shooter," said Lonely.

"Not if you're rumbled with a bird." said Callan. "You push off, old son."

Lonely looked at the sleeping girl.

"Might as well," he said. "Nobody's asked me to stay here."

Then he left, and Hodge came back with the shop keys. As he and Callan crossed the room, the Arab put down his glass left-handed.

Hodge opened the door and motioned Callan to enter. When he

followed, he left the door unlocked, but that, Callan was sure, was carelessness, no more.

"Now," he said. "Pick where you like."

Callan nodded to the red sticker. "I still like that one," he said.

"Matt—I Keep telling you— it's sold," said Hodge.

"Yeah," said Callan. "To an oil sheik. How much is he paying for it—a million?"

Hodge leaped for him then, and Callan met him with a karate kick to the stomach, a kick controlled so that Hodge wouldn't die, though the agony it caused might make him want to. Hodge screamed and staggered in front of Callan as the shop door flew open, the Arab leaped in and fired. Hodge screamed again, as Callan swerved round him, and the Arab turned too late. The Magnum spoke once, and the Arab fell.

Afterwards, the neighbours agreed, the ambulance arrived with commendable promptitude. As it should have done, thought Callan. Meres had been waiting long enough for the gun-shots. A. J. Meyler offered a reward for the Hodge painting that was stolen, but he never saw it again—or Hodge either.

"He had the papers between the painting and the frame," said Callan. "He was sending the whole lot to the Arab sheik—that's how I got on to it. Lonely broke into the shop and found the case for it already addressed."

"Did you have trouble making him tell you?"

"No," said Callan. "I said I'd rip the painting to bits if he didn't tell me. He told me at once."

"It's a terrible painting," said Hunter.

"He doesn't think so," Callan said.

"Did he say anything else?"

"Yeah," said Callan. "He did. He said he didn't like me any more."

File on a Reckless Rider

"Enjoying yourself?" Hunter asked.

"Not much," said Callan. He thrust his hands deeper into the pockets of his overcoat. "Too bloody cold" he said.

"They do choose rather bleak places for these country meetings I agree," said Hunter. "Still—there's something about an amateur steeplechase." He looked about him. A vast expanse of downland with a race track sketchily laid out, the jumps delivered by lorry; and Instead of a stand the gleaming cars of the rich drawn up in line to cheer on their equals. The three bookies with the stamina to stand the cold stuck out like Martians; and so do I, thought Callan.

"I've lost eight quid" he said.

"Allowable on expenses," said Hunter.

Callan said : "I don't like losing money to bookies. Even your money."

Hunter sighed. "Try *Pretty Lady* in the next one," he said. "A friend of mine owns her, and chap called Lawson's riding her. He's the best amateur jockey I've ever seen."

Pretty Lady, with Lawson up, led all the way and came in by six lengths at 100-8. Callan began to feel better.

"Lunch, I think," said Hunter, "unless you'd care to place another bet."

"Lunch," said Callan. "I know when I'm well off."

He lugged the picnic basket into the car. Hot soup in a flask, cold salmon, cold beef, salad, apple pie, a bottle of Beaune. When Hunter did things in style, he didn't mess about.

"I take it you don't ride." Hunter said

"If you mean horses, you know I don't," said Callan

"That's why I brought you here," said Hunter, "to get the feel of the thing. These people—" he gestured at the car window, taking in the fur coats, the British warms, shooting sticks, tartan rugs, the nervous expensive horseflesh and the well-born jockeys shivering in their silks—"These people are members of a hunt. I occasionally ride with them myself. For the most part they are rich, well-connected successful—and on the subject of horses completely insane. You are not like that."

"In no way," said Callan.

"In one way only. You are successful. That is why I brought you here. I wish you to observe tliem."

"Don't tell me you want me to knock off a horse?" said Callan.

"Hunter sighed, then sipped his Beaune. "Whatever target I give you will be - human," he said. "If, indeed, I give you one at all."

Callan looked at him. Hunter unsure of what he wanted was a rare sight indeed.

"Last month a man was murdered at a point-to-point meeting of this very hunt," Hunter said. "Perhaps you read about."

"Chap called Lyndhurst," said Callan, "Some bloke shot him with a rifle."

Hunter looked again at the window. A line of horses thundered past, kicking up divots, then streamed over a fence, floating in air. One horse pecked, and horse and rider went down, and Hunter waited in silence until they got up and the rider remounted, set the horse at the jump once more, and cleared it.

"Sir Francis Lyndhurst" he said. "Amiable but vacuous. Shot dead from cover with a high-velocity rifle. Murderer unknown. But the Press got a stream of pamphlets. Perhaps you remember?"

"If the fox, then why not the hunter?" Callan quoted. "I remember; all right. It sounded a bit too close to home for me."

Hunter grimaced.

"I was aware at it myself," he said. "Then there was some rigmarole about the evil of blood sports, and a life for a life. No further threats, and no confession of murder, but the Press drew its own conclusions, as did the public. The hunt was unimpressed. They met—and killed—next day."

"And nothing happened"

"Nothing," said Hunger.

"A nutter," said Callan. "It has to be."

Hunter poured more Beaune. "I hope so," he said.

Outside, the bookies were bawling the odds as if it were good news and the horses moved slowly, insolently from the parade towards the start and turned at once into nervous prima donnas whom the tape made more nervous still.

But it went up at last to the ritual cry of "They're off," and the field slowly lengthened, the huddle of silks that, had looked like a shattered rainbow resolved into individual colours as the leading horses gathered themselves for the first fence.

"Number Eight's the one to watch," said Hunter "Morrison. He's joint master. Beautiful hands."

The first horse cleared, then the second and third, and Morrison, lying fourth, came into the jump, the big grey he was riding took off effortlessly.

Callan put his glasses on it. Beautiful, he thought. Expensive, useless, maybe even stupid, but beautiful. Then at the height of the jump Morrison seemed to stiffen, the reins fell from his hands, and as the big grey landed he slumped sideways, one boot came free, his body fell like a stone as the grey galloped on, dragging him along the ground. In the crowd, a woman screamed.

"Let us hope he had a heart attack." said Hunter.

Callan said "He was shot."

Hunter sighed. "You would know," he said and left the car.

Callan finished his wine, and waited. Someone caught the grey by the bridle, men came running with a hurdle, and winced when they saw what was left of Morrison's face. An ambulance arrived, then one by one the cars left, some of them towing horse-boxes. The race was abandoned.

And still Callan waited, and brooded about the sniper. Got him from the side, he thought. In that clump of trees. All the cover, in the world. Three hundred yards range, telescopic sights. If you knew your business there was nothing to it. And this geezer knew his business. Must have done. Callan had seen it through his glasses. One shot. Straight through the brain.

Then off as soon as he'd fired, take the gun apart, and into a car behind the trees—or better still a motor-bike - kick the starter and away we go. Piece of cake and no way at all of stopping it as far as he could see. Then Hunter came back and they drove back to town, Callan told him about his broodings.

Hunter said "I'll pass it on," and picked up the radio-telephone, dialled Section H.Q. Callan heard him talk to the secretary, then waited as Hunter listened, said: "Thank you, Liz." and turned to Callan.

"More pamphlets to the Press," he said. "Delivered just after the shooting. Same as the last time. 'If the fox, why not the hunter?' with one addition—*Will they never learn?*"

"It has to be a nutter." said Callan.

Hunter said "Enderby rides with that hunt."

"Enderby?"

"Foreign Office," said Hunter "What they call a trouble-shooter nowadays. Middle East specialist Bright chap .Very bright. When the Egyptians kicked the Russians out, Enderby helped set it up. The Russians hate him."

"The sniper didn't knock him off."

"He wasn't riding." said Hunter "On either occasion. If he had been—and my theory is right—they'd still have spared him. They want this to look like the work of a maniac."

Callan said "But it he isn't riding—"

"He will be next week." said Hunter. "The Hunt Committee held an emergency meeting. There's a meet next week—it won't be cancelled."

"They must be out of their minds," said Callan

Hunter said, "I thought I told you. On the subject of horses—they are." He turned to Callan. "Enderby mustn't die, David," he said.

"Then tell him not to ride."

"I already have." said Hunter. "He refused."

"Have him kidnapped."

"I should like to, very much." said Hunter. "Unfortunately he's aware of it. And much too clever to allow it to happen. I want you to go to Langham."

"Where's that?"

"Langham Hall," said Hunter. "They meet there next Thursday. Lord Langham is the surviving joint-master. He is also a friend of mine. I arranged it with him before I left."

Callan said; "Come off it. The last thing I rode was a donkey at the seaside."

"You will go as an old friend of Langham's son Charles. He was killed in Malaya. You've always wanted to watch a hunt—and that's why you're there."

Calian said "Be reasonable, Hunter, it just isn't possible to stop a sniper."

"I know it isn't," said Hunter. "But I want you to try. Whatever you may need of course—"

"Toby Meres rides," said Callan.

"He does."

"I'll need him for a start". He thought for a while. "And I think it's about time Langham had a new stable hand."

"Anything else?"

"I'll let you know."

Hunter said: "I'm obliged to you," then thought for a moment. "How much did you win on *Pretty Lady*?"

"Fifty quid," said Callan.

"Which will be deducted from your expenses."

"Oh no it won't," said Callan. "I bet my own money."

Lord Langham was 73, and as lean and tough as a riding-crop. On foot he looked 60, and on Horseback 45. Whatever Hunter's told him about me must have been good, Callan thought. He doesn't even mind that I can't ride.

That night they dined twenty at dinner and of them all only Callan, Lawson, the rider of *Pretty Lady* and his sister were not to ride next day. Lawson was teased unmercifully about that. He'd taken a fall when out walking and dislocated his hip. His sister pushed him around in a wheelchair.

Callan watched him when the port came round, and the real teasing began. Lawson took it well enough but the smile on his lips never quite reached his eyes.

If he had the chance. Callan thought, he'd get on a horse tomorrow; stiff bandages and all. His whole life seemed directed down one channel only: the mastery of a beast for the killing of another beast, and anything else, even having to cope with the schoolboy teasing of men with less than half his skill, was something he couldn't hope to cope with—ever. Strength, mastery, the kill. They were all he cared about. All he knew.

At last Langham relented and took them to join the ladies.

Almost at once, one of them joined Callan: Lawson's sister pushed her brother to him in his chair.

"So you don't ride tomorrow either, Mr Callan?" he said.

"No," said Callan. "I never have, and I think it's a little late to start now."

"But you like watching a meet?"'

"Ask me tomorrow" Callan said. "I've never seen one."

Miss Lawson said "But how on earth will you pass the time? Follow on foot?"

"No." Callan said. "I'll watch them set out, then go to the library. Lord Langham's got some stuff there I find fascinating."

"Wouldn't you like to watch the kill?" Lawson asked.

"No," said Callan. "Not any more, I'll stay with the picturesque."

"I'm sorry if I seem inquisitive." Miss Lawson said, "but I can't help wondering—"

"Why I bother to come here?"

"I suppose that's rude. I'm sorry."

"Not at all," said Callan. "It's just that I'm fascinated by things I don't understand." They left him then, and Meres came over to Callan.

"Mixing with the nobs?" he said.

"They're just pitying a poor peasant," said Callan.

"Pitying?"

"I don't ride," said Callan.

Meres said, "And I do." He looked again at Miss Lawson "I might chance my arm myself—if I survive tomorrow. You still want me to stay close to Enderby?"

"As close as you can get," said Callan.

Meres said "I hope that sniper's as good as you say he is—damn you."

He moved away, and Callan left the room and went out of the house towards the stables. The night was chill, the stars brilliant and tiny, the air so clear after London that he breathed it deeply and gratefully. Then, suddenly, the air was far from clear. Callan stopped, a bush rustled softly and Lonely was with him.

"I might have known it would be you" said Callan.

Lonely said: "Of course it's me. You told me to meet you here. . . You better not come too close, Mr Callan. I think I'm niffing a bit."

"You're the expert," said Callan.

"Mr Callan, that's not fair." said Lonely. "Nerves is one thing and horses is another. Horses is disgusting. I tell you straight, that's the last time I'm working in a stable, even for what you say you're going to pay me."

Callan made soothing noises and handed over money, and had no doubt that Lonely would count it. Lonely could count money anywhere, even in the dark,

"Just right, Mr Callan," he said at last. "Ta."

"What you got?" said Callan.

"According to the grooms they're all good shots." said Lonely, "Even some of the birds. Up in Scotland," he added vaguely. "Stags and grouse and that."

"Lawson?"

He's supposed to be the best." said Lonely.

"D'you, find out who's hard up?"

"To hear them talk you'd think they all were," said Lonely. "Don't know where their next fifty thousand's coming from."

"Anyone in particular?" said Callan.

"Lawson again," said Lonely. "And his sister. Gambling mad they are."

"Thanks old son," said Callan.

Lonely said: "Can I go now Mr Callan? I want to have a bath."

"Off you go," said Callan.

As he moved into the darkness Lonely said: "Do you think after-shave would do any good?"

The meet was splendid—all Surtees and sporting prints and old-fashioned Christmas-cards—pink coats and thoroughbreds and eager, impatient hounds. To Callan it seemed an awkward and viciously expensive way to save the price of a few hens, but that presumably was the wrong way to look at it; the object of this exercise was pleasure.

He stood with the Lawsons as Langham swigged down his stirrup cup and nodded to the whipper-in, and the hounds moved off, the horsemen followed, Meres just behind Enderby's right shoulder: the bodyguard position, but even Meres had never bodyguarded on horseback before. . . At least they've got guts, thought Callan. Not one of them, either last night or this morning, has even mentioned the sniper. He looked down at Lawson in his wheel-chair.

"What will you do now, Mr Lawson?" he asked.

"Go back to bed." his sister said. "He says his hip is aching dreadfully."

Lawson said "She's a bully, Callan. She always was."

"Be that as it may," she said, "bed's the place for you."

She pushed the wheel-chair into the house. "Enjoy your reading, Mr Callan."

Callan went to the library, then out through the French window to where Lonely had left his scooter, and rode it through the lodge-gates to the stretch of common where the helicopter was waiting. The pilot opened the door, and Callan looked round approvingly.

"No spectators?" he said.

"All watching the hunt." the pilot said. "We did have a few, but I told them I was filming the meet for television. They said old Langham would have me flogged if I scared the horses—then they took off pretty quick. Guilt by association, or something. Ready?"

Callan took the old Mannlicher rifle from under the seat and tested it carefully. Getting on for 50 years old, and even better than the day it was made. Action, balance, telescopic sight, all perfect. The best big game rifle he had ever handled. He loaded the magazine, then fastened his safety belt. "Ready," he said.

The helicopter clattered, roared, lifted off in an ungainly lunge as the pilot sought the height that would give them maximum view, and Callan looked down. The hounds had found, and were streaming across bare winter fields, the hunters pounding after, clearing each obstacle as it came.

A horse went down, and another, and Callan reached for his glasses but Enderby was still there, with Meres hard behind him. By the look of things Enderby was telling Meres exactly what he thought about people who rode too close. But they were bunched in among other riders anyway— no need to worry yet.

Then Lord Langham, just ahead of Enderby, looked up and shook his fist at the helicopter and his horse slowed. Enderby and Meres shot ahead. Callan looked to where a deserted cottage stood, windows gone, roof tumbled In. Beside it was a metalled road.

Callan touched the pilot's arm and pointed—no use trying to shout above the racket of the rotor blades—and the helicopter moved abruptly as a dragon fly as Callan eased back the sliding door, picked up the Mannlicher.

Through the gaping hole of the cottage roof he saw a flash of blue and chrome, a motor bike—and he nudged the pilot again, his thumb pointed imperatively down.

He risked one glance at the horsemen.—Enderby had left Meres at last and was galloping alone, his hunting pink a perfect target,—then back to the cottage. By its window a figure crouched, a figure in worn tweeds with a rifle in its hands.

The sniper risked one look at the helicopter, then coolly, as unconcerned as if it wasn't there, took aim at Enderby. Callan lifted the Mannlicher and fired, and the tweeded figure fell. Enderby galloped on unaware, and the pilot sought flat ground, touched down the helicopter, the noise of its blades fading from a clatter to a whistling sigh.

"Bloody nerve," the pilot said, "setting up a killing with us watching."

"If I know that geezer he'd have had a go at us next," Callan said. "He didn't want witnesses. Let's take a look at him."

They walked towards the cottage, and Callan took the Mannlicher with him. It didn't pay to take chances with a bloke like that. As they reached the cottage, the pilot said: "Who is it anyway?"

"A bloke called Lawson," Callan said.

The pilot peered inside.

"I hate to contradict you, old boy," he said, "but it's a lady."

Callan looked, and felt sick

"A lady called Lawson," he said. "Her brother must really have dislocated his hip."

"What now?" said the pilot.

"We put her in the helicopter," Callan said. "We can't leave her here, not with a hole in her head."

"You dropped her, of course," said Hunter. "Where?"

"In the Channel," said Callan. "Five miles out."

Hunter said, "I've spoken to her brother. He's quite innocent."

"Does he know—?"

"That she's dead? . . . No. I told him she must have realised we were on to her—and run away."

"What made her do it, Hunter?"

"Money," Hunter said. "The KGB's money. And quite a lot of it—according to her bank account. Most probably he'll inherit it eventually. I've no objection."

"And I thought it was him all the time," said Callan.

"I know you did. May I ask why?"

"He was a perfect target on *Pretty Lady*—a far easier shot than Morrison—and yet the sniper didn't take it."

"She would hardly shoot her own brother," Hunter said.

"It never occurred to me she would shoot anybody at all," said Callan.
"Then it should have done." said Hunter. "You were really rather lucky in this one, David."

"Lucky." said Callan. "Yeah it's not every day I get a chance to shoot a lady."

File on a Weeping Widow

"How are you getting on?" said Hunter.
"All right" said Callan.
"The lady likes you then?"
"Seems like it."
Hunter sighed. "This isn't the time for maidenly coyness, Callan," he said. "I put you on to Pamela Ramirez for a reason."
"Yeah," said Callan. "So I gathered. She's in a red file."
"And you like her?" said Hunter.
"I like her."
"Then perhaps it's about time I told you that I'm not sure whether she belongs in a red file or not."
Watch it, Callan thought. He's about to get tricky.
"How many times have you seen her?" Hunter asked.
Seven, was it? Eight? The set-up encounter on the plane from Rome, then dinner that night; two theatres, three cocktail parties, and one more dinner. He ticked them off. "Eight," he said.
"And she believes you are—what you say you are?"
"Philbin Enterprises Ltd. Export and Import. Robert Philbin, Managing Director," said Callan. "Yeah, she believes it. Why not? It's what it says on my card." His voice was bitter.
Hunter said "I shouldn't have to say this—not to you, but don't like her too much, David."
"You want me to kill her?"
Hunter said testily "I've told you already. I don't know whether she belongs in a red file or not—so how can I possibly answer that question?"
"What do you want me to do then?"
"What has she told you about her late husband? " Hunter asked,
"Nothing."
"Not one word? Ever?" Callan shook his head. "Very well then. What do you know?"
"Enrique Ramirez" said Callan. "South American parents—brought up in Italy. Racing driver—and bloody good. Last year he was all set to be world champion, for the second year running—only he crashed instead. Car blew up. He died—and left her a lot of money."
"She also inherited his red file," said Hunter. Callan thought for a moment.

"It wasn't an accident, then?"
"No," Hunter said. "It was very carefully arranged."
"What was he up to?" Callan asked.
"He was a KGB courier," Hunter said.
"He was a Red?"
"No," said Hunter. "He was greedy. His driving made him a small fortune, but he wanted more—and the KGB were willing to oblige him, in return for his services of course. As a racing-driver his cover was perfect. They go all over the world to race—and nobody questions it. And he was based in Rome. He could take delivery of stuff from Italy, France, Germany, Austria, Yugoslavia, Switzerland, and deliver it wherever they wanted it to go. Even South America or the States."
"What kind of stuff?"
"Money, mostly," Hunter said. "But occasionally there were instructions—stuff they wouldn't risk even on a micro-dot." He paused. "Including executions. Three of our chaps died because of his instructions, David—and one of them took a long time to die."
"You think Pamela's in on it?"
"I think she might be. I want you to find out."
"I've met her eight times," said Callan. "She wouldn't tell me the stuff you're asking if it was our silver wedding anniversary,"
"All the same I want you to find out," said Hunter. "Perhaps she's innocent after all"
"Suppose she's guilty?"
Hunter said at once. "Then I'll take you off the case. I'm aware that you're incapable of harming her."
Callan stood up. "There are times when I detest my job." he said.
"There are times when we all do," said Hunter. "And they're not infrequent, I assure you."
Callan walked to the door then turned back, hesitant. "Just what have you got against her, Hunter?" he asked.
'Two facts," Hunter said. "The first that she has steadfastly refused to believe that Ramirez died by accident from the day it happened; the second that Ramirez died in England and she has remained here ever since—apart from one brief visit to Rome to sell up."
"What's so suspicious about that? She is English."
"She's hired a firm of private detectives to investigate her husband's death," said Hunter. "However, that doesn't worry me My chaps know their business. What does worry me is that she is considering entering motor-rallies, which is about as close to carrying on her husband's business as she can get—and I won't have her carrying on all his business." His eyes looked into Callan's. "Prove her innocent, Callan," he said, "or else hand her over to someone who won't care if she's guilty."
"Like Toby?" said Callan.
"Meres would handle this one admirably," Hunter said.

The little car eased its way through the traffic as if it didn't exist, and all the time she drove, Pamela kept up a stream of stories—about her housekeeper, her manicurist, a fat lady she'd collided with in Harrods'.

Her driving seemed to be done entirely by reflex, and yet was utterly sure. Callan risked a look at her as the lights flicked to green and the little car shot forward, leaving a Jaguar and an Aston-Martin standing.

Eyes brown, but with a hint of gold in them, the colour of the Amontillado sherry she liked so much, black hair cropped close, thick and springy to the touch—not that he had ever touched it, the nose pert, the mouth generous, the chin determined.

Put them all together, and they barely achieved prettiness, never mind beauty; but her figure could turn heads in the street and her charm was the kind that gets front row seats in the stalls even after the House Full notice has gone up. Callan knew; he'd seen it in action. She flicked a glance at him, then her eyes went back at once to-the road.

"What are you looking at?" she said.

"You," said Callan.

"What about me?"

"You're never on time, it takes you two hours to decide which dress to wear—and yet put you behind the wheel of a car, and you'd think every road was Brand's Hatch."

Her smile flickered, but came back quickly. "I like picnics," she said, and, anyway. I'm hungry . . . Oh, my God."

"What's wrong?" said Callan.

"I forgot the hamper."

"You did," said Callan. "I didn't."

She gave him another quick glance. "Dear Bob," she said, you have your uses." But her smile was tender.

A river bank and a clump of willows, green, rich grass and wild flowers neither of them knew the name of. Like a ruddy cigarette ad, thought Callan, but it was real enough, and nothing more real more wonderful than Pamela, setting out plates, nibbling at chicken, sipping wine. When she had done she leaned back on the motor rug and lit a cigarette.

"Gosh, this is good," she said. "It's—what I needed. Thank you."

"For what?"

"All this rural tranquility."

"You haven't been tranquil?"

"Not since Enrique died."

Callan said carefully, "Enrique?"

"My husband," she said. "He was killed in a race. Surely you read the papers?"

"A motor accident," said Callan. "I remember, I'm sorry—"

"Not an accident," she said," and he looked at her, wondering. "Believe me, I know."

"But how can you know?" said Callan. "The inquest—"

"Found that a bolt had sheared," she said. "It didn't. Somebody sheared it."

"You can prove this?"

"No," she said. "I can't. Not yet. But one day I will. And when I do—"

"What?" said Callan.

"They'll suffer for it," she said. "Believe me, they'll suffer."

And how the hell can I tell that to Hunter, thought Callan, and how the hell can I not tell him?

"You must have loved him very much," he said

"Enrique? I suppose I did. Sometimes. Quite often I hated him He wasn't an easy man. But he was my man. I won't sit by and let his murderers get away with it."

"But how can you—"

She sat up then, and held out her glass for more wine. Despite its abruptness, the movement was instinctive with grace. Callan could never remember her being clumsy, not once.

"How do you like my car?" she said.

He filled their glasses.

"So were changing the subject are we?" he said. "All right I like it. But you must have had it tuned."

"I did,' she said. Sacha did it for me," then laughed at his look of bewilderment.

"Sacha used to be Enrique's mechanic," she said. "In the racing world he was almost as famous as Enrique. When Enrique died—Sacha went home. Back to France. But now he's come to me."

"I see," said Callan.

She looked again at his face, and laughed: her laughter a gentle mockery.

"Silly," she said. "I mean he's coming to work for me."

"Doing what?" said Callan.

Tuning my car," she said, "I'm going to drive in rallies, I'm good you know. Even Enrique said so."

"I'll worry about you," he said.

"Thank you."

"This rally driving of yours— Is it because your husband was killed?"

Callan was certain she was about to say yes; but she stopped in time.

"You've never even tried to kiss me," she said. "I find, that vaguely insulting. I mean you might at least have tried."

Later she said, "You are an easy man." She felt him tense, and pulled him down to her. "Silly," she said. "That's a compliment. Honestly."

Lonely said "I don't think I can do it."

"Course you can," said Callan. "Look, I'll show you again." Deftly his fingers unscrewed the telephone mouthpiece; inserted the tiny bug, replaced the mouthpiece.

"See? Nothing to it. Now you have a go."

Lonely had a go, and another, and another. It was a slow, exasperating business, but half an hour later he could do it.

"Like you said, Mr Callan. Nothing to it," said Lonely, and Callan willed himself not to hit him. "Where's it for?"

"My bird's place," Callan said.

Lonely looked at him reprovingly. "Mr Callan, that's not nice," he said. "Not nice at all."

"I'm afraid she may be getting herself into trouble," said Callan, "and she's too proud to ask for help."
"Ah well in that case—," said Lonely. "Got a picture?"
Callan made the time honoured gesture of a man besotted, and took a photograph from his wallet.
"Very nice, Mr Callan," he said. "Very nice indeed."
There was envy in his voice, but there was admiration too. Mr Callan always went for the best.
"When's convenient, Mr Callan?"
"Tonight," said Callan. "I'm taking her out to dinner."
"Up West?"
"Yeah," said Callan. "Up West."
"Ludovico's is good," said Lonely. "You try Ludovico's,"
"You've eaten there?" Try as he could, Callan failed to hide his disbelief.
"Certainly I have," said Lonely, not without dignity. "I done the place last year. Try their sautéed lamb chops and pommes soufflés, Mr Callan. They're smashing."
"I'll do that" said Callan.
And don't you worry about me," said Lonely. "I'll be gone long before you get back." He picked up the bug again. "I feel like Cupid," he said.

The room smelt a little close, she thought, and opened one window further, but Callan knew that the closeness was due to Lonely, and relaxed. The little man had done well: come to that the cotelettes d'agneau sautés and pommes soufflés had been delicious, just as he'd said. You could always rely on Lonely, if he didn't get too scared. . .
"You can have another brandy." she said. "I can't."
"Turning teetotal?"
"I'm in training," she said. "The rally's on Saturday."
"I do wish you wouldn't—" he began.
"No you don't," she said. "Sacha says I might win." She watched, but he didn't smile.
"I have driven before, you know," she said. "I'm good. I told you. And the opposition's very amateur. All the same— if I win you'll be proud of me, won't you?"
"I'm proud of you every time we go out together," said Callan.
"Oh, you darling," she said. "I think you meant that."
"Of course I did," said Callan.
"But I wish you weren't so slow," she said. "It's embarrassing having to make improper suggestions to you all the time."
Later she said: "Do you want to marry me?"
"Very much," said Callan. The answer was like a reflex, no hesitation, no thought of Hunter and what he might say.
"Some day I think perhaps we will," she said. "Get married I mean."
"Some day?"
"There's such a lot to arrange first." she said.
"Such as what?"
"Some day I'll tell you," she said.
"Why not now?"

She reached across him for a cigarette. "I—can't," she said. Then: "I don't often talk about Enrique," she said, "but I talked about him to you. I told you I hated him—and it was true. But I owe him something—maybe we all do."

"I don't understand you," said Callan.

"I don't want you to. You know very well what I want you to do." And then: "It's late," she said "You'll have to go, darling."

"It's only eleven thirty," said Callan. -

"Before a race, that's late."

"What about after a race?"

"Ah," she said. "After a race our time stands still— yours and mine."

Next afternoon she was at her hairdresser's, working on a new style — "something chic and simple darling, to fit under a racing helmet." It was the ideal time to listen to the tapes of the telephone conversations the bug had picked up. When at last Callan did it, he found that he despised himself.

That she loved him was evident. She announced the fact to an aunt in Sonning, a girl friend in St. John's Wood, another girl friend in Kensington, and once, fleetingly, to her dentist.

She didn't announce it to Sacha. . . Callan listened to a highly technical conversation about compression ratios and four wheel drifts and overhead camshafts. All the wit and femininity had gone from her voice, but the eagerness and enthusiasm were there in full measure: would always be there. In the middle of it the phone rang.

"You're never at home these days," said Hunter.

"I'm on an assignment," said Callan. "You should know. You sent me on it."

"It's my job after all," said Hunter. "Just as your job is to report from time to time. You haven't done so."

"Nothing to report," said Callan. "I think she's clean."

"You're lying," said Hunter. "Come in and see me."

"Now?"

"No. Not now. . . I'm busy. Tomorrow. And get off the case. Callan. I'll turn it over to Meres."

"But you can't," said Callan.

"But I shall."

"Please, Hunter" Callan said. "Please. I've never asked a favour before."

"I rarely grant them, but I think you've earned one. Stay with her till tomorrow, then see me."

"She races tomorrow."

"After the race then." Hunter paused. "That's two favours, Callan. I shall expect to be repaid."

He hung up and Callan went back to the tapes. She still didn't announce that fact that she was in love: Sacha did.

Next day he spent with the radio and telly, hopping from channel to channel to find out how she was. He didn't care whether she won or lost; his only concern was that she should stay alive. But she was with the leaders from the start and if a Porsche and a Saab gave her trouble when she tried to pass, at least they couldn't snake her off. Callan watched when she finally scraped past the Saab, and found that he couldn't stand it.

He set off for the finish hours ahead of time, then realised he hadn't eaten all day and stopped at a pub for a Scotch and a sandwich.

What he really needed was three or four doubles, but even that solace was denied him. The only comfort he had was the solid weight of the Magnum .38 under his coat, and by the end of the day, he knew, he'd have given up either it, or Pamela. His world wasn't big enough to contain them both.

He parked, then moved to the finish, easing into the anonymity of the crowd. Sacha was easy to spot; he looked even tougher than his photographs.

Someone switched on a transistor, and Pamela was lying second, and the commentator was in ecstasies about the gallant and beautiful lady carrying on a great tradition.

Then she passed the Porsche and Callan thought he would die. But she came in first, dusty, grimy, spent, and disappeared under a sea of photographers and officials; roses and a sash and a silver cup and champagne. And Callan waited, as he'd promised, until the crowd ebbed at last, and there was time to walk to her hotel, up to her room, and knock and enter just as they'd arranged.

She still wore her overalls, and her face was still smeared with dust, and that was not what they'd arranged at all. But he still went towards her, unthinking, vulnerable; he was that much in love. And then she moved away.

"I know it's ridiculous," she said, "but Sacha says—Sacha says—,"

The mechanic appeared in the bathroom doorway. He was holding a 9 millimetre automatic.

"Sacha says you're a bloody agent," he said. "The bloody agent who killed Enrique."

Callan moved before he had finished speaking, in a flat dive that took him behind an over- stuffed chair, and the Magnum was in his hand before Sacha fired, the nine millimetre bullet slammed through the chair's cushion. Callan pushed the chair over and fired as Sacha appeared.

Sacha gasped as the bullet smashed his left collar-bone, but raised the automatic a thousandth of a second too slow. Callan's next bullet, drilled a small, neat hole in his forehead. But he fired again even so. Once more. Into the heart. It was what he had been trained to do. And all the time Pamela was screaming. . . .

Messy, stupid and bungling," said Hunter. "You've handled this atrociously, Callan."

"At least I killed Sacha Morel," said Callan.

"While she stood by and watched. You forgot everything you were ever taught "

Callan said: "No, Not quite everything— I killed him exactly the way I was taught —even if she was watching."

Hunter looked at him: the man's agony was unmistakable.

"Pour yourself a drink," he said, "and make it a big one."

As Callan poured, he said, "I take it you bugged her flat—on your own initiative?"

"Yes, sir."

"So did I. For God's sake Callan, did you think I didn't know about Morel?"

"I didn't think anything," said Callan. "Not about the job."

"We've been through his things," said Hunter. "He was KGB of course—Ramirez' controller—in time he would have been hers. I take it you know how he got round her?"

"Yes," said Callan. "Or at least I can guess from what I heard on the tape. He told her that Enrique was working for us—and the KGB killed him. When he found out about me I suppose he told her I was KGB too."

"He did indeed," said Hunter. "Do you think she believes it?"

"I think she does now," said Callan.

"You will find it difficult to persuade her otherwise," Hunter said.

"I'll find it impossible,' said Callan, "unless you help me."

"Which of course I won't," said Hunter.

"Somehow," said Callan, "I didn't think you would. How is she, Hunter?"

"In shock," said Hunter. "And of course she wept a great deal, till they put her under sedation. But I've no doubt she'll talk—once she recovers."

"You going to put Toby Meres on to her?"

"Why should I?" said Hunter. "It's really rather good for our image. Gallant racing driver brutally murdered by KGB—who follow it up by murdering his equally gallant mechanic, really. I rather like it."

Callan swallowed his Scotch; poured another.

"I really mean it, Callan," said Hunter. "She's quite safe."

Callan drank once more. "Yeah," he said. "She's safe. She'll never see me again."

File on an Angry Actor

"An *actor*?" said Callan. He sounded incredulous: Hunter enjoyed that.

"More of a film star really," said. "See for yourself. Perhaps you know him."

He tossed the file over to Callan, who turned at once to the photograph. The photographs in red files had often been difficult to come by: sometimes they were the only photographs of the subject in existence. But not this subject. Callan looked at the great shock of carefully careless mahogany-redhair, the thrusting beak of a nose, green eyes, cruel, reckless mouth that all added up to one of the best-known faces in the Western world.

"Of course I know him," he said. "That's Noel Empson."

He looked at the statistics: Age 33, height 6ft. 4in., weight 13st. 10lb. There was a hell of a lot of him.

"You saying he's naughty?" Callan asked.

"Extremely," said Hunter. "You know an awful lot of people are infatuated by what I believe is called show-biz." The last two words came out as if held in a pair of tongs. "Politicians, bankers, business men: people of that sort. If they go to the wrong sort of party they are peculiarly susceptible to blackmail. Empson is only too happy to arrange the wrong sort of party."

"Who for?"

Hunter said: "The KGB."

"The KGB?" Callan was incredulous again, and Hunter continued to enjoy it. "But this feller's worth a fortune."

"Indeed he is," said Hunter.

"And he's never made a political move in his life."

Hunter nodded.

"Then why—?"

"I believe the expression is 'for kicks,'" said Hunter. "He enjoys it—and he's very good at it. In that sense he's rather like you, David."

"What's he done?" *Call*an asked.

"He was responsible for Repton's suicide — and Repton would have been the best Foreign Secretary we'd had in years. Challow of the Treasury died the same night, you may recall. They had both been to the same party. You remember Onslow, the banker?"

"Yeah," said Callan. "He died in a car accident."

"His car hit a wall," said Hunter, "a month after Empson introduced him to a girl. I don't think Onslow hit that wall by accident."

"You want me to kill him?"

Hunter ignored it.

"He's shortly going on what I believe is called location, making one of those television spectaculars at a place called Axton Sands on the South Coast. Nearby is a place called Brent House. Olga Lubova is staying there. Do you know her?"

Callan shook his head.

"She's a remarkable old woman," said Hunter, "and she's writing her memoirs. They include her recollections of Beria, Stalin, even Lenin. The KGB have decided that they will be embarrassing. They are sending an executive."

"She's to die then?"

"Unless you succeed in keeping her alive."

"Know who it is?"

"Some protégé of Empson's; he has quite a few, I gather. That's all I got. Take care of it, will you?"

"I'll need help," said Callan.

"All you need."

Callan looked back at the sardonic, beautiful face.

"What about the actor?" he said.

"Take care of him, too." said Hunter. "But make sure he's in a condition to speak. I want a chat with him."

Empson's film was about the Peninsular War in Spain: Wellington versus Napoleon's marshals. Guns landed from one of His Majesty's ships to arm the Spanish guerrillas, and a handsome captain of infantry to teach them how to them: Noel Empson. Then there was the lovely Rosita who fell for the captain and spied on the French, and the fierce guerrilla leader El Moro and the wicked Colonel Lebrun.... Well, that took care of one thing. Callan knew that period of history backwards. Hunter pulled the necessary strings, and Callan was appointed technical adviser.

The trouble was to track down the KGB wet job boy—or girl. When it came to protégés, Empson seemed to be involved with just about everybody from the director down: El Moro, Colonel Lebrun, even the lovely Rosita. Even he must have had trouble getting her in the picture, Callan thought. Her name was Emma Marston, and she was beautiful enough, but as an actress she was an unknown. Empson had met her on a Safari picture in Kenya where her father was a white hunter.

Callan went on with the list. Empson had also asked for, and got, his own make-up man a well as designer, writer and sound man. His producer, it seemed, was receptive to Empson's ideas ... Noel Empson pictures grossed millions.

Callan took a trip to Axton Sands; a long uncluttered stretch of sea-coast with cliffs beyond it. Hidden in a rounded dip in the cliff-tops, Nissen huts and caravans were already assembled for the film invasion.

Brent House was less than a mile away: old rambling, its encircling wall already decayed. A KGB executive could walk in blindfolded.

And the only people in the house apart from Madame Lubova, were a housekeeper and a gardener, both pushing sixty....

Callan went into the village, found a phone, and asked to speak to Charlie. When Hunter came on he told him Madame Lubova would have to move: she hadn't a prayer where she was.

"You tell her that," said Hunter. "When I did, all she said was she was sick of running. And anyway she likes the house."

So Callan tried, and found himself arguing frantically, uselessly, with a frail old lady in dove-grey silk with dark, imperious eyes and a will of iron.

"You realise you could be killed?" he said.

"At my age, after what I have endured, death is not so important," she said.

"In fact, to be killed by the KGB would smear them even more than your memoirs?"

"You are a very clever young man," she said.

"Don't you think they've thought of that too?" said Callan. "You're due for an accident, madame."

"Then I rely on you to prove it was murder," she said.

Obstinate was right. Stubborn as a mule.

But he kept at her, and at last she gave way a little. She consented to having a bodyguard in the house, and when he told her what the bodyguard would do she laughed. Somehow it was the laughter that showed him how beautiful she had once been.

Back to London then for a chat with Meres, and Meres was every bit as angry as Callan had expected once he'd found out the part he had to play. But Meres knew that his only court of appeal was Hunter: knew, too, that he was under Callan's orders. It didn't make him hate Callan less, but at least he would do as he was told.

Time to visit a film fan. Spend hours in the cinema, Lonely could. Next to thieving and beer, it was his favourite occupation...

"Me?" said Lonely. "On the pictures?"

"That's right," said Callan.

"But how could I?" said Lonely.

"You'll be a natural, son."

"What I mean is," Lonely said and his face went scarlet, "if you're an actor, you've got to say words. Words what's written down, and you know I don't read all that good, Mr Callan."

Slowly, patiently, Callan began to explain what an extra did and Lonely began to look happier.

"I'd like that, Mr Callan. Honest I would. Only – "

"Only what?"

"Only how much do I have to pay to get on to the picture?"

"They pay you, son," said Callan. "So do I."

Suddenly there was far more delight.

"What do you pay me for, Mr Callan?" Lonely asked.

Callan told him and the atmosphere grew very close indeed, but all the same Lonely agreed. It never did no good to argue with Mr Callan and besides, this was his chance to get into pictures.

Empson said: "I've never seen you before."
"It's mutual," said Callan.
The producer scurried over to them, kicking little flurries of sand.
"Noel," he said, "this is George Tucker. He's an expert on period costume."
"Is that right?" said Empson. "How's my period costume, George?"
Empson was dressed in the green uniform of the 95th Regiment of the Rifle Brigade. Callan looked him over, taking his time.
"It's accurate," he said at last. "But it's too new."
"Come again?"
"You're supposed to have been in the Peninsula for over three years," said Callan. "Everything you wear should look used."
"Is that a fact?" said Empson and yelled: "Dino!" A small, wiry man came running.
"We've got an hour," Empson said and started to unbutton his tunic. "Take this gear away and make it look used." He continued to strip and halfway out of his pants turned to Callan.
"You ever do any hand wrestling?"
"No," said Callan.
Empson said, "I could break you in two."
He stripped down to minute under-pants and Callan was aware that his physique was every bit as perfect as the publicity hand-outs said: the man was iron-hard and graceful too, as he walked down to the icy sea, dived neatly in and swam beautifully, powerfully.
A woman's voice said, "And so another Empson legend is born."
Callan turned to look at Emma Marston, black-haired, beautiful, eyes only for the swimmer.
"His delights were dolphin-like," she said.
"I beg your pardon?"
"That's Shakespeare," she said. "*Antony and Cleopatra*. You know – literature. Noel doesn't go much on culture. I don't get much chance..." She broke off, then said: "But he's serious about pictures."
Callan looked at Dino, slamming the well-pressed uniform jacket at a rock.
"So I gather," he said.
"Poor old Dino – he spent hours on Noel's clothes. And mine. Are mine all right, by the way?"
He looked at her. Off the set she wore a T-shirt and jeans, but now it was a gown of golden satin, high-heeled buckled shoes, emerald necklace, black mantilla worn over a jewel-studded tortoiseshell comb.
"You are fine," Callan said.
"Dino will be pleased," she said, her eyes still on the sea.
After that, there was nothing in the world but the picture. The whole crew worked at it, slaved at it, from the moment the sun came up to give them enough light. Callan spent his day racing from one group to another, checking the authenticity of a half-pike, a musket, a *legion d'honneur* ribbon. And all the time Empson clamoured for his attention, and everybody else's, but all the same he worked, driving on director, co-stars, producer, with his own inexhaustible energy. And every dialogue with Callan—and everybody else he didn't know—

ended with the same six words: “I could break you in two.”

Lonely met him at the place on the cliffs they’d agreed on. It was night, and the moon was up, the sea heaved peacefully in grey and silvers. Lonely didn’t even look at it.

“I’m knackered,” he said.

Callan looked at him: he was still in costume, waiting for a night-shot. Lonely the terrible, with a straggling moustache, tattered shirt and breeches, and a heavy belt stuffed with daggers and pistols. Callan handed him a bottle of beer.

“Ta, Mr Callan,” Lonely said and swigged.

“You know, when you said I was going to be a guerrilla. I thought you meant a bleeding monkey,” he said, and swigged again. “Might as well have been,” he said bitterly. “Up and down those cliffs five times already. It isn’t human.”

“Find anything?” said Callan.

“Yeah,” said Lonely. Callan waited.

“Well?” he said at last. “Are you really going to tell me or has fame gone to your head?”

Lonely said at once: “Oh sorry, Mr Callan. I was thinking about that Miss Marston. She’s smashing.”

“Lot of people think that,” said Callan. “So what?”

“No, what I mean,” said Lonely, “she’s nice, Patient, like, when I moved wrong.”

Callan stirred impatiently.

“Save it for your memoirs,” he said. “Who’s got it?”

“That’s what I mean, Mr Callan,” Lonely said. “She has.”

It was in a box hidden behind the refrigerator in her caravan; it had a 6in. barrel and a magazine that held 10 rounds of what sounded like ·22 long rifle ammunition. From Lonely’s description it was either a Colt Woodsman Match Target Pistol or a Russian copy.

From the film H.Q. the assistant director began shouting through a loud-hailer: “Extras to Beach Assembly Point, please. Extras to Beach Assembly Point, please.”

Lonely hauled himself to his feet.

“The magic of the silver screen,” he said. “They must be joking.”

They parted then, and Callan went off to the village to phone Meres.

The next day the technical adviser had been recalled to London, or so the producer said. The director had no doubt that they could finish the picture without him. In fact, the technical adviser was crouched behind a bush in the gardens of Brent House, assembling a piece of equipment for which he needed no technical advice: an Armalite AR7 rifle.

Stored into the recesses in the stock were barrel, breech and magazine: a neat six and a half inch package that weighed no more than two and a half pounds. Deftly his hands assembled it, converted it into a deadly precision instrument, then he took a pair of field glasses from the grip beside him and looked at the drawing-room window.

A white-haired figure in a grey silk dress came into view, but it didn't linger, and Callan was glad of it. He put down the glasses and picked up the rifle there was nothing now to do but wait.

The waiting was the worst of it: the time when you cautiously eased your muscles to ward off cramp and worried about the hundred thousand things that could go wrong, even in a set-up like this one. Time crawled by, and he grew hotter, thirsty, but he dared not move: being too hot, being thirsty, was much better than being dead.

From the beach he could hear a thin crackle of musketry — Wellington's men going into action—and then, from much nearer, a soft rustle of grass. He waited, still as a stone, as a figure in jeans and T-shirt wriggled its way towards the drawing-room of the house.

Callan wiped his hands on his shirt and picked up the rifle as the figure drew nearer the window, rose to a crouch, and produced a Colt Woodsman Target pistol. Another crackle of musketry from the beach, and the figure rested the Woodsman over its left forearm and took deliberate aim—but it was Callan who fired.

The Armalite gave two whip-like cracks, and the figure in jeans was smashed into the ground.

Callan waited, but there was no more noise or movement in the garden. From the beach he could hear the voice of the assistant director calling the lunch break. Callan broke cover and ran to the figure in jeans, turned it over....

It was Dino. He over to the drawing-room and looked in to where the white-haired old lady in a dove-grey dress was pouring herself a Scotch with a not too steady hand.

"You all right?" said Callan.

"I'm fine," said Meres. "But I feel rather a fool." He sipped his Scotch. "You killed the girl."

"It wasn't the girl," said Callan. "Empson set her up as a decoy."

"And the poor bitch is in love with him? How very unpleasant."

"You better get rid of the body," Callan said.

Meres sighed. "Of course. Just as soon as I've slipped into something a little less formal."

Callan went to the edge of the cliffs and looked down: a beached longboat, cars and trucks, piled arms, cameras, sound-equipment cluttered up the sands, but it was lunch-break: it was empty of people. If he went across the sands he could be in the village in no time.

He dismantled the Armalite, put it in his grip, and went down, then walked along the wet, hard sand. In the distance a beach buggy started up and roared towards him, slewed round broadside on to a stop, and Empson got out. He wore his uniform, and in his hand was a long, slender bayonet, curving a little at the tip, that the Rifle Brigade calls a sword.

"You weren't in London," said Empson. "You were in Brent House." He waited. Callan said nothing. "What's in your bag?"

Above them a seagull screamed: Callan knew how it felt.

"An Armalite rifle," he said. "I just shot Dino with it."

Empson knew then that he had lost, but in defeat all he wanted was company.

"I can break you in two," he said, and moved in on Callan.

Callan dropped the bag and moved as Empson moved, all his being concentrated on the sword-bayonet, sliding aside as the sword-bayonet lunged, grabbing for Empson's wrist, but the big man was as fast as a cat; he slid away in his turn and aimed a kick that Callan only just avoided then came in again, crowding him, and his second lunge burned across Callan's ribs.

Callan's foot caught in the handle of the bag and he stumbled and fell. But even as he went down he rolled over, fingers digging at the hard sand.

Empson leaped at him and he flung the sand: it hit his face, bit into his eyes, and Callan kept on rolling, and leaped to his feet.

Empson was brushing at his eyes with his left hand and Callan rushed him: fist strike to the gut, left-handed, axe-blow with the edge of the hand below the jaw, and Empson went down: there was no defence against those blows delivered as Callan had been taught to deliver them. Callan knelt beside him. Incredibly, he was still—just—alive.

"You bastard," said Empson. "I didn't finish the picture."

Then he died. Callan heaved him into the beach-buggy. Another disposal job for Meres. "Film Star and Dresser Disappear Sensation."

He drove off. Hunter wouldn't like it. He'd wanted Empson alive. Well hard luck, Hunter. You never faced Empson with a bayonet in his hand.

File on a Lucky Lady

The row in the discothèque was appalling, but Callan endured it stolidly. He'd endured a lot worse than that, and at least the Scotch was good.

All around him, figures in velvet, in cotton, in jeans, moved and gyrated to a beat as obvious as a tank in a car park. A scruffy lot most of them. You wouldn't have thought the net worth of the people in the room ran into millions. And even the scruffiness was phoney. Most people wore tatty clothes because they had to: this lot had them made that way.

He looked at the two loads of tat coming towards him. Each was graceful, and each, in its own way, good to look at.

"David," said Toby Meres. "How nice to see you."

Callan stood up. "Hello," he said.

"May I introduce you," said Meres. "David Callan—Miss Angela Balboa."

She put out her hand as the psychedelic lighting muted and changed: black hair, white skin, red lips all became muted tones of purple. Even subjected to that indignity, she was beautiful.

"How do you do, Mr Callan?" she said. "Toby's told me so much about you."

A low-pitched voice, with more than a little arrogance in it: a reminder that a good slice of the net worth in the room was hers, tatty jeans or no tatty jeans. ... The music stopped, then started again: electric guitars shredding the silence.

"I think we'll go in to supper," she said. "We can't talk here. You needn't wait, Toby."

Meres didn't wait, and she turned to Callan, who was still seated.

"Well?" she said.

"Sit down," said Callan. "I haven't finished my drink."

"I do hope you're not going to turn out to be one of those masterful men one reads about," said Angela Balboa.

"Well, what d'you think?" said Hunter.

Callan said: "I think I'll never make a swinger."

"The girl," Hunter said. "What did you think of her?"

"I'm told she's rich," said Callan, "and I know she's beautiful, I also know she's scared out of her tights."

"You progressed so far?"

"Come off it," said Callan. "A poor peasant like me? She's healthy and she's arrogant—and she's scared. Because she's scared she wants to buy my company—on Toby's recommendation. Five hundred a week, Hunter, Tax free."

"Tempting?"

Callan shrugged. "That's up to you," he said.

Hunter said: "You'd better take a look at this." He threw Callan the file, and Callan turned its cover. Angela Balboa: a studio portrait; hair heavy, gleaming, long: eyes the colour of dark sherry. "Only child of and heir to Robert Balboa," he read. "Balboa is a financier, banker and recluse. His manner of life is such as to render him almost invulnerable: his daughter is vulnerable."

"What have you got on the father?" asked Callan.

"He's a widower," said Hunter. "Lives in a house with bodyguards and almost never leaves it. Doesn't have to. He's got a computer, Telex, direct lines: all he needs. He's little more than a money-making machine, but the machine is remarkably efficient."

"Odd sort of a name," Callan said.

"His ancestors came here from Spain 150 years ago," said Hunter.

Callan looked again at Angela's portrait: those Spanish genes must be strong.

"He's just gone into super-conductors." Hunter said "Do yon know what they are?" Callan shook his head. "It's a way of providing electricity at almost no cost at all," said Hunter. "The perfect answer to the energy crisis. It's been known for years—but it's full of bugs. Balboa's taken over a research team that might kill the bugs. If they do, even his fortune will double—every five years."

"Taken over?" said Callan.

Hunter allowed himself a smile: an indulgence he rationed severely. It was pleasant to have a subordinate who got to the heart of things as well as people.

"One of the early boffins was French," he said. "He was financed for a while by some chaps who'd been with the S.D.E.C.E."

French Intelligence, thought Callan. Known as *barbouzes*, some good, some bad, some terrible. But all of them rough...

"Corsicans," said Hunter. "De Gaulle hired them to combat the *Algerie Francaise* extremists. They were known as *l'Union Corse*, and they were very unpleasant—and damn difficult to get rid of. Even de Gaulle found that. When they did leave, they went into drugs—and invested their profits."

"In super-conductors?"

"Among other things, Super-conductors showed no profits, so they sold out to Balboa. Now it looks as if they'll show enormous returns, and the Corsicans want to buy back in."

"And if Balboa won't sell—they'll kidnap his daughter?"

"Precisely," said Hunter. "And if he still won't sell they'll kill her."

"He's that fond of money?"

Hunter nodded. "He's fond of his daughter too, but money takes priority. He's advised her to move in with him— and she's refused."

"I see," said Callan, "but surely these Corsicans aren't with the French security any more?"

"Indeed not," said Hunter.
"Then this is a police job."
"The police have asked for our assistance," Hunter said. "So have three Government Departments. They have no love for Balboa, David, but they ache for super-conductors. They're important."
Callan turned the pages of the file: Catalani, Motta, Neroni. Three names, three faces; but names can be changed—and so can faces.
"Stay with her," said Hunter. "Don't let her be hurt. We've guaranteed her safety to her father."
I bet you haven't guaranteed mine, thought Callan.

He went back to her flat in Eaton Square. Third floor, which he approved of, and with all the right locks and alarms. They would have taken Lonely an hour at least, but then Lonely didn't use a gun....
She was in a drawing-room that was furnished all in white; white curtains, white rug, white leather furniture. Even a white Old English sheepdog. In a red dress she glowed like a ruby.
"Like it?" she said.
"What happens to the dog if you change the colour scheme?" said Callan. "Do you dye it?"
"Did Toby tell you I like my men rude?" she asked. "I don't always."
"Toby told me five Hundred a week," said Callan. "So did you, Neither of you said what for."
"He—he said you'd done things," she said. "Last night I tried to ask you. I found I couldn't."
"What things?"
"He—he said you'd killed people." He made no answer.
"Is it true?"
"Yes," he said.
"With a gun. He said you were awfully good with a gun."
I bet he didn't enjoy saying it, thought Callan. "I'm good," he said.
"How good?"
His hand moved then: a 357 Magnum pointed at her like a blunt, accusing finger.
"Good enough for 500 quid a week," he said, and put the gun away. "Who do you want me to kill?"
"I want you to keep me alive," she said, and out it all came; her father and *l'Union Corse*, but nothing about super-conductors. The rich always keep something back, he thought. That's how they stay rich.
"I've heard about your father," Callan said. "He's got a house like a fortress. Why don't you stay with him?"
"If I moved in with Daddy," she said. "I'd never get away. I like to live, Callan." She hesitated. "But not necessarily with you."
Callan said: "It's mutual."

When you did a bodyguarding job you got all sorts, but this one was a real little charmer. Shopping—which meant either Bond Street or Harrods—lunch out, dinner out, theatres, discos, and always with

Gorilla Callan at her right elbow, always with his right hand free. And gambling; she was a gambling nut. At all the swish places they fell over themselves when she came in, and at all the new ones too, Callan couldn't understand why. She won far more than she lost. Poker was her game: any kind of poker you cared to name.

At the *Polka Dot* for instance - done up like a gambling joint in a forties gangster movie; potted palms, red plush, and a heavy on the door - roulette and blackjack and craps, and a poker table where he wouldn't have lasted five minutes, not even on the salary she was paying him. She went up to it as if she had a season ticket, and in a sense she had; they all had: Stavros the Greek broker, Mark, the heir to a viscountcy, Chuck, the inevitable American.

"Good evening," she said. "You don't mind if my mascot sits beside me? He's a bit big to put up on the table." She turned to Callan. "Say good evening, darling."

"Good evening," said Callan.

"You see," she said. "He's perfectly well-trained."

And that was their public relationship. Callan sat there drinking one cautious Scotch left-handed, making it last all night, whilst she with one eye cocked, watched him as if at any moment he might start searching his pelt for fleas.

When she was ready to leave she'd won over £6,000. It was three in the morning. Chuck rose and came round to her and found that Callan was on his feet too.

"One of these days –" he said.

"Oh Chuck, that's what you always say."

"I mean it," said Chuck.

She laughed and turned to Callan. "Say good night, darling," she said.

"Good night," said Callan. That made four words he had spoken all evening. He was the only one who seemed surprised....

Her Bentley was old, enormous, and chauffeur-driven. Her servants should have been able to retire on their overtime alone.

They sank back on the seats and the car moved off, elegant and discreet.

"You brought me luck tonight," she said, and kissed him. It was a pleasant kiss from the first, and one that gained in intensity. Suddenly Callan's hand moved and held her right wrist. The fingers of her right hand just touched the butt of the Magnum. She tried to pull her hand away and found she couldn't.

"Just testing," she said. "I don't like to see you too relaxed."

Callan said: "Miss Balboa, people like you always forget the one important thing about guns."

"And what is the one important thing?"

"They go off," said Callan.

The car whispered into the square and Callan kept his eyes on the road near the house. From the area a shadow flickered, once. Callan grabbed the speaking tube.

"Keep going," he said. The car went on till Callan told him to stop.

Then he left it and raced, cat-footed round the empty square, crouched by a car, took a silencer from his pocket and screwed it on to the Magnum, then eased his way towards her house.

His target was looking the way the Bentley had gone but even so Callan used all the cover the parked cars gave him.

There was a tap-tap of heels on the pavement and Callan cursed. She had no business to come back, not yet, but there she was, under the lights and behind her a car started up. In front of her the target moved slow and easy up the area steps, and she found herself facing a man with a gun. Behind her the car slowed.

Callan stood up and whistled, and the target spun round and there was a sound like a champagne cork popping.

The car accelerated and was gone. She looked at the dead man at her feet, a neat hole in his forehead, an almost equally neat hole at the back. The muzzle velocity of a Magnum revolver is tremendous.

"I didn't see anybody," she said, "and I thought you were just showing off."

Callan unscrewed the silencer.

"I told you," he said, "they go off." And he caught her as she fainted.

Later she said: "But what about the body?"

"Don't worry," he said. "It's been taken care of."

"You think of everything," she said and this time there was no gun to impede their kiss.

"It'll all go on the bill," said Callan.

"We rather think the one you got was Neroni," said Hunter. "He's the right height and weight anyway – and he's had a lot of plastic surgery quite recently."

"Why don't they hire talent instead of doing the job themselves?" Callan asked.

"Because they're the best," said Hunter, "and anyway, who could they trust? They're after millions, Callan. As I told you, super-conductors are important."

"Yeah," said Callan. "You told me. Did you check on last night's card players?"

"Not Mark Blane," said Hunter. "He's far too much of a gentleman – and not Stavros Lambaki either. He's too nervous. But Chuck Ebberly—he's a distinct possibility." He looked hard at Callan. "I can find no record of a Chuck Ebberly anywhere. Before he came to London he didn't exist." He paused, then added: "Motta ran the United States end of their drug-smuggling. He speaks fluent American. I think we can assume he's Ebberly."

"He's invited her to a poker-party in Kent too," said Callan. "On Thursday, House owned by a man called Martel. I have a feeling Mattel will turn out to be Catalani."

"Indeed?" said Hunter. "Where in Kent?"

"On the coast," said Callan, "near Hythe, about as close to France as we can get."

"Will she go?"

"If I let her."
"Dear me," said Hunter. "You've tamed the shrew very effectively," Callan flushed. "Let her," said Hunter.
"It'll be rough."
"I've no doubt. If you deal with them, it will also be over and done with."
Callan had a feeling that there were other reasons too, but he wasn't going to waste his breath asking Hunter for them.
"I'll need help," said Callan. "Toby."
"Very well."
"He'd better have a look at Martel's house, too—and let me know."
"I'll see it's done," Hunter made a note and looked up. Callan was yawning. "Weary, Callan?"
"Yeah," said Callan. "What with one thing and another I had a busy night."

At least now that she liked him they didn't go out so much, but that meant he couldn't get away either—till he told her he needed some gun-practice. Then she let him go without argument.
It was true, too. He and Toby met in the Section Headquarters Armoury—and after they talked, they practised all right. This one was going to be even rougher than he'd anticipated. The house was on a headland overlooking a bay, and surrounded by high walls of thick stone. Burglar alarms all over the place, from what Toby had heard, and the Frenchman who owned it very handy with a shotgun. Handy with a handgun too, if it turned out to be Catalani.
"Any sign of a boat?" Callan asked.
"Yes," said Meres. "I've seen it. If the weather's OK it should do 40 knots at least."
They began to plan.
He went to see Lonely the day she went for a beauty treatment, and Hunter sent a couple of Section operators along to see that she survived the ordeal of massage and facial and leg waxing.
Lonely enjoyed his beer, and the meat pie and crisps Callan bought him, but he was unwilling.
"It's not that I mean to be disobliging, Mr Callan," he said, "but I don't like country jobs. Never have."
"A hundred and fifty," Callan said.
"Then there's the shotgun," said Lonely. "Suppose I missed one of the burglar alarms and a Froggy come at me with a shotgun? I'm no good at violence, Mr Callan."
"You won't miss a burglar alarm," Callan said. "Two hundred, old son. Two hundred nicker for twenty minutes' work. Ten quid a minute. You'll have an inflation all to yourself."
Lonely said: "I'm not saying I'll do it, mind, but what would I have to nick?"
"Nothing," said Callan. "I want you to plant something there."
"Such as what, Mr Callan?"
Callan told him, and Lonely shot up in the air as if Callan had rammed a spike into him.

"I'm very sorry, Mr Callan," he said, "but the answer's No."

"Keep your voice down," said Callan. Lonely concentrated on his pie. "You remember when we were in the nick?" Callan said.

"Yes, Mr Callan."

"You remember Rinty?" Lonely nodded. "Look at me when I'm talking."

At once Lonely looked up.

"He was bothering you, wasn't he ... and I asked him to lay off ... asked him nicely ... you can't say I didn't ... only he was disobliging as well. What did I do to him, Lonely?"

The cold, grey eyes bored into his: no doubt about it, Mr Callan was angry.

"Well?" said Callan.

"You — you broke his arm," Lonely said and the smell came.

"No need to start stinking," Callan said gently. "Not yet, anyway, I know you won't be disobliging."

Lonely looked into his beer, "No. Mr Callan," he said.

"Good lad," said Callan. "Two hundred and fifty."

Meres was drunk when they picked him up, and stayed drunk all the way to Kent, if Chuck Ebberly resented it, he managed to conceal the fact, even when Meres produced a flask and went on drinking.

It was Angela who was furious: she wouldn't gamble with a drunk. We all have our standards, thought Callan, and submitted to her wrath. After all it was he who'd suggested they bring Meres.

They arrived at the house, and Martel helped Chuck and Callan to get Meres inside. There was a certain amount of bumping and jostling, and between them they managed to frisk both Callan and Meres. They did it unobtrusively and well, and the fact that neither man was armed left them at first bewildered, then relived. Once inside, Meres took another swig at his flask, staggered, then said in a voice of utter certainty: "I'm going to be sick."

Callan turned to Martel. "I'd better get him to the bathroom," he said.

Martel gave directions, and Callan picked up Meres and staggered upstairs.

One sniff inside the bathroom, and there was no doubt that Lonely had called. Meres lifted the lid of the lavatory cistern and Callan took out the waterproof box, tore off the wrappings. Two ·357 Magnums, clean, bright and slightly oiled. ... They raced down the back stairs to a green baize door and Callan squinted through a crack. Chuck had a gun on Angela, and Martel was putting on a coat—wrapping up warm for his sea trip. All three had their backs to him.

Meres and Callan went on through, and Callan shot Chuck without hesitation. If that one was going to die he'd want company, and Angela Balboa was nearest. Coat or no coat, Martel got a gun in his hand before Meres killed him.

The girl looked first at Callan, then at Meres. "You were right, David," she said. "Guns do sometimes go off."

Callan dialled the long, familiar number, and Hunter was delighted to speak.

"Excellent," he said. "Really quite excellent." Then, "Do you think you could do one more thing, David?"

"Let's hear it," said Callan.

"Keep Miss Balboa with you for a while—without letting her communicate with her father."

"Why on earth should I?" said Callan.

"Balboa might not compromise with Corsican gangsters," Hunter said, "but I'm sure he and I can reach an agreement."

"Do my best," said Callan. "I mean, it's like you say: super-conductors are important."

File on a Dancing Decoy

"That's her," said Hunter. "Fourth from the left. The one with black hair."

Behind them a balletomane said Shh! People saying Shh! seemed as much a part of ballet as the music.

Callan looked at the stage: *Les Sylphides*. ... Romantic never-never land: girls in white skirts, blokes in white tights and black velvet waistcoats, floating, ecstatic to the music of Chopin.

He looked at the fourth one from the left again. She was good—no question, but she would not make a prima ballerina yet. She was far too tense.

Before it started he'd looked down the list of names: Jane Sinkins, Marjorie Tomlinson, Valerie Prout, and in the midst of them, Varvara Arenskaya, about as inconspicuous as a dog at a cat show — and a borzoi at that.

Good looking, nice figure, but somehow, something was missing. He went back to the romantic ecstasy: the blokes in black and white were lovely movers, no question, but they'd have a hell of a time hiding a ·357 Magnum under those outfits.

After the ballet, Hunter took him to dinner, but that didn't mean they'd stopped working.

"Like it?" he asked. Callan shrugged.

"It was all right," he said. "I'm a *Petrouchka* man myself."

Hunter looked up from his smoked salmon. "You still have the ability to surprise me, Callan," he said. "I find that very refreshing." Then almost without a pause he added: "About Varvara Arenskaya. You've had a look at her file?"

"Yeah," said Callan. "Yellow cover - surveillance only. What's so special about her?"

"She defected," said Hunter.

"I remember," said Callan. "She was doing a tour with the Kiev Company."

"Rather a spectacular defection, if you remember," Hunter said. "She ran off the stage and into the auditorium in the middle of *Swan Lake* and the KGB made no move to get her back."

"How could they?" said Callan. "The place was packed."

"There were eight KGB men present at every performance," said Hunter. "They weren't there because they liked ballet."

"All the same..."
"My dear David," Hunter said, "you're not suggesting the KGB remained in their seats because they dislike making scenes? They've made scenes at airports, trade fairs, even embassy parties. An English theatre would be nothing to them. Why did they let her go?"
"Not worth the fuss?"
Hunter examined his roast pheasant as if it were a hostile witness. "Did you read about Routledge?" he asked.
"The Oxford professor. Yes ... I read about him."
"The correct word," said Hunter. "Is don."
"You'll have to excuse me," Callan said. "I'm ignorant."
"In the literal sense I suppose that's true," said Hunter, "but you're by no means a fool. Routledge met her in Moscow. They were lovers."
"Oh dear," said Callan. "One of them."
"Precisely," said Hunter. "That's why I'm having her watched."
"Has she tried to see him again?"
"Not yet," Hunter said. "Nor must she."
"Routledge is important?"
"Extremely," said Hunter. "He's an economist—specialises in economic planning. He sometimes does a little planning for us, too."
He'd got a Czech physicist out of Prague with a lot of good stuff about breeder reactors locked up in his head: arranged a set-up with a Polish metallurgist who had all sorts of interesting information about machine-tools: blackmailed an Egyptian who knew as much about SAM missiles as the bloke who made them....
"And you let him go to Moscow?" Callan said.
Hunter said: "His cover was perfect and in any case he had to go."
"And meet this bird?"
"A pity, that." said Hunter. "But he did his job. Of course his cover was blown after that. The KGB have marked him for a wet job."
That meant execution. Callan knew, and if they could smear him as well so much the better.
"You think they'll use the girl?"
Hunter poured more claret.
That is what I want you to find out," he said.

For a *Petrouchka* man it wasn't all that difficult to make contact with a dancer. He knew all the patter and Hunter laid on the necessary contact — Hugh Beaumont, an ageing though still beautiful premier danseur with a house off Cheyne Walk. He took one look at Callan and said, "Good gracious."
"Something wrong?" said Callan.
"You don't look as if ballet was your sort of thing," Beaumont said.
"You'd be surprised what my sort of thing is," said Callan.
"My dear, nothing surprises me," said Beaumont. "I worked for Hunter for years." He thought for a moment. "You can come to my party on Sunday," he said at last. "But you really must dress up a little."
Callan went to the party in dark blue slacks and powder blue sweater. Round his neck he wore a medallion of Mexican silver with

an amethyst in its centre carved to look like the head of an angry god. He was the most conservatively dressed man in the room.

Beaumont swooped down on him and gave him champagne, then studied his clothes, delighted.

"You see?" he said. "You can look quite pretty when you try—but you're out of luck. I'm afraid. Darling Varvara has failed me—she's doing extra barre practice instead. Oh, those Russians are so dedicated."

But most of the others were there: the pretty, indistinguishable girls with the dancers' floating grace and over-developed calf muscles.

Callan drew Valerie Prout. It wasn't the hardest contact he had ever made. All he had to do was keep on passing the canapes and listen, while Valerie told him about the rich fulness of her life, and how, at her age, it was necessary to achieve maturity.

She would be, he gathered, twenty next birthday. That lasted till the end of the party. After that he took her to dinner.

The way to Valerie's heart was through her stomach, all right. She at a dozen oysters with brown bread, the biggest steak in the restaurant with sauce béarnaise, pommes sautés and grilled mushrooms, had two goes at the dessert trolley and topped it off with celery, cheese and biscuits. Callan guessed her weight at seven and a half stone ... The only thing she refused was wine. Wine, he gathered, was *madly* fattening.

Her topic over dinner was the agony and ecstasy of being a dancer, even if one's father was a dentist in Tring, but he worked his way round to Varvara Arenskaya at last. After all, her defection had been an absolute sensation.

"Oh absolutely," said Valerie. "But she's very dull, you know, and she never seems to relax. I wish I could have publicity like that. But you can't defect from Tring, can you?"

Callan agreed that it would be difficult.

"I'm her best friend, you know," said Valerie, and ordered coffee with *lots* of cream. "Her only friend really and that's only because I share a flat with her. Not that she talks much."

"She speaks English then?" Callan asked.

"Quite well, actually." She spooned sugar into her coffee, one—two—three—four—and Callan watched, fascinated. "She has an accent, of course. Men seem to find it attractive."

"Men?"

Well, one man anyway. An absolute dish of a Frenchman who wanted to do a piece about Varvara for *Paris Match* or something... Jean-Claude was it? Or Jean-Marie? But she remembered his surname: Massenet. Like the man who wrote that dreamy ballet-music all those *hundreds* of years ago. But this Massenet was an absolute *dream*, and, Callan gathered, *totally* wasted on Varvara.

When they left the restaurant they walked for a while, then suddenly she turned to him and he kissed her: the inevitable follow-up to coffee and cream with four sugars. At last she said: "I think perhaps you're dreamy too, in a mature sort of way. Would you like to come back to the flat?"

"Very much," said Callan. "Even though Varvara will be there?"
Without a chaperon I wouldn't have a prayer, thought Callan, but he didn't say so aloud.

She was very beautiful and very Slav: high cheekbones, dark almond eyes: her body sturdier than Valerie's, but beautiful even so, controlled with the instinctive dancer's grace. And yet she wore a grey dress, as if she were retreating into the colour's neutrality. She was shy alright—or acting shy.

Behind the shyness Callan could detect a stronger, more primitive emotion. Rage perhaps, or fear, or both. Valerie brewed more coffee and opened a tin of biscuits; custard creams, chocolate fingers, macaroons, and Callan reminded his stomach that it too worked for Hunter.

"I was telling David about your boy friend," Valerie said.

"My boy friend?" Her voice was low-pitched, uncertain.

"Massenet," said Valerie. "Don't you see him any more?"

"No." Varvara said, "Not any more."

"But Varvara that's silly," said Valerie, and from the next room the telephone shrilled. "Blast," she said, and got up to answer it, and took the biscuits with her.

"I've seen you dance," said Callan.

"I am not yet very good," she said.

"Oh I wouldn't say that," said Callan.

"Why not? It is true. But one day I will be good," she said. "I hope you will be there to see."

Her voice was low-pitched still, but utterly certain.

Valerie came back furious.

"Some idiot asking for Mr Shillington again," she said. "It happens every week. I keep telling them they've got the wrong number but the bloody fools don't listen."

Varvara Arenskays retreated into her shyness: perhaps it was the bad language.

Callan left and hung about, and the night grew cold enough to make him glad that his powder-blue sweater was Cashmere. When she came out he gave her plenty of room, and followed her to a row of three telephone boxes. As she drew near he could hear the phone ring in the middle box, and she broke into a run and hurried inside.

Callan waited until she came out again. That emotion so much stronger than shyness was evident again. He followed her home, then waited until the lights in the flat went out before he went back to the telephone booths and dialled the number he knew best.

"Let me speak to Charlie, please," he said....

"Bugged," said Hunter. "Of course the flat's bugged."

"Learn anything?" Callan said.

"A great deal about ballet," said Hunter, "and even more about food."

"I think you ought to buy three telephone kiosks," said Callan and went on to talk about Massenet. Hunter listened, questioned, then agreed.

"I'll get on to it," he said.

"What about Routledge?"

"He's staying at his college," said Hunter. "There's been no contact. Not yet."

"Have you warned him?"

"Of course," Hunter said. "But the damn fool won't listen."

And you haven't seen her as I've seen her, thought Callan. So strong, so shy; so graceful, so vulnerable. And even if you had, it wouldn't make a ha'porth of difference.

Time to see another misogynist – and another good eater too. Chicken legs, cold sausages, pork pie and crisps. And beer. Lonely needed beer the way a plant needs soil.

"The bally?" said Lonely. "Me?"

He says it as if the word meant brothel, thought Callan.

"You don't have to go inside," said Callan. "Just follow a bird."

"What bird, Mr Callan?" said Lonely.

"This bird."

Callan showed him Varvara's photograph.

"Hey," said Lonely. "She's all right, Mr Callan. Your bird is she?"

"I'm not sure," said Callan. "She might be. One day."

He went back to his flat, set out the model soldiers and thought over the Battle of Salamanca. There hadn't been a bird in sight: or a Russian for that matter.

Hunter said "Cream and sugar?" and Callan thought of Valerie Prout.

"No thank you," he said. "Just plain black."

Hunter poured coffee.

"We can't find Massenet," he said. "But we'd like to, very much."

"He's a phoney then?"

"No," said Hunter. "He's a freelance journalist all right – among other things. He's a killer in fact. And I doubt he's French – even if his passport is."

"We'd better flush him out," said Callan.

"I doubt if she has Massenet's number," Hunter said.

"So do I," said Callan. "If she had he wouldn't call her. Why not try the old accident dodge?"

The story made the stop press of the late editions; not long before curtain time in the theatre. A woman who gave her name as Varvara Arenskaya, a dancer, had been hit by a car and taken to hospital. And there would be a woman, thought Callan, and she'd have the dancer's look. Hunter would see to that. Only the car wouldn't quite have hit her: not even Hunter was that thorough. The call for Mr Shillington came through just as she got back from the theatre, and she waited in a fever of impatience until Valerie fell asleep.

She hurried to the phone box and a little man in a raincoat scurried up behind her and stood at the bus stop: on his face the look of blank despair of one who knows the last one went ten minutes ago.

"He's at the Ilion," said Hunter.

"There's posh for you," said Callan.

"Yes, very decent hotel. As a matter of fact we've booked you in next door."

"Things warming up?"

"Near the boil," said Hunter. "He saw that piece in the paper. Checked at the hospital. It turned out the girl was a Barbara McIntyre. Stripper from Manchester. All the same it bothered him. He wants to get it over with."

"Get what over with?"

"Routledge."

"She's going to Oxford?"

"No," said Hunter. "He's coming here."

"Aren't you risking rather a lot?" said Callan.

"Possibly," Hunter said. "I want to get it over with, too... May be then Routledge will listen to reason."

If Massenet was at the Ilion, then Varvara would go there too. All the same, Callan thought, it might be as well to keep Lonely on her, just in case. And, anyway, he was enjoying his work. He left word with the little man that he was at the Ilion.

Routledge read the letter again: the Cyrillic characters were Varvara's, he was sure: the memories expressed in it were shared only by herself and him. Typical of Varvara, too, to say that she had deliberately kept away from him until there was no more trouble with the KGB—and equally typical to say that she hadn't dared phone because his phone—or hers—might be tapped. She had a lot to learn about this country. It would be a lifetime's delight to teach her.

He left his room and set off down the corridor, thinking of ways to lose those damn goons of Hunter's. Behind him his phone started ringing, but he ignored it. A man in love has no time for telephones.

Callan liked his room as well he might. It was costing Hunter £20 a day. He set up his scoop mike and looked at the view across the park, pretty in the sunshine, peaceful. He opened his suitcase and took out the .357 Magnum revolver, checked it, loaded it, stuck it in his waistband. No need for silencers, not in the Ilion. All the rooms were sound-proofed.

Massenet stayed in his room and ate lunch, and the scoop mike picked up every detail. Callan ordered a sandwich and drank coffee—black—no cream or sugar, and thought longingly of whisky. But that wouldn't come till after the matinée—if it ever came at all....

Lonely watched as they came out of the stage-door, chattering and gaudy as tropical birds: but the one he wanted wore grey as usual. Grey sweater, grey trousers, grey cloak with a hood pulled over her head. Ought to get yourself a bit of colour love, thought Lonely as he fell in behind her. You don't do yourself justice. A walker, she was.

Twenty minutes non-stop, but she pulled into a caff at last. Three buns and a cake, and tea with four sugars. She pushed back her hood and prepared to demolish the lot.

"Oh my Gawd," said Lonely, and streaked for a phone. Behind him a waitress sniffed, first in disapproval, then in outrage.

"I'm sorry, Mr Callan, honestly I am," said Lonely. "They must have like changed clothes."

"Not to worry, old son," said Callan.

"No charge Mr Callan. Not this time," Lonely said miserably. "I let you down."

"It'll all be right on the night," said Callan. "But one of these days somebody'll put that bird on a diet."

"Be a pleasure that would," said Lonely. "Mr Callan. I feel terrible."

So he spent five minutes soothing Lonely's feelings, then hung up as Varvara Arenskaya arrived. He went to the scoop mike and listened: not that his Russian was all that marvellous, but he could follow what was said.

"You know what to do?" said Massenet.

"Of course," she said. "I let him in then you take over."

"Exactly," said Massenet. "It shouldn't take long."

"I hope not," she said. "I have a performance at 7.30."

And where's the uncertainty now thought Callan?

Routledge's happiness was ecstatic. He grinned as he kissed her, grinned as she drew him into the room, and was still grinning as Massenet came in from the bathroom. But the grin died when he saw the Walther automatic in Massenet's hand.

"There is no need for that," she said. "You promised you wouldn't hurt him."

"There is every need." The barrel of the gun swivelled from Routledge to her.

"Peter, darling," she said. "I'm sorry. I tricked you. This man is from the KGB He says they will arrest my brother unless you—you give them some papers he wants. Just do as he asks and he'll leave us alone."

"I have no papers," said Routledge.

"I believe you," said Massenet. "But you do have information. You can tell me, for example, where Hunter is."

"I don't know anyone of that name."

The gun swung on him.

"It's no good shooting me," said Routledge. "I can't help you."

"Shoot you?" Massenet smiled. "Of course; but first I will shoot Arenskaya in the knee-cap. Her career as a dancer is finished anyway. Unless you care to tell me what I wish to know."

The girl's animation withered and died.

Routledge said: "Haven't you learned yet, darling? They always lie."

"Not always," said Massenet. "Only when the truth is of no use to us."

Callan put down the scoop-mike: it was time to move.

Lock and master-key alike had been specially oiled, and the lock yielded without a sound: but going in was the hardest thing he'd ever done. It always was: every time. Get on with it, Callan. The lady has a 7.30 performance.

His shoulder hit the door and he went in at a crouch, loosed off his first shot before he hit the floor. The first bullet's impact whirled

Massenet from the girl: the second one felled him as an axe lops off a branch. Callan got to his feet, picked up the Walther.

"We had you wrong," he said to the girl. "We thought you were setting Routledge up for murder."

"How could I?" she said. "I love him."

"Why did you change your clothes with Valerie?" said Callan.

"Massenet told me to," she said. "In case I was followed. He said British Intelligence would do anything to keep me away from Peter. Was he lying then, too?"

"You'll have to ask a man called Hunter," said Callan.

He looked at the dead man on the floor. For once in his life Massenet looked surprised.

"Why did you put off contacting Routledge for so long?"

"They said they would punish my brother if I went to him before they told me to," she said. "They will now anyway, won't they?"

Massenet had whisky. Callan drank some. "They right," he said gently. "But you knew that before you defected."

She put out a hand to Routledge and he took it at once. "You do know things," she said. "That is why they let me go. So that I could reach you—and they could hurt you."

"That's enough," said Callan. "We'd better go and talk to Charlie."

"But I can't," she said.

"I know, love," said Callan. "You have a performance—and I bet you'll be marvellous. But not tonight."

File on a Deadly Diary

"I WANT you to keep an eye on Lady Black," said Hunter.

"So I'm going into the aristocracy now," said Callan.

"I think one can describe it more properly as the gentry," Hunter said. "She is the widow of Sir Arthur Black. Foreign Office type. Attached to UNO. Knighted just before he died. Take a look."

He handed over a yellow-backed file. Surveillance only. That made a change: a nice change. There had been so many red files, so many deaths.

He opened the file at the photograph. It wasn't what he'd expected. Most of the aristocrats he'd met looked like the horse that came in fifth at Haydock Park when he backed it, but not this one. This one was a beauty. Black hair, brown eyes, full lips but not too full and a figure that filled an evening gown the way an evening gown deserved to be filled ... Pamela Black, aged 32, 5ft. 2in., estimated weight 118lb. And beautiful.

Hunter said dryly: "There's a photograph of her late husband too—if you'd care to look at it."

Callan turned the page.

Sir Arthur had been tall, lean, by the look of him intelligent, and 12 years older than his wife.

"How did he die?" asked Callan.

"Heart attack," said Hunter, "in the middle of a diplomatic party at the Romanian Embassy."

"Heart attack?"

"Natural causes," said Hunter. "There can be no doubt of it. Snell was at the post-mortem."

Snell, the section's doctor and psychiatrist, was the only person Callan had ever met with an assurance to match Hunter's, and it was equally well deserved.

"Then why the surveillance?" Callan asked.

"Black was able—extremely able. Like all the able ones he was grotesquely overworked. And he was in on things. Our sort of thing. Right to the limit. He was also extremely attached to his wife."

Who wouldn't be? thought Callan.

"And she to him so far as I can discover. It is possible that he talked to her about our sort of thing."

"Oh dear," said Callan.

"Oh dear is right," Hunter said. "It is even possible that she in her turn may be about to talk to others. Find out, will you David?"

Callan rose.

Hunter said: "You realise, of course, that if my suspicions are correct she'll move from that file to a red one?"

Callan put a team on her: surveillance round the clock. It was the only way. Two men with a car, two men and two women on foot. Lady Black had company wherever she went. The team were good at their jobs, but in two days their combined information was that she had had her hair done, eaten lunch with a woman friend at the Savoy, bought a book about archaeology, and gone to the Royal Ballet with an archdeacon who turned out to be her uncle. Bugging her phone hadn't helped either. She'd hardly used it.

Callan decided to slip one more ferret down the rabbit hole, though the way he smelled sometimes he was more like a stoat. All the same when it came to tailing he was unbeatable.

"Follow a bird?" said Lonely.

"Yeah," said Callan. "Ten quid a day and expenses. Twenty quid guaranteed."

"What's she like?" said Lonely.

Callan handed over a copy of the photograph. "Like this," he said.

Lonely did a very uncharacteristic thing. Right there in the boozer, with a draught enough to cut you in two, he took his cap off.

"You want me to follow *her* and you're going to pay me?" He sounded incredulous.

"That's right," said Callan. "Twenty quid minimum."

He handed back the photograph and replaced his cap.

"And wear your best suit," said Callan. "You'll be going to some pretty posh places."

Lonely looked outraged.

"Mr Callan," he said. "To follow her I'd always wear my best suit."

The phone bug told them that she'd been invited to a party at the Romanian Embassy, and had accepted. Callan thought it strange that she should go back to the place where her husband had died, and so did Hunter. He sent for a freelance who cost a fortune, but he had three inestimable advantages: he could speak Romanian, he could lip-read, and he could get himself invited at short notice to Iron Curtain embassy parties.

Lonely, resplendent in his best blue serge, pork pie and an I Zingari tie he'd lifted from a shop in Mayfair, followed Lady Black to Harrods, then took a walk with her to a hotel in the Brompton Road. The team had been warned that he had joined their ranks, and kept their distance.

At the hotel she went into the cocktail bar and joined a geezer who was all blondy and sun-tanned, who clicked his heels when he met her, and bowed over her hand. Lonely sat at the next table and ordered a gin and tonic: an heroic gesture—he was dying for a light and bitter—then followed them to a nearby restaurant, and had a bit of luck. He copped the next table. He didn't think much of the grub though. They didn't have any chips.

Callan bought him a pint of his favourite, and a packet of crisps.

"Let's have it," he said.

"Mr Callan, she's even better than her photograph," said Lonely. "You should just see her move."

"Take it easy," said Callan. "You'll be getting one of your hot flushes."

Lonely looked at Callan reproachfully: his heart was pure.

"She's a lady, Mr Callan," he said. "A real lady."

"Just tell it," said Callan. And Lonely did.

She'd met this geezer and called him Rudi, and that was all she'd called him, but in the restaurant he said he'd booked a table, and Lonely did his best to reproduce the sounds he'd made. It sounded like Von Kleist. Lonely said he'd got the next table, and Callan looked pleased. Lonely hated to disappoint him.

"The only trouble was," he said, "all through the meal they talked foreign."

"Foreign?" said Callan. "What kind of foreign?"

"Like Nazi," said Lonely.

Ever since a V2 had wiped out his family in 1945, and buried him alive, there had been no more Germans for Lonely, only Nazis – never mind how long the war had been over.

"They didn't speak any English at all?" Callan said.

"Only the once," said Lonely. "She was a bit, like, agitated." He scowled. "That Nazi had got her all upset."

"Get on," said Callan.

Lonely knew that voice, and felt the beginnings of terror.

Callan said, more gently: "Just tell it, old son."

"She said, 'The diaries are at the bank. I *think* they'd better stay there.'"

"Again," said Callan, and Lonely repeated it. Again the emphasis was on the *think*. Callan bought him another light and bitter.

"That was at lunch?" Hunter asked.

"That's right," Callan said.

"She went to the Romanian party last night," said Hunter. "My chap said she spent most of her time talking to a chap called Eminescu. He's on their books as cultural attaché—but I doubt it. Nothing known, but I doubt it. He also brought up the subject of diaries. She changed it.

"When she left, Eminescu had a word with another chap whom I *know* is Romanian security. He said: 'Any luck?' and Eminescu said. 'Have a heart. I've only just started.' I'm translating rather freely, but that was the gist." He consulted Lady Black's file. "I knew nothing about diaries," he said. "Your odoriferous little friend has his uses." He turned more pages.

"Ah," he said, "she banks at the London and Northern. The Mayfair branch. Do you know it?"

"I've been inside," said Callan. "It's a big one."

"Could you—er—break into it?"

This one must be bugging you, Callan thought. He said aloud, "Do a bank job?"

"Yes. *That* bank."

"I could," said Callan. "It'd be dodgy. But I could."

"Then do so."

"It would take a team," said Callan.

"Use anyone you like."

"Most of them are in nick," said Callan.

"Ah," said Hunter. "I thought you meant our chaps."

"Not for the London and Northern," said Callan. "For that you'd need specialists."

"Pity," said Hunter. "This chap von Kleist. Is there anything?"

"Yeah," said Callan. "He's the Herr Baron Rudolf von Kleist, and he used to have estates in East Germany before the war but now he's only a ski instructor. That's how he met the Blacks. They were both mad on ski-ing. He's supposed to be bright, and he's very successful with women, considering his age."

Hunter looked at him, head cocked.

"So are you," he said, "considering yours. I think you'd better visit Lady Black."

They began to discuss possible cover stories.

Lady Black said, "I have absolutely no talent for literature."

Callan risked one more glance round the room before he answered. He might have to break in here some time. ... Drawing room. First floor of a tall, narrow house in Mayfair. Curtains of dark red silk, chairs and sofa covered in gold silk, the perfect foil for her dark beauty. The only masculine touch was a photograph in a silver frame—the late Sir Arthur, and yet somehow it seemed to dominate the room. It was obvious that she'd adored him.

"Neither have I, Lady Black," he said. "But for the proposition I'm offering, neither of us needs it."

"Just what exactly are you offering, Mr Tucker?"

When he used the name Tucker, Callan had to be careful. Tucker had been everything from a lorry-driver to a merchant banker, but whatever else he was, he wasn't a killer. But the dark, beautiful eyes on his were shrewd, too. From her it would be dodgy to hide even that.

"I want a book with your name on it," he said. "All the inside dope about life at United Nations H.Q. — you know—parties, gossip, how much vodka the Russians' get through per day. But I don't want you to write it. Just put your name on it."

"Then who will write it?"

"I've got a ghost all lined up," said Callan. And it was true. Hunter had a tame hack in a fifth-floor flat, panting for the off.

"But how could he possibly? He doesn't even know me. Never knew my husband."

She moved in the chair, and Callan willed himself to remember that this was strictly business—and yellow file business at that.

"You can talk to him," he said, "and he'll take what you tell him on tape."

You bet he will, he thought. With two machines.

"And besides, your husband must have left papers perhaps even a diary ——" He broke off. She was laughing, but it wasn't happy laughter.

"I'm sorry," she said at last. "They say everything comes in threes, don't they?"

"So my mother used to say," said Callan.

"Perhaps she was right. ... Yours is the third offer I've had."

"Naturally I'll be prepared to discuss terms," said Callan. "Particularly if I have competitors."

"Only one," she said. "One wants me to publish, the other one thinks the diaries should be suppressed—and that was the better offer."

Callan willed his voice not to sound optimistic. "You'll take it?" he asked.

"I don't know," she said. "The diaries are all I have left of my husband."

"They must be very—controversial," he said. "If you're getting a good offer for suppression, I mean."

"They are."

"Maybe I could match it," he said.

"Maybe. I'll think about it—let you know."

"When?" said Callan.

"I'm going ski-ing," she said. "In the Cairngorms. I'll be back in a couple of weeks. I'll tell you then."

Again she moved in her chair: again Callan willed himself to remember her yellow file.

"I'm very fond of ski-ing," he said.

"Are you?" The clever, lovely eyes were alight with amusement. "Since when, Mr Tucker?"

"Since now," said Callan.

To her amazement Lady Black heard herself invite Mr Tucker to stay and have a drink.

"At first she treated me like a cross between an income-tax nark and the man who's failed to clear the drains," said Callan. "But it got better."

He reported in full, and Hunter nodded benignly.

"She's going to Scotland to meet von Kleist," said Callan.

"You're sure?"

"Yeah," Callan nodded. "Her phone bug."

"He's the one who wants her to publish?"

Callan shrugged "Looks like it."

"I think you'd better go ski-ing too," Hunter said.

"*Me?*" In outrage Callan knew, and cursed himself for knowing, that his voice resembled Lonely's. "I've never skied in my life."

"Now's your chance to learn," said Hunter. "Welcome to the over-privileged classes."

He went to see her once again before she left, and told himself that it was because of her yellow file, but it wasn't that. One day her file might be red, and he couldn't bear it. They talked, and this time when she laughed, it was happy laughter. They dined, and she invited him back for coffee, poured him brandy. ... It was the best night he could remember, but she wouldn't discuss the diaries.

Next day she took a train to Scotland, and the team reported that she'd stopped off at the bank en route. Hunter rang for Callan.

"About Lady Black," he said.

Callan's eyes went at once to the file Hunter held: it had a red cover.

"You can't do this," he said. "You can't."

"Not immediately perhaps," said Hunter. "Not if only von Kleist is involved. But if Eminescu's there–" he shrugged. "You'd better get up there. David. I've laid on an R.A.F. plane."

"No," said Callan.

"Would you rather I sent Meres?"

You bastard, thought Callan. You deal the hands and you take every trick. Slowly he fought his way back to calmness.

"All right," he said at last. "But I won't ski. And first I want to see Snell."

The request he made to Snell could have inspired anything from outrage to laughter, but Snell being Snell, all he got was a meticulous production of what he'd asked for. He left the Section, and a waiting Daimler 4.2 shot him off to the airfield. He was at the hotel hours ahead of Lady Black.

The only trouble was that Lady Black wasn't staying at the hotel. She was at a hunting lodge, the guest of a Scottish laird, and von Kleist was due there the next evening.

Not that Callan lacked for company. He'd studied the file carefully, and the man next to him at the bar could only be Eminescu: a short, roly-poly sort of man a little ridiculous in his après-ski costume, plump all over. But the plumpness didn't all have to be fat. A lot of it could be muscle.

He looked at Callan's left arm; the bandaged sling, the protruding edge of plaster.

"Had a fall?" he asked.

"Yeah," said Callan. "Off the train. Stumbled and fell and broke my arm—and I'm booked in for a week. You wouldn't care to hire a pair of skis, would you?"

Eminescu laughed.

"No thanks," he said. "I've brought my own."

He had, too. Callan watched him set off next morning. Roly-poly or not he was poetry in motion. Callan ordered coffee, and waited for the S.A.S. captain Hunter had procured for liaison. Upper-class tough, thought Callan. But nice with it.

Captain Lestrange said: "Sorry about your arm, old chap."

"I'll live," said Callan. "Tell me about the lodge."

The best way was on skis, it seemed, but something might be managed. ... One of Lestrange's chaps had got chummy with a maid there. The S.A.S. were doing a survival course near by, and what they had to endure had wrung every female heart for miles. Besides, he was a very handsome young man....

There was a ceilidh at the village near by, and the entire household was going, including the laird, but Lady Black didn't feel up to it. As a place for meeting unobserved, the house was perfect. And for breaking and entering it was a pushover. A chubby, foreign sort of chap had taken a toss on his skis just that morning, when the maid was coming in to work. It seemed he'd got through a lot of gossip before he left. The security at the lodge wasn't just awful, it was non existent.

The gallant captain left, and Callan went out for a breath of air as far as the first ski-lift, just as Lady Black walked up, skis over her shoulder, in cherry red sweater, white ski-pants, cherry red knitted cap with a white pom-pon.

"Why, Mr Tucker," she said. "This is a surprise." The mockery in her eyes was pure delight, and she was in a red file. She looked at his arm. "But what happened?" she said.

"I came to learn," said Callan. "I learned all right."

"Poor Mr Tucker," she said, and this time her smile was all compassion. Callan watched her walk to the ski-lift: strong, sure, and utterly feminine.

That night the moon was full, and the snow gleamed silver, the pine-trees were like exclamation marks cast in silver-gilt.

Eminescu ate early, and Callan didn't eat at all, but waited in the cover of the pine-trees, watched Eminescu set off.

Lestrange had a snow-cat waiting, and Callan climbed in, the snow-cat moved. In his ears Callan could still hear the hiss of the Rumanian's skis; harsh and dry. The damn snow-cat stalled. Lestrange cursed, then got out and fiddled, but even so they lost ten minutes before they churned their way on.

Lestrange drew the cat to a halt by the edge of a path to the lodge cut into the snow.

"Need any help old chap?" he asked.

"I'll manage," said Callan.

"With your arm in the state it is—"

"I'll manage," said Callan. "I've got to."

Lestrange drove off, and Callan slogged up the path to the house. One thing was certain. It could be opened up, quite literally, with one hand.

He went in through the kitchen, and peeped through a door that led to the only other room on the ground floor; a big room, dining-room and drawing-room combined, all stags' heads and claymores and pinewood floors, with stairs leading to the floor above. And there she was in a red woollen dress, a fine white shawl round her shoulders, and there Eminescu was, saying: "I assure you, Lady Black, it really would be best." Nice words, nice manners, but he had a gun in his hand as he said it.

Callan unzipped his windcheater took out the Smith and Wesson Magnum 357. No sense in hanging about. He kicked open the door and went in.

"Drop it," he said, and Eminescu did just that.

"Mr Tucker," said Lady Black, "we can't go on meeting like this."
Above them a voice said: "You drop it."
Callan looked up to where Baron Rudolf von Kleist stood at the top of the stairs. In his hands he held a Mannlicher hunting rifle, and his hands were rock-steady. Callan let the Magnum fall and von Kliest came down the stairs.
"The diaries please, Pamela," said von Kleist.
"I haven't got them," she said.
"But you told this man you went to your bank." The gun gestured briefly at Eminescu.
"I did," she said, "to cash a cheque."
"You're lying," von Kleist said. "Please don't lie, Pamela. I am your friend."
"I doubt it," she said.
"But I am," said von Kleist. "I heard that man say he wishes Arthur's diaries to be destroyed. I want them to be published."
"Why, Rudi?"
"Because this man destroyed all that I hold dear. Romanians, Czechs, East Germans, Russians, they are all alike. And Arthur knew what swine they are. His diaries prove it.
"He had a story about one of your lot."
The Mannlicher swung to Eminescu. "One of many. Your people did a job in Bonn. A very good job—and the best friend I had committed suicide."
Von Kleist turned to Lady Black. "Arthur told me that one night when he'd had too much cognac; and it's true—you know it's true.
"Our man was co-operating with British Intelligence," said Eminescu. "It concerned an ex-Nazi who had killed many Romanian Jews. The KGB for some reason wanted him left alone—but even so the job was done."
Suddenly Callan remembered that job. The Romanian wasn't lying. The Russians had been furious, but till now they'd held only British Intelligence responsible. If it came out, the Romanians would suffer, no question, and it had been a good job. A job worth doing.
And still Lady Black said nothing. Whether she knew about the Bonn job or not, she held her tongue.
Von Kleist said: "This is even better. For you and your masters to fall out—my friend would have liked that. The diaries please Pamela."
She made no move.
"Please," he said, "don't force me to hurt you."
Eminescu said, "Lady Black, don't do it. This man will smear your husband's memory."
The Mannlicher swung on him again.
"Speak again," von Kleist said, "and I'll kill you."
The roly-poly little man grew suddenly taller. "I think I'm going to die anyway," he said. Von Kleist put the rifle to his shoulder, moved in closer. "How right you are," he said.
Lady Black screamed out "Rudi!" and he hesitated just long enough for Callan to reach inside the plaster cast, pull out the Smith and Wesson 32 with the two-inch barrel. He fired twice, head and heart,

but outside that room only the snow could hear it. Von Kleist was dead as he fell.

"My friend," said Eminescu, "I owe you a debt. I promise it will be paid."

"A solitary," said Hunter, "what I believe they call a loner these days. Hated the Communists of course. They'd taken everything he had. But he shouldn't have gone after those diaries. That was naughty, especially as the Romanian tie-up with us has proved so useful. Did you get rid of the body?"

"Lestrange did," said Callan.

"What was the Romanian tie-up?"

"Romania doesn't always listen to Moscow," said Hunter. "Sometimes that's worth remembering. The KGB doesn't like it, naturally. But we are not in business to oblige the KGB"

"You might have told me," said Callan.

"I take it she really did have the diaries with her?"

"Yes," said Callan. "She lied to von Kleist."

"That must have taken courage. You have them now?"

"No," said Callan. "She burned them."

"A pity," said Hunter.

"She burned them," Callan said again. "In front of Eminescu and me. The diaries were his whole life, but she did it because she thought it was the right thing to do. That took even more courage."

Hunter reached for the Chivas Regal bottle. "Whisky, David?" he asked.

But Callan was remembering Lady Black, the way she'd gasped, but hadn't screamed, when he fired. She'd said: "My husband told me about your sort of person," and then, "I really must stop beginning every third sentence with the words 'My husband'. He's dead, and I've been alone too long," and then: "Let me help you off with that plaster."

Hunter coughed, and said again: "Whisky, David?"

"Eh?" said Callan. "Oh. No thanks, sir. I've got a date."

File on a Classy Club

""What I need," said Hunter, "is a loser. Would you say you were a loser, David?"

"Not yet," said Callan. "After all I'm sitting here talking to you, and nobody carried me in."

Hunter pushed the file over to Callan. Red cover. Now people in red files really were losers, thought Callan, the ultimate losers: because what they lost was their lives.

The picture showed him a young, lean man: wary eyed and elegant, black hair long, but disciplined. American, by the look of him.

Marty Rivers, he read, *age twenty-seven. Six feet one inch, one hundred and seventy-five pounds. Cover—gambler.*" Callan put the file on Hunter's desk. "What's he done?" he asked.

"Nothing as yet," said Hunter, "except gamble. Maybe he never will do anything. But we've had a flash from East Berlin. The S.S.D. have an operation mounted here—one I didn't even know existed, and whoever they are, they're damned good."

The S.S.D., as Callan knew only too well, was the East German Ministry of State Security, and they were good, all right, and better than good. That lot had brought about the ruin of a West German Chancellor. They were also lethal. There had been times when even the KGB had to put the brakes on the East Germans.

"You think it's Rivers?" he asked.

Hunter said: "I haven't the remotest idea. The flash I got told me two things: that whoever it is he's a gambler who's due to lose money, and that money will be lost at Renfrew's. Rivers dropped five thousand there last night."

"Renfrew's?" said Callan, and Hunter chuckled.

"What a sheltered life you lead," he said. "Renfrew's is a gambling club. Perhaps *the* gambling club. As I say, Rivers lost five thousand there last night. In dollars. He passes as an American, but he visits East Berlin quite a lot. And that place on Eighty Seventh Street in New York."

Hunter hated that place on Eighty Seventh Street. It was a KGB safe house, but the KGB were not lacking in hospitality. Polish and Czech agents were welcome too, and East Germans. And despite repeated requests, the C.I.A. had refused to close the place up. Largely, Hunter suspected, because the KGB targets were foreign diplomats and not native-born Americans. A deal had been made, and Hunter wasn't in on it. No wonder he detested the place....

"Renfrew's really is a club," said Hunter, "in the sense that you have to be proposed and seconded. Your election went through yesterday."

"I must have some posh friends," said Callan.

"It's all in the file," said Hunter, and added: "You'll need them, David. You'll need every friend you've got."

"To do what?" asked Callan.

"Lose money," said Hunter. "Lose rather a lot of money." He sighed. "Intelligence becomes a more expensive business every year."

"Too true," said Callan. "This one might cost me my life."

Hunter picked up the red file and offered it to Callan.

"Rid your mind of the idea that you've just made a joke," he said.

Callan went to the armoury. Practice was not only what made perfect, it was also what kept you alive. He worked on Prendergast, a dummy with a rubber head and a padded body. Callan shot Prendergast from a sitting position, then kneeling, then standing, then prone: he shot him in good light and bad, over and over, till his wrist and arm ached and the dummy was a shapeless mess from the chest up, and always he aimed for the same places, head and heart, over and over, until he was satisfied that his hand, eyes, and reflexes were still working. After that it was time to use his brains.

Renfrew's was something, no doubt about it. A George III town house in the best part of Belgravia, with a staff of servants on a scale George III might have envied, a French chef and an impeccable wine-cellar, and every item dedicated to the idea of making gambling losses painless—and enormous. The list of clients was breathtaking. Oil sheiks and millionaires and half Debrett. Callan noted without surprise that his proposer had been an Earl, no less, his seconder a millionaire many times over. He went back to Hunter's office.

"So I go there and I lose," said Callan.

Hunter sighed: "I'm afraid so," he said.

"Why, Hunter?"

"The man I'm after is a loser because he's been told to be," said Hunter. "Some kind of pay-off no doubt. Other people are after him too. If they should—"

"What other people?"

"I'm not sure," said Hunter. "And it has no relevant bearing. If they should turn their attention to you—you may pick up a few leads."

Or a few bullets, thought Callan.

Aloud he said, "They've already got one loser—Marty Rivers."

"He hasn't lost enough yet," said Hunter. "And you must see that he doesn't. It might lead to something. But even more important is that you go there and lose."

"How much?" said Callan.

"Fifteen thousand pounds."

Callan whistled.

Hunter said testily, "My dear David, an oil sheik dropped a hundred and twenty thousand pounds there in one night. Now please get on with it. Go away and lose."

But it wasn't that easy. Cards have a way of falling right only when you want them to go wrong, and even a roulette wheel can be embarrassingly generous when you least want it to be. It was time to consult his lucky charm.

"Cards?" said Lonely. "Never done much in that line, Mr Callan. The chap you need is Bulky Berkley."

"What's he do?" said Callan.

"Anything," said Lonely. "So long as it's bent. Three card trick, the Pullman dodge——"

"And what's the Pullman dodge?"

You go to a race meeting like Nottingham, say, and get the Pullman back. You and a mate," said Lonely. "In the carriage you and the mate have a game of cards, and you look a right mug. Lose every hand. Pretty soon the bookies in the carriage with you are itching to get at it—'cos you're carrying a roll of money would give you a hernia. By the time you've got to King's Cross you've emptied their satchels." Lonely grinned. "That's Bulky Berkley," he said.

Callan said: "I want to meet him."

"But he's big time, Mr Callan," said Lonely. "I don't know if he—"

"And what am I?" said Callan. "Some kind of midget?"

Lonely went to the phone.

Nice, airy flat in one of the nicest parts of Chelsea, and Bulky was the nicest thing in the flat: big and pink and genial, and with an air of innocence about him that would have made Mr Pickwick look cunning. But the eyes, though round, were bright, and a lot of that bulk could be muscle.

"Lonely says it's business?" Bulky said.

"That's right," said Callan.

The little pop eyes ran over him from head to feet, missing nothing.

"Lonely says you're a hard one," Bulky said.

"That's right too," said Callan.

"I'm not looking for a minder," Bulky said.

"And I'm not looking for a job," said Callan. "I'm offering one." He began to talk, and Bulky lay back in his chair and listened, as benign as a bishop.

At last he said: "Where do you want to do this?"

"Renfrew's," said Callan.

It was like saying Cartier's to a show-girl.

"Renfrew's!" said Bulky, then chuckled, a fat and comfortable sound. "Oh dear, oh lord, I've been trying to get in there for years and now you're paying me to become a member." He hesitated. "And all you want to do is lose?" Callan nodded. "Do you mind if I ask why?"

"Yes," said Callan.

"I see." Bulky squirmed in his chair, sought and found a pine and tobacco. "Sounds as if it could be tricky, even dangerous. If it gets too dangerous I get nervous—then my hands don't work."

"Mine do," said Callan.

His right hand moved in a short, abrupt arc, and Bulky looked into the unwinking eye of a .357 Magnum.

"You see it's this way," said Callan. "Now I've told you—you're in." The Magnum flicked down to Bulky's heart, then up again to a point between his eyes. "And there's only one way out."

"I'll do it," said Bulky.

"Good man," said Callan, then added, "You won't change your mind, will you?"

"Of course not," Bulky assured him.

"Because you're being watched, you see," said Callan. "And if you tried to scarper—well, put it this way. The bloke who's doing the watching makes me look like Santa Claus."

For the first time, Bulky looked less than benign.

"Now," said Callan, "tell me how we do it?"

The club was situated between an embassy and the headquarters of an international conglomerate, and better guarded than either. Just as well, thought Callan, that his millionaire seconder owned the firm that had installed the burglar alarms. All the same Lonely had his hands full. It took them a full hour to get in without leaving any marks. Not that he wanted to leave mark. He reckoned that place was real class.

Callan set off to the main gaming-room that had once been a ballroom, vast and elegantly painted, with a dome at either end. A Hepplewhite sideboard, the millionaire had said, and there it was.

"Open it," said Callan. But Lonely had found a picture, and behind the picture a safe.

"This is where you want to be. Mr Callan." he said. "There'll be nothing in no sideboards."

"Do as you're told," said Callan. "And don't leave any marks."

Lonely sniffed, but got to work. Barmy it was, stone barmy. Breaking into a place like this to steal silver. He set to work, and as always, he niffed, but the sideboard didn't take ten seconds: the door swung open. Pack after pack of cards, just as the millionaire had said. Callan took more packs from his pocket, added to them, and Lonely gaped.

"You're giving *them* playing cards?" he said.

"That's right."

"But what for, Mr Callan?" said Lonely.

"Because I feel like it," said Callan. "What I don't feel like is answering nosey questions."

The niff intensified.

"Lock up," said Callan. "Leave the place the way you found it." And Lonely did just that. Barmy it might be, but not so barmy as talking back to Mr Callan. When he'd done, Callan took an aerosol can from his pocket, sprayed the air round the sideboard, and then sprayed Lonely.

"Summer sweetness," he read from the label. "Keeps the air flower-fresh all day." He handed it to Lonely. "Souvenir for you, old son," he said. "And don't nick anything else...."

By night the gaming-room was full: men and women intent at baccarat tables, poker tables, roulette wheel; and the most refined types of dolly-birds handing out champagne as if it were election leaflets, and a few well-dressed hard boys who would ease out a trouble-maker so fast there'd be no more noise than cards shuffling. The hardest one of the lot was the short, stocky bloke running the place; smooth, polite, but carrying so much muscle that even a Savile Row dinner-jacket couldn't hide it.

Callan took a glass of champagne and went to the roulette wheel. Minimum stake 10 pounds. Callan bought 20 chips at 25 pounds a piece, and bet at random; rouge, impair, and a block of numbers. It just showed you could never rely on luck: all three came up. He bet again, and kept on winning, running it up to 3,000 quid, but at Renfrew's that was small change. The old bird next to him didn't even look up when he left; she was too busy losing four thousand.

They all had the look, Callan thought, the single-minded look of the born gambler, at once predatory and vulnerable: predatory because of their greed, and yet vulnerable because nothing will ever beat the house percentage.

He went over to the poker table, where Bulky sat, chubby and benign: looking about as safe as a lamb at a lions' convention. As Callan approached the Earl who'd sponsored him rose, offered Callan his seat, and Callan sat down next to Marty Rivers. They cut for deal, and Bulky won.

"If you don't mind," Bulky said. "I'd like a new pack."

The woman next to Callan waved to a dolly-bird, but Callan said: "Don't bother. I'll get it." He took a pack from the sideboard and gave it to Bulky, watched as the fat man unsealed them, shook them free, and clumsily, painstakingly shuffled.

"Keen to get on with it?" the woman said.

Callan looked at her: dark eyes, gleaming black hair centrally parted, a figure of rounded elegance, a suggestion of Spain in her looks and dress.

"It's what we're here for," said Callan, and Bulky finished his shuffle at last.

"Same bets as last time," he said, and fumbled out the cards. By the end of the night Callan had lost eighteen thousand pounds, a net loss of fifteen thousand and Rivers had won five thousand of it. If his change of luck pleased him, it didn't show. Bulky had won even more, and his face was beaming.

"Your luck was certainly out tonight," the woman said. "Let me get you a drink."

She signaled to a dolly bird and got champagne, Roederer Cristal, then raised her glass. "Better luck next time,

Mr ——?"

"Tucker," said Callan. Harassed, anxious Mr Tucker, the born loser. "And yours?"

"Amparo Soller," she said.

"Spanish?"

She laughed. "Was it so difficult to guess? You like the club?"

"Very much," said Callan.

"Then you must come again—if you're staying in town?"

"I'm at the Hilton," said Callan.

Hunter had created about that, too, but it was part of the cover.

"Do you come often?"

"Very often," she said. "It's—exciting." She rose then, and left him. On his other side, Marty Rivers said, "Last night I thought my luck was bad—but yours, oh boy!" He shook his head. "Did you say you were at the Hilton?"

Callan nodded. "Are you?"

"No," said Rivers. "I'm a Savoy man from way back. Well good-night. Mr Tucker; and thanks."

"For what?" said Callan.

Rivers gathered up his chips.

"For losing like a gentleman," he said. "I sure appreciate it."

It was a fine night, and Callan decided to walk. Gambling and champagne were the wrong mixture when you were up against the S.S.D. He strolled through the empty streets with the unconcern of man who had lost fifteen thousand pounds of somebody else's money.

In minutes, he knew he was being followed, and the tail was a good one, hard to spot. Callan moved into the shadows and kept on walking, and the Magnum got into his hand without any conscious effort from him. The tail must have had some kind of walkie-talkie, because when it happened it was fast, accurate, and efficient, a typical S.S.D. operation.

He walked down a side-street as a Mercedes 600 turned neatly into it. Suddenly, the Merc's headlights came on full, the engine roared, and Callan, blinded, remembered the man at his back. He leaped sideways, and the side of the car just clipped him, the merest whisper of a touch, that nevertheless slammed him into the railings of a house.

The car braked, went into reverse, and Callan leaped for the door-step of the house. A shot from the man at his back dented the shiny elegance of the door's brass knob, as Callan ducked and put three bullets through the Merc's rear window. It kept on coming, out of control, then veered towards the house opposite, headed straight for its door.

As the Merc passed him Callan could see that its driver was dead, but the man on foot wasn't. He was in the doorway the car was heading for, and he had no choice but to run for it. Callan shot him the way he shot Prendergast, head and heart, and the Merc veered again, ran right over him then slammed into a lamp-post. Two shots wasted.

Somewhere in the distance a two-note police siren blared, and Callan moved fast, brushing the dirt from his clothes as he went. Time to be tucked up for the night, once he'd spoken to Charlie.

It had been a rough day. ... But it seemed that rough days only got rougher. When he opened the door of his suite he saw that he had visitors, and they were passing the time waiting for him by fighting, two against one. And they were fighting in something close to silence. The one was good, but the two were crowding him, their backs to Callan. Sooner or later they'd win.

Oh God, thought Callan, who needs this?
He took out the Magnum, cooled off one of the pair left-handed, and chopped the second with Magnum's butt. That left their victim. Callan swung the gun on him.
"Hi," said Marty Rivers.
"Nice of you to drop in," said Callan.
"Yeah, well... You know how it is," said Rivers.
"Not yet," said Callan. "But I'm going to. Suppose you tell me."

Rivers was C.I.A. and had been planted to infiltrate the East Germans' London operation—or so he said. The C.I.A. knew far, far more than Hunter about that operation. And about Renfrew's. What they didn't know was why another man should turn up at Renfrew's and start to lose money.
"Mind you, you did it good," said Rivers. "You and the chubby guy. I broke in here to find out why, then these two hoods came in and jumped me. Who are you, Tucker?"
Callan said, "I thought the man with the gun asked the questions. Why are *you* losing money?"
"You thought wrong," said Rivers. "And you played it wrong."
"Go on," said Callan.
"The loser was supposed to be an American," said Rivers. "I guess your people didn't know that. You're about as American as fish and chips."
One of the men on the floor stirred, and Callan tapped again with the gun-butt.
"This is a rush-job," he said.
"I don't think so," said Rivers. "We've got lots of time."
Callan shook his head.
"Not any more," he said. "I just killed a couple just like this. I suppose my not being a Yank made them nervous. Soon their controller will be wanting to know what happened to them."
Rivers whistled. "Like you say, it's a rush," he said. "You want to go now?"
Callan bent to search the two unconscious men. They both carried Walther automatics, and he gave one to Rivers, kept one for himself. Walthers and Mercedes ... the East Germans still believed in West German technology.
"I'll just make a phone call first," he said and dialled the long, familiar number.
"Yes?" said the night-man.
"Let me speak to Charlie, please," said Callan.

Together they looked at Renfrew's. In the distance Callan could hear the police cars hooting like owls round the crashed Mercedes.
"What d'you fancy?" he said. "Break in or crash?"
"Crash," said Rivers. "That I can handle. I wasn't taught to be a burglar."
"Oh we are proud," said Callan, and went to the back of the house. He'd seen Lonely open it up once, and one demonstration was

enough—so long as Rivers supplied the diversions.

Rivers was good, at that. There were four men in the house, and he got past three of them, but the fourth one took him, and when Callan reached the gaming-room there he was, held by two thugs, looking at Amparo Soller.

She was worth looking at. In an evening gown she'd looked good; in the negligee she now wore she was sensational, but her eyes were the eyes of someone to whom pity was a meaningless word.

"So it was you," she said, "who killed my driver, killed the man who followed Tucker."

Rivers said: "That's right." He sounded like the man who deserved all the credit. "But I thought this guy was supposed to be running the place?" He nodded at the short, stocky man who held his right arm.

"Karl manages the club, certainly," she said, "but I manage Karl."

Callan didn't doubt it for a moment.

"And how did you know about the club?" she asked.

"I'm C.I.A.," Rivers said, and she shrugged, a lovely movement of shoulders and bosom, that meant "Who cared?"

"We did a deal," said Rivers "with the KGB. Your boys play too rough, Baby. You make them nervous. They gave us this place—for the house on 87th Street."

"You lie," she said.

Rivers shrugged.

"The 87th Street house doesn't bother us," he said. "They don't use it against us—and the way we've set it up, they can't. The KGB uses it for operations against UNO—mostly Britain, West Germany, and France. O.K., but this house—this you use against the United States, and the KGB think you use it wrong. Its over, Baby."

"It's over for you," Amparo said. "Kill him, Karl."

Karl put his hands to Rivers's neck and began to twist. Amparo Soller moved closer, to watch. It would seem that she enjoyed it, thought Callan, and shot Karl dead. She looked at him as he stood there in the doorway, the Walther in his hand, and he was aware only of the hate in her eyes: the near-naked, beautiful body was an irrelevance.

"So," she said, "the man who knew where the cards were kept—though he'd never been to the club before."

Callan made no answer, but cursed inside his mind. Rush jobs always led to carelessness....

"You could have got here a little earlier," said Rivers His voice was hoarse.

"Better late than never," said Callan. "Now let's go and speak to Charlie."

The woman said, "I speak to no one."

"Darling," said Callan. "You don't know Charlie."

Hunter was furious. He'd known that the C.I.A. was up to something, and that they should mount an operation in London was bad enough, but that the S.S.D. should have a safe-house in London, and he didn't know it and the Yanks did...

Callan said: "You better watch it, Hunter. The only time I ever saw a colour like yours was on hot-house grapes."
Hunter fought for, achieved, control.
"It could be worse I suppose," he said. "We've cleaned out that nest of vipers, thanks to you—and that woman and her men-friends will have lots to tell us."
"Amparo Soller," said Callan. "Why's she working for the Germans?"
"What better cover?" said Hunter. "Who would suspect a Spaniard of working for the S.S.D.?"
"Freelance, was she?"
"Yes," said Hunter. "That's why they wouldn't tell her the name of her courier. All he had to do was go to the club, lose fifteen thousand – and leave. That would finance her till the next operation. But he had to lose it to *her,* of course. I'm sorry, David. I didn't get that bit of information. Rivers did."
"Then why did she have me followed?"
"Greed," said Hunter. "A spot of blackmail on her employers."
"She's got guts to take on that lot," said Callan.
"She'll need them," said Hunter.
It took Callan all the will-power he had not to react.
"By the by," said Hunter, "your friend Berkley. Did you reclaim our cash from him?"
"I did," said Callan.
"No trouble?"
Callan shook his head. "He cleaned up £27,000 on top of what I lost," he said. "He's happy."
"I should think he should be," said Hunter, then added: "What about the money Rivers won?"
"I sent Meres for it," said Callan.
"Good man," said Hunter. "Really David, we simply have to cut down." He pressed his buzzer. "Send Rivers in," he said.
Rivers was unrepentant. It was a C.I.A. job, and it was over, and what was Hunter going to do about it?
"What can I do?" said Hunter. "Unless your people would care to let me destroy that house on 87th Street in return?"
"Forget it," said Rivers. "Not a chance. No way."
Hunter sighed.
"I rather thought you would say that," he said. Then he brightened. "But it doesn't matter."
Rivers' eyes became guarded at once.
"Go on," he said.
"Rather a sad accident," said Hunter. "About an hour ago some careless idiot started making explosive in that house. I think it may go off."
"Are you telling me——?" Rivers began.
Hunter said, "I'm telling you that the C.I.A. can have no possible objections," said Hunter, "after what they've just done to me."
The phone rang, and Hunter listened, said, "Thank you," and hung up.
"The explosive did go off," he told Rivers. "There were no survivors.

Neither we nor the French, nor the West Germans, will send wreaths."

"You tricky bastard," said Rivers, and lunged at Hunter, but somehow Callan was in his way, and neither Callan nor the Magnum he held seemed inclined to move. Rivers fought for control, as Hunter had done, and, like Hunter, achieved it.

"O.K.," he said, "you won this one, but—" he glared at Callan "I'll see *you* again."

Callan put the gun up.

"I'll be here," he said.

File on a Fearsome Farm

"A *health* farm?" said Callan.

There was no way he could keep the outrage from his voice.

"I think so; yes," said Hunter. "You're getting quite podgy, David."

To save his life Callan couldn't stop himself from looking at his waistline. "You're kidding," he said.

"Not at all," said Hunter. "All that rich West Indian food—and the beer you had to drink when you were a school janitor. My dear fellow, if you're not careful you'll become obese."

Hunter paying off old scores was the most insufferable Hunter of them all.

"Ah well," said Callan, "at least it'll be a rest for me."

"Not at all," said Hunter. "We may as well combine business with pleasure."

"Pleasure?" said Callan.

Hunter ignored it. "Last year we hired a freelance," he said. "An American called Odell. He was rather good. In fact better than good. He got us some rather useful stuff. Then he went double. The rouble is not without its attractions, even for an American. I sent Meres to deal with him, but unfortunately he heard him coming. He killed himself. All Toby got was a diary."

"Better than nothing," said Callan.

"Not much," said Hunter. "What I'd hoped for was a list of new agents at that wretched Russian Trade Mission in Hampstead."

"But if he'd gone double—" said Callan.

"The list was his insurance," said Hunter. "The KGB never pay till they must. With that list of names they'd have to pay."

"Wouldn't it be on micro dot?"

"Not possible," said Hunter. "I'm quite sure."

When Hunter used that tone of voice you could believe every word.

"Nothing in the diary either?"

"It was in code," said Hunter. "Rather ingenious. Took our chaps all day. Repeated reference to a person called 'K.' One reference said: 'Safe with K. Bet your—'" Hunter grimaced—"'ass.' Then another one yesterday: 'K at Mince.'"

"Mince as in pie?"

"It's a French word meaning thin or slender," said Hunter. "It's also the name of a health farm—the one you're going to." He handed over a sheaf of papers. "I've had Odell's diary typed up for you."

Callan took them. "Who's K?" he asked.

"That's what I want you to find out," said Hunter. "It'll be something to do while you're losing weight."

Callan took the notes from Odell's diary and read them while he ate. Odell had been careful, even if he had used code. K was always K, just that. No description, no name. Nothing. Not even a hint whether the list of Russian names had been planted or K had taken them knowingly.

But then Odell had reason to be careful. The Ivans he dealt with had been a wet job squad, and they were boys who liked value for money. If you didn't give value you didn't get money: but you might get dead. And so might K, if the wet job boys knew K had the list....

There has to be more of a lead than that blasted diary, thought Callan. Maybe Odell's flat.

He ordered steak and salad and Perrier water, and on the way home he bought a pair of bathroom scales – and found to his fury that he was 5lbs overweight.

"I'll have a pint, please," said Lonely. Callan went to the pub counter and bought him one.

"Ta, Mr Callan," Lonely said, then noticed that Callan had bought nothing for himself. "Aren't you having one then?" he asked.

"I'm not thirsty," said Callan.

Lonely looked at him as if he'd gone finally, utterly barmy, then caught the look in Callan's eye.

"You don't mind if I drink mine, Mr Callan?" he said. "I've been thirsty all day. Must be the heat."

"It's October, and it's raining," said Callan. "But go ahead and swill if you want to. Pack in the calories. Why don't you let me buy you a pork pie as well?"

"Oh ta, Mr Callan," said Lonely, and Callan gave up and bought him his pie. There were some battles you just can't win.

"I've got a job for you, old son," Callan said, as Lonely chewed and swigged. "Opening up a drum up West."

"I'll need a minder," said Lonely.

"You've got one," said Callan. "Me."

"That's all right then," Lonely said.

Callan thought: Well at least *you* don't think I'm too fat for thieving, and stopped holding his stomach muscles in.

To do a place like Odell's requires a bit of nerve and a lot of practice. Most of the nerve is expended on opening the lock of the door leading into the block of flats, but the owners hadn't got further than a simple snap-lock, and Lonely, with Callan beside him, fiddled that with a strip of hard plastic. He might have done it faster with a key, but Callan doubted it.

After that they took the lift to the top floor, and Lonely had a good sneer at the burglar-proof locks on Odell's door and opened instead a window that looked out on to the well of the building. As he did so Callan took off his raincoat and unwound from his middle a length of cord with a hook at one end. Lonely risked a joke.

"You look better now you're on your diet, Mr Callan," he said, and Callan willed himself to smile and handed over the rope. Lonely scuttled on to the fire-escape, hooked the rope to it and swung down to Odell's window. Good lock on the window, but the window itself was just glass—no wire mesh. Suction cup and a glass cutter and all you needed was two minutes. ... Lonely reached inside and turned the catch, then called out softly: "All yours, Mr Callan."

Callan swarmed down the rope and into the kitchen, and told himself he could climb as well as ever he could: to worry about extra weight was ridiculous. As he went through the window, he wondered if he'd just told himself a lie....

The heavy curtains were drawn tight as befitted a house of death, and Callan risked a light, and prepared to go to work.

"Remember," he said. "No thieving."

"You know me, Mr Callan," said Lonely.

"Yeah," said Callan. "I do. No thieving."

Lonely, offended, stuck his hands in his pockets and looked at the pictures on the walls. There were plenty of them....

If you're looking for a needle in a haystack at least you know what you're looking for, but Callan didn't even know that. He went on searching....

"Blimey," said Lonely. "He was fond of birds, Mr Callan."

Lonely was right, Callan thought. Every single picture in the drawing room was of a naked woman. More skin than a tannery. Might as well do them next, he thought, and took down the pictures, took off the frames. Nothing. And again nothing. Same in the dining room, bathroom, kitchen, bedroom. Odell was the most anonymous man who'd ever lived—and died.

That left the hall: a desk with a telephone, a plant with a stand—and more pictures.

Lonely looked at the pictures.

"Stone me," he said. "This one's a feller."

And indeed it was. A man with a sour expression and a wig. Portrait of the composer George Frederick Handel by Thomas Hudson, bang in the middle of another bevy of birds. Judging by the look on his face and the way he was clutching his stomach, naked birds gave Handel indigestion. Callan said so.

"Maybe it's just that he can't get at them," said Lonely.

At the end of two hours, Callan gave up. There was nothing–not a damned thing, except this K at the health farm.

It was a nice place: you had to admit that. A manor house of middling size, eighteenth century, with a plastered frontage ornamented by statues of Greek gods and goddesses who'd never been on a diet in their lives by the look of them. Nice room too: comfortable bed, telly, bathroom en suite, and a view of the grounds: parterres and lawns, trees in landscaped groves: there was even a lake with boats on it—if anybody had the strength to row. The only things missing were food and drink.

Callan changed into a dressing-gown that everyone in the place seemed to wear like a uniform and went to join his fellow sufferers. Do the obvious first, he thought. The only K listed was an Alistair Kennedy. Odell would never have been as obvious as that, but there was nothing else to do. He tracked Kennedy down in the drawing-room, where he was one of a four at bridge. He proved to be an elderly and enormously fat Negro. So much for the obvious.

Callan sat down on a sofa and reached for a magazine, peeped round it at the sufferers. Obese to a man and woman, he thought, and whatever Hunter says. I'm not like that.

A woman took the seat next to him.

"Just arrived?" she said.

Callan lowered the magazine. She was a blonde in a tight-fitting robe that followed the lines of her figure, and she was not obese. Maybe she could lose a pound or two, but if you admitted that you'd have to ask where from, and there was none of her Callan wanted to lose.

"Yeah," he said. "Just arrived."

"You can always tell," she said. "The new ones always look so fed up."

Also you haven't seen them before, he thought. So you're a dumb blonde. ... But she was something to look at all right.

"I'm David Callan," he said.

"Natasha Biscayne."

She held out her hand, and he took it. Her skin was soft, with the texture of peaches. ... I really must stop thinking about food, thought Callan.

Dinner that night was half a grapefruit, with a walk to a phone box for dessert. Maybe the KGB didn't know about K and the health farm, but it was too much of a maybe, and at bugging phones they were unbeatable. He dialled the long, familiar number, went into the ritual.

"Let me speak to Charlie, please."

"He's at dinner," said Liz.

"Good," said Callan. "Interrupt him."

But Hunter was benign.

"How are you, David?" he said.

"Starving," said Callan. "And out of luck." He told Hunter about Kennedy, and Natasha Biscayne.

"That's the most preposterous name I ever heard," said Hunter. "Obviously an alias."

"Yeah," said Callan. "It is. She told me herself. Her real name's Bertha Cheeseman. She does photographic modelling and she's going to be a hostess on TV – hence the diet. She's a right little chatter-box."

"You don't usually react like that to attractive young women," said Hunter.

"I am starving," said Callan.

"And you can't expect me to investigate her because she chose a Russian first name.

"That's all I've got," said Callan.

"Then get more," said Hunter. "You'll forgive me David, but my dinner is getting cold." He hung up.

Callan slogged back up the road to Mince, turned into the drive. In the moonlight the house looked magnificent, the line of statues gleaming like ice on a cake. Food again. From behind him came a soft, popping sound. He heard the whisper of a bullet past his face, the hard slap it made as it hit a tree, and Callan was off, running, no messing, dodging through the grove of hardwoods to the safety of the lawn where the sufferers strolled. Starving or not, he found he could still run.

So somebody knew who he was, and why he was there. An impetuous sort of chap who fired and missed, but almost certainly wouldn't miss twice, and the only chance Callan had was to stay with the crowd, and how could he do that and look for that list?

Breakfast was lemon juice and water, and after it a sauna and massage, and after that a talk on flower-arranging. Callan talked to Natasha Biscayne instead. To him, he thought, she would always be Natasha Biscayne. Nobody who looked like that could possibly be called Bertha Cheeseman. And she was restful, too. When she talked you didn't have to listen at all. And it all came out; all the fabulous men in her life.

"And then there was this other chap," she said. "Honestly, he was an absolute kook. Except that that's what he used to call me, but really he was the kooky one," She waited. It was his turn to say something.

"A chef was he?" said Callan.

"No, silly, you're not listening," Natasha said. "Kook's a word Americans use. It means—you know—far-out."

Suddenly Callan was listening hard.

"Tell me about this American," he said.

"Well, he used to be lots of fun," said Natasha. "Honestly, he did. You know—parties and discos and champagne. And then he got all moody—you know—like worried."

"What was his name?"

"Chuck," she said.

"Chuck what?"

She shrugged. "That's all he ever said. Just—call me Chuck. You know. Like they do."

But she did manage a description.

Callan said: "Will you excuse me a minute?" She nodded. "You won't go away, will you? I really am enjoying our chat."

"I'll be here," she said. "I fancy you an' all."

Mince had a library, and a good one; it even ran to an American dictionary, the Random House Unabridged, 1967 edition. He turned to the K-L section.

Kook, he read. *Slang. 1. an unusual, peculiar or foolish person. 2. an insane person, (? alter of cuckoo).*

Then lower: *Kooky. Slang of or pertaining to a kook.*

And Natasha was the kookiest of them all, but she was lovely. Now

all he had to do was find that list. He went back to the kookiest.
"Feeling better?" she said.
"Much," said Callan. It was no lie.
"What were we talking about?" she asked.
"Americans."
"Oh yes ... They get everywhere don't they?" she said. "There's one over there. His name's Linder. He just arrived."
Callan looked where she nodded, at a big, bald man with a sour expression, and knew he'd seen him before.
"How d'you know his name's Linder, then?"
"He tried to pick me up," she said. "Just now, when you went out. But he isn't nice like Chuck." She grimaced. "Can you imagine? Trying it on in a health farm!"
Callan tut-tutted, and said: "Chuck's really nice?" Careful to use the present tense.
"Super," she said. "He's always giving me things ... Crazy things."
"What things?"
"Oh, like ten pairs of boots I liked, and a crazy jewelled egg made by some Russian before they had their revolution—"
Fabergé, thought Callan. Hunter, old sport, Odell really cost you money.
"—and my album," she said.
"Album?"
"For my photographs, silly. It's made of baby crocodile skin. ... It's got a gold lock."
"It must be valuable."
"Oh, it is," she said.
"I hope you take care of it."
"Oh, I do. I take it everywhere with me."
"Even here?" Callan asked.
"Even here."

And after that all he had to do was wait till the evening, when it was time for her massage, and time for Callan to go back to his room and collect his Magnum .357 – except that someone had been there before him. The Magnum was gone. That made it time to make a decision whether to ask Hunter for another gun, or break into Natasha's room without one. Callan decided that there was no way known to man that he would admit to Hunter that he'd lost his gun. He went to Natasha's room unarmed, and terrified.
The door was easy, but as he opened it there was a blast of gunfire that sent him diving for cover, but when he looked round the room was empty. Natasha, running true to form, had left the telly on, and cowboys were blasting hell out of Indians.
He locked the door and set to work. Natasha, bless her, was no Odell. The album was in her suitcase, and the suitcase had the kind of lock Lonely could have opened with a sneeze. After that it was just a matter of find the lady. ... Callan thought of what he knew about Odell, and chose the picture in which Natasha wore nothing but a look of hauteur and a pair of boots. ... Right first time. The list was

tucked neatly behind it. All he had to do then was put everything back and leave, except that the handle of the door started to turn just before he touched it.

Callan moved into the angle of the door and waited. The man who came in was a man he'd never seen. Squat, chunky, but silent as a cat. Not one of the sufferers. Unlike Callan, who wore the uniform dressing-gown, he was fully-clothed, and his shoes were the kind of heavy brogues that could stamp the life out of you. The only edge Callan had was surprise.

His left hand slammed the door shut and his right aimed a fist strike at the back of the chunky man's neck, but Chunky was already moving and the blow thudded into his side as he twisted away and countered with a blow to Callan's stomach. Callan swerved, only just in time, but Chunky kept on coming, and the next blow hurt, a fist like a hammer beat into Callan's shoulder. He was trapped in the angle of the door too, and Chunky had the whole room to manoeuvre in. ... Chunky backed off, and Callan knew what was coming, a low and agonising kick, but backing off had given Callan room too, and he used it to twist aside once more. The brogue thudded into the wall.

Chunky opened his mouth to yell his anguish as Callan's spear-strike took him in the gut, and the yell was stillborn. Even so he was still on his feet until Callan landed the blow behind the ear that ends all fights.

Chunky went down like the Titanic. ... And still cowboys shot Indians, Indians shot cowboys, and Callan went through Chunky's pockets. A Smith and Wesson revolver, his own gun, and a Makarov with a silencer. So Chunky was the one who'd tried to kill him. ... Too much hardware for a dressing-gown, but he couldn't leave them there. They went in his pockets. ... And that was about it.

He took Natasha's hand mirror, held it to Chunky's mouth. No clouding. Chunky was dead. Callan bundled him into a cupboard and locked it, and as he did so a bland, professional voice said: *"The Great Composers,"* and music soared, civilised, majestic. Hallelujah ... Hallelujah. *Hallelujah.* Callan looked at the telly: a hefty fellar in a wig and a sour expression, left hand at his stomach.

"George Frederick Handel," said the voice.

And Callan knew where he'd seen the sour American before: put a wig on him and he was the face on the telly, on the picture in Odell's hall. Odell had left a message after all—and wet job boys always hunt in pairs. He looked at his watch. Natasha's massage should be over. Callan ran.

That night there were yoga classes, and the place was deserted except for the drawing-room. Callan met her by the health club, grabbed her wrist and kept on running.

"Come on," he said.

She pulled back. "Where?"

"Out of here," said Callan. "Somebody's going to try to kill you."

She wasn't so kooky at that. One look at Callan's face and she ran, too.

The cars were parked at the main door of the house, and so was Linder. Callan dragged her round to the side of the house, then skidded to a halt. If he started a gun fight the girl might die: she deserved better than that. But the moonlight was strong, there was no cover nearer than the trees. ... Callan looked up to curse the moon, then dragged her to a drain-pipe.

"Up you go," he said.

Linder came round corner, Makarov ready, stopped, appalled. It was impossible, but they'd disappeared. His eyes flicked up to the line of statues, then he turned to the grove of trees. Too far. Even if they were Olympic athletes. Too far....

Above him a standing Apollo with his back to a crouching Venus took off in a flailing dive. Linder hit the grass and was unconscious at once. If it had been anything harder he'd have been dead. Callan tied his hands with his tie, then went back up the drain-pipe for his dressing-gown, and Natasha. But the crouching Venus had turned into a reclining Venus. Natasha had fainted.

All's well that ends well, I suppose," said Hunter. "But you were careless, David. Linder and his friend were watching Odell's flat the night you broke in. They even followed you to Mince."

"It's been done before," said Callan. "But I bet they used two cars. Did they?"

Hunter nodded.

"Of course," he said "You weren't *that* careless."

"And I did get rid of the body. And delivered Linder."

"That was luck," said Hunter.

"I also got on to Natasha Biscayne," said Callan.

Hunter said: "That was luck too."

Callan thought of Natasha.

"Maybe it was," he said. "Who've you got interrogating Linder?"

"Snell," said Hunter.

Callan thought of Snell, the section psychiatrist, and shuddered.

"So he's singing?" he said.

"Very, very sweetly," said Hunter.

"Why did he pretend to be an American?" Callan asked.

Hunter shrugged. "They often do," he said. "If anything goes wrong they can blame it on the C.I.A. Besides his American accent is perfect: his English accent is not."

He looked at Callan more closely.

"You appear to have lost weight," he said.

"Five pounds," said Callan.

"Extraordinary," said Hunter. "You were there for only two days. How on earth did you manage it?"

Callan remembered the moment when he found that his Magnum .357 had gone.

"Mostly fear," he said.

File on a Careful Cowboy

It was quiet on Main Street. The saddler's and the Wells Fargo office were empty: at the blacksmith's the forge fire flickered and died: even in the Dirty Shame saloon the only one there was the gambler, duded up in cravat and frock-coat, dealing out an endless series of poker hands. ... The gambler won every time, but there was nobody there to see him win, not even a barman.

From outside there came the clop-clop of a horse's hooves.

Callan stirred in his seat. This is ridiculous, he thought. The worst collection of cowboy cliches I've ever had to sit through. But Hunter's eyes never left the screen, and that meant business. Callan, too, settled down to watch.

A baddy riding a palomino. He had to be a baddy—he had a Mexican moustache and his hat was black. He was hard and he was dangerous, and Callan knew it at once.

Clop clop went the hooves, and hey presto! there we are by the sheriff's office, where the sheriff sits out on the board-walk, seat tipped back, spurred heels hooked on the hitching rail, white hat tipped over clean-shaven face, because the sheriff is a good guy, and on him facial hair and black hats are unthinkable ... *clop clop.* And the sheriff wakes, yawns, reacts, checks the ·45 on his right thigh.

Into the saloon then, where the gambler listens, the horse's hooves are still at last, and the gambler leaves the table, pours a drink at the deserted bar and crouches behind it.

Footsteps now, slow and easy, and we're back on Main Street, black hat approaches white hat, and black hat's tethered horse moves restlessly, whinnies in apprehension. ... Long shadows in the sun, close-ups of wary hands hovering over gun-belts. Black hat; white hat.

Then suddenly the hands claw for Colt .45s, two tall men crouch in the sun, and the hand guns boom like cannon, White Hat falls, twitches, dies....

Hunter pressed a button on the arm of his chair, and the picture faded and died.

"Like it?" he asked.

"Every time I see it," said Callan, "and that can't be more than two thousand times. But at least they had a new twist—the baddy killed the goody."

"You recognised the-er-goody?"

Callan thought of all the spaghetti Westerns Lonely had conned him into going to see. "He's never off the screen," he said, "but I haven't seen this one before."

"It's never been released," said Hunter. "The-er-baddy paid for it himself."

"Must have cost him a bit," said Callan.

"Quarter of a million dollars; a hundred thousand just to persuade the actor to die. How vain actors are — but they are greedy too. As you can see, he died. This baddy always wins. His name's Martel ... Nap Martel. I want you to kill him."

"You mean you're going to get me into the movies, Mr. Goldwyn?" said Callan.

"I mean you're going to do a Section job," said Hunter. "What you saw on film was a dude ranch—or so I am instructed they are called — in the Camargue. That, as I've no doubt you are aware, is a cattle-raising district in the south-east of France. Martel is a devotee of the cowboy myth. He goes to the ranch at least twice a year — and every time he goes he enacts that little scene. He will be there next week."

"And I just fly to Marseilles, take a car to the ranch and knock him off?"

"Precisely," said Hunter.

"Would it be too much trouble to ask why?"

"At one point," said Hunter, "I thought it would: but then I remembered your passion for demanding reasons. Martel is—on paper—a citizen of France, but in fact he was born in Naples—hence his nickname: Nap. His real name is Martello, he is an important executive in the Mafia, and his millions—he has many millions—are the result of his exporting heroin."

"He'll have minders," said Callan.

"Of course he does," said Hunter, "but when he goes to the — er — dude ranch he relaxes, and so do his—er—henchmen."

"A bit off your usual beat, isn't it sir? Knocking off the Mafia?"

For the first time since Callan had known him. Hunter blushed.

"Actually," he said, "I'm doing this to oblige the C.I.A."

"They got the movie, did they?" said Callan.

Hunter's blush, if anything, intensified.

"As a matter of fact they bought it," he said.

"Bought it?"

"From Martel's rivals. Another group of Mafiosi. Led by a man called Sordi. His group are attempting to muscle-in—I believe that is the expression — on Martello's drug operation."

"So now I'm a hit man for the Mafia," said Callan.

"Not at all," said Hunter, "for the C.I.A., and God knows they have cause to worry about drugs—particularly drugs destined for the U.S.A."

"So why don't they go and knock Martello off?" Callan said.

"Their operation in Marseilles has been blown," said Hunter. "They had to put the execution out to contract. It was my good fortune that they chose us."

"And suppose I knock off Martello and they muff the follow-up?"

said Callan. “Do I have to go back and knock off Sordi as well?”

“I hope so, David,” said Hunter. “They pay extremely well. Information and dollars. And vast quantities of each.”

“Even so I don’t like it,” said Callan.

“But you’ll do it,” said Hunter, and Callan had no doubt that he would.

And after that the paperwork: Martel in a red file. It was funny the amount of paper-work you had to do just to kill somebody. Not that Martel didn’t need killing: he was all Hunter had said he was, and more. Raw opium run in from Turkey, or Burma, for that matter, to Marseilles, cooked in kitchen factories till it became heroin, shipped to the U.S. inside Citroen-Maseratis, antique furniture, even dead bodies, and then hustled on the streets for a one thousand per cent profit: men—and women too, ready to rob for it, kill if they had to.

Martel had been responsible for as many deaths as a localised war. And the dead were all innocent, that was the point. Except for the gangsters who’d tried to take over from Martel in the past. They were only after his empire of corruption, but they’d failed, and paid the penalty of failure—death: mostly by a slug from a Colt 45.

It seemed that Martel carried his passion for cowboys even into, his business affairs. Callan wondered if Sordi knew how many rivals Martel had murdered. But this was no time to worry about Sordi. Now was the time for Martel: as dangerous as a rattlesnake, and as vicious.

All right then. But he, Callan, had to kill him. And it wouldn’t be easy. Not with the kind of talent he hired as bodyguards. He read on through Martel’s file and made a decision. He’d need an assistant, and maybe the assistant might even have to take over the starring role. Time to go back and talk to Hunter....

“Meres?” said Hunter. “A *cowboy*?”

“Englishmen went to the West too,” said Callan. Some of them could even read and write.”

“Even so,” said Hunter. “*Meres*?”

But Meres loved the idea and when they went down to the armoury Callan found to his bewilderment that he loved it too.

Partly, no doubt, it was the clothes. Boots, denims, plaid shirts and the cut-away leather holster tied down to the thigh with pigging string, the unbelievable weight of a Colt .45 in the holster.

All his working life Callan had been used to a light-weight gun in shoulder harness or trouser waistband: the .375 Magnum revolver with three-and-a-half inch barrel, weight 41 ounces - and he’d take one with him when he went to the ranch, even though he’d be expected to handle the cowboy gun as well as the Colt Single Action that Martel played with, which had a five-and-a-half inch barrel and weighed three-and-a-half pounds.

Trying to draw that after the Magnum was like giving up the violin and learning the cello. Practice, practice, he told himself. That’s what gets you to the Albert Hall.

Meres practised too. Meres dressed in black pants, black boots, white shirt, black shoestring tie, black leather waistcoat, black flat-brimmed hat; the epitome of the cowboy dude. But even so it was

Callan who was always faster: Callan, as he well knew, who would have the starring role.

When he knocked off, he went to see Lonely; not that Lonely could help him, but he'd arranged to see the little man anyway and he made a nice change from the Mafia. Lonely accepted a light-and-bitter, raised in in a ritual gesture of greeting.

"You look worried, Mr Callan," he said.

"Hard day at the office," said Callan.

"Anything I could do to help?"

When he'd said it he'd looked terrified out of his mind, but he'd said it. A good mate. Callan thought of the dude ranch: of saloons and barbecues, gun-fights at the O.K. Corral, and the kind of horse that would never accept the role of man's most faithful friend. Not even for Hunter would he get on one of those horses.

"No, old son," he said, "for this one I need someone who can ride."

"Ride?" said Lonely. "Like horses, do you mean?"

Callan considered then rejected several witty answers. The little man was his mate.

"Yeah," he said, "like horses."

"I can ride a horse, Mr Callan," said Lonely.

"*You?*"

The little man accepted Callan's incredulity with composure, even pride.

"When I was at Reform School," he said, "they had a scheme for teaching the little 'uns to be jockeys. We rode every day."

"Weren't you scared?"

"Terrified," said Lonely. "Funny thing was the horse and me got along. Every time. Good stuff they were 'n all, once you got the knack. Racing stable up the road."

"So why didn't you become a jockey and make your fortune?" said Callan. "Did you nick one of the horses?"

"Who told you, Mr Callan?" asked Lonely, intrigued.

Let it lie, thought Callan. But even so he decided to take Lonely with him. If you went among the Mafia, a thief might come in handy. And there weren't any arguments from the little man either: not this time. For a chance to dress up as a cowboy Lonely would even risk a job for Mr Callan.

They flew to Marseilles but Meres had insisted on getting on an earlier flight. Nothing, he said, would ever get him into the same aircraft as Lonely, much less the same car...But Lonely enjoyed the flight. He even enjoyed the food. Lonely, thought Callan, the human incinerator.

The ranch – the Lazy B – could have been designed by Warner Brothers.

Ranch house, bunkhouse, Main Street, corral; all like you saw in the movies. And the cattle were all long-horns, the horses tough and sure-footed as the ones on Remington paintings. But the bunkhouse had separate bedrooms, all air-conditioned, the saloon sold champagne, the ranch-house chef was worth two rosettes in Michelin.

This was a ranch for millionaires, and Callan, Meres and Lonely were the only Englishmen there. Just as well the C.I.A. were paying expenses.

Nap Martel was the life and soul. Wrestling steers, branding, shooting, you name it, he could do it, and do it as well as the genuine cowboy instructors. Or maybe they just let it look that way. After all, he was paying. And always with him went his three bodyguards, who did nothing at all except keep their hands close to Colt .45s they knew all about how to handle.

After lunch it was target practice, firing at bottles: claret and burgundy instead of rye, but the target was the same.

Callan stood next to Martel. Careful, he told himself. Don't let him know you're too good ... The trick was to keep your hands near your belt. It made the draw longer, slowed you up. Callan and Martel hit bottle after bottle, but always Callan was slower. At last, hating himself for doing it, Callan missed. Martel chuckled: a displeasing sound.

"*Vous étes anglais*?" he asked. Callan nodded. "I am better than you," said Martel.

Callan thought: And you could be right.

"But even so you are not bad," said Martel. "Tomorrow you and I will play the scene together—the gun fight on Main Street."

"Oh, I don't know—" said Callan.

"But I insist," said Martel. "I will not take no for an answer."

He meant exactly what he said.

Lonely in chaps was unbelievable: the great leather leg-coverings flapped about his lower half like the wings of a giant bat. Somehow he managed to waddle to a waiting horse, and Callan watched, appalled.

The horse looked meaner than Meres. Martel moved in close to watch, enjoying every minute, as Lonely moved up to where the horse was hitched, stroked its muzzle. The brute shied, then grew passive, as Lonely stroked it again, unhitched it, climbed into the saddle.

Oh my God, thought Callan. What have I done?

But the horse trotted off as if tranquillised. Martel hated it.

Callan took a walk round the ranch. Behind the ranch-house was the service area, kitchens, offices, and a squat stone-building that could only be the armoury. Nice lock on it too, but Lonely could handle it. He walked back to the corral, where a big roan was giving Meres a rough time. Then Callan looked at Lonely, cantering home as if his saddle were an armchair. It shouldn't be possible.

Night time was saloon time: gambling, champagne, dance-hall girls. The simple pleasures of the rich. Callan stuck to Chivas Regal, but he acquired a dance-hall girl even so. Her name was Yvette, and she was French, but her can-can costume was absolutely in period; Tombstone Arizona prettied up by Hollywood. She went off to dance, and Lonely swaggered up to Callan. Even without his chaps. Callan still couldn't believe he'd sat on that horse.

"How in hell do you do it?" he asked, and bought the little man a beer. Lonely pondered.

"Horses scare me," he said, "and you know what I'm like when I'm scared, Mr. Callan, I stink. I reckon the horse does what I want 'cos it hopes I'll get off."

He broke off as Meres limped over. It was pleasing to watch Meres limp when Lonely was free from pain.

"A message from Charlie," said Meres. "He wants you to call him—but not from here."

"All right," said Callan. "But there's a job on." He told Lonely what it was.

"I can do it," said the little man at last.

"Course you can," said Callan.

"Only I'll need a minder," said Lonely.

"Meres will oblige," said Callan. Meres looked outraged and Lonely knew it.

"You sure?" he asked.

"Positive," said Callan. "You give him a few tips on how to stay on a horse and Meres'll do anything for you."

"First off," said Lonely earnestly to Meres, "you got to smell right."

Callan fled, but at the door Yvette was waiting.

"You are leaving me," she said.

"Not possibly," said Callan. "I'll be back. Believe me."

She believed him. After all Martel had decreed he'd be in the big scene tomorrow. Callan drove to the nearby town, found a hotel, and spoke to Charlie.

"Bit of bad news. I'm afraid," said Hunter, "Sordi's dead. Shot in the back of the head, body mutilated. Typically Mafia stuff. I'll spare you the details. They are not pleasant."

"Did he know about me?" said Callan.

"Not you particularly. He knew in general terms that there was a contract out for Martel."

"I reckon Martel knows a bit more than that," said Callan.

"It's a possibility. The C.I.A. gave me some other charming news. Martel owns that ranch. Everyone in it works for him. I've called the deal off David."

"No," said Callan.

"If you're blown—"

"I was followed here," said Callan, "and if I try to leave they'll kill me anyway. And Lonely and Meres. And Martel will go on peddling heroin, I'd better go back and do what I came to do."

"Very well, David," said Hunter at lost, "but I hope Martel has read your script."

Me too, thought Callan. And even more I hope that I've read his.

He had company on the way back, too; unobtrusive, correct, nobody tried to hustle him, but all the same he felt like a sheep with a sheepdog all to himself.

When he got back to the ranch the watchman on the gate seemed surprised to see him, and that made sense too. Would you walk into my parlour, said the spider to the fly... Lonely and Meres were still in the saloon. So was Martel, but if he was surprised that Callan had come back, he didn't show it.

Callan ordered champagne and three glasses, and Lonely swigged

happily at his share even if he was still drinking beer at the time.
"Got it like you said, Mr. Callan," he said. "Your friend's not a bad minder—when he puts his mind to it."
"Nobody saw you?" said Callan.
"Nobody," said Meres. His voice was arrogant, but then it usually was. It didn't stop him knowing his job. Yvette joined him then, and Callan went to the bar for more champagne. As he walked back past Martel's chair, Martel stretched out a foot, Callan tripped and fell and the champagne bottle shattered to fragments.
"You're mighty clumsy, friend," said Martel. Despite the Italian accent, his voice achieved the authentic Western drawl.
"Only when I'm tripped," said Callan.
"You saying I tripped you?"
Callan knew that he was close to death, maybe now, and if not, certainly tomorrow but even so he enjoyed the next word.
"Yup," he said.
"I did not," said Martel.
Unhurriedly, Callan got to his feet.
"Mister," he said, "you tripped me."
At once the group at Martel's table scattered: the classic call-down in the saloon scene.
"You're not wearing a gun," said Martel. "Wear one tomorrow friend—or get out of town."
Callan went back to their table: Yvette had gone to the bar.
"You were smashing, Mr. Callan," said Lonely. "Good as John Wayne any day." He looked at Meres, "Exciting, isn't it?"
Such innocence must not be imperilled, thought Callan.
"I want you to do your starring bit tomorrow," said Callan.
"Beg pardon, Mr. Callan?"
"Get on a horse and ride into town. Only make it look like the horse is taking you."
"I'd look a right Nana riding a horse into town," said Lonely.
"Then you'll look a right Nana," said Callan, "but you'll do it."
Lonely looked into Callan's eyes, and knew that what Mr. Callan said was true.
"And you watch your step," said Callan to Meres. "I don't want you falling asleep when I play my big scene."
"I'll be there," said Meres. "Wouldn't miss it for the world, old boy."
Then Yvette came back with more champagne, and the lovely idea that they should drink it somewhere more private—like his room in the bunk-house.
"You were wonderful," she said. "Really you were, sometimes people don't know how to play the saloon scene, and it makes Nap so angry. But you were terrific." She raised her glass. "I wish you success for tomorrow."
And maybe you do, thought Callan, but it didn't stop you doping my champagne tonight ... Getting rid of the champagne when she wasn't looking was tricky, and wouldn't do the rose in the pot by his bed any good, but he managed it and went into the Act.
Slurred speech, dazed look, collapse on the bed. She began her

search at once, and found the magnum 357 in no time at all. But she didn't find the little package Lonely had thieved for him. Not that you could blame her: it wasn't in Martel's script.

Meres missed Lonely's big scene. The night before he'd acquired a dancehall girl with champagne too, and he also was supposed to be asleep: so he acted a man sleeping. It was a very boring role.

At the corral Callan watched as Lonely, wearing his terrible chaps, approached a raw - boned grey that whinnied nastily. The only other spectators were Martel and his three bodyguards. By the look of things they were the only ones on the ranch. Lonely mounted and the horse snorted, reared, then set off at a gallop, and Lonely looked by no means in control, even when it leaped the corral fence and went off down the road.

A bodyguard moved towards his own horse, but Martel stopped him.

"Later," he said in Italian. "First the big one."

Then in English to Callan: "I told you to wear a gun."

"I'm sorry," said Callan. "My head's a bit thick this morning. I forgot." He looked about him. "Where is everybody today?"

"Gone," said Martel. "You and I will play out our big scene alone, my friend."

He turned to a bodyguard and said, "Get him a gun." The man sped off, came back with a gun belt and a Colt .45. Callan buckled them on.

"We do it here?" he asked.

"No, no," said Martel. "Go to the sheriff's office. We do this always on Main Street."

He sounded angry that a tradition should be so nearly broken, and Callan willed himself not to show relief. On the way back, as soon as he was out of Martel's sight, he took out the gun, ejected the blank cartridges, and fed in the live ones Lonely had stolen from the armoury. ... At least now he had a chance....

Meres left his bedroom, and sped silently to Main Street, retrieved from under the board walk the loaded Winchester Lonely had stolen for him from the armoury the night before, then went into the empty saloon, up its stairs, through a trap door to its sloping roof.

Costume right, weapon right, setting absolutely perfect. He settled the shallow black hat to shade his eyes from the sunlight. This could be fun."

Callan heard the clop clop of hooves, then silence. Time to go. He moved, slow and easy, down the board walk, but his heart hammered in terror. At last Martel came into sight, but there were no signs of his bodyguards. Up the alleys on either side of the street, thought Callan. I hope to God Toby's awake.

Meres, up on the roof, saw it all. Martel's sudden, dramatic appearance, and his three heavies working up towards Callan, two on the right side one on the left. Blanks in Callan's gun, he thought, and odds of four to one. You don't believe in taking chances, Mr. Martel.

Then Martel yelled: "I warned you mister. Go for your gun." His own hand moved, fast and sure, but Callan's hand was like a striking snake as the big Colt filled it, boomed in the sunlight.

Martel went down as if he had been swiped with a girder, but even so his trigger-finger twitched, a bullet smashed into the dirt road inches from Callan's feet. Strange, thought Meres. His face bore a look incongruous for a dead man: amazement perhaps, or was it outrage? Meres had no time to look. Carefully he shot the two men on the right, but the one on the left had already run in behind Callan.

"David!" Meres yelled "Behind you."

Callan dropped, swirling round as he did so. Again the big Colt boomed over the whip-crack of the Winchester, and the last bodyguard fell like the lead inside him.

Callan walked back to the saloon, where Meres was already pouring Scotch. Callan drank and said: "Well, I guess we cleaned up the town."

"We sure did," said Meres. "What happens now?"

"We re-arrange a massacre," said Callan, "then we pick up a horseman, then we go back to the twentieth century."

"The bodies," said Hunter. "What about them?"

"We set them up so it looked as if they killed each other," said Callan. "Thieves fell out, that's all."

"No witnesses?"

"None," said Callan. "Martel had sent them all off before the shoot out."

"I was thinking of Lonely."

"All Lonely knows," said Callan, "is that he's saddle sore."

"You've done very well, David," said Hunter. "Very well indeed. The C.I.A. are delighted."

"Yeah," said Callan. "Martel won't push any more heroin ... I hate that stuff."

Cautiously Hunter looked at Callan.

"It won't last, of course," he said. "Sooner or later someone will take Martel's place."

"Oh sure," said Callan, "and sooner or later you'll send me to kill him."

File on a Doomed Defector

Callan sat in the car and looked across at the great cathedral; the most incredible piece of Gothic he'd ever seen. Beside him in the driving seat, Meres yawned, resenting his boredom, itching for action, but the only possibility for action was spite, the only possible victim Callan.

"How can you just sit there?" he said.

"I can sit here because nice, kind Mr. Hunter told me to sit here," said Callan. "So why don't you just shut up and look at the nice cathedral?"

"So everything's nice today, is it?" said Meres.

Not everything, thought Callan. You're not nice for one, and neither is Ostrava. But he kept his thoughts to himself. He had enough on his mind as it was: he didn't need a punch-up with Meres to top it off. Meres looked around the square.

"What a boring place Milan is," he said.

Callan let it ride. Any place is boring when all you have to do is sit in a car and keep a look-out for a geezer on a sight-seeing tour, and both men knew it. They'd done it often enough before. But this time there was a chance that the geezer might get shot at, and if he were. Callan and Meres were supposed to make sure that he didn't die, and there was nothing boring about that.

Callan thought again about Ostrava. If there was one geezer in the world whose death he would do nothing to prevent it was Ostrava. He'd even give his assassin shooting lessons, come to that—but nice, kind Mr. Hunter had said that Ostrava must stay alive, so Callan sat in a car and made sure that the Magnum .357 under his coat was nice and handy. If it came to a gunfight then he was going to be among the survivors. No way would he get his head shot off for that bastard.

Ostrava was a Czech, and on his passport it said that he was a member of the State Purchasing Bureau, which was why he was on a guided tour of Milan with a banker as guide, and two goons from the Czech Secret Police for bodyguards.

But Ostrava had done a lot more for his State than just purchase—interrogation, torture, killing; you name it, Ostrava had done it. Started young, too: not much more than a lad when the Nazis went into Czechoslovakia, but inside a year he was in the SS, doing his bit—and more than his bit—for the Third Reich.

Jews, left-wingers, liberals; it was all the same to Ostrava. Find them, interrogate them, send them to the gas chamber. Then when the war ended and the Russians moved in, Ostrava disappeared for a while, then bobbed up again with the KGB, doing exactly what he'd done for the Nazis. Only the uniform was different: the KGB knew talent when they saw it.

And now here he was, pushing 60, with more than 35 years of torture and murder behind him, and a cushy State Purchasing Bureau job instead of a pension. And I have to keep him alive, thought Callan. Thank you, Hunter. Thank you very much.

Meres said: "They're coming out."

And so they were. The banker in a silk suit that had been cut in Savile Row, Ostrava in a blazer and flannels that he wore like an SS uniform, the two goons in the kind of dark grey suit that can only come from Eastern Europe, the kind that looks as if it had been cut and sewn by gorillas with hangovers; but their Makarov pistols would be the best. Bunched together, the goons herding them like sheepdogs, Ostrava and the banker moved to the banker's Ferrari. Meres looked at his watch.

"Seven minutes they were in there," he said. "That must be a record."

"Yeah," said Callan. "So much for culture."

But it seemed there was still culture to come. The Ferrari moved off and Meres followed, not pushing it, through the city and on to the Autostrada, leaving it at last for a minor road that wandered through vineyards, and finally turning off into the courtyard of what had once been a monastery and was now one of the best—and dearest—restaurants in Italy.

Meres parked his hired Alfa-Romeo not too close, took his time about locking it up, and never once looked at the group from the Ferrari as they went inside. Say what you like about Meres, thought Callan—and there isn't much I couldn't say about him—but even so he's great with a car. Never obtrusive, always at least two other cars between him and the subject, but always there, clinging like an adhesive bandage. If only he could be like that with people.

They went inside, into a tall, cool room. Ostrava and his entourage were already seated, the two goons with their backs to the window, facing into the room, like the excellent bodyguards they were. Callan and Meres copped a table for two, nearer the door, which was exactly where they wanted to be. They might have to leave in a hurry.

They ordered *spaghettini al vongole*, calves' liver with herbs, a salad, and a bottle of Barolo. Spirits were out till the job was over. Callan dug into his *vongole*. It was just about perfect.

He looked up, and as he did so, a man came into the restaurant from the door to the kitchens: a tall, lean man wearing the kind of dark suit and discreet tie that says successful restaurateur: the *"I've probably got more money than you but I'll still call you sir because it'll make me even richer"* look. It was Jan Neruda.

Callan was positive he'd said nothing out loud, but even so Meres put down his fork. He'd smelt trouble, and he wanted both hands free.

"Something's wrong," he said.
Callan forced himself to go on eating.
"Wrong?"
"Come off it," said Meres. "Something's happened. What was it?"
I suppose, thought Callan, he has to be told. After all it's his neck on the block as well as mine.
"The geezer who just came in," he said. "I know him, and he knows Ostrava."
Meres' eye got that glittering look that foretold the chance of danger; the chance to hurt.
"Do we take him?" he asked.
"No," said Callan. The denial was hard and final. "We don't do anything. He's had enough for one lifetime. I'll talk to him."
Meres picked up his fork.
"What an old softy you are," he said.
Neruda had looked once at Ostrava, a glance that flicked the way a lizard's tongue catches a fly, and from then on he didn't look back. But that didn't fool Callan. Neruda had looked once at Ostrava, and Callan *knew*. He went on eating and thought about Neruda.
Once, Neruda had been the best restaurateur in Prague. Now—so it would seem—he was the best in Milan.
But, like Ostrava, he'd been a lot of other things too. Like the best British agent in Czechoslovakia, thought Callan, until 1968, when the Russians came in, and Ostrava had picked up Neruda's wile and interrogated her—an interrogation Ostrava had undertaken personally, because it was the kind of thing he enjoyed doing: the kind of thing he did best.
Neruda's wife had held out long enough for Neruda to get away to the West, because she had loved Neruda as he had loved her. But in the end she had died, and her death had been as agonising as the last three days of her life. Callan knew it all, in minute detail. He'd been one of Neruda's debriefing team after Neruda had escaped to the West.
Callan pushed away his plate. Neruda had sat down at a table laid for one: a waiter had supplied him with antipasto and white wine. Callan pushed back his chair.
"You can't," said Meres. "If that bird and Ostrava know each other you could blow the whole operation."
Callan got up. "He's a good man," he said.
Meres poured out more Barolo.
"First they're nice, now they're good," he said. "What on earth is the matter with you?"
But Callan was already walking over to Neruda's table.
"I just wanted you to know how much I enjoyed my meal," he said.
Neruda bowed sitting down, a feat only restaurateurs can achieve.
"You're very kind," he said, then more softly. "How are you David?"
Callan replied with the voice he'd learned in the nick, the voice that is softer than a whisper.
"I'm fine," he said, and thought: I mean it. Either I'm fine or I'm dead. Aloud he said: "Ostrava's fine too."

Neruda said, "Ostrava? That was a long time ago, David. I have almost forgotten such things."

"Yeah," said Callan. "And that bulge under your left armpit is a wallet full of lire."

Neruda put down his glass, his hand reached towards his coat.

"Stop acting, like a berk," said Callan in the same soft voice. "Ostrava's two goons have had their eyes on you since you came through the kitchen door."

Neruda's hand kept on travelling, reached into an inside pocket for a wallet, took out a card and gave it to Callan.

"You can reach me at this number," he said. "A banquet for 200 or a little intimate dinner for two. I shall be happy to arrange."

He was a pro all right, thought Callan. But he was no match with a gun for Ostrava's goons. More softly Neruda added: "You think those two goons could stop me?"

"Maybe not," said Callan. "But I could."

"You would protect such filth?"

"That's what I'm here for," said Callan. "I like you, Jan—I really do. But start anything and I'll kill you."

"There will be no charge for your meal," said Neruda. "I owe you that at least. But I do not want to see you again."

Callan found he had no appetite left, but he chased the food round his plate till the goons escorted Ostrava back to the Ferrari. At once Meres stood up.

"Leave it," said Callan. "We're conspicuous enough."

Meres started to argue.

"That's an order," said Callan. "You remember orders? They're the things I give and you take."

Meres went back to sulking.

One thing about being in the passenger seat, thought Callan, it gave you time to think. About Ostrava and Neruda for example, and about how little Hunter had told him about this mission.

When they got back Callan booked two calls to London.

"Come to Milan?" said Lonely. "On me tod?" He sounded appalled. If it gets any worse, thought Callan, I'll be able to smell him through the telephone.

Gently he said, "It's easy, old son. All you have to do is pack an overnight bag, passport, bit of money—oh and that bug I left at your place."

"Bug, Mr. Callan?"

"That plastic job," said Callan. "The one with the wire-recorder. You can leave your cockroaches in the sink. You know they hate flying."

"Mr. Callan," said Lonely, "that's not nice. You know I keep my place spotless. Eat off the floor, you could."

Dazedly, Callan heard himself apologise. It was a relief to get his other number.

"Neruda?" said Hunter. "Oh yes. I remember. And, he saw Ostrava you say?"

"Yeah," said Callan, "and Ostrava saw him. And his two goons."

There was a silence: Callan knew that Hunter was thinking hard.
"Ostrava is about to defect," Hunter said at last.
"You might have told me before," said Callan.
"There was no reason for you to know it before," said Hunter. "Now there is. His trip to Milan is to be followed by a trip to London. A normal business trip, except that he will defect when he gets here. That is why you are in Milan now: to make sure that he does get here."
"What about the two goons?" said Callan.
"I had intended to eliminate them here," said Hunter. "Now that they've seen Neruda I think that you and Meres had better take care of them in Milan."
"Just like that?"
"Precisely like that," said Hunter.
"And what about Neruda?"
"There was a time when Jan Neruda was valuable," Hunter said, "but that time is past. Ostrava, on the other hand, is very valuable indeed."
"He's a butcher," said Callan. "Neruda was one of the nicest men—"
"David," said Hunter, "as of this moment Neruda is in a red file." The phone went dead.
Meeting Lonely without Meres knowing should have been a nightmare, in fact it was a breeze. That night Ostrava and his goons were entertaining girls, and Meres, in his room across the hall from Ostrava's suite, was so consumed with envy he wished for nothing but to stay there and sulk. Callan left him to it, and drove out to the airport.
The little man came out of Customs oozing triumph. Ciggies, aftershave and a half bottle of Scotch for Mr Callan—he'd got the lot. The way he goes on about it, thought Callan, you'd think they were giving the stuff away. But nonetheless he thanked Lonely for the Scotch, even though he couldn't drink it till the job was over.
They found a cafe that sold beer that wasn't too bad, Lonely assured Callan, provided you didn't try to taste it. Then they got down to business. Callan talked and Lonely listened, and was amused, even indulgent.
"All this way?" he said. "Just for that?"
"And a hundred quid and expenses," said Callan, and thought: My own money, too. But Neruda's a good man; one of the best.
"You're too good to me, Mr Callan," said Lonely. "What else do you want me to do?"
"Go home," said Callan.
"Go home?" said Lonely. "But I only just got here."
Callan said. "Once you've done your job it's liable to get a bit physical, old son."
The cafe was redolent of garlic sausage, cheap wine, and even cheaper perfume, but even so Lonely came through loud and clear: the real, vintage niff.
"Just as you say, Mr. Callan," he said, and swigged off his beer, studied the dregs. "You know I feel sorry for these Italians," he said. "They must be glad when they've had enough."

After that he went and did his duty like a little soldier: not that there was any trouble bugging the goons' room; they were too busy having a good time in Ostrava's suite—then Callan drove him out to the airport.

"Will it be very physical, Mr. Callan?" he asked.

"Could be."

"You take care of yourself," said Lonely.

"Don't I always?" said Callan.

"Yeah," said Lonely. "But there's always a first time. And just you remember that, Mr. Callan."

Callan drove back to the hotel, watched Meres sulk for a bit, then went to bed. To judge by the sounds across the half, Ostrava's party was just warming up.

Get rid of the goons, Hunter had said. No problem in that. No problem at all. But Neruda in a red file—that was something else. He looked at the half bottle that Lonely had given him, a short cut to oblivion. But as always, oblivion would have to wait.

Eliminating goons is easier when they have hangovers, and easier still if you can intercept the floor waiters, hand out a wad of lire, and take over their breakfast trays. After that all you do is put on the waiters jackets, knock and enter.

Callan and Meres walked in on two men who would have bartered their mothers for the pots of steaming coffee on the trays. They had no eyes at all for floor waiters. It was all so easy. Callan slammed the barrel of his magnum behind his goon's ear, and Meres did the same with his.

The two men pitched forward. By the time they came to, their coffee would be cold.

Callan unscrewed the telephone mouthpiece and took out the bug. Meres' eyebrows rose.

"You never told me about that," he said.

"You never asked," said Callan. "Come on."

They went into Ostrava's room. He looked worse than his minders, but even in the state he was in he recognised the guns they held, and lay very still. Callan watched Ostrava sweat in fear, and enjoyed it. So often Ostrava had made others do the sweating.

"You have come to kill me," he said at last.

Meres chuckled: a sound that made Callan think of a silk cord twisting round a neck, and Ostrava turned green.

"Actually no," Meres said at last. "Rather the reverse as a matter of fact. We've come to save your life—I can't think why."

"We're from Hunter's Section," Callan said; "Hunter thinks it's time you got on with your defecting."

"My bodyguards," Ostrava said.

"All taken care of," said Callan, and Ostrava began, cautiously, to relax; though they had to pour some of the goons' coffee into him before he could get his clothes on and set off for the airport.

On the way Callan checked for tails, but there was none.

Meres said: "I've been thinking about those two goons. Shouldn't we have killed them?"

He says it like it was shouldn't we have asked them to tea, thought Callan. Aloud, he said: "What would be the point?"

"When they recover they'll squawk," said Meres.

"They've lost a geezer they were sent to guard," said Callan. "A very important geezer. They won't squawk, mate. They'll scarper."

And as he said it, their off-front tyre blew out, and once again Callan had a superb opportunity to admire Meres' skill as a driver as he wrestled the wheel, forcing the car to stay on the road—except that he was too busy worrying about what was coming next.

Meres made the car limp towards a lay-by; a lay-by with one car in it. For once the road was deserted, but the geezer in the car wouldn't have been deterred by an audience of thousands, and Callan knew it. Beside him Ostrava was cursing in Czech, or maybe he was praying. Callan grabbed him, rammed him on to, the floor as their car reached the lay-by.

Callan said to Meres: "Stay out of this."

"I rather think you'll need help, old boy," said Meres.

"Stay out of it," said Callan, and got out of the car.

Neruda was already out waiting for him, a Walther PP automatic in his hand. Callan's glance flicked to the road that was sprinkled with vicious triangular spikes.

Neruda, it seemed, had had his own spy network watching and reporting on every move made by Ostrava. A network better than anything Callan could have imagined. But after all, Neruda had been trained in the hardest school of all.

"We can't go on meeting like this," said Callan. Neruda wasn't even listening.

"I want only Ostrava," he said.

"Sorry," said Callan. "You can't have him."

Neruda moved forward, kept on coming.

"Then I am sorry too, David," he said, "but I must take him."

The Walther came up, and Callan fell into a crouch, clawed the Magnum from its harness as a bullet whipped its way over his head. A thousand feet per second, thought Callan. At least it doesn't take long.

Neruda squeezed off another shot that hit the car. There was no chance of winging Neruda. Callan knew that Neruda was there to kill or be killed; and that if he failed, he would not want to live. Callan fired twice, head and heart. Neruda's body jerked as if it had been pounded with hammers, then he fell to his knees and pitched slowly forward. It never took long.

Callan walked over to Neruda, and scooped up the Walther. Both the Magnum bullets had gone precisely to their targets.

"Wipe our car off, he called to Meres. "We're taking his." He noticed without surprise that his voice was shaking.

Mere came over at last, half-carrying Ostrava.

"No wonder you didn't want any help," he said, and looked down at Neruda. "He was terrible."

"Would you do me a favour?" said Callan. "Would you please shut up?"

Ostrava said, "I am most grateful to you."
"Oh dear God," said Callan. "That's all I needed."
They travelled back first class. Callan and Meres had ditched their guns well before the security check, but Hunter had allowed for that one, too. The flight steward did Hunter a favour from time to time, in return for money, and he did him one then. He slipped Callan and Meres two more .357 Magnums.
Callan opened Lonely's farewell present, poured and sipped.
Behind him Meres said, "Oh lord. We're not going to get maudlin are we?"
Callan poured and drank once more, then put the cap back on the bottle. For once Meres was right: Neruda's death demanded something better than a drunken wake.
They had nothing but hand-luggage, and were first off the plane: out through the Green Customs section, then on to where Hunter would have a car waiting; but even so they were intercepted.
A small, wiry man hurried, towards them, and called out: "Ostrava."
You cast practise all your life, thought Callan, but your own name will always get a reaction. Ostrava turned, and the small, wiry man started firing.
Two stiff doubles was two too many, thought Callan, but even so he went through the motions as people on either side of him scattered and Meres brought down Ostrava in a flying tackle.
As his hand reached the Magnum he felt an appalling blow on his left shoulder, followed at once by numbness, but even so he got the gun out, its weight just about as much as he could lift, so heavy that it dragged him down to his knees.
Callan loosed off one shot then it seemed as if somebody switched off all the lights in London Airport.
A priest bent over him. Callan looked up, stirred on the bed, and his left shoulder reminded him that it had by no means healed.
"Mr. Callan," said the priest, "I am Father Kollar. You went me a wire-recording."
"Did I?" said Callan. "Pop or classical?"
Father Kollar said, "You are right to be cautious, my son, and in any case it is your trade—but this time there is no need. Mr. Hunter said I might visit you. I am the head of the Czechoslovak Freedom League."
Callan remembered that he was in a hospital; remembered too the fight at the airport, that he did not know who had lived and who had died.
"Oh yeah," he said. "I bugged Ostrava's bodyguards."
"Mr. Hunter wishes me to tell you what it contained," said the priest. "For much of the time they were drunk—but, I think, truthful. They knew all the time that Ostrava was going to try to defect. They thought it funny. They knew also that their Secret Police had told our Freedom League where Ostrava could be reached. Even persuaded him to take lunch at a restaurant owned by one of our members. They found that funnier still. They laughed, and Dobrovsky died."
"Dobrovsky?"
"The man you killed," said the priest, then saw Callan's look of

bewilderment and added, "At the airport. His sister was married to Jan Neruda."

Callan moved on the bed, then winced as his shoulder reacted. "I killed him, did I?" he said.

"One bullet," said Father Kollar. "Through the heart."

Callan closed his eyes, and the priest said. "Perhaps I should not ask you this, but what happened to Neruda?"

"He's dead," said Callan.

"You are sure?"

Eyes still shut, Callan said, "Yes, Father. I'm sure." When he opened his eyes the priest had gone. This time there was a nurse bending over him. She was prettier than the priest, but much less relaxed.

"You have another visitor," she said accusingly.

Like it was my fault, thought Callan, and found that maybe it was. The other visitor was Hunter.

"You spoke to Father Kollar?" he said.

Not even a bunch of grapes, thought Callan. Not even - how are you?

"Yeah," he said. "He told me the whole set-up."

"They are in exile," said Hunter, "It makes them naive. They believe, what everybody tells them—even their enemies. Milan-London. Wherever Ostrava went he'd find an avenger waiting. Quite neat in its way."

Callan closed his eyes again, and Hunter said: "Look at me, David." Callan looked at him. "Meres tells me you bugged the bodyguards' room."

"Meres did not speak with forked tongue," said Callan.

"Why didn't you tell me?" said Hunter.

"Because I don't speak Czech," said Callan, "and in Milan I didn't know anybody who did."

"So you posted it to Father Kollar and the Czech Freedom League instead?"

"They speak Czech," said Callan.

"David," said Hunter, "I'm in no mood for flippancy. Why did you do it?"

"I liked Neruda," said Callan. "I told you that before, remember? I liked him and I killed him—for a swine like Ostrava."

"Neruda was both likeable and valueless," said Hunter. "Ostrava was appalling, but his value was immense."

"Was?" said Callan. "You mean he's dead?"

"He was shot in the head," said Hunter, "but he didn't die."

"Too bad," said Callan.

"Let me finish," said Hunter. "His brain is damaged extensively. He cannot communicate with us in any way. Does that make you happier, Callan?"

Callan closed his eyes and slept, and the nightmares began at once. When he awoke it was to find Lonely peering at him anxiously over an enormous bunch of grapes.

"'Cor Mr Callan," he said, "you weren't half having bad dreams."

"I can even do that when I'm awake," said Callan.

"I bought you some grapes," said Lonely. They must have weighed about a stone.

"I can see you have," said Callan. "Thanks, old son."

Lonely pushed them at him, and Callan took one: it was delicious. Lonely coughed.

"All right, Mr. Callan?" he asked.

"Smashing," said Callan.

"Only don't want you to think I thieved them," said Lonely. "Not a present to a mate. Bad luck that would be."

"They must have cost you a fortune," said Callan.

"Mind you," said Lonely, "I had to thieve the money to buy them." Then he added anxiously, "But that wouldn't count, would it, Mr. Callan?"

Callan said soothingly, "Of course it wouldn't. It's only the thought that counts, old son."

He took another grape.

File on a Pining Poet

Hunter said: "Have you ever been interested in poetry?" Callan looked at his drink: Chivas Regal and Malvern water mixed fifty-fifty, with ice. And he'd only had two sips. It couldn't be that. Cautiously he said: "Poetry, sir?"

"Poetry," said Hunter. He sounded pettish; maybe because he was embarrassed. "It does exist you know. I should have thought that even you ..." This was unkind.

"Oh, *poetry*," said Callan. "Of course I know poetry:

"There was a young man of Calcutta,
Who mixed raw green chillis with butter.
But he mixed them so strong.
That when he smelled the pong —"

"Spare me your barrack room ballads," said Hunter. "Take a look at this."

He passed over a yellow file — surveillance only. Subject: Arthur Lewis. Age: 50. Profession: Economist attached to the Foreign Office. Special aptitude: trade agreements. Callan looked at the photograph. It was the kind of face whose one reaction to Hamlet would be to add up the number of words in the play.

Callan looked again at Hunter. "Poetry?" he said.

"Look at this, too," said Hunter.

Another yellow file. Subject: Luba Varenskaya. Age: 30. Profession: Poet. Special aptitude: Survival. There was more: a lot more, but this wasn't the time to read it. And besides, there was the face. No man living could ignore that face.

Black hair close-cropped, brown eyes wide-set, slanting a little (a touch of Tartar blood?), high cheek bones, small determined chin, small, straight nose, lips full but not pouting—together they made beauty, but a beauty that had been tormented, driven to the very edge of destruction.

"I see what you mean," said Callan. "Poetry."

"That was taken just after she was released from Siberia," said Hunter. "She was in Moscow. So was Lewis. They met at a party given by some underground painter or other—it's all in the file."

"He doesn't look much of a one for iambic pentameters," said Callan.

"It wouldn't bother her," by said Hunter. "Her husband was an atomic engineer."

"Was?"

"He went to Siberia too," said Hunter, "but he's still there. She divorced him as soon as she got out. And now she's in Switzerland—and Lewis is going there to see her."

"Maybe it's love," said Callan. "It does happen."

"It has happened," said Hunter. "To Lewis. It's all on tape. You'll listen to it before you go."

"Go where?" said Callan.

"Froissart," said Hunter. "It's a little town on Lake Geneva."

"You want me to break up love's young dream?"

"I think Varenskaya's about to take Lewis where we can't get at him. I want you to find out I'm right—and stop her."

Not even stop her *if* I'm right, thought Callan, Mr Know-All Hunter. But then that's what he was. Callan gathered up the yellow files.

"If the Ivans sent her to Siberia why should she help them?" he asked.

"Greed," said Hunter. "Or fear. Or the conviction even after all that Marx was right. Or even a vulnerable relative."

They were all incentives, and Callan knew they all worked. The knowledge had put his life at risk more than once.

"If you're right," he said, "she'll have a couple of minders at least. KGB minders."

"Of course," said Hunter, "And that will show that my suspicions are justified."

"Yeah," said Callan. "It might also show that I am dead."

He took the flies away and went through them. Lewis was a type he'd dealt with before. Good grammar school, Cambridge scholarship, double first. Only child. Both parents dead. No holds on him except his job, and he could do that anywhere in the world, including Moscow, if he paid for his admission with the kind of inside information his job yielded all too freely.

Brilliant, conscientious, hard-working. Several liaisons with women: all discreet. Even gay lib hadn't got him. Only hobby: chess. Political affiliations: nil. This geezer was too good to live. And maybe that was the point. Maybe if it came to the crunch he wouldn't live. Once Hunter started having intuitions there usually weren't all that many survivors.

Highly strung. Tense. He would be. A lot of specialists are, thought Callan. Look at me. He thought longingly of another Chivas Regal, but that wasn't on. Not if the KGB were involved.

Better, much better, to read about Luba Varenskaya. Her beauty was of a grave, reflective kind, but there was humour, almost mockery, in the dark, slanting eyes, the curve of the lips. Or maybe that was reading too much from a photograph.

He looked at the body that supported the lovely head: thin, far too thin for his taste, even thinner than a fashion model: but then not even the most dedicated of fashion models took her weight off by going to Siberia. Feed her up and she'd be perfection, he thought. And trouble. He reached for the tapes.

Hunter had had Lewis's flat bugged from the moment he got the first whiff of the romance. That was routine stuff after all. What wasn't, was the amount of it.

Hour after hour of the stuff, all dated and timed. All the poor devil's salary gone on telephone bills. Callan picked one at random, fitted it to the tape deck. It was eves worse than he'd imagined. The poor devil had even tried reading poetry to her: Shakespeare, Byron, Elizabeth Barrett Browning. That gravely beautiful face didn't look the type to read much Elizabeth Barrett Browning ...

"How do I love thee?
Let me count the ways.
I love the to the depth
and breadth and height.
My soul can reach..."

And he means it, thought Callan. It's the most terrible reading I ever came across, but he means every word.

"It really gives you pleasure—my reading this?" Lewis's voice asked.

"Of course."

Her voice was low, the accent faint but enchanting.

"I'm a terrible reader," said Lewis. "Always was. Even at school, I used to dread when it would be my turn to read aloud."

"There is more to reading than making pretty words," she said.

But Lewis' love was the kind that wanted always to give; never to take. He went on as if she hadn't spoken.

"I know I'm terrible. I was terrible just now—but poetry's your sort of thing and I had to show you I was trying to make it, my sort of thing — no matter how badly I—"

There was a pause then the rush of words gushing out so fast that Lewis literally choked on them. At last he said: "I'm making myself vulnerable to you ... I always will ... I'm in love with you, you see."

"You can only be vulnerable to those who wish to hurt you, Arthur," she said. "You will never be vulnerable to me."

Clever, clever lady, thought Callan, and listened once more as Lewis poured out his hopes, his dreams, his triumphs, his despairs: hour after heart-breaking hour. Then Callan went back to Hunter.

"You've heard it all?" Hunter asked, and Callan nodded. "Ghastly, wasn't it?" said Hunter.

It hadn't been Callan's word, but he let it pass.

"I've never understood this love business," said Hunter, and again the voice was pettish, because Hunter hated to admit that there was anything, anything at all, that he could not understand. "It seems to me a kind of madness."

"In this case I think it is," said Callan, and Hunter understood that all right.

"Go on," he said.

"He's obsessed by her," said Callan. "Her wish is his command. If Varenskaya told him to streak across London he'd have his pants off before he reached the front door. Are you sure you're doing the right thing in letting him go to Switzerland?"

"How can I stop him?" Said Hunter. "He can take his leaves where he likes."

"There are ways," said Callan. "We've used them before."

"Not this time," said Hunter. "I've suggested it to the F.O. people at the top. They say love's good for Lewis. Makes him work even better. Besides —" He hesitated.

"Yes?" said Callan.

"Never mind," said Hunter. "You've had one reason. I rarely give more. He leaves for Switzerland on Saturday night. Mind you're there before him."

Callan left wishing that Hunter hadn't hesitated after "Besides." It wouldn't be a reason, because Hunter's reasons were backed always by impeccable logic that felt no need for hesitation.

It would be a gut-feeling: a hunch sparked off by something in Lewis' file—or Varenskaya's. He'd have to go through them again; but first there, was a more immediate problem: Varenskaya's minders. They'd be well planted, unobtrusive — and deadly. Someone would have to smell them out. And when it came to smelling, he knew a feller who could take it almost as well as he could dish it out.

"Switzerland?" said Lonely. He sounded appalled. It might almost have been the moon.

Callan sipped at his whisky and water.

"And what's wrong with that?" he said. "A lot of people pay money to go there. I'm going to pay you."

"Switzerland's foreign," said Lonely. "Funny food and no beer and that."

"They've got beer," said Callan.

"Don't tell me," said Lonely, "that German muck." He gulped at his light and bitter, seeking courage at the bottom of the glass. "I'm sorry, Mr. Callan—"

"You will be if you turn me down," said Callan, then sniffed and added hastily: "And for Gawd's sake don't start."

"You know I can't help it, Mr. Callan," said Lonely. "Not when you look at me like that."

"Just tell me what's wrong with Switzerland," said Callan. "First class hotel, good nosh, beer. The holiday of a lifetime."

"You wouldn't take me on no holiday," said Lonely. "When you and me go off together it's work."

"All right," said Callan, "a little light work."

"Depends what you mean by light," said Lonely.

Callan signalled for refills.

"Sussing out a few heavies," he said.

"*Heavies*?"

This time the little man was so appalled that he spilled what was left of his beer. Callan handed him a fresh one.

"Nothing to it," said Callan. "I'll do the rough work. You know that. I always do."

"Oh, granted, Mr. Callan," said Lonely. "I only hope I don't have to do the sweeping up after you've finished."

"You'll be all right," said Callan. "I guarantee it."

God help me, he thought, I meant what I just said.

Getting Lonely aboard the plane was not easy. Lonely had nothing against planes: indeed, when it came to scheduled services from

Heathrow he was pretty well in favour and ate all the free food.

It was the cover story he didn't like. For the purpose of the exercise, Callan, was an account executive with an advertising agency which was considering a TV soap commercial shot in Switzerland—and the Ivans could do all the checking they liked.

The advertising agency existed, and Hunter's Section owned a piece of it, and Callan was on its books. At first the idea pleased Lonely. Mr Callan, it appeared, would be classy. Lonely asked, "And what would I be?"

"My assistant," said Callan. "Sort of an account executive's mate."

That was also pleasing especially when Lonely learned that he could wear all the brightest clothes he owned. The trouble was the shoulder-bag. Patiently Callan explained that all account executives' mates carried them, that all they held was tape-recorders, notebooks and pocket-calculators. Lonely was in no way convinced.

"It makes me look poofy," he said.

"Believe me, son," said Callan, "nothing could."

Even so he almost had to carry the little man aboard the plane.

At least he liked the hotel: elegant, quiet, warm as toast and with a super view of the lake. The bathroom was entrancing: bath almost big enough to swim in and a shower. He stripped off and was soon happily splashing. A chambermaid came in, took the tape-recorder from his shoulder-bag and replaced it with another. Callan knew all about it but said nothing to Lonely. For Lonely, ignorance was rather more than bliss: it was the smell of after-shave.

The bar was busy but discreet. Luba Varenskaya sat alone sipping dry sherry, making it last. Callan pecked at his whisky and water in the same way looking for her minders. They weren't easy to find. At last Lonely appeared, smelling of roses.

"This Lowenbrau isn't all that bad, Mr Callan," he said. "If you eat enough crisps you can hardly taste it."

"Spot anybody?" Callan asked.

"Geezer at the bar," said Lonely. "Grey suit. Blondy feller. Sun tan. Him and the bloke on the bar-stool in the corner. Fatty. Drinking vodka and tonic. Next to the tall bird with the muscles. They're heavies, Mr Callan, and they're mates – even if they don't speak to each other."

No good asking how the little man knew: he just did, and that was that. Suddenly Lonely stiffened.

"What's wrong?" said Callan.

"There's a third one, Mr Callan," said Lonely. "I know there is. The trouble is I can't spot him."

Callan fetched him another Lowenbrau and a bowl of crisps but Lonely was still worried. He'd never failed to spot a heavy before.

They dined and Lonely turned in early. Callan went to the lounge: heating just a little too hot, leather chairs just a little too warm, but the sense of wealth piled up over generations was overwhelming. And there was still wealth about: the place was crowded. So much so that when Varenskaya came in, every table was full, not a place to be had. She looked around her and came over to Callan.

"If I may?" she said.

"Of course," said Callan and rose to his feet as she took the vacant chair.

And if this is a coincidence, he thought, I'm the Queen of the May.

"You are English?" she asked.

"Does it show that much?"

She chuckled: it was a rich and earthy sound.

"There is a niceness," she said. "I know that the English detest that word – but it exists."

He bought her coffee and they talked, or rather he did. She had a way of asking questions that made refusing an answer unthinkable; so he found himself telling her all about the agonies or account executives, and when she asked him about the sad, wary little man he'd dined with he told her all about account executives' mates.

But she didn't believe him: of that he was sure; and when she'd made her report the blondy feller and the fatty wouldn't believe him either—and they were between him and the door.

And somewhere there was a third one that even Lonely had failed to spot. Somehow or other they were on to him and, despite the enchanting company, he was worried. But the company was enchanting, no question. Swiss food had given her back her figure so that now the body was worthy of the face. Lewis would have no chance at all.

Nothing else happened until Saturday. Varenskaya smiled when they met, but there was no more coffee, no more cosy talk. Then on Saturday Varenskaya, Blondy and Fatty took a drive. It didn't look as if she were all that keen on going, but she went, and Callan followed in the Mercedes he'd hired for his stay, taking Lonely with him. There'd be trouble, Callan knew, but trouble he could see was better than leaving Lonely back at the hotel with an unidentified third heavy.

Blondy drove, fast and accurate, on the motorway to Zurich, then headed up to the snow line. The traffic was heavy, and Callan hung on three cars back and kept on going. Even if they spotted him he had an answer. After all, you can shoot soap ads in snow if you want to....

The thing was that Varenskaya hadn't wanted to go, and somehow Callan knew that that fact tied in with Hunter's hunch: knew, too, that he should have brought another section operative with him to wait for Lewis at the hotel. But it was too late for that, and Varenskaya too beautiful....

They left the motorway, and were suddenly among the snows: banked up, limitless, above them only the peaks of the mountains, the ice-blue sky. Callan stayed glued to the stretch of road the snow plough had cleared. There were no other cars now to hide behind: no way to pretend that this was a trip to see the sights. He'd been conned because the woman was beautiful. Conned like Lewis—and God knew who else.

Lonely said, "I don't like it here, Mr. Callan."

Carefully, Callan negotiated the twisting, bending road.

"Winter Paradise," he said.

"No caffs, no boozers, nothing," said Lonely. "I'm scared, Mr. Callan."

"All right," said Callan. "I'll let you out."

"Here?" said Lonely, petrified.

"Follow the road," said Callan. "There's a village two miles back. You've got money — get yourself a taxi."

"On me own?"

Gently Callan said: "Believe me old son, you'll be better on your own."

The niff was pure, vintage Lonely but even so the little man said, "I'll stay if you need me, Mr Callan."

"No, old son," Callan said. "You get off at the next bend. Just let me have what's inside the tape-recorder before you go."

Lonely unsnapped the shoulder bag, opened the recorder. Inside was a Magnum .357.

"I might have known," he said.

Callan eased for a bend, slower, slower, and Lonely opened the door, dived for a snow drift. As he did so there was a shot from the hills above them, and the little man fell.

Callan accelerated, then braked, grabbed for the Magnum and crouched on the car floor. Suddenly snow began to fall, silent, deadly.

From above there was another shot, and his offside tyre went; then another that ripped into the back of the seat, inches from his heart. Callan screamed and in the scream was rage for what had happened to a smelly, loyal friend: frustration at what a woman could do if she were beautiful enough.

From above there came a crunching sound. Callan looked up. On the hillside a skier was edging towards the car: a white-clad skier who held a machine-pistol. White against white, with white snow falling. An impossible shot, but Lonely was dead, and it was Callan's turn next.

He rose to a crouch, and fired just before the skier loosed off a burst, knocking the white figure backwards so that the bullets went up to meet the snow as it fell....

Callan left the car, slithered over the snow, and looked at what he had killed. "There's a third one," Lonely had said. "Trouble is I can't spot him." And earlier: "Next to the tall bird with the muscles." Lonely male chauvinist to the end, had failed to equate a bird even a tall bird with muscles, with machine pistols.

He'd never been taught to think that way, but Callan had. He'd allowed Varenskaya to distract him, and because of it Lonely had been shot. That the tall bird too was now dead gave him no consolation. Callan unzipped her ski-ing costume, dumped her in the car, then settled down to wait. If only it wasn't so cold. If they didn't come back soon his fingers wouldn't work.

They were back in twenty minutes, and so far as his fingers were concerned it was only just in time. White against white in the tall bird's ski-clothes he rose up and sprayed the car. Blondy died at once and Fatty had a smashed shoulder, and that Varenskaya escaped was her good luck; with Lonely gone he could have killed them all....

The car swerved and smashed into the snow, and Callan raced to meet it, knocked Fatty unconscious, looked into Varenskaya's eyes.

Even getting up from the car floor she was beautiful.

"How did you know it was me?" he asked.

She wasted no time in pretence: "Yuri," she said. "The man you killed. He had what they called a nose for danger ... it didn't help him."

"Oh yes it did," said Callan. "My mate had a nose like that too. And they killed him."

He took the car keys and went to look for Lonely; but there was too much snow. He'd have to wait till summer. But there was one thing he could do—talk to Fatty. After what had happened it would be a pleasure.

"I never wanted to trick you into following us," she said.

They were in his room, drinking brandy. In a corner Fatty sat, doing his best not to listen. After what he'd told Callan, Callan was the only friend he had—if Hunter wanted him. Fatty was no trouble at all: even when his shoulder hurt, he did his best not to groan. Callan looked back to Varenskaya.

"You may not believe that," she said.

"I believe it," said Callan.

"They still have Oleg, you see. My husband. It was the KGB who made me divorce him—to show people like Lewis that I am—available. But I love my husband very much—and the KGB know it. Poor Lewis. It was wicked to do such a thing to him. But Oleg—if I get Lewis for them, Oleg will go free."

"You're making yourself vulnerable to him ... You always will ... You're in love with him you see," said Callan.

"I've heard those words before," she said.

"Lewis spoke them," said Callan. "To you."

The phone rang. Hunter checking up. Callan gave his report then listened. It seemed that Hunter could use Fatty, and Fatty heard it in Callan's voice, and relaxed.

"I think you should tell me your other reason for sending me here," said Callan.

"It occurred to me as a wild surmise that the lady's husband might be dead, and that they had withheld that information from her," said Hunter.

"Your surmise is by no means wild," said Callan.

"You're sure?"

Callan looked at Fatty.

"I'm sure," he said.

"Bring her to me," said Hunter. "I'll let Lewis know his journey is no longer necessary." A pause, then: "I'm sorry about your friend."

"Yeah," said Callan. "Me too."

It was a lousy epitaph.

He hung up and turned to Varenskaya, to tell her what she must know: what Fatty could prove. Even when she wept she was beautiful.

More brandy, and Varenskaya grew calm at last, then at one in the morning, a knock at the door. The woman shivered, and Fatty turned green and hid in the bathroom. Callan took out the Magnum and opened the door. The sodden object on the threshold was Lonely.

He looked at the woman, and said. "Sorry to bother you, Mr Callan, only I've forgotten the word for beer."

"Where the hell have you been?" said Callan.

"I scarpered like you told me," said Lonely. "I couldn't help it if me taxi broke down, now could I? I tried to tell the driver it was urgent but he only talked in foreign."

"But you were shot," said Callan. "I saw it."

"Bruise as big as a turkey egg," said Lonely, not without pride.

"Bruise?" said Callan. "What do you mean bruise?"

"Hit me shoulder bag," said Lonely. "Right smack on the buckle." He looked again at Varenskaya. "Mustn't keep you," he said. "Only I thought I better let you know I was back. What was the word for beer again?"

"Bier," said Callan.

"It just goes to show," said Lonely. "They can all talk English when they want to. Well—goodnight all.

"Goodnight, old son," said Callan, and went back to Varenskaya.

File on a Powerful Picador

Callan crouched on the roof-top, waiting. The roof of a Belgravia mansion was no place to crouch on a cold night in April, but if Hunter told you that's what you had to go and do, that's what you went and did, even if the assignment was as barmy as this one.

A man came walking up the deserted street, a big man, Hunter had said, with the look of a horseman about him. What a horseman looked like once he'd left his horse, Callan had no idea, but this man was big, all right, he wore the clothes Hunter had described, he headed for the house converted into service-flats just as Hunter had said he would.

And even more important, he carried the parcel: brown paper wrapped round a square case or box.

Callan reached for the rifle.

Always he hated dumdum bullets, but Hunter was the one who gave the orders. Callan looked through the telescopic sights at the figure that grew clearer in the porch light, and in the distance a taxi obligingly backfired: he squeezed off a shot.

The bullet sped to the target. Its tip, sawn in a criss-cross, opened up on impact into four vicious claws, and kept on going smack into the middle of the box.

Whatever was inside is would be a total wreck, but Callan didn't have time to find out what it was. He slung the rifle over his shoulder, crawled up and over the eaves to a drain-pipe.

As he moved he could hear a man's voice swearing. At least he assumed it was swearing: the voice was speaking Spanish, a language Callan didn't understand, but he knew a lot about anger—and fear.

When he got back to the Section Hunter was still up, still working.

"He appeared?" Hunter asked.

"Yeah."

Callan rubbed his hands: he was still cold.

"And you hit the box?"

"With a dum-dum," said Callan. "Dead centre."

"Excellent," said Hunter, and went back to work.

Callan left. He knew Hunter far too well to ask for an explanation: knew too that the thing Hunter enjoyed most was to say 'No' when explanations were asked for.

That had been a month ago. Now here he was again in Hunter's office, looking at the little Dégas dancer on the wall, sipping Chivas Regal and Malvern water.

"You may recall that I once asked you to put a bullet through a parcel in Belgravia," said Hunter.

Somehow Callan managed not to choke.

"I do recall something of the sort," he said.

Hunter pushed a red file across to Callan. "The man's name is Escobar – Luis Escobar," said Hunter. "The details are all in the file ... I think I want him killed."

Think? thought Callan.

Aloud he said, "Let me know when you make up your mind."

Hunter continued as if Callan hadn't spoken.

"Your little exhibition or marksmanship was of course a warning," he said. "He chose to ignore it, and that is why I think he must be removed. On the other hand, if we could frighten him enough, he could be of value to us," Hunter sighed. "He appears to be a difficult man to frighten."

"What is he then?" said Callan.

"An agent," said Hunter. "An agent for profit. His best employer is the KGB. He kills for them in Central and South America."

"And his cover?"

"It's all in the file, David," said Hunter. "Go away and read it and then we'll talk."

Callan picked up the file.

"Just one thing," he said. "That parcel I smashed. What was in it?"

"A head," said Hunter. "A shrunken head. Rather a good example, I'm told. Done by a Jivarao tribe of Amazonian Indians. It was Escobar's most treasured possession. That was why I had you destroy it."

"Sounds like a nut," said Callan.

"An analyst would no doubt describe him as a psychopath," said Hunter. "I prefer more old-fashioned words. The man is a sadist." He turned back to his desk.

Luis Escobar. Aged 34. Six feet two. Thirteen stone ten. Occupation: picador. Good at his job. Travels with all the best matadors to Mexico and Peru as well as in Spain. Takes his holidays always in Latin America and wherever he goes, men die, and women too. And some of them work for Hunter.

His latest victim, Litri, a Mexican, was the best Hunter had ever had in Central America, and the KGB had had him marked for death for months. And at last Escobar had done it.

Immensely fit and strong, read Callan. Reported lover of Amparo Sanchez, widow of Onofre Sanchez. ... Callan sat back. Onofre Sanchez. The name rang a bell. A bullfighter...a - what was it? – a matador. Killed a few years back at the height of his career.

The bravest and best—till a bull got him, and when it did, all Spain went into mourning.

Callan read on. Escobar had been in the bull-ring when Sanchez died: had ridden his horse straight at the bull, but he'd been too late. Callan went back to Hunter.

"He's a hard one," he said.

"Indeed he is," said Hunter. "But all the same I think you should talk to him first. It he defected to, us he'd be extremely valuable."
"He killed four of our lot," said Callan.
Hunter looked at him: the dark, cold eyes told him nothing at all.
"I'm aware of that," said Hunter. "But he has information, David. Information about KGB operations in South America. I want it."
"Written information?"
"Coded," said Hunter. "Inside a first edition of a novel about bull-fighting called *Blood and Sand*."
"Then why don't I just steal it?"
"No," said Hunter, "Not unless you must. I'd prefer him alive. But take a thief with you—just in case."
Callan went to consult with his thief. Consulting was thirsty work: so he took the necessary lubricant with him. Lonely examined, approved of, the serried ranks of canned beer.
"Ta, Mr Callan," he said. "Ta very much."
Callan examined Lonely's pad. In a changing world, it never changed. Lonely still thieved junk, and still kept the worst of the junk for himself. Grotesque clocks, transistors with no batteries, naked ladies holding up light bulbs: the place was booby-trapped with them.
Callan took off his dripping coat and hung it on a hanger marked Tel Aviv Hilton—God knew where the little man had thieved that from—then looked out of the window at the rain-sodden sky as Lonely bustled about, opened beer for himself, poured whisky for his guest.
"Here you are then, Mr Callan," he said. "Cheers." He gulped at his beer. "To what do I owe the pleasure?"
"It's wet," said Callan.
"Ah," said Lonely. "Been raining for days. Still—they say the farmers like it. Gawd knows why."
"How's your rheumatism?" said Callan.
"Awful," said Lonely. Gets me right in the back. Like knives it is."
"What we need is a bit of sunshine," said Callan.
"I did nick a sun-lamp," said Lonely. "Only the bulb wouldn't work. Terrible the junk they turn out these days."
"Spain," said Callan. "We ought to go to Spain."
"Yeah," said Lonely bitterly. "And pigs ought to fly.
"I've got tickets," said Callan, and at once the smell came. "Oh gorblimey," said Callan. "All I said was—"
"You got a job on?" said Lonely.
"Not, quite," said Callan. "We've got a job on. Five hundred quid, old son."
"What for?" said Lonely.
"A little light thieving."
"That's too much just for thieving, Mr. Callan," said Lonely. "And you know it."
He hadn't the nerve to say that five hundred was danger money, but Callan knew the thought was there.
"The bloke I'm working for can afford it," he said, and that at least was true.
"What d'you want me to thieve then?" said Lonely.

"Documents," said Callan. "Hidden in a book. This geezer's being blackmailed."

As Callan well knew. Lonely abominated blackmailers.

"Blackmail?" he said. "That's dirty. That's wicked."

He sucked at his beer. "Bit of a good deed we're doing?"

"That's right," said Callan.

"You know I've always wanted to go to Spain," said Lonely. "Do you think I might meet one of them matadors?" Gravely Callan agreed that it was not impossible.

The way to Escobar, Hunter decreed, was via Amparo Sanchez, and it was a pleasant enough route to take. She was dark, slender, very lovely, and very rich.

Successful matadors may die young, but their widows rarely have financial problems. One of her many possessions was a ranch in Castile, a ranch whose sole function was the raising of fighting bulls. Hunter had arranged it so that Callan, agent for a wealthy foreigner, should go on a visit to the ranch, where Escobar had a permanent suite.

They flew to Madrid, and Lonely was no trouble at all: the flight was tranquil, he'd copped Mr. Callan's duty free ciggies as well as his own, and there was beer.

They stayed over-night at a hotel near the Puerto del Sol, an old hotel of shabby elegance with big cool rooms: but first Callan took Lonely out to eat. The thought of Spanish food appalled the little man, but Mr Callan took him to a place that sold sucking pig, that was almost as good as the roast pork, his Aunty Gertie used to make. They even served beer with it. Lonely ate and was so happy that Callan ordered him another plateful. Lonely ate that too.

"It beats me where you put it," said Callan.

"Energy, this is, Mr. Callan," said Lonely. "Like fuel. Keeps the engine going. Geezers like me burn it up fast."

"Doing what?" said Callan.

"Thieving," said Lonely, reproachfully. "It's what we're here for, remember?"

Callan hadn't forgotten: but thieving came well down in the list of Hunter's priorities.

They slept in a big, cool room that Lonely regarded as palatial. A refreshing change, as he reminded Callan, from the time in the Scrubs when they'd been three up with a religious maniac. Beer and sucking pig took their toll, and Lonely's sleep was sound.

The man came in with a pass key he'd had to steal from a maid's room. Breaking in, stealing, were no novelty to this man. He'd done both, many times.

Cautiously he took out a pencil torch with his left hand, shone it on the nearest figure. The one he'd been sent to kill had been pointed out to him at the restaurant: it wasn't this stupid little runt with the idiot grin on his face.

Slow and soundless he moved to the other bed, used the pencil torch once more. This job had to be done right. The one who'd hired him wasn't the kind you made excuses to.

Lonely ceased to grin. Even in his sleep the antennae were still at work. Light had touched his face; was still there in the room, and his dreams turned at once to nightmares of danger: appalling, horrible things were about to happen, and Lonely yelled out for his saviour—and even in his sleep, his voice was a scream.

"Mr Callan!"

Callan erupted from the bed aware of a figure above his, a figure whose arm was lunging down at him where his heart had been. Pain scalded across his ribs and the fist strike he aimed was spoiled, reduced to a glancing blow that made the man gasp, no more.

Callan kept on moving as the man drew his arm back for another blow. He swerved instinctively so that the knife arm missed again, then stumbled over a bedside table and his hands missed their grab, but he managed to knock away the pencil torch, and there was darkness again.

The geezer with the pencil torch was now as blind as he was—or he would have been, except that Lonely, now wide-awake and niffing like a glue factory, decided to be helpful and switched the light on, and the geezer with the knife didn't even wait to say thank you. He just rushed straight in.

Again Callan swerved, and this time his throat punch found its target and the geezer with the knife stopped in his tracks.

Callan's hand opened, became an axe-blade that smashed behind the ear, and the knife fell, the geezer swerved, falling, and Callan linked his hands and brought them down on the other man's neck. Callan hated knives.

"Blimey," said Lonely, and Callan discovered a more urgent need even than that of bandaging his ribs. He opened a window, then sent Lonely for the iodine, gauze and tape in his suitcase. The little man was still niffing but his hands were deft.

"Good thing I had the presence of mind to put the light on," he said.

Be fair, Callan told himself. Be fair. At least you're still alive.

"It's like I told you," said Lonely. "Geezers like me we've got to eat a lot, Mr Callan. It keeps us on our toes."

Callan knelt by the knifeman.

"Yeah," he said. "Fuel. I remember." But his voice was distracted. The knifeman was dead. He looked up at Lonely. "Go and nick a laundry basket," he said.

Lonely went ashen. Mr Callan had finally and utterly lost his marbles. "What for, Mr Callan?"

"Him," said Callan and looked at the stranger. "I just croaked him."

"He's dead?"

"You catch on quick," said Callan. "Must be all that fuel. He's dead, yeah. But you and me won't be going to his funeral. Now go and nick a laundry basket."

Lonely knew that voice. He and Callan looked around the room: a red carpet, so the blood wouldn't show – but a dirty great hole in the mattress.

After that cut on the ribs he would have to wait for Lonely to help him turn it over. He bent and looked at the knife: plain wooden handle, heavy, short, triangular blade. He'd heard of knives like that, but it was the first one he'd seen. It was the kind of knife they used to finish off the bull if the matador missed his kill.

Lonely remained unsurprised that Mr Callan and he had disposed of a body down a dark alley. After all, he'd come to Spain to thieve himself, so why not get on with it? And calling the rozzers was against every principle he held and anyway, foreign rozzers, from what he'd heard, were even worse than the home-grown variety.

Callan let him think the foreign geezer had come to thieve, but he doubted it. The job was blown. Callan called Hunter to tell him so, but Hunter wouldn't wear it. The man that Callan had killed made him the more formidable one and besides, he only had to talk to Escobar. The way Hunter saw it the job was still on.

Callan hired a Seat and drove across the harsh landscape of Castile - scrubland, parched grass, gnarled, stunted, enduring trees: the whole lot framed by the high Sierras. Lonely hated it; not a boozer in sight.

But the ranch impressed him: stone-built, big as a manor-house, with deft, unobtrusive servants, and every possible comfort behind its austere façade.

Senora Amparo Sanchez impressed him even more. She was dressed for riding: white silk blouse with a red scarf, red, flared riding pants over boots of Cordoban leather. Her face retained an imperious beauty that was very Spanish, her body was invincibly feminine.

"You are welcome," she said, and Lonely sighed with relief. She spoke English. "Luis — Senor Escobar—is out working the young bulls. Perhaps we will join him later.

"But first—do I understand you wish to buy a place like this?"

"As an agent," said Callan, and thought: so Escobar's her partner ... in what?

This ranch is not for sale," she said, "but you are welcome to look around. May I ask who you represent?"

"He's Mexican," said Callan. "That's all I can say."

She shrugged, and Callan wished she would do it more often.

"Let us join Luis," she said. "I have horses waiting—or perhaps you would prefer the jeep?"

The jeep, Callan assured her, would do splendidly.

She drove through more parched grass, more scrub; and still it stretched unending before them, till they reached a herd of cows with bull calves, and Lonely wished that jeeps were armour-plated.

Near the bulls a bunch of geezers on horseback, dressed like Mexican baddies in cowboy pictures, separated one calf from the herd. It snorted, head down, and found itself facing another cowboy, who held a long pole like a blunted lance. The bull calf, more than half-grown, compact with muscle, snorted again and charged.

At once the rider dug spurs into his horse, charged obliquely, and tripped the bull with his lance. It fell and charged again, and again was tripped.

"Luis is testing the courage of the bull," said Amparo Sanchez. "If it turns away after a fall it is no good. But this one is very brave."

And Escobar enjoys his work, thought Callan. That bull calf's going crazy and the big man's loving it. No wonder he collects shrunken heads. Anything sadistic makes him happy. In the end the woman, after one quick glance at Callan, yelled at the big man to make him stop.

He was like that all day: spurring, over-working his horses, tripping, teasing bulls. The only good thing about him was his courage ... men and horses alike were afraid of him.

When his own horse stumbled he quirted it savagely, and one of the ranch-hands, Callan noted, had a bruised jaw.

They left the harsh sunlight at last for the cool of the house, then bathed and met for drinks. Escobar drank heavily, but it didn't seem to affect his balance—or his sadism. Both were very much in evidence.

All he wanted was the name of Callan's client, and when Callan wouldn't give it, he talked of bulls: how they died, how they were weakened and tormented by pics—the picador's lance.

On and on it went through dinner, and the brandies that succeeded dinner, and all the time his eyes were on Amparo Sanchez: he was never far from her side. And the woman took it all, until suddenly Escobar fell asleep in his chair like a switched-off light. Callan nodded to Lonely who excused himself at once. Best time in the world to open up a drum–when the mug was stoned.

"You are wondering," said Amparo Sanchez, "why I endure this indecency."

"Not my business," said Callan.

"No," she said. "It is mine. And I am wondering too. Onofre, my husband, was in love with him. And Luis can prove it. The greatest bull-fighter in Spain ... Mexico ... Peru. A—what do you call it? A fairy. And so I keep quiet. I accept."

"To preserve one man's name?" said Callan.

"To preserve a legend," she said. "A man is not worth it, and beside. I can always find another."

Later she said: "Perhaps it would be better if Luis were to die."

"He lives dangerously," said Callan. "He's near death all the time."

Her arms came round him.

When he left her he stopped by Lonely's door. The little man had had no luck.

"Right Mother Hubbard it was, Mr. Callan," he said.

"Come again?"

"The cupboard was bare," said Lonely.

"Blimey," said Callan. "First it's fuel, now it's poetry." But he had other plans for Lonely, and the little man was not averse; by no means averse.

When Callan got back to his room, he found that Escobar was there, no longer drunk, not yet sober.

"That Mexican," he said. "I demand you tell me his name."

Callan said. "I could take you. While the brandy's still in you—you're mine."

Escobar's eyes roamed over him, considering. At the back of the eyes was the first hint of despair.

"You have been with her?" he said.

Callan walked over to his suitcase, opened it. "Yes, I have been with her. And I'll tell you one thing more. The name of the man who's responsible for my being here. It's Litri."

Litri: the last man Escobar had killed. At the sound of it he came at Callan with a rush. Callan's hand dipped into the case, came out holding the matador's knife. Escobar skidded to a halt, and Callan's hand moved: the knife point pierced the big man's shirt, just touched his skin.

"You were telling me all about bull-fights," said Callan. "Maybe you know what this is? It's got your initials on the haft."

"Not mine," said Escobar. "My brother—Leon. He was with me when we worked for Onofre."

"And where is he now?"

"Holiday," said Escobar, and shrugged. He did not shrug like Amparo Sanchez, thought Callan.

And then—"And you have his knife."

Escobar's eyes held an expression Callan couldn't read.

"People die," said Callan. "Every person dies and you have helped to prove it. You're getting too old, Escobar. It's time to talk money."

Escobar's hands moved, and Callan leaned on the knife, let it just pierce the skin. Escobar was still.

"Who are you?" he asked.

"I'm a million pesetas," said Callan, "and political asylum."

"Tomorrow," said Escobar. "We talk tomorrow. Tonight is too much brandy."

"You lost your head once before," said Callan. "I wouldn't let it happen again."

Escobar stiffened. "You know about that?" he asked.

"I did it," said Callan. "Believe me son — money's better."

"Tomorrow," said Escobar. "First I—" he hesitated, then said again: "Tomorrow."

"O.K." said Callan. "Tomorrow, But don't get it mixed up with *manana.*"

But the next day first brought Lonely bearing rich gifts in the shape of Callan's .357 Magnum.

"Found it just where you said it would be," he said, but it was funny. Mr. Callan didn't look all that pleased. Still, Mr. Callan and the posh bird and the big geezer were going out that morning, which left the coast clear for him to get on with his thieving, and then back to good old England. So far as Lonely was concerned, you'd seen one bull you'd seen the lot.

She wanted to show Callan the bull-ring, the small, private ring attached to the ranch which her husband had used for practice. They walked across its sanded floor, and she talked, her voice clear in the still air—of Onofre's triumphs, the shame that Escobar could bring to her; then the door crashed open and Escobar appeared, in the full picador's costume, lance in hand, mounted on a massive chestnut.

"Luis," she said, "What...?"

Escobar rammed his spurs into the horse and charged. And that wasn't in the textbooks at all, thought Callan. According to the book, the picador was supposed to wait for the bull to charge him, but it seemed that Escobar had thrown the book away. Callan pushed the woman aside, grabbed for the Magnum and ducked as the lance whipped over his head.

Escobar pulled his horse round and charged again, as Callan aimed the Magnum two-handed. Chivalry versus technology: romance versus science. Science bellowed twice in the bull-ring's stillness, and Escobar rose high in his stirrups and hurled the lance wide of Callan, at a point just below Amparo Sanchez's left breast. Man and woman fell together. Callan ran.

"Find anything?" said Callan.

"Yeah," said Lonely. "That book you were on about. Under her knickers it was. You never seen nothing like them. Why she bothered putting them on...."

But Callan held out his hand for the book. Lonely's sex life could wait till they were on the plane.

"So it was the woman all the time?" said Hunter.

"She was controller; he was the hit-man," said Callan.

"And Sanchez's supposed love for Escobar?"

"About as real as hers for me," said Callan. "She just wanted to see which of us would win before she decided who to sign on with. Mind you she did give Escobar the edge—she stole my gun when we were—when we were—"

"Otherwise engaged," said Hunter.

"Thanks," said Callan. "But Lonely nicked it back. Anyway, seeing she seemed to want it, I left it with her—in her hand. Made it look like they killed each other."

"Neat," said Hunter. "Very neat. Thank you, David. The book has some useful stuff in it by the way—including the fact that she drugged her husband before his last fight."

"Good Lord, why?" said Callan.

"She preferred Escobar," said Hunter. "He could be manipulated. Sanchez could not. With Sanchez out of the way it was all so easy."

"I'd never have spotted her for a Red," said Callan.

"Of course not," said Hunter. "She was simply a sadist—a more academic one than Escobar, but a sadist nonetheless. She enjoyed planning a killing as much as Escobar enjoyed committing one."

"And you sent me to her," said Callan.

"To get at him," said Hunter. "I had no idea of her involvement — but you coped admirably, my dear fellow."

Callan bowed, then winced as his wounded ribs objected.

"I killed Escobar's brother," said Callan, "and I as good as told him. I didn't realise at the time, but the look in his eyes wasn't rage. It was jealousy. Because she'd chosen his brother for the job, not him. He was mad for her. Hunter, and I don't say I blame him. That's why he killed her. He couldn't bear to let her go."

File on a Difficult Don

"You know about soldiers, don't you? Models, I mean," said Hunter.

"I make them," said Callan.

"How about battles?" Hunter asked.

"War games. Yeah, I've fought a few."

"That may not be enough. What I want to know is, do you understand battles?"

"Nobody does," said Callan. "Not till they're over. Then everybody does."

Hunter considered the statement. "Not bad," he said at last. "Cryptic, but accurate. I think you'll do. I've put you down as a military historian. Amateur, of course, and not of the first rank, but competent. Do you think you could sustain that role?"

"Sustain it where?" said Callan.

"St. Giles College, Oxford," Hunter said. "There's a conference of historians there. The Military Historians' Society. Bit of a treat for you, mixing with the real experts."

"Which one do I kill?" said Callan.

"Now, now," said Hunter. "Always jumping to conclusions. Then there's Santarem House as well. The roses should be just about perfect now. You're a very lucky fellow, David."

"I'd be even luckier if I knew what you were on about," said Callan.

Usually Hunter reacted badly when Callan used what he considered to be vulgarisms, but this time the whimsical mood went on. He handed over a yellow file: surveillance only.

"Read, mark, learn and inwardly digest," he said, "and afterwards we'll talk."

The file was on Routledge. Oliver Stanley Routledge. Aged 27. Former scholar of St. Giles. First in Mods, first in Greats. Callan read on and discovered that that meant he was some sort of expert on Latin and Ancient Greek and on classical philosophers. And a Rugger blue. A real diligent lad.

He read on to discover that Routledge was now something called Reader in Classics at a university up North. He was also Hunter's cipher expert and somebody from the S.S.D.—East German Intelligence—had gone double and leaked the knowledge that he was somehow going to be taken to East Germany soon, but Hunter's informant had died from an S.S.D. operator's bullet before he could tell how and when.

At least that explains Hunter's whimsicality, thought Callan. Hunter hated the idea of attacks aimed at members of the Section, hated them so much that exaggerated whimsy was his only barrier against berserk rage. Callan read on.

Santarem House was the home of the fifth Earl of Burgos, whose ancestor, then Sir Harry Davenant, had taken part in several spectacular victories in the Peninsular War and had been granted the earldom.

The present earl was a noted authority on his great-great grandfather's victories. His house was near Oxford, and every year he invited the members or the Military Historians' Society to dinner. Even so it seemed an unlikely place to look for an S.S.D. operator. Time to go back to Hunter.

"You sure they'll try to make contact with Routledge in Oxford?" Callan asked.

Hunter put ice, Chivas Regal and Malvern water into a glass and handed the mixture to Callan.

"Quite sure," he said. "He's thoroughly watched—and bugged at his place of work—and the S.S.D. know it."

"Then why not have him watched and bugged at Oxford?"

"Because I want this thing out in the open," said Hunter. "I want whoever's been sent to do it destroyed. An attempt made here – on my own territory—I won't tolerate it, David, and I want the S.S.D. to know that."

"They seem to be going to a lot of trouble just for one cipher expert," said Callan.

"He's the best one alive," said Hunter. "He's broken every KGB code, every S.S.D. code there is." Callan whistled. "That's why I kept his existence a secret, even from you."

"Does he go abroad much?" Callan asked.

"Quite a lot," said Hunter.

"Surveillance?"

"When I can—but he's difficult, David. In fact he's a damn prima donna."

"So the S.S.D. could have reached him already?" said Callan.

"I have him checked from time to time. That's all I can do."

"It could be it isn't enough," said Callan.

"With the Routledges of this world one must take risks," said Hunter. "The Americans have, offered me any price I want for him—but he's priceless."

"And yet you're putting him at risk?"

"I have to, David," Hunter said. "No man can be protected indefinitely—and Routledge least of all. The young fool's been warned time and again what can happen, but he just won't listen. In such a situation even a genius must take his chance."

And not just geniuses thought Callan: geniuses' minders too. The S.S.D. plays so rough they even bother the KGB.

Oxford in high summer. Too hot, too damp, but with the undergraduates gone at least there was enough space to breathe. Callan put his suitcase down in a battered room normally inhabited by a young man who, to judge by the evidence, was interested solely in

Zen Buddhism and Rugby football, then went to call on his host and sponsor.

Dr Odgers was old, spry and immensely learned. In ten minutes he put Callan through an interrogation on Peninsular battles that left Callan dripping with sweat. Everything from North Portugal to Toulouse. And after that the grilling switched to uniforms: light infantry, line regiments, dragoons, hussars: their uniforms, weapons, colours, equipment. At last he paused, and looked at Callan in surprise.

"But you really know about these things," he said. "God bless my soul. I could well have made a historian out of you." He poured out two glasses of sherry even paler and drier than the one Hunter preferred, and offered one to Callan, who detested the stuff, but forced himself to drink.

"What has Hunter made out of you, I wonder?" Odgers asked.

Odgers, Callan knew, had been involved in the Section throughout the war. His security clearance was absolute, yet even so Callan hesitated before he answered; the habit of secrecy ingrown.

"I'm the man who has to keep Routledge alive," he said at last.

"Routledge," said Odgers. "A remarkable young man—really extraordinarily gifted. You think you can perform the task Hunter has set you?"

"I've got to," said Callan.

"But even despite that imperative you may fall."

"Then I'll die," said Callan, "and so will Routledge."

The old man put down his glass.

"Only the dead cannot be hurt," he said. "At my age one prefers one's battles to be already fought and over."

Yeah, thought Callan. At my age too.

At dinner that night Odgers had arranged the seating so that Callan sat between Routledge and Odgers. Routledge, Callan thought, was even more good-looking than his photograph had suggested. Hair longish but disciplined, firm mouth and chin, eyes ablaze with an intelligence itching to be used. He was there because of his knowledge of Greek and Roman battles, but he turned the conversation at once from Salamis and Actium to Callan's own field.

Once again Callan found himself being grilled and was grateful for Dr. Odger's interrogation. He looked across the gleaming silverware into the eyes of an antique gnome opposite, whose dinner jacket might well have bees created to celebrate the end of the First World War. Not for the first time Callan wished that he wasn't so overdressed. Dons, it seemed put evening wear very low on their list of priorities. Velvet jackets, frilled shirts might never have been invented: there was even one old boy wearing a winged collar.

Callan sipped at his Burgundy. Military historians did themselves well. Except for Routledge. Throughout the meal he drank only water.

After dinner Routledge disappeared with a group into the Senior Common Room, and Callan and Odgers followed. Routledge was the centre of the group, now deep in an argument about Julius Caesar's strategy against the Nervii, and he was for the moment, safe. Callan and Odgers went out into the moonlight to stroll in the Old Gardens of the college, and listen to the sweet, melancholy notes of its nightingales, that sang oblivious to the crash of lorries hammering in from Cowley.

"A determined young man, Routledge," said Odgers.

"He didn't drink wine," said Callan.

"You find that significant?"

"Not especially," said Callan. "Just a fact."

"He wishes always to be fit," said Odgers. "And he is fit. Fit for almost anything he may wish to achieve."

"Hunter thinks so too."

"Hunter had always had a high regard for excellence. Now, about Santarem House. We shall be visiting it tomorrow, and as you know, the present Earl, like yourself, has a deep preoccupation with the Peninsular War—particularly those battles in which his distinguished ancestor..."

Beneath the trees in which the nightingales nested a twig cracked. Lorries still hammered by, the nightingales were yelling their heads off, but Callan heard the twig go, and reacted at once. One-handed, he knocked Odgers to the ground, a terrible thing to do to an old man, but the alternative was far, far worse. Then he dropped flat as a bullet swirled through the air between them and slammed into a tree.

Callan lay prone, waiting; the .357 Magnum transferred from the webbing holster beneath the velvet jacket to his hand. Ahead of him a shadow appeared where before there had been no shadow, then from outside another lorry hammered on its way, and Callan fired, once, then again. A body fell on to the meticulously shorn grass of the Old Gardens.

"And to think," said Odgers, "that I was foolish enough to inquire what Hunter had made out of you."

Callan made no answer, but moved in on the supine body like a hunting leopard, and crouched beside it. "He's dead," he said at last.

"I don't doubt you," said Odgers.

But Callan hadn't wanted him dead: not before he talked.

With an old man's care Odgers not to his feet. "The body may prove an embarrassment,'" he said.

Callan looked across the shaven turf to where the river lapped. A punt nudged gently at the bank. "We'll manage," he said.

Odgers chuckled. "And to think I also said I could have made you a historian," he said.

But Callan wasn't laughing. The S.S.D. were supposed to be after Routledge. So why had they picked on him?

The body was just a body, Callan discovered: a body with a hundred pounds in notes, a Walther automatic and English clothes. He took it by punt to a tangle of weeds, dumped it there, then punted back, found a phone-box, and told Hunter what had happened, and the location of the body. Hunter promised to get rid of it, but he was disturbed, and said so.

Callan, too, was disturbed, and with reason. His dinner jacket was a mess, and he was afraid.

He went back to the college, and checked the Senior Common Room where Routledge was still giving Caesar a rough time. By then Odgers had joined the group. Callan went back to his room and poured Chivas Regal from the bottle in his suitcase. He had a lot to think about.

Half an hour later, Routledge knocked and came in. Callan offered him a drink and he shook his head, impatient.

"Look here," he said. "You may know your stuff about the Peninsular—but Hunter sent you here."

Callan pondered. "Boy at my school?" he said. "Terrible adenoids? Used to call him Snuffy Hunter? Would that be him?"

"Not a boy," said Routledge. "A man. Whatever else he is he's a man. He sent you here to bodyguard me. Go back and tell him I don't need you."

Callan managed to look at once nervous and bewildered. "Me?" he said. "A bodyguard? Do I look like one?"

"Yes,' said Routledge. "You do. Go back and tell Hunter I said so."

"A bodyguard?" Callan said again. "*Me*?"

"Oh for heaven's sake," said Routledge. "I know it's you."

"But how?"

"Observed facts," said Routledge. "Inferences. Now please go away."

He slammed the door when he left, and Callan pondered further. People were getting at him, and he needed a friend. For the second time that night he went to a phone-booth.

"Oxford?" said his friend. "I couldn't nick anything in Oxford. That's all parsons and that. Bad luck to thieve from a parson."

"No it's not," said Callan. "You remember that bloke who was on our landing. Six months for insulting behaviour. He was at Oxford."

"So he was," said Lonely, "but wasn't he a parson n'all?"

"Never mind what he was," said Callan, "you get yourself down here."

Lonely sighed. "Just as you say, Mr Callan."

"Good lad," said Callan. "Just do as you're told and you'll cop fifty quid."

"What about me expenses?" said Lonely, but Callan hung up. Lonely's beer was the least of his worries.

The roses at Santarem House were as beautiful as Hunter said they would be, and there seemed to be about a million of them. And among them one very English rose, tall, blonde, elegant, even in patched jeans and a sweatshirt that proclaimed Power To The People across her admirable chest.

She walked, moving beautifully, across the lawn to a balcony where the guests stood, sipping their drinks and looking at the roses, procured a glass of Chivas Regal about twice the size of Callan's and came up to him.

"You look like the man who wears the wrong sort of dinner-jacket," she said. That could only have come from Routledge.

"On the contrary," said Callan. "I'm the only man who wears the right sort of dinner-jacket."

She laughed, then gulped at her drink. "A bit of a bounder," she said and Callan knew she was quoting.

A tall, vague, ageing man came up to them. "Excuse me, my dear," he said and turned to Callan. "Buffet supper I'm afraid," he said. "Not mad about them myself, but with the servant shortage as it is what else can one do?"

Callan recognised his host and swore that he loved buffet suppers.

"Decent of you to say so," said the Earl, undeceived. Very decent. Are you a Peninsular man, Mr – er - ?"

Callan spoke his name and admitted that he was indeed a Peninsular man.

"I dabble a bit myself," said the Earl. "We really must talk later. Look after him, Conchita." He ambled off.

Callan turned to the very English rose once more. "*Conchita?*" he said.

"Lady Conchita Sarah Elizabeth Davenant," she said. "The first Earl married a Spaniard called Conchita. So there's been one in the family ever since. God knows why. They gave each other hell. Conchita...what a name! It means little shell."

Callan looked again at the location of Power To The People. "Does it indeed?"

Again she laughed, then gulped at her drink. "Oliver's right, you really are a bit of a bounder," she said. "What's your first name?"

"David," said Callan, and Routledge came over to join them, sipping at his lemonade.

"Oh goody," said Conchita Davenant. "You can get me another drink." She held out her glass, and Routledge took it at once and went back to a bar engulfed by historians. He looked delighted to obey her orders.

"Strange," said Conchita. "He didn't even scowl—and Oliver hates to see me drink."

No observed fact in that, thought Callan, but there might be an inference. When Routledge came back Conchita was holding forth on the People, whom she was for, and the Establishment, which she was against.

It seemed to Callan that she hadn't met many of the People, but Routledge stood beside her and listened, not interrupting: his look one of tender and very loving amusement—except when he looked at Callan. More inferences?

The dreaded buffet turned out to be cold salmon, cold capon, cold roast beef, and salad. They were all as good as the St Emilion Callan drank with them. He moved over to Odgers, who still limped from his fall of the night before.

"Nobody warned me about Conchita Davenant," he said.

Odgers looked at the jeans and sweatshirt, and winced. "She takes her political—er—avocation very seriously," he said. "Strikes a rather jarring note, don't you think? As a matter of fact I'm surprised she's here at all. I thought she was still at the Peace Conference."

"Peace Conference?"

"One of those Third World things," said Odgers, "where rich young Britons and Americans have a high old time denouncing their parents. This one was in Amsterdam."

Just the place, thought Callan, to make contact with an S.S.D. controller.

"Routledge seems very keen on her," said Callan.

"Indeed?" said Odgers. "One had begun to suspect that young Oliver was beyond human emotion."

He moved off, and the Earl came vaguely over, motioned Callan to sit beside him, and looked round his long drawing-room in despair. Callan thought this arose from seeing so pretty a room used as a buffet, but he was wrong.

"They do eat, don't they?" said the earl. "I sometimes think I'm the only historian left who gets three decent meals a day." He looked at Callan's glass. "You like the St Emilion?"

"Very much," said Callan.

The Earl looked at Routledge, obsessively close to Conchita. "Our young perfectionist drinks water," he said. "Stuff you wash in. No good for Conchita, young Routledge. She's very like the first Conchita, you know."

Callan looked at the Romney portrait on the wall of a small, dark woman, her beauty very different from that of the Earl's daughter. The Earl smiled.

"Not in looks, I grant you," he said. "But the first Conchita was also a confused but loveable brat. Not exactly the ideal mate for a man of action. My daughter has no future with Routledge." He paused. "She's taken up good works, you know."

Callan looked round the long drawing-room: at the Regency furniture, the Vermeer, the Goya, the two Romneys. "I suppose it's expected," he said.

"A centre for the mentally disturbed," said the Earl. "Over by the Parks somewhere; every Wednesday and Friday. I hope to God she isn't mentally disturbed herself."

Callan looked up from the fifth Earl to the portrait of the first, directly above him. Tall, lean men, both of them with eyes that might have been vague, or perhaps the vagueness was a concealed intelligence.

The fifth Earl stood up. "I suppose you'll have to start herding these fellers into their charabancs, or however they travelled," he said. "Come again when we can dine properly. I really would like a chat about the Peninsular one of these days."

More inferences, thought Callan. What he needed was observed facts.

He got them after the military historians were driven back in their coach to the college, after he'd watched Routledge safely to his room.

The walls of Oxford colleges are lavishly equipped with spikes, rather to deter undergraduates from returning after midnight than to repel invaders.

Lonely was neither deterred nor repelled. He'd gone over the spikes as if they were a puddle in the road. Callan opened him a can of beer.

"You got it?" he asked.

"Course I got it. Mr. Callan," said Lonely, affronted. "Beats me why you think I couldn't."

"You're not niffing," said Callan.

"Went back to me digs and had a bath after I done the job," said Lonely. "You know I like to keep meself fresh, Mr. Callan."

"Let's have it," said Callan, and Lonely handed over his haul. Two passports, two airline tickets, that's all he'd nicked. And the little case he'd opened had more then two thousand quid in it an' all. He knew because he'd counted but Mr Callan had told him straight: if there's money there don't nick it. He sucked at his beer. Barmy it was—but not as barmy as crossing Mr Callan.

Callan looked at the passports and tickets. Observed facts. Conchita Davenant and Oliver Routledge were on their way to East Germany on Thursday; the day after tomorrow. Sooner, much sooner, than Hunter had anticipated.

Inference: something had happened to gee them up—like the disappearance of an S.S.D. man? Further inference: Hunter would be displeased and therefore they must be stopped. Tomorrow was Wednesday. Conchita's day at the health centre. It would be no hardship to see her again.

Callan counted out ten fivers, added four more for expenses, and gave them to Lonely.

"That," he said, "is your lot. If you drank more beer than that since you got here you can sue me."

The health centre was drab and ugly, a place of many doors, all with numbers, none with names. But Callan had talked with Odgers. 4-12 was the one. From other doors there had come the sounds of madness: laughter, weeping, pain; but this door was silent.

He pushed it open, drew out the Magnum, and went inside. At once an inner door opened, but it was Routledge who came out, not Conchita. He was in a raging temper.

This barracks was like the Scrubs—for Lonely a real home from home—and yet somehow Routledge too belonged; but not as a prisoner. Callan forgot about fact and inference. Suddenly he *knew*.

"You're sure you don't work for Hunter?" said Routledge.

Callan said: "I work for him."

Routledge moved closer.

"Just like me," he said.

"Well not exactly," said Callan. "You're important. You had two minders."

"Two?" Routledge achieved an intensity of stillness. That incredible brain, Callan knew, would be clicking like a computer.

"Yeah," said Callan. "The other one was sent by the S.S.D."

"Was?"

"I killed him," said Callan.

Routledge said politely, "Oh put that thing away," and Callan restored the Magnum to its webbing harness. At once Routledge leaped at him.

He was young and hard and fit; he'd studied all the manuals and undergone all the training, and his blows hurt because his hands were hard. Callan took a fist strike on the close-packed muscle of his shoulder, grunted with the pain and countered with a kick straight out of the book. Routledge swirled like water to avoid it, and came in again, crowding him, throwing punches that Callan only just had time to block. This learned teetotaller was a little too good. Better, thought Callan, to throw the book away.

He sucked in his stomach to avoid a fist-strike to the gut, grabbed Routledge's shoulders and brought his forehead down hard into Routledge's face—elementary rough-house stuff that the books don't even bother to mention and so Routledge had no answer.

Callan pushed him away, swung his hand in an axe blow to find the nerve at the tip of the jaw, and Routledge became jelly, but even so Callan hit him twice more before he fell. Then Callan bent over him, feeling for his heart.

There was a sound at the inner door, and the Magnum filled Callan's hand of its own volition. Conchita Davenant looked into its unwinking eye.

"Did you—" she said. "Did you—?"

"Yeah," said Callan. "I killed him. He was trying to kill me."

"He'd just asked me to run away with him," she said. "I told him No. It seemed it was a word he didn't understand. *'But you must,'* he said. He was furious. As if I were one of his pupils who couldn't understand his lecture. And then you came in." She began to crumple.

"Get out of here," said Callan. "Go home and tell your father he's dead ... But don't tell anybody else."

"How did you know?" said Hunter.

"That health centre," said Callan. "It was the dead spit of the Lubyanka. You may remember. Hunter, the KGB held me there for a month."

"I remember."

"And it fitted Routledge like a glove. It was what he was for."

"You find a strange use for architecture," said Hunter.

"Oh I had facts as well," said Callan. "Lonely found passports and airline tickets in his briefcase."

"You didn't think that could have been at the girl's instigation?"

"No I didn't," said Callan. "Her passport was a forgery." He paused, then went on: "And somebody knew who I was, remember? Somebody called in an S.S.D. goon to shoot me. That meant somebody had access to the file on me the KGB gave the East Germans."

"That could have been the girl."

"I talked to her father about her," said Callan. "Conchita was a confused but loveable brat, he said. Not the type for a man of action like Routledge."

He reached for his drink, winced as his shoulder hurt him. "Only Routledge was supposed to be a don, no more. Even I thought that till he jumped me. Yet the Earl had him tagged as a man of action. Don't worry. The girl's clean, Hunter."

Hunter sighed in what could have been relief.

"But the Earl isn't," said Callan. "How long's he been working for you?"

Hunter wasted no time on denial. "I consult him," he said, "from time to time. I—"

"He set me up to kill his daughter's boy-friend."

"He advises me on Oxford academics occasionally," said Hunter. "No more. It was he in fact who first suspected Routledge might go double."

"And you didn't tell me?"

Hunter said, "I didn't believe it ... I didn't want to believe it."

"He suspected that Routledge was guilty and used his daughter to prove it?"

"You did a good job," said Hunter. "Leave it at that."

Callan finished his whisky.

"A good job," he said. "Yeah, I killed him. If he'd gone to trial Conchita Davenant would have been up to her neck in scandal."

"Then her father will be obliged to you, as I am."

Callan rose. "Tell me something," he said, and his voice was bitter. "Are you related to him by any chance?"

For the first time since he'd known him, Callan saw Hunter flush.

"I sometimes forget how astute you are," said Hunter, "but we've talked enough. Please go away."

Callan had reached the door when Hunter called out, "David!" Callan turned.

"The Earl has asked me to tell you he really would like you to dine with his daughter and himself."

"His daughter—any time," said Callan, "but not the Earl ... Somehow I don't think I'm ready for the Earl yet."

File on a Darling Daughter

"YOU'LL like Nice at this time of year," said Hunter. "Everybody does."
"You're giving me a holiday?" Callan asked.
"Holiday?" Hunter considered the word. He might never have heard it before. "Oh—holiday. No, of course not. You wouldn't know what to do with it."
"What then?"
"Drugs," said Hunter, "and an addict."
Callan grimaced. He hated drug cases.
"A girl," said Hunter. "A girl called Angela Lawson. Rather a nice girl before she got on to heroin. A little inadequate perhaps."
"They always are," said Callan. "That's why they get on to it. Who's her pusher?"
"Ultimately," said Hunter, "the S.S.D."
The S.S.D. were an East German operation and hard enough to make the KGB nervous.
"The S.S.D." said Callan. "That's all I needed."
"It's her father you see," said Hunter. "Her father's a general. Knowledgeable sort of chap—knows all about our NATO commitments and so on. Contingency plans, that sort of thing. Stuff the S.S.D. would very much like to know."
"Does he know his daughter's on heroin?" Callan asked.
"It would seem so," said Hunter.
"Then why doesn't he do something about it?"
Hunter sighed. "It would also seem," he said, "that he loves her."
He reached out for a file—yellow cover, surveillance only—and threw it to Callan.
"Read it and come back for a chat," he said Callan scooped it up and stood, ready to leave. "There's just one thing," said Hunter. "The general really is very important. If you can't think of another way, Miss Lawson goes into a red file."
A red file meant death and both men knew it.
"And I'll still be running the operation?" For once Hunter didn't look at him.
"There's nobody else I could trust to evaluate the necessity for a killing," he said.

Angela Lawson, 23 years old. Only child of Sir Richard Lawson and the late Lady Lawson. Educated at various schools, including a girls' public school and a crammer. The longest she'd lasted at any of them had been 18 months.

Her mother had been killed in a car crash when she was three years old. Her father had been driving, and Angela had been in the car—and her father loved her as he'd loved no other human being.

Callan looked at the list of her boy friends. It was comprehensive, but he had no doubt he could whittle it down to a short list.

He looked at the photograph. A weak, pretty face, but not without intelligence; even if she had gone to a hell of a lot of schools.

At present on holiday with her father in Nice.

She'd tried sniffing the stuff, he read, then gone on to injections, and now she'd reached the top: she was main-lining. The ones who injected the stuff straight into the bloodstream never lasted long. The S.S.D. would be in a hurry. Callan willed himself to remain calm, detached, then read through the file again, made a phone call, then went to talk to Hunter.

"We don't know her pusher," said Hunter. "Not with certainty. And anyway you should be on your way to Nice."

"A pusher's the obvious link with the S.S.D.," said Callan. "I'd like to know who I'm after."

"You're after the girl."

"Only if I must," said Callan. "If I take the girl it could destroy your general—and from what the file says you don't want to lose him."

Hunter said. "I'm to liaise with the General Staff about the general. Naturally if you can save the girl they'll be happier—but no room for pity, Callan. Not on this one."

"There never is," said Callan. "Now about the pusher—."

"We have a possible," said Hunter.

"Let me guess," said Callan. "Billy Bone."

"How very perceptive of you," said Hunter.

But it hadn't been: not really. Billy Bone was a young man with money who lived the life of an elegant Chelsea layabout, without any evidence of inherited wealth. He described himself as a pop group manager, but the pop expert Callan had called had never heard of Billy Bone, not even as a joke.

"I'd like to work on him," said Callan.

"By all means," said Hunter. "Provided you're quick. Will you need assistance?"

"Yeah," said Callan. "Meres and FitzMaurice."

"Good gracious," said Hunter. "I hope the poor chap isn't brittle."

At first Billy Bone thought it was a nightmare. It was his flat, there could be no question of it, and there was his quadrophonic sound system and the switches for his psychedelic lighting and everything, but the room had been ransacked. And the three creatures in it—they had to be a nightmare.

It wasn't just the stocking masks they wore, though heaven knew that was frightening enough; it was the way they moved, the way they behaved, as if all this were just as much a part of a job as making a telly. And like making a telly, there was no reason why the job wouldn't be over as soon as they'd put the pieces together—or taken them apart.

The slim, elegant one said: "You're late."

Behind Billy the big one, the positive giant, the one Billy was pretty sure was a spade, shut the drawing-room door and leaned against it. That left the other one; average height, average build, and yet after one look at him Billy was even more afraid of him than the others.

The slim, elegant one spoke again. "I said you're late."

Behind Billy the giant moved, picked him up like a clumsily wrapped parcel, searched him in a manner both painful and degrading, and dropped him on a sofa.

"Tell us why you're late," said the slim, elegant one.

Billy heard himself say that he'd dined at the Terrazza, danced at that new place everyone said was marvellous.

"It doesn't matter," the slim, elegant one said. "It gave us time to look around. You have got guilty secrets, sweetie."

He gestured, and Billy looked at a table with wrought iron legs and a marble top. On it were some white packets that looked like tea-bags, only the stuff they contained was white. Billy Bone knew then that this wasn't a nightmare: he was already awake.

The slim, elegant one said: "You're going to tell us, sweetie. You're going to tell us everything."

"I don't know what you mean," said Billy Bone.

The slim, elegant one laughed: just that, no more, and yet Billy found that he was sweating, and the sweat was cold. The slim, elegant one drew on a pair of thin, leather gloves.

"Oh dear. Manual labour again," he said.

"You need us?" asked the one of average build. His voice was bored, and that, for Billy, was the most frightening thing of all. "I mean we'd rather like a cup of coffee."

"Go ahead," said the slim, elegant one. "Twosomes are by far the most fun."

Callan and FitzMaurice drank coffee, and listened to the sounds from the drawing-room. They were very nasty sounds.

"There are times," said FitzMaurice, "when I dislike my job."

"That's heroin he's selling," said Callan, and FitzMaurice drank his coffee in silence. When Meres called them back in, Billy Bone was weeping.

"Billy Bone has a *chum,*" said Meres. "A perfectly adorable chum called Helmuth. Helmuth gets him the dream powder so cheap one would think it must be love—but Helmuth isn't like that, is he, sweetie?"

"Helmuth's tough," said Billy Bone. "My God he's tough."

"Tougher than us, sweetie?" said Meres, and Billy Bone was silent. "No, no. Tell us all about Helmuth," said Meres. "I promise you we'll be as quiet as mice."

Billy Bone told them, and Callan said: "That's it then." He looked at Billy Bone. "Shall we keep him?"

"Oh I think so," said Meres. "There's still lots about heroin that he can tell us about." Meres hated heroin as Callan did. He reached down and patted Billy's cheek. "Sweetie," he said, "you've been overdoing it. We're going into the country for a while. Good, wholesome food and fresh air. And do you know what? When you're feeling strong enough you're going to tell all."

Billy Bone groaned.

"Oh, but I mean it," said Meres. "Every single thing; to the last teeniest detail."

Callan and FitzMaurice took Helmuth's room the way they had been taught, a neat, even elegant break-in, the only sound a tiny splash of glass. But they needn't have bothered. Helmuth had gone, and so had some of his clothes. All they found was more heroin, and a British Airways timetable that included flights to Nice. Callan sighed.

"I'd better go there too," he said.

FitzMaurice looked at the little white bags. "If you need any help you just yell," he said. "I'll even pay my own fare."

"But I don't want to go to Nice," said Lonely.

"How do you know?" said Callan. "You've never been."

"It's abroad, isn't it?" said Lonely, and Callan nodded. "You know I don't like abroad, Mr Callan."

"Sea air," said Callan, "sunshine. Good food. Wine."

"I don't like wine," said Lonely. He looked round his gaff. Nice gaff it was. All mod cons and a lot of things you might call collectors' pieces an' all. And here was Mr Callan saying he had to leave it and go off to Frogland. It wasn't bleeding fair.

"Two hundred quid and expenses," said Callan.

"It'll get physical," said Lonely. "When you go to abroad it always gets physical."

"I'll look out for you, son," said Callan. "Don't I always?"

Reluctantly Lonely nodded.

A pleasant flight, thought Callan, though he could have done with a bit more sleep before he joined it. Still, Hunter had booked him first class for a change. Callan lounged back in his seat and considered his cover. A business man who'd made his pile in nuts and bolts. Only hobby: clay-pigeon shooting. The general was a clay-pigeon shooting nut.

The plane came in on time, and Callan yawned his way through Customs and passport control, then wandered out, blinking, into the sunlight, looking for the car Hunter had assured him would be waiting. It would have been easier to leave the whole thing to Avis, but Avis didn't supply a ·357 Magnum as standard equipment.

He found the car at last, an elegant Citroen, and used the key he had been given, loaded up his suitcases and took the road to the town. As he drove he opened up the glove compartment. It held maps of the district, and a *fiche* for the car: and that was all it held. No ·357 Magnum. He might as well have gone to Avis after all.

His hotel, the Rialto, was an old one near the Albert I Garden:

high-ceilinged rooms, big comfortable beds, the kind of bath in which you could life full-length. Callan's sort of hotel, but that wasn't why he was booked in. The general and Angela were staying there too.

He bathed, took a nap, then allowed himself one drink from his duty free bottle. No Magnum revolver. He stuck his hands out in front of him; looked at the toughened ridges of skin that ran from wrist to little-finger tip, the hard, flattened knuckles. Karate hands; the only weapon he had left.

He went down in a vast, elderly lift, all gold paint and crimson velvet, to look into the dining-room where a sixty-year-old of boundless energy was trying to coax an exhausted twenty-three-year-old to eat just a little bit more: General Lawson and his daughter. That was one battle the general wasn't winning. Callan walked along towards the Quai des Etats Unis and found the restaurant Hunter had recommended. The food was delicious, but he was glad that Hunter was paying the bill.

He picked up his car, and drove along the Promenade des Anglais, took the road to Cannes, and turned off where the map in his glove-compartment told him to, passed some road-works the map didn't know about, drove up to the club. Admission was for members only, but Hunter had fixed that too. Hunter was in a hurry. Callan parked his car among a gaggle of Bentleys and Mercedes and Maseratis.

He went in and declined to play tennis or golf, swim, or ride a horse. He'd come to shoot clay- pigeons. A page took him to the armoury, and he hired a shotgun, an American job, the Sears automatic 5-shot. For some reason automatic shotguns were considered unsporting in England, but they were more than adequate for shooting clay-pigeons.

Callan went over to the attendant who worked the treadle, told him to pull. The disc came out low and curving, travelling fast. Callan fired and missed, called "pull" again, and again missed, but he was nearer. Next time he knew the gun, and the next time, and the next. With each shot the disc that is a clay-pigeon disintegrated. Callan reloaded, and behind him a voice said, "You're really awfully good."

Callan eased in the last cartridge and turned, taking his time to confront an energetic sixty-year-old holding a French imitation of a classic English shotgun, old-fashioned, double-barrelled, with hammers. General Lawson had come for a spot of shooting, just as Hunter had foretold.

"As a matter of fact I'm not too had myself," said the general. "You wouldn't fancy a match, I suppose? My name's Lawson – Richard Lawson."

"David Callan. A match by all means."

They shot four each, and didn't miss one, then the attendant had to go to load in more clay-pigeons. Callan waited as the general inserted two more cartridges, eased back his shotgun's hammers, began to turn to face him.

"Good a chance as any to have a chat," the general said.

Callan said: "Bit of a cheat these American guns, aren't they? I've still got one shot left."

The general looked at the way Callan handled the Sears Auto and froze. "Were you ever in the Army?" he asked at last.

"Yes," said Callan.

"What rank?"

"Corporal," said Callan, and it was true.

"Bloody waste," said Lawson, then added: "I'm a general. I suppose you didn't know that?"

"How should I?" said Callan. "What did you want to talk about?"

"Old men will talk about anything." General Lawson said. "That's what makes them such bores—and I won't inflict boredom on you today. I don't think I'll shoot any more either." He broke his gun, took out the cartridges. "Good day to you."

Callan watched him go. His back was still ramrod straight, but the bounce in his step had gone.

Callan gave him a couple of minutes' start then followed him. Lawson drove an elderly Mini with a right-hand drive, but driving on the right held no terrors for the general. He stuck to the middle of the road all the time. Callan followed him to a café, and watched unseen.

Lawson might know all about NATO commitments, he thought, but he hadn't a clue about being tailed. What the general did know about was drinking brandy. He ordered one neat, and told the waiter not to take the bottle too far away.

Callan went back to the hotel, but not to his room, which was on the fifth floor. The general and his daughter had a suite on the third, and Hunter had booked the room next door to it. Its occupant was a large, lethargic lady who woke up and left as soon as Callan came in. Callan switched on the little receiver on the table by the bed, and at once the voices came through. The suite was well and truly bugged.

"... grateful to you. Of course I'm grateful. You must know that." A woman's voice, soft and weary. That would be Angela.

"*But you do not show it.*"

A man's voice, hard and alive, with just a hint of accent ... Helmuth?

"I've paid you in full, haven't I?" the girl's voice said. "And it's very expensive here. ... Not like London."

"Money," said the man. *"I do not like taking money from a young lady."*

There was a silence.

"I can think of an easier way," the man said at last.

The girl laughed then. There was bitterness in her laughter: self-disgust, despair. "If it's what you want," she said at last, "but I'm not really much fun any more. Honestly I'm not."

The man's voice was full of outrage when he spoke. *"I did not speak of making love,"* he said.

"I somehow didn't think you were," said the girl. "You're far prettier than I am." Another pause, and Callan thought: Say his name. Miss Lawson. Let me know who my target is.

"What were you speaking of?" said the girl.

"*Information.*"

"I don't have any," the girl said.

"*Your father does.*"

"Oh dear God," said the girl.

"Listen," said the man. *"It is not so very bad."*

"It's awful."

"Please listen. I'm not spy or anything like that," said the man. *"Believe me."*

"Oh I do," said the girl. "How could you be? You're a friend of Billy Bone."

"But I have certain—business contacts," said the man. *"One of them is with the Defence of the Constitution. That is the West German Security Service."*

Oh you cunning bastard, thought Callan. That one was worthy of Hunter.

"What possible use could my father's knowledge be to West Germany?" the girl asked. But there was no doubt she was nibbling.

"It is possible that Britain does not tell us quite everything," said the man. *"And there is no harm in keeping a check on one's friends."*

"No," the girl said. She didn't mean it.

"Think about it," said the man.

"But I don't know anything about Daddy's work."

"You could find out," the man said. *"And in any case I think you lie. I think your father tells you many things."*

"Not any more," said the girl, and Callan found himself sweating. Those three words had put her in a red file.

"Next time you will pay with information," said the man.

"But next time's tomorrow. You promised me you'd bring the stuff tomorrow."

"Think about it," said the man.

Callan switched off the receiver, and sped, cat-footed, to the door, peered through a crack as the man left: blond and handsome—and six foot three and thirteen and a half stone, and none of it fat. And all I've got to take him with is my hands, thought Callan. The blond giant headed for the lift, and Callan raced for the stairs, hurtled down in a fury of speed to the lobby, and thanked God he didn't meet anybody coming up. He slowed to a halt when he reached the lobby, turned away as the elderly lift creaked to a rest and the blond man went to the desk left a key and went out. Callan went to the desk as the clerk reached for the key. Room 507. The fifth was the spy's floor.

"Wasn't that Gunmar Bjornsen who just went out?" said Callan. "The Swedish film actor? I've always been a fan of his."

"No. sir," said the clerk. "Mr Bauer is a West German gentleman. I do not think he is in films."

"Pity," said Callan, and meant it.

He went back to the room next to the Lawsons, to hear the general come in and kiss his daughter.

"Did you go for a swim?" the general asked.

"No, Daddy."

"You don't think exercise might help?"

No answer. The general tried again. "I met a chap at the club," he said. "We were shooting clay-pigeons together. He was the best shot I ever saw in my life."

"As good as you?" Angela asked.
"Maybe better. Dangerous sort of feller."
"Dangerous? But you shoot—"
"I shoot clay-pigeons," said the general. "And anyway, I'm dangerous too, aren't I?"
"Not to me," said his daughter.
"This chap bothers me," the general said. "I think someone's running a check on me."
"Daddy, who could possibly do that?" said Angela.
"Security," said Lawson. "They sometimes do run checks on generals — and their daughters."
The girl said nothing.
"You're still getting the stuff, aren't you?" the general said. "I brought you here to get away from it—and you promised me—you gave me your word—but all the same you're still getting it...." There was a silence, then: "Oh, my darling. My poor, poor darling," said the general, as Angela Lawson wept.

Callan met the plane, and reacted, in duty bound, to the full glory of Lonely in his abroad gear: lightweight suit in a delicate shade of green, shirt of deeper green, canary yellow socks and tie, shoes and snap-brim straw hat of chocolate brown.
"Very nice, old son," he said. "Very nice indeed."
Lonely smirked. "What I always say, Mr Callan," he said, "is if you're going to mix with foreigners, you've got to show 'em Old England's still on top."
Callan took him to dinner and watched him work his way through shell-fish soup, duck a l'orange, three kinds of cheese and a basket of fruit.
"So all I have to do is lift these little paper packets?" said Lonely.
"That's about it," said Callan. "Except I may want you to give me a hand later on."
Lonely was at once suspicious. "Doing what, Mr Callan?"
"Getting rid of some rubbish," said Callan.
Lonely tried, failed to find a catch as Callan finished his wine.
"You really like that stuff?" he asked.
"I do."
"I wish I did," said Lonely. "The beer's awful."
Callan took him back to the hotel, and the room next to the Lawsons, and they listened as father and daughter prepared to go out to eat. Angela wasn't hungry, but the general insisted. ... When they'd gone Callan switched off the receiver.
"In you go, son," he said. "Do a nice, tidy job."
Lonely preceded Callan to the door, then turned. Mr Callan was looking down at his hands. The face told nothing, thought Lonely. It never did. And yet he knew. Mr Callan was worried.
"It's going to be all right, isn't it, Mr Callan?" Lonely asked.
"It's going to be all right," said Callan, and looked again at his hands. "It has to be."
Callan watched Lonely go into the general's suite like a weasel

going down a rabbit-hole, and with much the same smell, he thought, then went to the desk, checked that Helmuth Bauer's key wasn't there, and went up to floor five.

Whoever lived in 509, next door to Bauer, was watching a Western: the kind where the Indians and the cavalry use enough ammunition to keep El Alamein going for a fortnight. And that was a bit of luck, he thought. He would need all the luck he could get. He knocked on the door of 507. Bauer's voice spoke in French: "Who is it?"

Callan made his voice high and whining. "Helmuth," he said. "It's Billy Bone. I've got to talk to you."

There was a muttered exclamation, then Callan heard a lock turn. As the door started to open he hit it with all his weight and kept on going, kicked the door to with his foot.

Bauer lay on the floor, in his right hand was an automatic pistol. Callan dived at the wrist, levered and pulled, and Bauer struck left-handed as the pistol slid from his grasp. Pain scalded across Callan's biceps as both men scrambled to their feet. Callan kicked the pistol out of reach. From the sounds next door it seemed as if the Indians were using tanks, but he didn't dare risk the sound of a real pistol-shot.

Bauer aimed a kick and Callan swerved just, only just in time to miss it, and grabbed for the foot, but Bauer pirouetting away, grabbed Callan's attacking hand instead, levered and pulled, and Callan allowed himself to go up and over, landed on the bed in a break-fall, hurled himself from it to avoid Bauer's follow-up dive, rolled and scrambled to his feet—but Bauer had used the bed as a spring-board, jack knifed to the floor, and threw a fist strike that would have ended the fight if it had landed properly.

But Callan had swerved just enough to take it on the shoulder. Even so he gasped with the pain, gasped again as Bauer aimed another kick that took him high on the thigh. I'm five inches shorter, thought Callan, and three stone lighter, and God knows how many years older—and it's my turn to lose.

Then the big man rushed him again and Callan swerved and struck, and landed a good one under the heart, but even so the big man kept on coming, his hands striking like axe-blades, forcing him into a corner from which there was no way out. And that's the end of it for me, thought Callan. Now I'm cornered he can finish me. I hope Lonely doesn't hang about waiting....

The big man dived, and Callan's luck improved. Bauer caught his foot in a strand of lamp-flex and stumbled. The lamp added to the uproar or next door's TV, and Callan swirled round the German, his foot slammed into the small of his back, pushing him prone: then he knelt on top of him, knees and hands found the vulnerable places and Callan levered and pulled....

The crack sounded very loud when it came: the cowboy film had ended. Callan limped across the room and picked up the familiar weight of metal. Now he didn't need one, he had a gun.

"Two," said Lonely. "Two packets was all there was. I reckon it must be her emergency ration."

"How do you know they were hers?" said Callan.

"Hidden in her bath salts," said Lonely. "You didn't tell me it was heroin, Mr Callan. Heroin's nasty."

"It's filth," said Callan, and flushed it down the toilet.

"You're limping," said Lonely severely. "You want to know what I think—I think you've been fighting."

"I know I have," said Callan. "Let's get rid of the refuse."

They went from the third floor to the fifth, and Lonely stared down at the dead German. "My Gawd," he said, "what d'you use? Not just your hands?"

"He died of bad luck," said Callan. "Go and fetch a laundry trolley from the service room."

"But it'll be locked," said Lonely.

"What d'you think I brought you for?" said Callan.

They loaded Bauer on to the trolley and covered him with sheets, ran him down in the service lift and waited in the corridor that led to the goods entrance till there was no one in sight. And all the time Lonely stank.

"Mr Callan," said Lonely. "We got a corpus delicti."

No sense in wondering where Lonely had learned Latin. Callan braced himself and hauled Bauer from the trolley.

"What we've got is a drunk," said Callan. "Help me get him to the car."

Somehow they hauled Bauer to the waiting Citröen, and Callan drove along the Cannes road, turned off on to the road that led to the country club and stopped by the repair works. Lonely watched as Callan fetched sand and cement, added water.

"What we doing, Mr Callan?" he asked.

"We're conducting a funeral," said Callan. "No flowers by request."

"I'm sorry," the girl said. "My father's asleep." Callan pushed past her. It was very easy.

"Yeah," he said. "He takes pills for that."

Angela Lawson moved towards the telephone. "You seem to know a lot about my father," she said.

"I know everything about your father. I know everything about you."

The hand that was reaching for the telephone fell. She turned to face him.

"Did Helmuth send you?" she asked.

"Helmuth's dead, Miss Lawson," said Callan.

"Dead?" She said it as if a were impossible.

"I killed him," said Callan. "It was one of the reasons I was sent here."

"You killed him?"

Callan nodded.

"But he gets me the stuff," she said.

And there, thought Callan, is a junky for you. No room left for compassion or even pity: only a terrible, obliterating need. Aloud he said, "Not any more."

She thought for a moment, then her tensions eased.

"I know what you're thinking," he said.

"How can you?"

"You're thinking there's two packets left," said Callan. "If you're careful they can last till you meet Helmuth's successor—but you won't. Helmuth isn't just dead. He's disappeared. I saw to that. It'll be days before they'll send anybody else."

But she still hung on.

"You're thinking you'll go back to England—to a geezer called Billy Bone. But you can't love. We've taken care of him too."

She began to sweat then, the need for the drug making her shiver.

"I—you'll have to excuse me for a minute," she said.

"I took the two packets from your bath-salts as well," said Callan.

"Give them to me," the girl said, and knelt before him. It was almost more than he could bear.

"I destroyed them," said Callan.

"You're destroying me."

"No," said Callan. "I'm trying to save your father."

He told her then what his trade was, about Billy Bone who worked for Bauer, and Bauer who worked for the S.S.D., and all the time she sweated. Her body shivered. Callan kept on trying.

"Your father knows about me," he said. "He told you about me this afternoon."

"But how could he?" she said.

"A pal on the general staff," said Callan. "You see they know all about him. And you. It would be better if he resigned his commission."

"He mustn't," she said.

"He can't," said Callan. "He's needed too much." Better tell it all. "He must have some good friends on the staff. One of them saw to it I didn't get a gun."

In his mind he begged her: Please see what I'm trying to tell you. But nicely brought up generals' daughters never think they can die by violence, the way the Helmuths did. He waited, and at last she said: "What do I have to do?" In her voice there was nothing but despair.

"A clinic," said Callan. "A cure."

"There is no cure," she said. Her certainty was absolute.

"You've got to try, otherwise—they'll get to you again. They'll get to your father. Miss Lawson, you've get to try."

Callan's voice was desperate now, as hers had been. Hunter's instructions had been explicit: already he had exceeded them.

"Junkies find it impossible to try," the girl said. "Didn't you know that—and you so clever?" She sighed then, and Callan realised how much he hated Helmuth and Billy Bone, how much he hated Hunter—and himself.

"All I can do is go for a swim," said the girl. "Daddy's always telling me to go for a swim."

"I'd have to come with you," said Callan.

"You're the only one I'd want to," she said. "I know you won't try to stop me ... Please, may I say goodbye to Daddy?"

Callan watched as she kissed her father. He stirred, but the sleeping pills were strong. He didn't wake.

Callan drove her along the road to Beaulieu, and a deserted beach. She stripped then, and put on a swimsuit and looked down at her body. The marks on her arms were like wounds.

"I used to be pretty," she said. "I wish I'd met you when I was pretty."

She plied her clothes neatly together, left her hangbag on top to be found in the morning, then moved down to the beach.

"Please say goodbye," she said.

"Goodbye," said Callan. "You're very brave."

Her voice floated back over the dark water. "Not brave," she said. "Just very tired."

The moon came out then from behind cloud and Callan watched as she swam, strongly at first, then more and more slowly as the drug-weakened body refused to respond. She submerged and then surfaced, and Callan looked away.

When he looked back there was no sign that she had ever been: only dark sea, white moonlight.

There were worse places to rest.

File on an Awesome Amateur

Callan looked at the woman: middle-aged, tough as old teak, in a coat and skirt of derelict tweed and a felt hat she must have bought when she joined the Girl Guides before the war, knitted stockings, and a pair of brogues that would have terrified a skinhead.

"Ms," the woman said, and Callan wondered if it were some sort of password.

'I beg your pardon," said Hunter.

"You always say that," the woman said, "and I always have to repeat myself." She glared at Callan, who felt aggrieved. He hadn't said a word.

"I will not respond to the useless appellations of outworn shibboleths," she said. "Miss and Mrs. are labels pasted on to obscure the reality of one's essential persona."

"I quite agree, Ms Widgery," said Callan.

"I don't suppose you do," said the woman, "but at least you've got more tact than Hunter. How d'you do?"

She held out her hand and Callan took it. She had a grip like a wrestler's.

"This lady," Hunter said carefully, "has just returned from Russia. She's been doing some work on—er—birds."

Ms Widgery reached for the teapot.

"Have some tea," she said. "It's no more a woman's job than a man's, but I suppose if I don't pour out we'll all die of thirst."

She poured out tea with a ladylike elegance, and Callan observed that a succession of nannies, governesses and finishing-school teachers had not laboured quite in vain.

"Birds of prey actually," she said. "Hawks and eagles. They're my sort of thing. Done a couple of books on them. Don't suppose for a minute you've read them."

"Well as a matter of fact ..." Callan began.

"Thought not. Time you did though. Bit of a bird of prey yourself by the look of you."

Hunter coughed, and tried again.

"While she was there Miss – Ms - Widgery met Lubov."

"In the Crimea," said Ms Widgery. "He's got a dacha there. He's interested in birds too. Of course, once I turned up he always had somebody with him – interpreter he called himself, though Lubov speaks better English than most of us. But we climbed pretty high one day to get a look at a falcon. Rather un-useful species really. Don't see many of 'em – not even in Russia." She sipped at her tea, remembering the falcon, then asked abruptly: "What was I talking about?"

Hunter sighed again. "Lubov," he said.

"Oh yes. We climbed rather high and the interpreter feller turned giddy, and we had a few moments to ourselves. He wants to defect."

Callan's face showed nothing but bewilderment.

"Lubov," she said. "He wants to defect ... Great God Almighty, don't you know who Lubov is?"

"Well, as a matter of fact ..." said Callan.

"You said that before," Ms. Widgery said acidly. "He's a poet. I take it you know what a poet is?"

"Yeah," said Callan. "There was a young man from Penang..."

Ms Widgery flushed an instant scarlet, then erupted into barking laughter like a demented sea-lion. "Sorry," she said. "I'm very impatient, you see, and that occasionally makes me rude. Sorry. Why the devil should you have heard of a Russian poet, except he's rather good."

"And he wants to defect," said Hunter.

"He got an invitation to the Venice Biennale," said Ms Widgery. "He thought he could hop it from there if we laid on a gondola or something."

"Has he permission to leave Russia?" Callan asked.

"He's a Category Two," said Ms Widgery. "He has to apply for permission. I told him not to bother."

Callan waited.

"The invitation came from some very important Italian lefties," Ms. Widgery continued. "The sort the Ivans like to keep sweet if it doesn't cost too much. And a poet's about the cheapest thing they've got."

"But you told him to say 'No'?" said Callan.

"Obviously," said Ms. Widgery. "If he'd started acting keen they'd have assumed at once that he wouldn't come back. They really are the most predictable people. So he said No and they've *ordered* him to attend."

She took one more dainty sip of tea, then put down her cup and looked at Callan. "If I were you I'd bone up on your culture," she said, and rose.

"Don't get up," she said, but Hunter and Callan had already risen to their feet. She clumped in her massive brogues to the door, turned on them and glared. "I wish you'd try to forget I'm feminine," she said.

The door slammed. Callan found that he was mopping his face with his handkerchief.

"Is she reliable, sir?" Callan asked.

"Cynthia Widgery is one of the most competent persons it's ever been my misfortune to meet," said Hunter, "and the only amateur I've ever used more than once."

"Amateur?" said Callan, and Hunter grinned at the note of horror in his voice.

"I wanted her full-time," he said, "but she wouldn't have it. She's too busy with her damn birds."

He flicked a file over to Callan. Blue cover, which meant that Lubov wasn't a danger to be removed, not even a potential danger. Boris Lubov ... poet.

"You really want me to go to Venice and lift a poet?" said Callan.

"Everyone wants to go to Venice," said Hunter, "and you could use a little culture."

"What possible use can you find for a poet?"

"Pasternak, Solzhenitsyn, Mandelstam," said Hunter. "They all got out—or their work did. The Praesidium were very annoyed with the KGB. There was even talk of a shake-up. That pleased me, Callan. If Lubov were to defect there might even *be* a shake-up, and that would please me even more. The KGB in its present form is much too efficient. Go away and see if it's possible to lift a poet."

If Lubov got to Venice it should be dead easy, thought Callan, but Hunter hadn't made it sound like that, and the file didn't make it sound like that either.

When Lubov went to Venice it would be as part of a cultural mission and half of that would be KGB executives with only one order: bring him back alive. He would stay in a room in a hotel where the KGB had booked a whole floor, and the meetings he addressed would be jam-packed with Italian lefties, and when the Biennale was over he would go by private motor-boat to the Piazzale Roma, then by car to the airport, and then back to Russia.

So far as Callan's chances of lifting him went, he might as well have stayed in the Crimea.

He looked at the picture of Boris Lubov. Young and fit, hair cut short, nice smile: he looked more like a dentist than a poet. But the file said he was a good one. Now and then the word genius appeared. Lyric poetry. Forests and cornfields, lakes and bird songs; but he'd known and talked with a hell of a lot of people and he had a photographic memory...Callan wondered if Hunter might not want him for rather more than annoying the KGB.

Did he have to call his fellow bird-watcher Ms Widgery? Or would 'Comrade' do? Ms Widgery was a caution all right, but she was also an amateur, and Callan never had gone much on them. Hunter was an utter professional. Lonely was a smelly professional; even Meres was more than just detestable, he was a pro too, and you knew where you stood with all three of them. Yet Hunter had said she was competent. All the same, there was no harm in checking.

"You want me to follow an old bird?" said Lonely.

"That's right," said Callan.

"Where's the fun in that?"

"No fun," said Callan. "Just fifty quid a day and expenses."

Lonely signalled for more beer, more whisky. "What's she look like?"

Callan reached out for his whisky, but kept his eyes on the door.

"She'll be along in a minute," he said. "And when she does I scarper—and you start work."

"Old birds is murder," said Lonely. "They keep going into Harrods."

"You can go into Harrods."

"Not into the ladies' lingerie, I can't," said Lonely. "People might talk."

Callan chuckled. "I don't think you'll have any problems," he said. "What this one wears next to the skin is barbed wire."

He finished his Scotch and turned so that a bunch of dart-players shielded him from the door. "Here she comes now," he said.

Ms. Widgery strode in and ordered a pint of Guinness.

"Blimey," said Lonely.

"Good luck, old son," said Callan, and left by the side-door....

He'd traced her easily enough: the Royal Ornithological Society had been more than helpful, and the porter at her block of flats had a few things to say as well ... like where her local was. Now it was up to Lonely. And if she was clean, and Hunter ever found out, he'd be in dead shuck. But she was an amateur, and amateurs were chancy at the best of times.

He went home and cooked himself a meal, and concentrated on the problem of detaching Lubov from his KGB goons. The file said that Lubov had begun his life as an historian who had specialised in the eighteenth century. A lot of his poems too were about the past.

There might be something in that, if Hunter would wear it.

"I can't possibly lay on a reception," said Hunter. "The money just wouldn't stretch that far."

"Ms Widgery might," said Callan.

"What on earth do you mean?"

"She's got a sister," said Callan. "Married to the Conte di Alassio. They've got a palazzo in Venice—and they love giving parties."

"How the devil do you know that?" said Hunter.

"I looked her up," said Callan. "Opened a file."

"May one ask why?"

Hunter hadn't raised his voice, but there was no doubt of it: he was furious.

"Because she's an amateur," said Callan, "and amateurs make me nervous."

"I've already told you—"

"Yeah," said Callan. "She's very competent. All the same, I'm happier with the pros. Amateurs have ideals, Hunter. That means they take risks. They're even ready to die in a good cause."

"And you?"

"I'm like the feller in the French Revolution," said Callan. "When it was over somebody asked him what he'd done—and he said: 'I survived.'"

But Hunter wasn't listening. His mind was still dealing with the problem Callan had put to him, and the solution Callan had suggested.

"I'll talk to Cynthia Widgery," he said at last.

Callan stayed silent: he'd won. There was no point in harping on it.

"It means you'll be working with an amateur," said Hunter. "I thought you disliked that."

"I do," said Callan. "But you said you wanted me to fetch you a poet."

Time to bone up on his culture. For the Biennale that meant new paintings, new sculpture, new music. No pleasure in that for Callan, but work. For him the contemporary world was one of danger, defectors, assassins, double-agents, death: the feel of a Magnum ·357 in his hand, or just the hand itself as a lethal weapon, clubbing, subbing, breaking bone.

Art for him existed only in the past, where death could have no terrors, because it had already happened. But he worked on modern art because he had to look right; because if he didn't look right he might die. When he couldn't stand it any more he called up a friend.

Lonely cut his meat pie into sections, spread mustard over each section, then doused the lot with thick brown sauce and ordered pickles. Once the little man got started, thought Callan, he could make as ostrich look dyspeptic.

"First decent meal I've had in days," said Lonely, and looked reproachfully at Callan. "You didn't tell me she was a vegetarian." The anguish in his voice was such that Callan found himself apologising.

"I am sorry, old son," he said, "I didn't know."

"Chopped nuts," said Lonely, "and shredded carrots and that. Thank Gawd she wasn't teetotal."

"So it was vegetarian restaurants and pubs," said Callan. "Where else?"

"The British Museum," said Lonely. "She spent hours there, reading about birds. The seats ain't half hard," he added, and Callan ordered him more beer. "Ta, Mr Callan."

"Did she meet anybody?"

"A bird," said Lonely. "I mean a real bird. Not one with feathers on. Mind you she'd have looked all right in feathers."

"Never mind your strip club memoirs. Who was she?"

"Redhead," said Lonely. "About eight and a half stone. Five feet three without her platforms." He consulted a piece of paper. "Barbara Jackson," he read, "17, Kensington Mansions."

"How d'you know?"

"I followed her an' all," said Lonely. "No extra charge. Made a nice change from the other one."

"Did you hear them talk?"

"Your bird called her Barby," Lonely said. "The redhead sounded American–but classy with it. She's daft on birds an' all. Woodpeckers and kingfishers and owls and—" he hesitated.

"And what?" said Callan.

"Great tits," said Lonely, and blushed scarlet.

"Anything else?"

"Your bird told Miss Jackson she was going off to Venice," said Lonely. "Miss Jackson said she might go there an' all."

"What's all this Miss Jackson?" said Callan.

Again Lonely looked reproachful.

"Mr Callan," he said, "she's a lady."

That she was a beauty there was no denying. Red hair worn to her shoulders, neatly rounded figure, long All-American legs, Callan tailed her to a secondhand bookshop off the Charing Cross Road, and burrowed into the military history as she went through the section on birds like a devouring flame, and talked to an adoring assistant as she did so.

Her voice was musical, low-picked, the cultivated New England accent just pronounced enough to be pleasing. And she knew the hell of a lot about ornithology, thought Callan as he listened. But that proved nothing. For the moment he knew the hell of a lot about modern art.

He found an old copy of Sir Edward Creasy's *Fifteen Decisive Battles of the World* and bought it before he could decide he couldn't afford it, then lingered as Barbara Jackson stacked together her enormous pile of books, tripped as she walked, and fell on to his chest.

Books cascaded in all direction, the adoring assistant raced to the rescue, and Callan found himself clutching Miss Jackson, and enjoying it enormously.

"Oh dear I'm so sorry," said Miss Jackson, "so clumsy of me. I didn't hurt, you, did I?"

Callan assured her that he had survived without pain, and they went out together to seek coffee. The adoring assistant looked disgusted.

Over coffee Barbara Jackson told him even more about birds. She could talk almost as well as Callan could listen, the only trouble was she never told him anything–except about birds.

He left her after they'd lunched together, a lunch for which she'd insisted on paying her share. No vegetarian nonsense with this ornithologist. There'd been highballs and wine and brandy with the coffee—and an implicit, if not precisely defined, promise of more goodies to come when Barby got back from a little trip she had to make.

Callan took a walk. There were things to think about, and he had to work off some of the alcohol inside him. Walking was good for both. He cut through a maze of Soho streets, past the strip-clubs and dirty bookshops, and thought that maybe there was something in modern art after all, then turned down an alley that would lead him to Old Compton Street, and from there to Shaftesbury Avenue and the Piccadilly Tube.

It was in the alley that they jumped him: two good men who knew their job: workers who were both eager and willing to take advantage of anyone as filled up as he was with Scotch, wine and brandy.

They raced up behind him and one of them wrapped his arms round Callan's body—Callan could see nothing of him but the arms and they were like steel hawsers—and the other one moved round to face him, a long-haired gent in a denim suit who looked like a useful light-heavyweight.

"You follow ladies," the light-heavy said. "That's not nice. For that you get punished."

He moved in on Callan, and the man who held him clamped his arms even tighter. At least he wasn't going to let him fall. Callan swung both feet off the ground, and they landed side by side in the light-heavy's midriff. The light-heavy made a sound like a paper bag bursting some way off, and Callan felt the other man's arms slacken as his own feet touched the ground. He ducked his head and pulled forward, and the blow from the man behind him hit his left shoulder instead of his head.

Callan felt an explosion of pain, pitched forward on top of the light-heavy and kept on rolling. A shoe just missed his ear as he rolled on and scrambled to his feet just in time to face the other man's rush. He was a solid barrel of a man, a cube of approximately 5ft. 6in., and when Callan landed a fist strike to his gut he just grunted and kept on coming, looping a right that Callan swerved too late to avoid.

It slammed under his ribcage, jerking his torso forward, Callan willed himself to continue the forward movement, and the top of his head smacked into the face of the cube, then he brought up his knee, but the cube was ready for that and swerved away, aiming a kick as he did so.

Callan took it high on the thigh, and hobbled round to face the cube's next rush. The cube's nose was bleeding, and the sight of his own blood flowing seemed to upset him enough to make him angry, and maybe, Callan thought later, that was what saved him, Callan, from annihilation. For the cube came in with both hands spread wide to crush, and Callan balanced on his sound leg, kicked out for the gut with the one the cube had hurt, and groaned when he connected, groaned again as he hobbled over to where the cube crouched, writhing in pain, and chopped behind his ear.

Callan limped his way to the Tube.

"So it's all clear?" said Hunter.

"I think so," said Callan. "We go to the party at the Alassio Palace and I switch Meres for Lubov and put him aboard the ship off the Lido."

"It should be quite straightforward," said Hunter.

"Provided Lubov goes to the party."

He's already accepted," said Hunter. "So have the entire Russian contingent. It seems Alassio's a member of the Italian Communist Party. You know. Callan, all Italians puzzle me, but rich ones are a positive enigma."

"No they're not," said Callan. "They just like to cover all their bets."

He got up and went to the door. He did his best, but he couldn't hide his limp.

"Have you been fighting?" said Hunter.

Now was not the time to admit he'd had Ms. Widgery followed; that he'd met her friend. Callan looked hurt.

"I slipped," he said, "getting out of the bath."

The Biennale was pretty well what he'd expected. The little white buildings in the Giardini, each the exhibition centre of a different country, housed what each considered best in contemporary art.

The Russians, it seemed, still went in for pictures that looked like pictures. On the day Callan went there he saw heroic peasants, soldiers of the people, the battleship Potemkin.

Then he went into the American Pavilion, which was dominated by a vast statue, perhaps 10ft. tall, which appeared to be constructed largely out of beaten-out tincans. It was called The American Eagle, and if you viewed it from precisely the right angle it did look a bit like a bird of prey, but not nearly so much as Ms Widgery, who stood beneath it deep in conversation with Barbara Jackson and Lubov.

Even with two KGB goons six feet away, Barbara Jackson seemed to be making a lot of headway.

"I adore fancy dress parties," said Meres, and adjusted his cravat with finicking care.

Callan looked at him: knee breeches, buckled shoes, a waistcoat of black and gold; all he needed was a tie-wig to be the perfect Casanova. But Meres wasn't due to be Casanova till later. For the moment he donned a scarlet robe that covered him from head to toe, and little buttoned hat and became a slim and elegant cardinal.

"You look all right," he said.

"You too," said Meres. He sounded surprised. Callan was dressed as a corsair: soft leather boots, baggy trousers, white shirt, embroidered waistcoat, and a broad red sash round his waist stuffed full of plastic daggers and pistols, and hidden within its folds a ·357 Magnum and silencer.

"We'd better go," said Callan.

"In a minute."

Meres picked up a little bag of scarlet silk and inserted into it another Magnum, another silencer. "There," he said. "I'm ready."

They put on their masks, and left their hotel, walked to the quay where gondolas were parked like cabs. Neither gondoliers nor passers-by reacted. In Venice nothing is surprising. A gondola took them to the Palazzo Alassio on the Grand Canal. It was near the church of San Samsone, and Callan approved of that. It was about as near the Lido as he could hope to get.

They arrived to join a queue of gondolas, bobbing like black swans before the palazzo's steps as one by one the guests disembarked: pierrots, Columbines, doges, Desdemonas. As Callan and Meres took their place in the queue a motor-boat moved gently in, long and sleek and powerful.

Aboard it were the Russian contingent. Gondolas it seemed were bourgeois deviationist, Callan sighed. He could have done without a motor-boat full of Russians.

Ahead of them the count and countess waited: he a portly *condottiere*, she a slender and elegant Portia. Beside her stood her sister, Ms Widgery, the most improbable Moorish slave-girl Callan had ever seen.

Callan and Meres kept on going into an eighteenth century ballroom where a rock group blared out amplified sound. Callan winced, then winced again as an eighteenth-century courtesan red-haired and gowned in cloth of gold, headed straight for him.

But the red-haired charmer walked past him, to watch the arrival of the Russian contingent of mouzhiks and Tolstois, and a masked Casanova, slim and elegant in knee-breeches and buckled shoes, coat and waistcoat embroidered in gold.

"That's our boy?" Meres asked, and Callan nodded. "Really not bad," said Meres.

The masks came off at midnight. At 11.30 Meres and Lubov would switch characters and that would be that—if all went well. If it didn't the best thing they could hope for was an international incident, and Hunter detested international incidents. All the same, thought Callan, once you start lifting poets you have to take chances.

The ball dragged on, and Meres and Callan found girls and danced a little, drank a little, and kept a cautious eye on a Casanova who drank a great deal, but always with a mouzhik to keep him company. At 11.25 Callan put down his glass.

"Oh dear," said Meres. "I always get stage fright just before we start."

He went up the wide, elegant staircase. Callan followed him more slowly, and looked down at the ballroom.

Casanova too was heading for the staircase. He still had a mouzhik with him ... Meres turned into the second room on the right, and Callan paused to examine a little picture of Venice by Longhi as Lubov and his mouzhik walked past him, plucked a cosh from the array of weapons in his sash and laid it behind the mouzhik's ear, then caught him and dragged him into the second room on the right, and Lubov followed. He could just about walk, Meres. Casanova in shirt-sleeves, held a cardinal's robe in his hands.

"Jolly good," he said. Callan dumped the mouznik on the bed as Lubov swayed.

"I don't think I want to go," Lubov said.

Meres swore, but Callan gestured him to silence: the rock group thumped below.

"Why not?" said Callan.

"I'm afraid," said Lubov. "It is a very shabby reason."

They wasted five frantic minutes arguing with him, but Lubov just stood there swaying, saying No. Then Callan saw the handle of the door beginning to turn, and motioned to Meres, who took his Magnum ·357 from its scarlet bag, and waited behind the angle of the door, watched it open to admit a red-haired courtesan in cloth of gold, holding a Colt Agent revolver, the one with the two-inch barrel, that should have been too much gun for a woman to handle, only they'd forgotten to let this woman know. She kicked the door too behind her, and aimed the Colt at Callan.

"Hold it still," she said. "Mr Lubov's coming with me."

Without hesitation, Meres brought the barrel of his gun down on the woman's head and caught her as she slumped to the floor. A real pro, thought Callan, then belted Lubov gently as he opened his mouth to yell.

"We do have fun," said Meres. "Where do I put her?"

"On the bed," said Callan.

"Pity about your poet," said Meres, and dropped Barby Jackson beside the mouzhik.
"Help me to get that robe on him," Callan said. "He's passed out. I'll see he gets home."
"What a resourceful fellow you are," said Meres, and looked at the bed. "And what an odd couple they make," he said.
"Yeah," said Callan. "The eagle and the bear. Let's get on with it."
Together they robed Lubov as a cardinal, then Meres donned Casanova's coat and wig and they eased the Russian into the corridor, where an enormous Moorish slave girl stood fuming.
"You took your time," Ms Widgery said.
"We had a visitor," said Callan. "A Miss Jackson."
"What happened to her?"
"She got belted," said Callan.
"You struck a woman?" Ms. Widgery's voice held nothing but outrage ... Amateurs.
"We tried to forget she was feminine," said Callan. "Now help me get Lubov downstairs. Meres has work to do."
Between them they managed it, though on the way down the stairs another mouzhik passed them. Callan would have liked to check the ballroom for his mates, but there was no time. ... They reached a side-door with a tiny jetty where a motor-boat and pilot waited, and Callan heaved Lubov aboard, then jumped in after him. Behind him, Ms Widgery clucked. "Be careful you fool," she said. "He's a genius."
The motor-boat roared off then joined the procession of vaporetti, gondolas, private craft that moved down the Grand Canal. The pilot was a lieutenant R.N. who knew Venice far too well to make speed just yet.
"Everything O.K.?" he asked.
Callan thought about Meres and the questing mouzhiks. "We'll manage," he said, and looked behind him. Another motor-boat processed sedately on their tall.
"I think we've got company," said Callan, and the lieutenant risked a quick look over his shoulder, as they passed Santa Mariadella Salute, moved into open water.
"Better lose them," he said, and opened up, but their pursuers had more power. They hung on, began to gain, as they sped past gondolas and power-boats, setting them frantically bobbing in their wash. They headed for the Lido flat out, and suddenly there were no more pleasure-craft, only their pursuer closing in.
"Did you bring anything?" Callan yelled.
"In the locker aft," the lieutenant shouted, "but the orders are it's only to be used in an emergency."
From the other craft a searchlight flicked on, swivelled, and held them. A man dressed as a mouzhik loosed off a shot with a Makanov semi-automatic that came far too close for comfort.
"This is an emergency," said Callan. He opened the locker and took out a Mannlicher hunting rifle, the one he preferred ... Hunter had gone to a lot of trouble over this one. He crouched on the bottom boards and shot out the searchlight. The other boat kept on coming.

Callan lay still, breathing slow and easy as a cloud switched off the moon, switched it on again as it passed, then he shot the other boat's pilot, and it sheered away as the pilot slumped on its wheel, making it rock so crazily it spilled out a mouzhik.

"My God," said the lieutenant R.N.

They moved on to the open sea and the waiting ship.

"Lubov doesn't remember that you hit him," said Hunter. "He thinks he passed out. As a matter of fact he's grateful to you for making up his mind."

"And Meres?" said Callan.

"Oh, Meres had lots of fun," said Hunter. "He claims that a mouzhik accosted him. I gather there was quite a scene. A pity you let the others get on to you."

"We were held up," said Callan, "by a bird, a C.I.A. bird."

"You know about her, do you?" said Hunter.

"She was pretty obvious," said Callan.

"Yes, she was," Hunter said. "That's why I told Cynthia Widgery to make contact with her. I thought it might provide a useful distraction."

Callan thought of the Colt Agent she had held. "It was me that was distracted," he said.

"Pretty women always distract you," said Hunter. "All the same it was a neat idea to put her to bed with a KGB man. They're such brutes," said Hunter, and he smiled for rather less than a second. "She had assistants," he continued. "I think you fought with them ... Perhaps you'd been following her and she put them on to you."

Callan said nothing.

"Come, Callan," said Hunter, "the police found two very large Americans beaten up on the day you came in limping."

"All right," said Callan. "I had Ms Widgery followed. She led me to Barby. It you'd told me about her—"

"She would have taken your mind from your work," said Hunter, and Callan knew he was right.

Hunter shifted in his chair. "I trust that now you've revised your opinion of Cynthia Widgery," he said.

"She did a nice, smooth job," said Callan, "but she's still an amateur."

Hunter was at once alert.

"In what way?" he said.

"She's all for Women's Lib," said Callan, "but she doesn't like birds getting belted."

File on a Joyous Juliet

The television set began to produce its usual pattern of waving lines, and as usual Hunter got up to slam it open-handed on its side. At once the waving lines vanished to be replaced by a test card.

He still knows how to hit, thought Callan, and where.

Aloud he said, "I didn't know you understood electronics, Hunter."

"I understand force," said Hunter. "So do you. It'll last my time. If you're lucky, it'll last yours. Watch the set."

The test card faded, and gave way to a commercial. Somebody, it seemed, was out to save Western civilisation by marketing a new brand of deodorant. "Fresh," a poofy voice was saying. "Get Fresh. Keep Fresh."

And as the poofy voice was saying it, a leggy blonde wearing a thigh-length sweater and not much else, sailed in slow motion past a barrow-boy, a traffic cop and a loveable old cockney char, then twirled balletically into the arms of a good-looking geezer wearing a sweater exactly like hers.

Each of them then began sniffing the other while the barrow-boy, the traffic cop and the loveable old char looked on, approving. "Get Fresh," the poofy voice said, "and keep that way."

Maybe I should get some for Lonely, thought Callan.

The screen went blank.

"Like to see it again?" said Hunter.

"Gawd no," said Callan.

Hunter got up and switched off. "You found it distasteful?" he asked.

Callan shrugged. He wasn't there to be a TV critic, and both men knew it. "I've seen it before," he said. "Several hundred times."

"You haven't seen the blonde before," said Hunter.

Long-legged sweet-smelling blondes who flogged deodorant were as alike as cigarettes in a packet, but if Hunter was watching her then there was something different about her, and Callan was all too aware of what that difference would be: *trouble.*

"Her name's Jo Bright," said Hunter. "She's going to Italy soon—Verona. Doing a TV film of *Romeo and Juliet.*"

"She's Juliet?" Callan asked, and Hunter nodded. "On the strength of that?" Callan gestured at the blank TV set.

"Oh, she can act," said Hunter. "Act very well; maybe too well."

Callan watched Hunter intently. From the tone of his voice it would seem that Jo Bright didn't confine her acting to the theatre.

"She's got a boy friend," Hunter said. "In my day we would have described him as her lover, but in my day we used language with precision. Harold Manning ... ever heard of him?"

"No," said Callan.

"Industrialist," said Hunter. "Started out as a research chemist—still does a bit. He invented 'Fresh.' It made him a lot of money. He's on to something now that could make him even more. A hell of a sight more." The thought of it seemed to depress him, and he poured out drinks: Chivas Regal and water for Callan, very dry sherry for himself.

"Nerve-gas," he said at last.

"Science-fiction stuff," said Callan.

"If only it were," said Hunter. "We've got it, and so have the Russians, and the Yanks. Trouble is it's too damn clumsy to operate and too expensive to make. Manning's won't be."

"He hasn't perfected it yet?"

"He will," said Hunter. "And soon."

"And we'll have it and be happy."

"I hope we'll have it," said Hunter. "I doubt if we'll be happy. The stuff's appalling."

"Why shouldn't we have it?"

"I got a flash," said Hunter. "The KGB knows what Manning's after—and they want it."

"Can't you stop them?"

"In London they haven't a prayer," said Hunter. "But Miss Bright is going to Verona. In Italy, as you probably know, kidnapping is now almost a national sport. If she's lifted, Manning would do anything — and I really do mean anything — to get her back." He grimaced. As always with Hunter, human emotion was incomprehensible but it had to be allowed for.

"Can't you stop her?" said Callan.

"No," said Hunter. "She sees the part of Juliet as the beginning of a great career."

"Can't Manning?"

"As I said, the man is besotted. He wants her to go." He threw a file over to Callan—yellow cover — surveillance only.

"It's all in there," said Hunter. and finished his sherry. "You've never been to Verona, have you?" he asked.

"Never," said Callan.

"You'll like it," said Hunter. "The old city is quite lovely."

"You want me to act for the telly?"

"In *Romeo and Juliet*? Somehow I don't think that's quite on. How much I should have enjoyed seeing you in doublet and hose...."

The file on Jo Bright was the usual stuff: ballet-school, drama school, career. At present she was appearing in an experimental theatre production in a pub off Oxford Street — a play called "Circles"—lunch times only. Hunter had even included a ticket: clipped to the paper was a note signed by him. "It's time you had a little intellectual stimulation...." At the end of the file there was a memo on Manning's nerve-gas, written in Hunter's own hand. Callan read it, and managed not to vomit.

He'd seen and endured just about everything, but even by his standards, this stuff of Manning's was appalling. The last sentence of Hunter's memo was: "Now burn this." Callan did so, but the flames could not erase this memory.

He went to see "Circles." As Hunter had sent him a ticket, he had no choice. He'd expected an audience of perhaps three, with himself as an all too identifiable fourth; but the place was packed. He eased his way into what, in more conventional times, would have been the pub's singing-room, past a crowd of blokes who looked as if they'd never been intellectually stimulated in their lives.

The ones who didn't wear dirty macintoshes looked as if they were in disguise, he thought, and went to the bar, bought Scotch and a sandwich, then fought his way to his seat. The man in the seat next to his, a fresh-faced, burly looking feller, eased up to let him pass, and Callan nodded his thanks, not just in gratitude for three more inches of leg room: the fresh-faced feller looked as if he'd never worn a dirty macintosh in his life....

"Circles" was all about how awful Western society was. Its values were going, its stability was going, and its morality was almost gone. It was up to men and women of good will to give Western society a good kick in the teeth and finish it off.

The five men and women of good will on the stage, three actors, two actresses, said so over and over again, and from time to time took their clothes off to prove how uninhibited they were, which accounted for the dirty macintosh contingent.

Jo Bright's body was beautiful ... She was also a remarkably good actress, investing even the tiredest left-wing clichés with life, even with originality. Not that the dirty macintoshes were worried: if Jo Bright had spoken in Esperanto it would have been all the same to them, and the fresh-faced bloke next to him had the bored look of a man who'd seen it all before.

You and me both mate, thought Callan, and left at the end of Scene One. "Circles" was no place for squares.

He went back to the Section H.Q. and worked on Jo Bright's file till he had it by heart, then sent for Harold Manning's and worked on that.

Harold Manning, solicitor's son, was 43. Double first at Cambridge, Ph.D. from Berkeley, California. Specialist in inert gases, but he'd made his money in detergents. Married to Julia Bowman, who had much more money than he had, and who still financed his operations. No children. Mrs. Manning adored her husband. She was 52. Jo Bright was 24. He looked at Mrs. Manning's photograph, and remembered Jo Bright. Whichever way you approached this caper there'd be trouble.

At seven, Hunter looked in. "Hard at it?" he said. "Good, good. How was the play?"

"Terrible," said Callan.

Hunter nodded as if he'd expected no other answer. "We're dining with Manning tonight," he said. "His wife's at the theatre. The legitimate theatre." He moved forward to look more closely at Callan's suit. "For heaven's sake try to smarten yourself up a little," he said.

At least I'm not wearing a dirty macintosh, thought Callan.

Harold Manning was an impatient eater. Food to him was fuel to be shovelled down as fast as possible so that other, more important business could be done, like getting rid of the butler and talking about Jo Bright. But Callan resented having to wolf down such excellent *tournedos rossini* and nothing in the world would force Hunter into gulping domaine bottled Romanee-Conti.

Manning had to wait, and being rich and influential he made little effort to hide his impatience. He was a big man, and still looked powerful—with a big, handsome head. When the butler put the port on the table and left them alone at last he said at once: "It's all nonsense."

"No," said Hunter.

"Oh I daresay you've picked up gossip." Manning said, "that's what you're for after all—but all the same it's nonsense. I've got Security S.A. looking after her. She'll be all right."

Security S.A. was a Swiss firm. They were the best private protection money could buy, and they cost a bomb. There was also a buzz that they'd do a lot rougher work than just provide security, but whether it was true or not they were a hard bunch, and very professional.

Callan flicked a glance at Hunter. He was still busy effacing his annoyance at being called a gossip-monger.

"I know my business as you know yours." said Hunter, "and I know an attempt will be made. It is not nonsense."

Manning shrugged. "You could try talking to Jo if you like," he said at last and pushed the port on to Callan. "She won't listen, she wants to go. More precisely, she *has* to go."

As he spoke the door opened and a woman came in, a woman who still moved gracefully and on whose face still survived a mixture of attraction and shrewdness; an ageing autocrat with no intention of yielding one lot of her power — or her authority. Mrs. Manning.

Manning's hand shook slightly. A drop of port splashed on to the mahogany.

"Ah Julia," he said, "we were just talking about you."

"Were you?"

The voice was low, and soft in pitch. It was the business of others to strain to hear.

"This passion of yours for the theatre." Said Manning. "It seems to have been a very short play this evening."

"I found it displeasing," she said. "I left after Act One. Nowadays the experimental stuff can be much more diverting." She turned to Callan. "Do you agree, Mr er——?"

"Forgive me," said Manning, and performed introductions. She acknowledged them graciously.

"The two gentlemen from British Intelligence?" she asked.

"Quite so," said Hunter.

"You have come to discuss the nerve-gas?"

"You appear to know all about it," said Hunter.
"All about my husband you mean?" Julia Manning thought for a moment. "Is it ever possible to know all about one's husband, or one's wife?" She sat down next to Callan. "I will take a little of that port," she said.

She was there to stay, and there could be no arguing the fact. It seemed that she knew all about the nerve-gas: where the lab was, where it would be produced, what it would cost. Everything, in fact except the formula, and Callan had no doubt she could put her hands on that at any time she wanted. Breaking free from Julia Manning would be the hell of a job, thought Callan. There was no more talk of Jo Bright.
When they left, Manning went with them to the door and Hunter made one more try.
"About that other matter," he said. "I'll come to your office —"
"No," said Manning. "I'm sorry. It just isn't on."
Hunter went to the waiting Bentley, but Callan walked. There was a lot to think about, and he thought best on his feet.
His way took him through a series of fashionable streets, and as he walked he became aware that he was being followed, and by somebody good enough to do it without being seen. He turned into a mews, and as he did so a car drove past him, reached the far end of the mews, and stopped.
A geezer got out, a squat, heavy-shouldered geezer built like a wrestler. He made no move towards Callan, just waited. By the way he held his hands Callan was quite sure there was a knife in one of them. Callan risked a glance over his shoulder.
The man who'd tailed him on foot had broken cover, and stood full in the lamplight: a fresh-faced, big muscled feller, the kind who might sit next to you if you went to see a play called "Circles" in a pub off Oxford Street. No gun showing—a gun might be a bit noisy in a Belgravia mews—and no knife either. The geezer by the car would be the one to do the rough work.
Callan walked on down the mews. He wouldn't have minded being noisy—with a .357 Magnum say — but Hunter had said they were paying a social call, and guns would not be worn. Ah well, better get on with it.
Suddenly his easy walk became a sprint, and he raced towards the knife man. That wouldn't worry the fresh-faced geezer too much. Towards the knife man was where he wanted Callan to be. Callan went cannon-balling on and swerved at the last possible moment, so that the knife-man's upward-scooping lunge sliced empty air and Callan checked, steadled himself one-handed against the car and kicked, the point of his shoe landing precisely in the knife-man's armpit.
The knife-man screamed, and lurched sideways into Callan's second blow, a fist strike to the back of the neck. The scream died.
Callan leaped his body and confronted the fresh-faced feller. He'd been racing up the mews behind Callan, ready, willing and able to

back up his mate, but now his mate was down and he hesitated, his run lost impetus.

Jump Callan, or go for his gun. While he was thinking about it Callan moved in on him crowding him so that he had no time to go for his gun and hit him with a fist-strike, but the blow was mistimed, catching him on the right collar-bone instead of the gut.

Fresh-face grunted with the pain, fell back against the wall and lashed out with a kick that Callan just, and only just, managed to avoid, retaliating with another fist strike to the already damaged shoulder. Fresh-face grunted again, and swung left-handed but the pain he felt had slowed him. Callan grabbed the fist and threw him and his damaged right shoulder slammed on to the ground.

As he opened his mouth to yell, Callan came up behind him, his interlocked hands came down in the ultimate blow, and the yell never materialized. Callan grabbed for fresh-face's pulse, and sighed with relief. It was faint, but it was there. This one had to speak to Charlie, and if he were beyond speech. Charlie would be displeased.

He began heaving them into the car. Nice car—it even had a radio-telephone. Useful, that. He could let Charlie know he was on his way.

"Extraordinary," said Hunter. "Really quite extraordinary."

"Yeah," said Callan. "That's what I thought when they tried to clobber me."

"You were very rough with them."

"They were trying to be very rough with me."

Hunter allowed himself one thin-lipped smile. "I told you that force might last your time," he said, and the smile flicked off. Back to business. "They both say they were set on you by Miss Bright," said Hunter. "They also claim they are operatives of Security S.A. and I'm inclined to believe them."

"Is that all they say?"

"So far," said Hunter. "But Snell is working on them. He's not without hope of more."

Snell was the Section's psychiatrist, and what he would be doing to the two operatives Callan neither knew nor wanted to know.

"You talked to Jo Bright?" he asked.

"Unfortunately," said Hunter. "She has already left for Verona. Rather hurriedly. I gather. I suggest that you go too."

"How can I?" said Callan. "She's on to me. I'm blown."

"There's nobody else available," said Hunter. "I'm afraid I'll just have to risk it."

"*You'll* have to risk it?" said Callan. "What about me?"

Hunter continued as if Callan had not spoken. "There's a vacancy for a production accountant," he said. "I feel sure you'll be an admirable production accountant." Callan tried to speak. "That's an order, Callan." That was it then.

"Instructions?" Callan asked.

"Let her finish her picture and give her back to Manning," said Hunter, "as intact as possible."

Callan signalled for more beer.
"Of course you can do it," he said. "It's a doddle."
Lonely sucked at his pint.
"Would be if I had the right minder," he said.
Callan waited till the little man's glass was empty, and pushed across another pint of light and bitter. "I've told you," he said. "I've got to go to Italy."
"It's all right for some of us." said Lonely. "Some of us can go on our holidays—but the rest of us has to graft for a living."
"I'll be grafting," said Callan, "and so will you mate. Or do I have to get physical after all these years?"
Lonely instantly turned suet-white, and Callan said hastily. "Now don't start. You just do as you're told and nobody'll hurt you. Anyway, you'll be coming to Italy and all."
"Will I?" said Lonely, intrigued. "What for?"
"To tell me how you got on."
"Why don't I just write to you?"
"The post in Italy is terrible," said Callan.
"Worse than ours?"
Callan nodded.
"Gawd," said Lonely, "it must be bad."

Being a production accountant was dead easy, really. You just wandered around with a clip-board and looked disapproving and everybody thought you were part of the landscape ... It was nice in Verona, very nice. Churches, palazzos, castles and a two-thousand-year-old arena that looked good for another two thousand at least. A quiet city, restful except for the Montagues and Capulets charging all over the place - and him having to charge after them.
They were doing the fight scene first and that meant Jo Bright wasn't working much. The only public appearance she made was in the courtyard of the Capulet house where she posed on Juliet's balcony for publicity pictures.
Callan tried to hide behind his clip-board but the mob of photographers pressed him up against her on the way out and she looked right at him—and didn't bat an eye. She could act, all right. He saw her back to the hotel, walled round by Security S.A., and went in his hired Alfa Romeo to the Piazza del Signori where they were rehearsing the big fight scene of Montagues and Capulets.
The Piazzi del Signori is one of the glories of European architecture, an airy, graceful square flanked by exquisite buildings, and all the space in the world for forty or more extras armed with rapier and dagger to knock seven bells out of each other.
It would have been nice just to sit there and watch other blokes get clobbered for a change, but he had a date at the air terminal.

"How do you say beer?" said Lonely.
"*Una birra,*" said Callan.
"*Una birra,*" Lonely said to the waiter and it appeared in no time at all: cold pale, topped with froth. "Not that it'll be any good," said

Lonely, then sipped and grimaced. "Told you," he said.

"Never mind. Think of all the money you're making. And tell me what happened."

Lonely looked round the café: jam-full of Eye-ties jabbering nineteen to the dozen: all the same it was better to be careful.

"The male subject had a stack of letters, and photos," he said. "All signed Jo. Juicy stuff they were an' all. Had 'em hidden in a box of cigars." He grimaced his disgust. "Amateurs," he said.

"What about the women?"

"The female subject," Lonely said severely, "had a photo. Underneath her smalls it was. You should have seem them. Disgusting, a woman of her age."

"Tell me about the photograph."

"Same bird," said Lonely, "prancing about in a sweater. Daft, innit? What would a bird keep another bird's picture for?" He sucked distastefully at his beer." Funny thing—they was both on my plane."

"Who was?" said Callan.

"The subjects."

"You sure?"

The two words struck him like blows.

"Positive," Lonely said, and if Lonely was positive it was so.

"Of course they was travelling first," said Lonely.

"Did you hear where they went?"

"Ferrari waiting for them," said Lonely. "They said they was going straight to the fight scene."

Callan rose. "Come on," he said.

"I haven't finished my beer," said Lonely.

"You don't like it," said Callan. "Come on."

He left, and Lonely followed. When Mr Callan talked like that you did as you were told.

The little Alfa scuttled its way to the hotel where Callan had a room and Jo Bright had a suite, and Callan raced in and went over to the desk. Jo Bright's key was not on the rack, but the desk clerk handed him his own—and a letter.

Cailan ripped it open. "Re. Security S.A. takeover," the message read. "Ivan is now the major shareholder." It was signed only with the letter H. So Security S.A. was now a KGB unit.

Snell had got more, just as Callan knew he would.

He stuffed letter and envelope in his pocket, and as he did so the lift doors opened, and Jo Bright walked out between two Security S.A. goons. She was smiling happily, and still smiled as she walked past Callan, handed in her key and went out.

Callan followed and watched the three or them get into a big Mercedes, then joined Lonely in the Alfa and followed.

The start was easy. The Merc was an easy car to spot, and he could lie back, a couple of cars behind, as they went through the town and on to the autostrada. But when they left the autostrada he had trouble. They were on a minor road where traffic was minimal, and in the end he had to take a risk he hated, pull out and pass them, tailing from in front, watching them in his rear-view mirror.

When they turned off on to what looked like a farm track he kept going till the next bend, did a three point turn and came back to the track, parking near by, but out of sight, then reached under his coat and took out the .357 Magnum. This time he was fully dressed. Lonely let out his breath into a soft sigh.

"The hard stuff," he said. "I might have known."

Callan reached under the dashboard, brought out another Magnum he'd taped there, and gave it to Lonely.

"This one's yours," he said.

For a moment he thought the little man was going to faint, and so did Lonely.

"I couldn't," he said at last. The niff was awful.

"Course you could," said Callan. "All you do is come with me, fire a few shots when I tell you, then belt back to the car and wait for me?"

"I couldn't," Lonely said again.

"*You will,*" said Callan.

Lonely, looked into Callan's eyes, and found that he would.

They crawled up to the narrow track, and Callan reconnoitered cautiously. It led to a farmhouse an old one, built to last. Round the back would be the best place. He left Lonely behind a bush to niff by himself, and worked his way through the cover of peach trees and vines till he reached the rear of the building ... almost a ruin, he thought, but solid.

Warily he moved in on it ... No dogs, thank God. He tried a shutter. It was bolted of course, but it was loose. Lonely had showed him long ago how to deal with loose, bolted shutters. He took out his knife and got to work, then when it swung loose, wriggled back to where Lonely could see him, gave their agreed signal and hoped to God the little man was watching.

The shots came like a burst from a machine-gun, and Callan raced back to the shutter, wriggled through and fumbled his way through a musty kitchen, and down a corridor that led to the front of the house.

He reached a door, and stood listening. Men's voices. They were speaking Russian. Callan's hand went to the door-knob. One more shot came from outside and Callan twisted the knob, and dived into the room.

Two men with automatics by the window and the girl in an armchair looking scared—but out of the line of fire. The men turned, and Callan fired once, then dropped to his knees as the second man loosed off a shot that smashed through the door-frame. The first man was already on his way down.

Still on his knees Callan fired twice more, the Magnum pointing like an accusing finger. Two whiplash cracks and the second man went down, wearing that look of surprise they sometimes have when they think they're the best there is, then run into a feller who's just a little bit better. Cautiously he rose and kicked their guns away and found there was no need: both men were dead. He scooped up the two automatics and turned to the girl. She was standing now, ashen, ready to faint, but she didn't niff like Lonely.

"But that was real," she said.
"It's all real," said Callan.
"They told me it was just a stunt — for publicity," she said.
"No publicity," said Callan. Jo Bright fainted.

He'd put her back in the chair and left it at that. She was better off unconscious not knowing, as he went through the dead men's pockets. Money cigarettes, lighters, and that was it. KGB goons travel light. He stiffened at the sound of a car, bumping up the track, and risked a look from the window. Not the Alfa—a Ferrari.

Callan hid behind the angle of the door as car doors slammed, footsteps came up the steps and into the house. A voice called out, and Callan spoke in accented English. "It's all right. Come in."

They entered on what looked like an even bigger massacre than it was - Jo Bright still looked as dead as her escorts. Behind them Callan slammed the door shut and the man and woman spun round to look down the barrel of the Magnum.

"We never did finish our chat about experimental theatre, Mrs. Manning," said Callan.

She ignored the Magnum completely as if it could have no possible relevance to her life and glanced back at Jo Bright.

"You appear to be something of a critic," she said.

Harold Manning made as if to turn to Jo then swung round on Callan.

"You killed her," he said. "You killed Jo."

Callan aimed the Magnum at a point between Manning's eyes, and the big man was still.

"Be nice," said Callan. "Let's all be nice."

As he watched, Manning crumbled and began to weep. Mrs Manning took a handkerchief from her bag and gave it to him, saying nothing. Callan waited.

"But why did she come here?" Manning sobbed and turned to his wife. "You said we were just going for a drive. How did you —?" He wept again.

"I lied to you," Julia Manning said. "I'd arranged to have the girl brought here. The silly child thought it was just some publicity stunt."

"You knew about Jo?" Manning asked.

"She's even got her picture," said Callan. "She keeps it under her smalls."

That got to her all right: Mrs. Manning blushed, but even so her voice showed no emotion.

"It was not a publicity stunt," she said. "I wanted to see the two of you together. Confront you if you like."

Behind her Callan saw Jo Bright's eyes open, but she lay still.

"Why Mrs. Manning?" he asked.

"To show poor Harold that it must cease," she said.

"And how did you do it?" Callan asked.

The woman said: "These men you appear to have murdered — I had bribed them." She might have been discussing her account at Harrod's.

"But they're Security S.A.," said Manning. "I hired them."

"I paid them more," Julia Manning said. "After all—most of our money is mine."

Behind them Jo Bright stirred in her seat as Julia Manning turned to face her husband.

"They were to pretend to force you to choose," she said. "That pretty little tart—or me."

"And if he'd chosen Jo Bright?" said Callan.

"They would have disposed of her," said Mrs Manning. "Harold is mine, and I don't propose to share him."

"Murder costs quite a lot," said Callan. "Especially from Security S.A."

"I'd have paid quite a lot," said Julia Manning.

"More than you thought," Callan said. "Security S.A.'s a KGB operation, Mrs Manning. The only thing they want is the nerve-gas formula."

For the first and only time, he shattered that glacial calm.

"They lied to you, Mrs Manning," said Callan. "I wonder where they got the nerve."

"I disliked you from the moment I met you," Julia Manning said. "It was perfectly apparent that you were dangerous."

"That's right," said Callan. "You did. You disliked me so much you arranged a little surprise for me — in Jo Bright's name."

"I arranged to have you beaten. I assume it was bungled."

"You don't beat people with knives," said Callan. "Never mind. As you say, they muffed it. But why say you were Jo Bright?"

"After all, they were under her orders," said Julia Manning. "If they'd been caught, she'd have been discredited and I could hardly use my name in such an affair."

Behind her Jo Bright said: "My God, if you want him that much you can have him."

Julia Manning turned unhurriedly to face her. "My dear," she said. "I've got him—I always will have." She looked at Callan. "Isn't that so?"

"Yeah," said Callan. "All right. Only take him home—and keep him there. Foreign travel's not good for him."

Jo Bright moved then with her dancer's grace, and looked at Julia Manning. It was as if Harold Manning had no existence.

"Please—" she said, "may I finish the film?"

"Of course," Julia Manning said. "It should make rather a lot of money. Only keep out of my sight and my husband's."

She went out to the Ferrari, and Harold Manning followed her. He didn't look back.

"Rather neat idea of yours," said Hunter, "making Julia Manning her husband's keeper. I've had a word with her. I think it'll work." Callan remembered Mrs Manning, "I'm sure it will," he said.

"And this Jo Bright person—will she keep quiet?"

"She's jumping up and down with joy," said Callan. "She's a star."

"She won't ever recollect your encounter with the KGB?"

"Stars look down on such things," said Callan. "They're bad for the image."

"That's it then." said Hunter. "Oh, one thing more: what happened to the KGB men?"

"There was a fire," said Callan. "The farm burnt like a torch. I believe they did find two bodies—but they were never identified."

"Have another whisky," said Hunter.

File on a Mourning Mother

““My son was killed in a motor accident,” said Mrs Browne.
“I know,” said Callan, “and I'm extremely sorry to intrude on you at a time like this—”
She sighed, and looked at him: a neat man in a neat suit, carrying a neat briefcase, his eyes brimming with sympathy. But she was utterly sure that he would not go away until he had asked his questions and she had answered.
“May I know your name, please?” she asked.
“Tucker,” Callan said, and handed her a piece of pasteboard. “My card.”
J. G. Tucker, she read, Ministry of Defence.
Callan followed her across a parquet hallway that was all oak-chests, stags' heads, foxes' brushes, and a pair of matched shotguns above the fireplace, to a living room that was spacious enough without being ostentatious: an elegant, French-windowed room.
It was a room that had been polished till it glowed and yet in one corner there was an occasional table on which stood an old vase of Waterford crystal filled with roses, deftly arranged. The roses were dying.
Mrs Browne motioned Callan to a chair, then sat facing him.
“My son really did die in a motor accident,” she said. “There was an inquest. The coroner said so.”
Callan looked at her. Forty-five if she was a day, blonde and tall. Meres, who was an expert, maintained that tall blondes faded quickly, but Meres hadn't met Mrs Browne. Before tragedy had touched her she must still have been a very beautiful woman.
“We always have to check,” he said, keeping his voice gentle, sympathetic.
“Check what Mr Tucker?” the woman asked.
“Your son was a scientist,” Callan said. “He worked for us in a rather sensitive area.”
A new jump-jet fighter, Hunter had said, even better than the old one. Worth hundreds of millions with the right foreign sales. Maybe even thousands of millions.
“Are you by any chance in Security?”
“We don't exactly call it that,” said Callan. “More like Records, really.” He smiled and even in her grief the woman responded to his smile.

"In my department they call me the human tape-recorder. I write it all down and send it upstairs and the chief writes No Further Action on the bottom and has it filed."

Callan listened to his own voice and marvelled that he could lie with such conviction.

"Now if you'll just tell me—"

Mrs Browne looked at her watch. "Of course," she said. "Anything. It's rather late for tea, Mr Tucker. May I offer you a drink?"

"Thank you," said Callan. "A little whisky and water would be very acceptable."

She poured him a big one, added water, then took another for herself. He'd have sworn her tipple was medium dry sherry.

"About your son's father," said Callan.

"His father's dead too," said Mrs Browne, and gulped at her whisky.

"Yes," said Callan. "We have that on record, of course and I'm sorry to revive even more painful memories. It's just –"

"The drill," she said, and drank again. "My husband taught me all about the drill, Mr Tucker.

"He was in the army. Acting Major when he died. Sooner or later he would have got the battalion if he'd lived. But he didn't live you see. A sniper got him. In Londonderry."

She rose with a grace that was completely natural, and walked to a sofa-table on which was an array of photographs in silver frames, and Callan followed her.

"That's my husband," she said.

A handsome, efficient-looking geezer in mess kit. Hard as nails by the look of him, and utterly devoid of imagination. Callan looked at the next photograph. Mrs Browne with a younger edition of her soldier, except the younger edition wore academic dress and looked far too imaginative for his own good.

"You must have been proud of your son," said Callan.

Mrs Browne was silent for a moment, then said: "Martin—my husband—hoped Roddy would go into the regiment. But Roddy preferred science."

"Physics," said Callan.

"He took a first," said Mrs. Browne. "Peter Carteret persuaded him to go into the Civil Service. My husband would have approved of that."

"Why, Mrs. Browne?"

"Peter was Martin's closest friend. I rather gather he promised to keep an eye on Roddy."

Callan's eyes went back to the photographs.

"Your son was very like his father," he said.

"They weren't alike in the least," said Mrs. Browne.

Callan asked more questions then: about Roddy's interests. There was his hi-fi, he learned, and his cameras, and his car. No girls, at least no particular girl. After all he was only twenty-three. But Callan was more interested in the car.

"A Mercedes," said Mrs. Browne. "What they used to call a sports coupé."

"But your son wasn't driving it when he was killed?"

Mrs. Browne filled up her glass, and his.

"It was a hit and run," she said. "Surely you know that?" Callan knew it all right. "Anyway," said Mrs. Browne, "Roddy never drove the car to work. He said it wasn't a civil servant's sort of car."

"I don't wish to upset you," said Callan, "but might I see it?"

She took him to the garage, then on to the room that had been Roddy's, to show him the hi-fi, and the pictures he had taken: shots of birds, of buildings, of ships in the Thames. There were no shots of girls. Callan wondered how he could work the questioning back to girls.

Mrs. Browne took him back to the drawing-room and her third drink. Callan hung on to his second.

"Can't you tell me anything about his girlfriends?" he asked, and again Mrs. Browne gulped at her drink.

"What possible reason —?" she said, and left it hanging there. For the first time, she looked less than sober.

"I think you know," said Callan, but she made no answer. "Your son worked on classified stuff," Callan continued. "There's been a leak."

For a moment he thought she was about to attack him, and so perhaps did she, but she drank instead.

"I like you, Mr Tucker," she said. "It's about time I started liking people again." She tried, but failed to smile at him. "My son was homosexual," she said, "but I daresay you know that." Callan stayed silent. "What you probably don't know is that he told my husband so—on his last leave. Roddy was 21, you see. A man. He felt he had a man's rights, owed his father a man's honesty."

Callan willed himself not to see the agony in her eyes. "What happened, Mrs Browne?" he asked.

"My husband beat him unconscious," she said, and finished her drink, went back to the decanter ... Callan stood up. He'd got all he needed and she'd taken more than enough.

Mrs. Browne took the stopper from the decanter, then let it fall back again, put the decanter down. "The funny thing is I don't even like the stuff," she said. "I'm a sherry lady—but sherry takes too long."

Callan moved towards her. "I'd better be off," he said. "Thank you very much for your help."

"Oh must you go?" she said, and took a step forward, tripped on the Shiraz rug. Callan caught her, smoothly and deftly, and she sagged in his arms so that he couldn't let her go.

"You're awfully strong for a clerk," she said, then suddenly her body straightened, her arms came round him and she kissed him on the mouth. Her lips were soft, and tasted of whisky. "Oh dear God," said Mrs. Browne.

Callan drove back to London in a mood of savage self-disgust.

Through the trim and elegant home-counties' villages, sleek with wealth, he drove in a fury turned inward on to himself and his trade, driving by instinct, but even so driving as Mr Tucker would have driven, competently but with care.

A motor-cycle roared past him in a perfectly preserved High Street and he cursed High Street and motor cyclist both, then turned off into the sort of leafy lane that was straight out of a Christmas calendar, and cursed that too.

Ahead of him, a long way ahead, the motor-cycle glinted in the sunlight, rose to a dip and disappeared. Callan turned off the hatred: hatred of oneself or anybody else was futile and worse than futile. It made you vulnerable.

He looked in his mirror. Nothing behind him but a Jaguar. He couldn't remember whether the Jaguar had been behind him for long, or not. He hadn't looked. And anyway why shouldn't a Jaguar be there? This was Jaguar country—except that it could pass him any time it wanted to, and it hadn't.

Callan accelerated the elderly family saloon that was Mr Tucker's lot, and at once the Jaguar accelerated too, but still it kept its distance. Rage made you vulnerable all right. Callan reached for the glove compartment, took out a ·357 Magnum, and laid it on the seat beside him.

The leafy hedges ended and he was driving between empty fields; grass on one side, plough on the other. From the grass to his left he caught a silvery flash, the flash that might come from a motor-bike's chrome if the bike is inexpertly hidden.

Instinctively Callan slowed, and the Jaguar slowed too, and from his left there came the whipcrack of a rifle, and then another, followed by an even louder bang as his front tyre went.

Callan wrestled with the wheel and headed for the ditch. If he hadn't slowed he might have been dead. The Jag accelerated: he still might die. He switched off his engine.

The car's near front wheel ploughed into the ditch as Callan opened the door, and went out in a tumbling dive, holding the Magnum.

The Jag accelerated, and suddenly a stubby barrel appeared in its open rear window, bullets sprayed from it, thudding into what was left of poor old Tucker's family saloon.

Callan crouched in the ditch as the car went past, then held the Magnum two-handed, his rage now canalised into a cold and deadly hate as he loosed off at the Jag's rear tyres.

He got them both. ... The Jag reared crazily, and Callan fired again. It was extreme range for a Magnum, but even so he hit the driver, and the Jaguar dived nose-first into the ditch.

Incredibly the rear-seat passenger fumbled his way out still clutching his machine-pistol. Callan raced up the ditch and shot him too—then remembered the motor-cyclist.

He dropped flat, swirling, and looked towards the field. From across its empty distance came the stutter of a motor-bike's engine, as the bike bobbed up a cart track. Apparently the motor-cyclist was a car tyre specialist. Callan went on up the ditch and looked over the men in the Jaguar. They were just men: one ugly, one handsome, both tough, and anonymous, and dead. Callan scurried back to dispose of Mr Tucker's car.

"Guns cause such a fuss," said Hunter.

"I wish you'd warned me," said Callan. "I'd have told the geezer in the Jag not to fire."

Hunter shot a quick look at Callan, poured Chivas Regal, added water and handed him the drink. Callan sipped.

"You disposed of the Section car?"

"Totally," said Callan.

That was something, Hunter thought. With a bit of luck it could be blamed on mere criminality, perhaps even the I.R.A.

"You talked to Mrs Browne?" Hunter asked.

"Yeah," said Callan, and sipped again. "I talked to her. I'm a lovely feller, Hunter. Did you know that? A really lovely feller."

"Indeed?" said Hunter.

"I call on bereaved widows who've lost clever, homosexual sons and because I'm so lovely they trust me and get drunk and —"

"And what?" said Hunter.

Callan looked at his glass: put it down. "And tell me everything I ask," said Callan, "because I'm so lovely."

"Personally I find you rather maudlin," said Hunter. "Get on with your report."

"He had a Merc. 250 SE coupé," said Callan. "They cost over seven thousand quid. He had about fifteen hundred quid's worth of hi-fi equipment and another five hundred's worth of cameras."

"Mrs Browne's house is large," said Hunter. "She must have some sort of means."

"Mrs Browne's living out her time on an annuity," said Callan. "Her son never took a penny from her, but he bought her a mink stole."

"So it was him," said Hunter. "Except —"

"Except that three other geezers set up an ambush," said Callan. "That means it was him and somebody else."

"Quite so," said Hunter. "I'll have all those research people checked for alibis and so on. It would be nice to know who's trying to kill you."

"I do so agree," said Callan.

"Mr Carteret's still in conference," the girl said. "Can I send out for some coffee or something?"

Callan looked at her: another tall blonde – Mrs Browne 20 years ago - dressed with a neat and casual elegance.

"That's very nice of you, Miss er—?"

"Miss Townley," said the blonde, and went out, leaving Callan to yawn his way through a magazine, then came back with coffee. It was terrible. The girl watched him sip and grimace and said, "I'm sorry. I should have warned you." She fidgeted with a file in front of her, then asked: "Mr Tucker. Is it about Roddy?"

"Roddy?" said Callan.

"Roderick Browne," Miss Townley said. She said it gently, as if saying the name was a source of pleasure.

"Tell me about Roderick Browne," said Callan.

"I don't think I...perhaps we should wait for Mr Carteret," she said.

"You're seen my clearance," said Callan. "Tell me about Roddy."

"He was a colleague," Miss Townley said at last. "And he was a friend of mine. Just that; a friend. No overtones ... I suppose you know that he was gay?"

Callan said deliberately: "A poof. It's on his file."

The girl flushed, and said angrily. "He was a person. A human being. A very nice human being." She went on, and Callan listened. Roddy had been sweet and sympathetic, a real friend, and a near-genius at his job. A very simple person who had nothing but contempt for the tyranny of possessions.

"What does that mean?"

"His working life was bound up with one of the most sophisticated pieces of machinery ever made," said Miss Townley, "and he was good at it. Better than good. But in his personal life he lived very simply. He didn't even own a car."

He never told you about the Merc., Callan wondered? Or hi-fi, or the cameras? Then Callan remembered that Miss Townley possessed a degree in applied psychology. Was Miss Townley applying it now?

Then, in the middle of it all, Carteret erupted in on them and Callan was swept on a wave of nervous energy to Carteret's office.

"I've got twenty minutes," Carteret said.

"I've got all day," said Callan. "Maybe all year."

Carteret scowled. "Now look, Tucker," he said, "I cannot accept that there is a leak in my department merely because one of my assistants is involved in a hit and run."

"Why should you?" said Callan. "But there's rather more than that."

"May I know what it is?"

Callan said easily, "This time you may," and again Carteret scowled.

"We got a flash," Callan said. "Never mind from where. The Ivans have just started a jump-jet research project: a 20-million-rouble investment."

"Couldn't that be coincidence? Everyone wants a good jump-jet fighter."

"They're not starting from scratch," said Callan. "They're only a few months behind you; and heading in the same direction."

"My God," said Carteret.

Callan decided to risk a flier. "We've got a line on the car that killed Browne."

But Carteret's mind was on Russian research. "You're saying they've got it?"

"I'm saying they're getting it," said Callan.

"And that Roddy was implicated?"

"He had too much money," said Callan, and went on to outline exactly how much money Roddy Browne had had.

"But this is awful," said Carteret. "His father was the closest friend I ever had. I trusted that boy."

"So did his country," said Callan. Carteret winced.

"Well at least it's over—now that he's dead," said Carteret. Callan stayed silent. "It is over, isn't it?"

"We haven't got his contacts," said Callan.

"But surely, Tucker, now that they no longer have information—" he hesitated. "Surely they'll give up?"

Everybody gives up when they're dead, thought Callan. Aloud he said, "Even so, we'd like a word with them."

"I expect you would," said Carteret, "and I hope you find them. But you've no leads, have you?"

"That's right," said Callan. "All we've got is Roddy Browne." He moved softly to the door, jerked it open. In the door frame stood Miss Townley.

"Oh!" she said. "I do beg your pardon," then looked over his shoulder seeking for Carteret as a groupie would seek for a lead guitarist. "I have Dr Stokes waiting for you, sir," she said.

"Turning over birds' drums isn't nice, Mr Callan," said Lonely.

"She's a good-looking bird," said Callan and passed Lonely the chips. Lonely emptied the lot over a plate that already contained two fried eggs, three rashers of bacon, four sausages and a double helping of baked beans, then reached for the tomato sauce.

"That makes it worse," said Lonely as he shook. "What I mean, Mr Callan, it's not like I was going to nick anything, is it?"

"No," said Callan, as the ketchup flowed like blood. "It's not."

"So what I mean—I'm no better than a Peeping Tom," said Lonely, and put the sauce down at last. "No offence, Mr Callan."

"None taken," said Callan and tried not to look as Lonely ate. "But you'll be a Peeping Tom who's a hundred quid better off."

"Oh, well in that case," said Lonely with his mouth full, "you're on."

Callan stood up. "I'll get us a couple of teas," he said.

"There's just one thing, Mr Callan," said Lonely, and Callan prepared for war. A hundred quid and not a penny more....

"A hundred's top rate."

Lonely impaled half a sausage and gestured regally with his fork. "Am I denying it?" he said. "You're a prince, Mr Callan. Only—"

"Only what?"

"When you go for the teas, could you bring me back a pudding as well?"

While he waited for Lonely to do his stuff, Callan read: about Roddy Browne, about Carteret, about Miss Townley, about Dr Stokes, who was director of the Research Lab and had come visiting Carteret so opportunely.

Callan abandoned Dr Stokes for Mrs Browne. Hunter even had a file on her — yellow cover — surveillance only. He was not happy, by no means happy, that Mrs Browne had never queried her son's sudden wealth. And neither am I, thought Callan.

"Diana Browne," he read. And like all good Dianas, she was fond of field sports. And her son. And once upon a time, so the file said, her husband. Only she had been forced to choose. He looked at the photograph again. She was beautiful and unhappy. He went back to Miss Townley.

Twenty-five and lived in Battersea. Father a car-worker in the Midlands. No known politics, not even at university — but ambitious.

Liked to live well; perhaps beyond her means. Who doesn't, he thought? He yawned and looked at his watch. Time to go to the boozer and wait for Lonely.

When he arrived the little man was waiting.

"You don't believe in hanging about, do you?" said Callan, and ordered light and bitter and whisky as Lonely smirked.

"She went out," said Lonely. "Just as I arrived. Bit of luck that." He reached for the pint glass and sucked thirstily. "Your very good health, Mr Callan."

Callan waited: thieving always made Lonely thirsty, unless it went wrong. Then it made him niff. Tonight he smelt only of after-shave. Just as well. Callan had enough on his mind without Lonely niffing. The little man emerged from his glass.

"She's got a nice little gaff," he said, "and she keeps it nice an all. But she ought to move to a bigger place, she should really."

"Why?" said Callan.

"Clothes," said Lonely. "Silk and cashmere, you never saw anything like it. And underwear. Cor, you should have seen—"

"You've been at the red meat again," said Callan.

Lonely coughed. "Sorry, Mr Callan," he said. "I was just wishing I'd got a proper look at her. From what you were saying she'd have filled them out a treat."

"Get on with it, Bluebeard," said Callan.

"She had some nice tomfoolery an' all," Lonely said.

"What kind of jewellery?" Callan said. "Costume stuff?"

"No," said Lonely, regretfully. "This was all real. I looked it over special."

That was enough for Callan: when it came to jewellery Lonely could make a pawnbroker look ignorant.

"Tell it," he said.

"One ring, ruby and diamonds, one pair sapphire ear-rings, one silver and turquoise bracelet, one pearl necklace. Look nice on a blonde that would—especially if she got a bit of a suntan."

"How much?" said Callan.

"I could have got three grand for them easy," said Lonely, "—if I'd nicked them." Then added hastily, "which I didn't Mr Callan. Word of honour."

Multiply that by three at least, if you got your jewellery from a jeweller's, thought Callan.

"From what you told me she'd have looked real nice with that black silk dress she had—and those pearls," said Lonely. "Pity I didn't see her."

"But you did see her," said Callan. "You said so."

"Not properly I didn't," said Lonely. "She had the gear on."

"What gear?" said Callan.

"You know," said Lonely, "the leather. Like a blooming Hell's Angel she was. Crash helmet, the lot."

"You mean she had a motor-bike?"

"Of course she had a motor-bike," said Lonely. "All over chrome and that. Nasty, dangerous thing. What a nice, refined girl like —" he broke off. Callan was heading for the door.

"Mr Callan," he said. "You haven't finished your drink." But Callan was gone.

Lonely finished off the whisky; not that he liked it, but he hated to waste good drink, especially when it had been paid for.

"I'm sorry, Mr Callan," Liz said. "Mr Hunter's at a Cabinet Security Meeting. I can't interrupt him there."

Callan looked at Hunter's secretary — the third tall blonde in twenty-four hours—and knew that what she said was true.

"Is Meres in?" he asked.

"Mr Meres and Mr FitzMaurice flew up to Scotland," said Liz. "A Russian trawler's just collided with an oil-rig. Mr Lang's the only one on stand-by." She hesitated. 'It's lucky you called in. Mr Hunter left orders—you're on stand-by too."

"But I'm off duty."

"I'm sorry," said Liz, "but Mr Hunter's orders are you're on stand-by as soon as I could reach you."

"Have you got the checks on the movements of those people I'm working on?"

"They're in your office," said Liz.

"Right," said Callan. "I'll be there too." Then, as Liz opened her mouth again. "On stand-by."

Stokes, Carteret, Miss Townley: they were all there, and so were fifteen others, and a written report from the forensic lab on the Jaguar. Laboriously Callan began to compile a time-table of movements, of absences explained, unexplained, inexplicable. And always at the back of his mind something nagged: something he had said, a calculated risk taken ... and then suddenly he had it. He'd been in Carteret's office, and they'd been talking about hunting down young Browne's contacts.

Carteret had said, "You've got no leads at all," and after he'd said it Callan had heard his own voice saying, 'That's right. All we've got is Roddy Browne.' And Miss Townley had been listening at the door. And now she'd gone off on a motor-bike.

Callan got up and headed for the door.

Liz said at once: "You're not to leave. That's orders."

"I'm sorry, I've got to."

"David," she said. "Don't be a fool. I'll have to log you out. David, *please*."

He kept on going to the garage. What he wanted now was speed, and there it was, waiting for him: a blood red Lamborghini Miura, four-and-a-half litre engine; 12 cylinders, top speed of a hundred and eighty miles per hour. Callan's only worry was that it might be too slow.

He broke every speeding law there was, but even the traffic cops in the souped-up Rover 3500's couldn't catch him: couldn't get near, and he reached the house in 37 minutes flat, parked the Miura in a side road, and went across the garden to the French windows of the drawing room, hesitated, and went back to the vehicles in the gravelled drive: a 500cc. motorcycle and a stolid saloon that could only belong to a civil servant.

He immobilised them both, and went to the windows. It was a warm night, and one of them was ajar.

Callan looked in on the trio: none of them was drinking. Carteret sat suave and helpful in a dark grey suit, Mrs. Browne looked restless in a twin-set. Miss Townley was all too aware of how much at odds her leather gear was with the elegant drawing-room.

".... his friends, his mother," Carteret was saying, "Really rather vile insinuations."

"Appalling," Miss Townley said. "Believe me, Mrs Browne, I really got to know Roddy well. We talked about so many things. He would never do what Tucker said. He couldn't."

"I'm grateful for your loyalty to my son," said Mrs Browne, "but it's over; finished."

"They'll come back," said Carteret. "Tucker and his friends—looking for proof."

"They'll find nothing," said Mrs Browne.

Carteret said: "If you would allow Miss Townley and I to undertake a search—now—we could perhaps stop Tucker from pulling Roddy's room apart."

Mrs Browne winced, and Carteret's voice grew gentle. "I loved that boy, Diana. Loved him as my friend. I couldn't bear to have his personal secrets revealed to strangers. And there will be secrets."

Mrs Browne shook her head. "Believe me there will," said Carteret. "We all have them. ... Now just you let me pour you a drink." He rose and went to the drinks table. "We'll be very quick, Diana, and you know we'll be discreet." He picked up the whisky decanter.

"No," said Mrs Browne.

Carteret poured a drink, put it into her hand. "Don't be foolish, Diana," he said.

"You're not to go into Roddy's room," said Mrs Browne, and Miss Townley sighed, Carteret's hand went to his pocket.

Time for the big entrance, thought Callan, and went in through the French windows.

"Evening all," he said.

Carteret's hand kept on going, but Callan's hand moved fast and accurate as a striking snake, and came out holding the ·357 Magnum. Carteret froze.

"Sensible feller," said Callan, and relieved him of a Bernadelli revolver, a small, mean gun for a small, mean man, then turned to Miss Townley.

"What a mug you are, love," he said. "You believe what people tell you."

"I don't understand."

"Take Carteret here," said Callan. "He said he wanted to help preserve Roddy's memory—right? So, you leap on your bike and away. Or take Roddy. He gave you things and told you he wanted nothing for himself; why?"

"He liked me," said Miss Townley.

"He wanted you in," said Callan. "Him and Carteret."

Mrs Browne put down her glass.

"The time might come when they might need you, love."

"Need me for what?"

"Pinching secrets," said Callan. "Pinching them for money and ruby rings and pearl necklaces."

"But he didn't," said Miss Townley. "He was—sweet."

"You know what I think?" said Callan. "You were too much like his mother—so he couldn't bear to do it. I think he told that to Carteret here—and Carteret killed him because he was a risk. Knocked him down with a Jag. Tell me, darling, did Carteret ever give you a ride in a Jag?"

"He said he was thinking of buying it," said the girl. "He even let me drive it."

"Of course he did," said Callan. "It's got your prints on it. Handy that—if it came to court. He borrowed your bike too - when he tried to kill me. Him and a couple of Ivans in the Jaguar. More evidence against you. And bringing you here—that was clever too. If he'd found anything you'd have had a choice, love—either join him or there'd have been a struggle and you'd have died—and you and Roddy would be blamed for the lot—and your boss could have taken his time and made one more haul—and lived happy ever after."

"I don't believe it," said the girl.

Callan looked at Mrs Browne: she believed it all right. He turned to Carteret. "We'd better go and talk to Charlie," said Callan.

But Carteret had other ideas. He put his head down and charged for the door, and kept on going. Callan moved after him and thought: he wants to die, and Charlie won't like that at all.

Mrs Browne followed him, moving like quicksilver, out into the hall and unhooked a shotgun in one fluid movement as Callan stood on the doorstep, taking his time, watching Carteret wrestle with a car door that refused to open, though he hadn't locked it.

"Give up," said Callan. "Nobody's going to shoot you."

Behind him a shotgun boomed and what had been Carteret disintegrated.

"I doubt if you will ever be so wrong again, Mr Tucker," said Mrs Browne.

"A mess," said Hunter. "An absolutely appalling mess."

Callan shrugged.

"We've plugged the leak," he said.

"That woman's on a murder charge."

"She'll say nothing about us," said Callan. "So far as she's concerned Carteret corrupted her son."

"He did indeed," said Hunter. "She found the boy's diaries, I believe."

"She found a lot of things," said Callan, "including the stuff that tied Roddy in with that good looking Ivan I killed. Carteret should have listened to her. She said there was nothing to find. She meant it."

"That still leaves Miss Townley," said Hunter.
"Miss Townley wasn't even there," said Callan.
"Who says so?"
"Me," said Callan. "Carteret planted evidence on her – and I'm using it."
"That's something I suppose," said Hunter, then dredged up another grievance. "You were on standby."
"If I had been," said Callan, "Miss Townley and Mrs. Browne might be dead – and Carteret would be safe – even from you."
Hunter looked at Callan in disgust.
"If you didn't always have an answer," he said.

File on an Angry American

““You’ve fed us very nicely,” said Hunter, and took another sip at his coffee.

The C.I.A. controller looked at his bodyguard and snorted. “Nicely, the man said.” He turned to Hunter. “That’s the first time I ever gave a dinner for four that cost a thousand dollars.”

Callan warmed his cognac to the cupped palm of his left hand. It was very old cognac: the label on the bottle read VVSOP, and the bottle had been left on the table.

There were four of them in the small, elegant, private dining room that was part of a restaurant which even by French standards was superb. Before they had sat down to eat, he and the junior C.I.A. man had gone over it for bugs, and there was none.

The C.I.A. men had called themselves Mackley and Stone, and that was just about as meaningless as Hunter and Callan. Who they said they were wasn’t important: it was what they were that counted. And what they were was two very good men indeed. Callan shifted in his chair. The weight of the ·357 Magnum against his chest was a very comforting thing.

Mackley, the C.I.A. controller, said: “Come to that, it’s the first time I ever gave a dinner party where the guests chose the restaurant and the menu. Even the wine.”

Callan’s stomach reminded him that there had been seven courses and four wines. Mackley had a right to be bitter.

“You wanted to ask me a favour,” said Hunter. “The least I could do was help you put me in the mood where I might grant it.”

“But why Paris?” said Mackley. “Don’t they have food in London any more?”

“London,” said Hunter, “is my territory, just as Langley, Virginia, is yours. I thought we’d be more comfortable where neither of us has commitments.”

Callan finished his cognac, and Mackley said: “Give him some more of that stuff,” and continued in the same breath, as Stone rose to pour. “I have a health alteration assignment.”

Hunter said testily: “You mean you want to have somebody killed. I wish you’d say what you mean.”

“Mr Hunter,” Mackley said, “you have your vocabulary and I have mine. Neither of us may like what we’ve got, but we’re stuck with it.”

"I hope I shan't need an interpreter," said Hunter, and Mackley scowled.

"I'll try to keep it simple," he said. "I want a guy knocked off - in the U.K."

You had to know Hunter long and well to know when he was displeased, but Callan had known him longer and better than any living man, and put his brandy glass down. Better, far better, to have his hands free.

"You want to come over to England and kill somebody?" said Hunter.

"That's right."

"Preposterous," said Hunter. "Out of the question."

"Why?"

"Because things are quiet," said Hunter. "If I allow you to kill someone the victim's employers would no doubt seek revenge. These things escalate."

"We'd be very discreet."

"So would your enemies," said Hunter. "But they'd kill."

"I could just have done it," said Mackley, "instead of picking up the biggest tab in history."

"No," said Hunter. "You couldn't."

"Why not?"

"Because I'd have found out," said Hunter, "and when I'd done that I'd have made life very unpleasant for the C.I.A. in England; and elsewhere."

"Unpleasant," said Mackley. "Oh boy." He put back his brandy in the way that made Hunter wince, and said: "O.K. It's horse-trading time. You two vice-presidents take a walk."

Callan waited for a confirmatory nod from Hunter, then went with Stone to the ante-room, and percolating coffee, and another bottle of cognac labelled VVSOP, Callan waited till Stone had sampled both before he poured his own.

Once Stone said; "What kind of gun do you use?" and Callan said "One that works," and that was all they said until Hunter came out and it was time to go.

The hired Citroen drove them through the worst traffic jams in Europe and Hunter didn't say a word; still silent they went aboard the Lear executive jet and took off; then the plane levelled off and Hunter said, "There's a vacuum flask somewhere. Pour some coffee."

Callan poured: it was nothing, like as good as the coffee in the restaurant. Hunter sipped, grimaced, and said: "They want to kill Ventris."

Callan considered what he'd heard of Ventris: Greek and cheerful and handsome. A freelance: a good one.

"What on earth for?" he said.

"They have reached the conclusion that he was responsible for the death of a Hungarian called Arani. Arani was a scientist the Russians used quite a lot in their space-shots. The Russians didn't know that he told everything he knew to the C.I.A.—not till Ventris told them."

"The KGB got him?"
"He killed himself as they broke in," said Hunter. "I suppose in a way he was lucky."
"Ventris did it for the money?"
"He did indeed," said Hunter, and told Callan how much he thought it would be. Callan whistled.
"Ventris happened to be working for the C.I.A. at the time—as Arani's controller," said Hunter. "It's hardly surprising the C.I.A. want him dead."
"And he's in the U.K. at the moment?" Hunter nodded.
"They already know where he is," Hunter said viciously. "And I don't. That annoyed me, David."
"Yeah," said Callan. "I can see that it would."
No wonder Hunter had been so silent, he thought.
"You going to let them do it?" he asked at last.
"Yes," said Hunter. "I'm going to let them do it. In return they've given me some bits and pieces. Really quite valuable bits and pieces. Stuff I've got to have."
The warning lights went on, the plane began its descent, and Callan risked one more question. "Did they say who was going to do the job?"
"The man who dined with us," said Hunter. "Stone."
Callan considered Stone: lean and hard and fast, by the look of him, and filled with youth's desire to excel. He fastened his seat belt. "I should think he'd do good job," said Callan.

That was Tuesday. Callan woke on Wednesday morning without either a hangover or indigestion, and blessed the restaurant's chef and sommelier.
Wednesday was a rest day, and that was pleasant too. He re-fought the battle of Gettysburg, and this time Lee won. But Thursday—Thursday was different, from the very beginning, when he went into Section Headquarters. Liz, Hunter's secretary, was waiting for him. He was to go in at once.
Hunter didn't look nearly as rested as Callan. "I trust you slept well," he said at last.
"Like a top," said Callan. Hunter scowled.
"I had a wretched night," he said. "This Ventris business; it bothers me, David."
Callan waited: it was far too late for Hunter to start developing a conscience: an event as unlikely as a pig with wings.
"Not knowing where he is bad enough," said Hunter. "But the C.I.A. *do* know and that's worse. And now there's this."
He scowled at a memo on the Sheraton sofa-table he used as a desk. Seconds ticked by, then Callan coughed delicately. It seemed a monstrous thing to intrude into such monumental gloom.
"There's what, sir?"
"We did a spot check on immigration, at Heathrow last night," said Hunter. "No particular reason. It's just that we sometimes dredge up something useful. Last night's chap was rather bright." He sighed.

The thought of last night's chap's brightness seemed to cheer him not at all. "He found us a possible."

"Yes, sir?" said Callan.

"Mrs Ventris," said Hunter. "He followed her to the Savoy. She's staying there. It seems she's looking for her husband."

Callan said carefully: "I suppose that does rather complicate matters."

"Dear boy," said Hunter "Don't try to be nice to me. I don't think I could bear it."

Callan gave up trying to be nice. "I didn't bring my crystal ball," he said, "and even if I did you'd probably have it bugged—so why don't you just tell me what's bothering you?"

"I made a bargain with the C.I.A. to let them kill a man. One man. No women. If this Ventris creature reaches her husband before Stone does—he'll kill her too. For aiding and abetting."

Callan willed himself not to shrug—but even so he didn't understand the fuss. If Mrs Ventris had aided and abetted she'd be sure to be on the death-list.

"Maybe they'd pay you off with more information, sir."

"They could give me a ton of diamonds and I'd still lose," said Hunter. "Mrs Ventris—" he broke off, and stared gloomily at the memo once more. "She wants a private detective to find her husband," he said at last. "I've fixed that. You're the private detective. It would be nice to know where her husband is, but your main job is to keep her alive."

Callan stood up. "If I could just have a look at Ventris's file, sir—I suppose she's in it?"

For the only time since Callan had known him. Hunter looked shifty.

"You won't need the file," he said. "Just do it."

This time Callan did shrug.

"I'm sorry, David," Hunter said at last, "but this one is marked Most Urgent. Get over to the Savoy at once."

Callan left. On the way out he passed Liz's desk: she was compiling a yellow file—surveillance only. There were two names on the cover: Mackley and Stone.

Private Eyes, he decided, should not arrive at the Savoy in too much style; he took a taxi, walked past the commissionaire to tread the hallowed ground, and was glad that he was wearing the best of his three suits. It didn't impress the receptionist much, but then the ·357 Magnum he was wearing under the coat didn't exactly help the fit. He waited humbly and was told at last that Mrs Ventris would see him.

He had expected glamour—after all Ventris lived dangerously, was shortly not to be alive at all, and that way of life tended to insist on its compensations—but what he got was beauty, but beauty so ill-clad as to look like a surrealist joke: a perfect rose wrapped in soiled paper....

She was a blonde: medium height, medium build, with her hair pulled back in an untidy bunch. She wore shapeless tweeds and a sweater two sizea too big for her, woollen stockings, and court shoes that must have been going out of fashion when she'd bought them ten years before.

And yet; her hair really was like sovereign gold, her nose short and straight, her complexion flawless, her eyes wide-spaced and dazzling blue behind their granny glasses. And she opened the door to him herself. Callan shuddered to think what easy meat she'd make for Stone—or even one of Stone's assistants.

"I'm Callan," he said. "The private investigator you sent for."

"Do come in," she said, and the three words were enough. Mrs. Ventris was a very English rose, the expensive kind nurtured by all the right schools. He followed her in, and felt better once the door was closed. Her movements as she crossed to a chair and sat were not without elegance, but her clothes still looked terrible.

"There's coffee over there somewhere," she said, and gestured to a table. "Help yourself."

Callan helped himself and as he did so the woman wriggled in her chair, reached down to pick up a book and dropped it on the floor. The book was *Philosophical Reflections* by Ludwig Wittgenstein. Dimly Callan remembered Hunter once telling him that Wittgenstein was the sort of philosopher even other philosophers found heavy going.

"It's about your husband, isn't it?" he said.

"His whereabouts," she said. "I want you to find him."

"You have reason to believe he is in England?"

"He telephoned me," she said, "from this hotel, some days ago."

"Telephoned you where, Mrs. Ventris?"

"Is that relevant?" she asked.

"It's a little early for relevance," said Callan.

She shrugged. Like her wriggling, it should have been pretty to watch, but the tweeds eliminated the prettiness. Maybe that's what they were for.

"At our house in Palm Springs," she said, and added kindly. "That's in California."

Callan thanked her, sipped his coffee and asked, "May I ask why you want to find your husband?"

"No," she said. Callan found that he was beginning to sweat.

"Have you any leads you can give me?" he asked.

"Leads?—Oh, clues. Surely that's your job—"

"There are over fifty million people in this country," said Callan, "and quite a lot of them are adult males. If I have to look at them all it might take some time."

The woman got up, and went to a briefcase near the coffee-pot, took out a photograph. The briefcase's locks were the kind it would take a Lonely to open.

"Find one that looks like this," she said.

He looked at the photograph: Paul Ventris in swimming trunks by a pool. A sleek man who smiled a lot to show how good his teeth were: one look at him and you heard the splash of heated water, the tinkle of ice-cubes, pretty women's laughter. But he wasn't hard, like Stone.

"That narrows it a bit," he said.

"He has a passion for clocks," said Mrs Ventris.

Callan found he was sweating again.

"He collects them. At the last count I think he owned 43. When he called me he said he was about to visit a fellow collector. The fellow collector will be female, certainly rich, probably pretty, possibly both."

"Did he say where the fellow-collector lived?"

She made a sound that from anyone less beautiful would have been a snort.

"Had he done so," she said. "I wouldn't have needed you. Please get on with it." She reached for Wittgenstein, and Callan put down his cup and went to the door. "You made no notes," she said.

"I shan't forget this conversation," said Callan. "Believe me."

"I suppose I was insufferably rude," said Mrs Ventris. "I often am when I'm worried." She didn't say 'I'm sorry.'

Callan went out. In the corridor, a large and very black West Indian was vacuuming a carpet that had already been cleaned. His name was FitzMaurice, and he could—and had—beaten Callan at karate, but not with a pistol. Hunter really wanted this bird secure, thought Callan, and kept on walking. Neither man spoke.

Callan went back to the office and phoned a mate in Sotheby's. The mate said: "I'll call you back," and phoned an antique dealer who put him on to a man who listed his profession as horologist. The horologist went through his records, dithered and came up with a name at last, and the bloke from Sotheby's called Callan back.

"Mrs. Bennington," he said. "Haverton Hall, Northumberland."

"She pretty?" asked Callan.

"My informant describes her as personable—but then he's over 70."

"How many clocks?"

"Dozens," said the bloke from Sotheby's. "David, what is this?"

"Research," said Callan. "Thanks. I'll buy you lunch next week." He hung up.

The bloke from Sotheby's knew Callan as the researcher for a national dally, and read it for a month. There wasn't anything about Mrs. Bennington; there wasn't very much about clocks.

Hunter said: "I'll get our man in Newcastle to check," then buzzed Liz, and gave precise instructions.

"Suppose he is there?" said Callan. *"What do you want me to do?"*

"Do your best to keep Mrs Ventris from her husband," said Hunter, "but above all keep her alive."

"You want me to lift her?"

"Unfortunately that's not possible, David," said Hunter. "I wish to God it were."

"So she can go where she likes?"

Callan got no answer to that one, and tried again.

"I see you've got FitzMaurice in on the act too."

"Meres is also lending a hand," said Hunter.

Mrs Ventris got the cream all right. So why was Hunter so worried?

"Turn over a drum in the Savoy?" said Lonely. The little man was obviously horrified.

"It's not Buckingham Palace," said Callan, but Lonely could see very little difference.

"It's all lords and film-stars and heads of state and that," he said, and sucked at the dregs of his beer. Callan signalled for another.

"Guarded like the Crown Jewels, the Savoy is," said Lonely. He looked at the Annigoni portrait of the Queen above the bar, and raised his fresh glass in salute.

"Her Majesty goes there herself sometimes," he said. "So what chance would I have? I mean who's going to look after me?"

"I am," said Callan.

"Oh well, that's all right then," said Lonely.

Not for the first time Callan marveled at Lonely's faith in his, Callan's, abilities.

"And just to keep your hand in you can follow the bird round till it's time to do the job."

"Just as you say, Mr Callan," said Lonely equably. He liked following birds. "Fifty quid extra."

"Thirty and expenses," said Callan.

"Done," said Lonely, before Mr Callan could change his mind. Callan finished his Scotch and was ready to go.

"And Lonely," he said, "wear your best suit."

Lonely looked hurt. "I trust I know what's expected, Mr Callan," he said. "After all, it is the Savoy."

At Hunter's H.Q. Liz told Callan that Mr Hunter was not available, but that the Newcastle man had confirmed that Ventris was staying at Haverton Hall. Mrs Bennington was pretty, rich and divorced, the Newcastle man said. Ventris had it made. They played with the clocks all morning and every afternoon he went out to shoot and always by himself—probably because he was such a terrible shot.

Callan didn't give much for his chances. He thanked Liz and went into records: the Ventris file was out of circulation but the one on Mackley and Stone was there. Mackley it seemed was a first-rate controller: his only weakness a tendency to anger if one were ill-advised enough to betray him.

Stone — John Arlington Stone: 6ft. 1in., 180lb.—was a better than average C.I.A. plumber: killer rating A. There weren't that many pure A's around. Callan read on: 'Known associate James Luard. Killer rating B+'. Callan took another look at Luard, then went to the armoury till it was time to meet Lonely.

"Antique shops," said Lonely. "She couldn't get enough."

"Any special kind?"

"They was all full of clocks," said Lonely. "Barmy—half of them didn't even work."

"Anywhere else?"

"She had tea at Fortnum's with an old bird," said Lonely. "Acted like she'd been her teacher one time. They talked about something called moral obligation, whatever that is."

Callan asked for—and got—a description of the old bird. It was unflattering but, he had no doubt, accurate.

"Anywhere else?"

"Car rental place," said Lonely. "She hired a Jaguar. Told them to drop it off at the Savoy tomorrow morning. They were swarming all over her."

"Right," said Callan. "Let's get on with it."

Lonely hesitated. "Do I look all right, Mr Callan?" he asked. Callan looked at him: peacock blue safari suit, cream shirt, peacock blue tie, cream shoes. Gawd knew where he'd nicked them.

"Perfect," said Callan.

Lonely sighed his relief. "I always say there's only one thing gets you into the Savoy—and that's class," he said.

Callan told himself that Lonely was disguised as an eccentric millionaire.

He checked the grill-room. Mrs Ventris, who appeared to be wearing a blue tablecloth with a hole in the middle, was reading a menu as if it were Wittgenstein. At the next table Toby Meres was deciding between Chambertin and Pomerol. They went on to Mrs Ventris's room.

Lonely did a beautiful job: dexterous, professional, unobtrusive, worthy of the highest traditions of the Savoy, and Callan went through her terrible clothes, took photographs of the documents in the briefcase Lonely had opened: put everything back the way he'd found it.

On the way down, he said: "Thanks, old son. Fancy a beer?"

"How about in the bar here?" said Lonely. "On me."

"I doubt if they'll sell your beer," said Callan.

"*Beer*?" said Lonely, horrified. "Mr Callan. This is the Savoy. We're having champagne."

Mrs Ventris believed in an early start. Callan was waiting for her at six, and at 6.10 they were on their way, nosing through the early traffic to the North Circular, and on to the M1.

Mrs. Ventris knew all about handling a Jaguar, granny glasses or not, and if the E-Type she drove wasn't exactly in its first youth, it still had plenty of punch left. Callan was glad he'd made a fuss and insisted on the Lamborghini Miura that was the transport department's pride and joy. They'd sprayed it black since the last job, but it still wasn't exactly invisible.

Callan settled down to drive. Mrs Ventris it seemed, was keen on driving. She left the M1 to fumble her way through Newcastle, and Callan wished she'd stop for breakfast or even a cup of coffee. But Mrs. Ventris was in a hurry.

She headed north-west, reached a road at last that was far from considerate of a Jaguar's needs—or a Lamborghini Miura's—and still kept going. The road dwindled to something little better than a cart-track, and on either side of them the moorland streched. The two drivers were the only visible living things. Callan had no doubt at all that she knew he was there.

They were going down a shallow slope when he heard a rifle-crack and she swerved. Not just a skid: the whole car, seemed to decide suddenly to go crabwise. She lost speed and Callan braked as she wrestled the car back to the left and then he heard a second shot, and the E-Type started playing crabs again.

Callan accelerated, and passed Mrs. Ventris, still wrestling the wheel, on the inside. The Lamborghini whined its pleasure at being allowed to go, but already he was braking, wrenching the car to a stop beside a gnarled and stunted tree, the only cover in miles. He was out and running as the wheels stopped turning, pounding down the road, hand reaching under his coat, hoping to God there was only one of them.

The enemy was quite visible. He stood in the road, holding an Armalite carbine: the lightweight job with the fibre-glass stock, and he held it right. It was aimed into what was left of Mrs. Ventris's E-Type.

Callan fired and missed, and the man with the Armalite turned. Callan swerved as the other man fired, and still kept on coming. The rifleman was still out of the Magnum's range, and he had to keep going ... The rifleman fired again, and Callan lurched drunkenly, made a few more yards, and fell.

The rifleman left the E-Type and walked towards Callan, unhurried. Callan lay prone, and the rifleman drew closer, closer, began to lift the Armalite to his shoulder.

From the E-Type there came a scream, but the rifleman ignored it: he had been trained to do things one at a time, and do them right. Callan rolled over as the rifleman fixed, came up holding the Magnum two-handed feeling it pulse once, then again between his hands as he fired. The rifleman's hands opened, and the Armalite fell as he lurched backwards, spinning with the impact of the Magnum's bullets, landing hard on the empty road.

Callan shambled to his feet, grimacing from the pain that burned across his ribs. He willed himself to move in: pick up the Armalite. And all the time the Magnum covered the man he'd hit until he staggered up closer still, and turned him over with his foot, put the Magnum up. The rifleman was dead. Time to look at Mrs. Ventris.

She was not in the best of positions for a lady philosopher with an Oxford first. The E-Type had gone into a ditch that was both broad and deep, and Mrs. Ventris was swinging sideways in the car, supported by her seat belt. Somehow the hem of her skirt had got entangled with the seat belt too. Her legs, Callan noted, were good enough for an ad for tights but her language was deplorable.

He reached out to turn off the ignition key, found it had already been done, and released her seat-belt. Mrs. Ventris fell in an undignified heap, but at least she stopped swearing. Callan got on with the business of helping her out of the car, and the graze across his ribs hurt more than ever.

She wriggled free at last and yanked down her skirt—today's offering, Callan noted, appeared to have been made from sub-standard billiard table cloth—then looked at the body of the rifleman.

"You killed him?" she asked.
"Yes," said Callan.
"I always knew you weren't a private detective," she said, and went closer to the body. Her face was white, Callan noticed, but she was steady enough. Suddenly, as she saw the dead man's face, she began to shake. "But that isn't him," she said.
Callan found that he was using the Armalite as a kind of crutch, to stay upright.
"Do you mind fetching my car?" he said. "There's some first-aid gear I need."
She took one look at his side, and ran up the road. Callan heard the disciplined roar of the Lamborghini as it started, and sat down at the edge of the road, eased off his coat, pulled up his shirt. It was what they called a graze, but it hurt like hell and it was bleeding.
Her fingers were deft, but the antiseptic stung: he was glad of a gulp from his whisky flask when it was over, and so, he noticed, was she. Mrs Ventris sat down beside him, not touching him, but there, and touchable. She took a cigarette from her bag, lit it, dragged in the smoke.
"It's the wrong man," she said.
"It's the man who shot up your car, tried to shoot you—and did shoot me," said Callan "He'll do."
"There's another one," said Mrs. Ventris.
"Of course there is," said Callan. "The rifleman let me pass you—he wouldn't have done that unless there had been somebody else up ahead to take care of me."
"That somebody else is here to kill my husband," said Mrs. Ventris. "You know that, so please don't bother to deny it."
Callan didn't bother to deny it.
"My husband's innocent," Mrs. Ventris said. "I came here to try to save him. I suppose we're too late."
Callan pushed the butt of the Armalite into the ground, ready to lever himself to his feet. "Let's go and find out," he said.
"You're going on?"
"I've just killed a man," said Callan, "I have to go on." Carefully, so as not to start the bullet graze biding again, Mrs Ventris kissed him.

They drove on for another mile, and then they abandoned the car and crawled up a ditch. This time Mrs Ventris carried the Armalite. Around them the moorland stretched, apparently for ever, except for one dip in the hills where a grey-stone house stood in a huddle of trees, warming itself in the meagre sunlight.
Callan settled in the ditch, wary, watching as Mrs Ventris picked twigs from her billiard table skirt.
"What do we do now?" she said at last.
"Wait," said Callan. "He's here. He has to be."
"I could drive the car up," she said. "If he tried to shoot me you could get him."
Callan took the rifle from her. "You really must love your husband," said Callan.
"Paul? I'm divorcing him," she said. "But he's innocent."

"So am I," said Callan. "So are you. But Luard—the one I killed is a B plus killer—this one's an A."

"Then what do we do?"

"Wait."

They waited for more than two hours. Jane Ventris had never seen before so furious a concentration of energy in a man. Like a cat, she thought: alert, contained, and deadly; and like a cat, when the time comes he will kill. She tried to emulate his stillness. It was a very difficult thing to do.

A Land Rover bumped its way across the moorland ahead of them, seeking a track that led to the house. The man who drove it wasn't smiling, but if he did his teeth would gleam. Paul Ventris. He had a shotgun and game bag beside him: the game-bag looked empty.

Suddenly the Land-Rover back-fired, and to its right the heather stirred: there was the dull gleam of a rifle-barrel and a man's head just visible. The Land-Rover back-fired again, and Callan squeezed the Armalite's trigger, the other rifle barrel dropped. Like a cat, she thought: precise, elegant, and quite pitiless.

The Land Rover bumped on, and Callan left the cover of the ditch, moved in warily on what was left of John Arlington Stone. "What kind of gun do you use?" Stone had asked, and he, Callan, had said: *"One that works."* He went back to Mrs Ventris.

"What do we do about my husband?" she asked.

"Let him go home for his tea," said Callan. "As a matter of fact I could do with a cup myself."

They found a pub that sold tea, and eggs and bacon that were ready as soon as Callan had made his call to Newcastle. He began to eat at once.

"Aren't you going to ask me anything?" she said.

"No," said Callan. "I know my limitations. Save it for Hunter." She blushed.

Later she said, "You shouldn't travel any more today—not with that wound." He went on eating, and she added, "They do rooms here. I asked." He poured more tea.

"Look," she said, "I know my dress sense is terrible, but clothes aren't everything." She took off her granny-glasses. "Are they?"

Mackley was furious. He bought Callan and Hunter another dinner in the same restaurant just to tell them so. There was a time when Callan thought he would literally die of sheer frustrated rage, but when he at last paused for breath, Hunter said: "This is all nonsense, you know."

"Nonsense?" Mackley howled. "You cheated me."

"Stone cheated you," said Hunter. "He and Luard sold Arani to the KGB. Ventris was innocent." He scrabbled in his briefcase: dealt out photostated documents like playing cards. Mackley grabbed for them, and turned white.

"My God," he said. "Where did you get this stuff?"

"Never mind," said Hunter. "We got it and we used it. To your advantage, I think you'll agree."

"My God," said Mackley.

More silence in the Citroen, more coffee in the executive jet. At last Hunter said, "I have behaved disgracefully."

"You didn't have much choice," said Callan, "once you knew Ventris was the target. Your niece should never have married him."

Hunter slopped coffee into his saucer. "How the devil did you know she was my niece?" he asked.

"I spied on her," said Callan. "The way you taught me. Opened her briefcase—had her followed—telephoned her old tutor at Oxford."

"Entirely without instructions," said Hunter, then added, "I'm more grateful than I can say. You can imagine how I felt when I heard of her marriage."

"At least she's going to be a divorcée now," said Callan. "Keep her that way." Hunter winced. "But I bet you knew she was on her way over from California," Callan continued. "That story about the pickup at London Airport. It was far too crude for you, Hunter. She was on her way over with the goods on Stone—and you knew it."

He sipped his coffee and grimaced: it was still terrible.

"Like the way I could never get hold of Ventris's file, because she was in it, and the story about Jane needing a private detective. She knew who I was from the start—because you'd told her. Only she thought I was going to save Ventris. You knew I was going to kill Stone."

Hunter accepted it all without a blush: he had a grievance. "Why the devil did she go do there herself?" he asked.

"She talked it over with her tutor," said Callan. "She called it moral obligation."

Hunter snorted. "At least you disposed of the bodies," he said.

"The Newcastle man did," said Callan. "He couldn't quite cope with the Jag."

"I've fixed that," said Hunter, and found another grievance. "You were a day late getting back," he said.

The warning lights came on, and not irrelevantly thought Callan. "I had to help your niece choose some new clothes," he said.

File on a Deadly Don

"What you're saying," said Callan, "is that you want me to go over to New York and knock off a Mafioso."

"Precisely," said Hunter.

Calmly, Callan told himself. Calmly and reasonably. No use losing your temper.

"In other words you want me to go to the place that's got more C.I.A. men to the square foot than any other place in the world except Washington, make sure they don't see me while I find this Mafia geezer—separate him from his bodyguard—I take it he does have a bodyguard?"

"Bound to," said Hunter.

"And then, come back here. You do want me to come back?"

"Very much," said Hunter.

"Even though his bodyguard, and the C.I.A. will use every trick they know to stop me." Despite himself Callan found he was yelling.

"You do rather go on about the C.I.A.," said Hunter.

"I know I do," said Callan. "It's the way I'm made. I can't help it. You annoy them and they fire guns at you. It upsets me."

He looked round Hunter's office: the Sheraton table, the little Degas dancer, the Aubusson carpet, all remembering the days when the pound was still worth money. The Mafia seemed a long way away—but they weren't, not if Hunter decided to bring them close. Callan looked at the red file on the sofa table's gleaming walnut surface, and tried again.

"All right," he said at last. "So the target's a gangster and I'm a hit-man. But this isn't *Gangbusters* — whatever rackets this geezer's in wouldn't matter a damn to you. If you want him dead he's done something political and if you're on to it the C.I.A. will be too, and they don't like us on their patch any more than you like them on ours."

Hunter said: "You were never a fool, David."

"Only once," said Callan, "when I got into this game."

Hunter ignored him, reached out for the red file and opened its cover.

"Peter Valence," he read, "United States citizen. Has homes in New York, Florida, and Rhode Island. Estimated wealth: fifteen million dollars. He pays taxes on a third of it—road hauliers and a chain of bakeries, more or less legal. He is also what is called a don, a Mafia chief. The rest is vice: prostitution and what I believe is called porn—"

"Pornography's too long a word for the ones that need it," said Callan.

"No doubt," said Hunter. "That doesn't concern us. He is also very active in the heroin market."

"That does concern us?"

"Burma," said Hunter, "Thailand, even mainland China; wherever the poppy grows. He buys in bulk, and does the refining himself. But South-East Asia is where he goes shopping. And Red China knows it—of course they do.

"He's one of their best customers, and a dollar customer at that. And now and again he gives them something extra—what is called, I understand, sweetening the deal. And one of the things he gave them was our man in Shanghai. He lasted two days, but he told all he knew—and he knew a great deal. All because this man sweetened a deal; like giving a tip to a waiter."

Hunter closed the file and handed it to Callan. "I want him dead. David," he said. "See to it, will you?"

The file was an inch thick, and most of it conjecture. The only facts were that Peter Valence was fifty-three years old, had had an expensive education in business and accountancy, and had been baptised Pietro Valenti.

His father, Luigi "Scusi" Valenti, had worked for a while with Capone, but had moved on to New York. Capone's attitude had made no sense to him, it seemed. Making money was far more important than killing.

Even so, he was known as "Scusi" (Excuse me), because that was the word he used each time before he pulled the trigger on a victim—and he'd pulled the trigger 19 times. And Pietro, it seemed, was a true son of his father. He too, in his turn, had said "Scusi" before he pulled the trigger, though nowadays he told his minions to say it.

Florida, it seemed, was for a little winter amusement, and Rhode Island provided a little nostalgic summer fun to celebrate his birthday, but most of the year he stayed in New York and chased another million to add to the 15 he already had, and where he stayed was the apartment block he owned—and the ones who looked after him were his very own security service.

To kill a man was easy, thought Callan. It was to get next to him that was difficult—and to get away was sometimes impossible....

He went over to Notting Hill, to Lonely's favourite boozer. After a hard day's intellectual exercise the little man's company could be very restful. ... And sure enough there he was, on his own as usual, nursing a half and a packet of crisps as if they had to last till Christmas.

Callan ordered, and went over to him, and Lonely looked in incredulous surprise at the pie and pickles and the pint of light and bitter in front of him. Callan raised his whisky glass. "Cheers," he said.

"Oh ta, Mr Callan," said Lonely. "Ta very much."
The pie went in seconds.
"You not working then?" Callan asked.
"Work?" Lonely's voice was bitter. "There's no bleeding point, Mr Callan."
"I thought thieving was the only growth industry we had left."
"Growth?" said Lonely. "How can you have growth when the mugs is skint? Three jobs I did last night, Mr Callan. Really grafting. And what do I end up with? Eighty-nine pence and a set of fish knives—and the knives was electro-plated." He chewed moodily on a pickle. "I'd do better on the dole."
"Why don't you then?"
Lonely swigged at his beer, then looked at Callan, reproachfully.
"I have my pride, Mr Callan," he said. "And anyway—where would I get the stamps?"
"Nick them," said Callan.
"That's about all there's left to nick in this country," said Lonely. Then he added, unexpectedly: "Let them eat cake."
"I beg yours?"
"A queen said that," Lonely explained. "Like historic she was. Her subjects had no bread—so let 'em eat cake, she says. They cut her head off."
"Who told you that?" Callan was fascinated.
"You did," said Lonely. "In the Scrubs."
Callan sought enlightenment. "What's it got to do with nicking insurance stamps?" he asked.
"It's the same thing, innit? Posh word for barmy."
"Ironic," said Callan, but his brain was racing. He bought more beer, another pie, and Lonely thanked him nicely, but stayed immersed in economic gloom, and Callan encouraged him. There was no future in thieving until the economy took an up-turn.
"What you need old son," he said at last, "is a holiday."
At once the smell came.
"Oh my God," said Callan, "can't you ring a bell or something?"
"I know your holidays," said Lonely. "If you don't like the way I niff you shouldn't have said it."
"What about my holidays."
"Duffing blokes," said Lonely. "Croaking them even. You're physical, Mr Callan. Always were. And you can't help it—any more than I can help niffing."
It took a long time to persuade the little man that a holiday was a good idea.

And maybe it wasn't, but it was the only idea Callan had.
Valence had a house in Newport, Rhode Island, and most of the year it was just a tax loss, but once a year Valence opened it up and gave a party that lasted for days. A Gatsby party; Twenties stuff. Girls in cloche hats, men with spats, vintage motor-cars and booze served in coffee-cups. There'd still be bodyguards, but with any luck they'd be a bit more relaxed than usual, and if he could wangle an invitation,

there'd be no problem about getting close to his target. Lonely's cake might come in handy too. Valence's one weakness was pastry—maybe that was why he owned a bakery chain....

"I agree absolutely," said Hunter, "but how do you propose acquiring an invitation?"

"Valence likes cars," said Callan. "The real vintage stuff. Pierce-Arrows, de Sotos, Isotta Fraschinis. To get the cars he has to invite the owners. All you've got to do is get me the right car."

"And how would I do that?"

"Buy it," said Callan.

"Good God," said Hunter, appalled. "Have you any idea what the damn things cost? In dollars?"

Hunter and Lonely, thought Callan, singing duets. The country must be in a mess ... In the end Hunter settled for a vintage Rolls, paid for it in sterling, and had it shipped.

Callan and Lonely went by Jumbo, and if they hadn't Callan doubted whether Lonely would have gone. But the chance to add such a plane to his collection was too much for him, and he went—in terror, but he went.

Over and over Callan reassured him that violence would take place only in his absence, that the visa he'd got for him was even better than the ones supplied by the U.S. embassy, that the one little job required of him was totally devoid of risk—and worth five hundred under-valued pounds—and at last Lonely relaxed, and ate and drank and watched movies—and was happy.

He had a nasty spasm going through immigration at Kennedy, but the air-conditioning had broken down anyway, and nobody noticed. Not in New York, not in summer time. Not with the garbage collectors on strike.

By the time they joined Spencer Percival FitzMaurice at the car-park he'd almost recovered, but the sight of the big Barbadian upset him again: it always did.

FitzMaurice was massive, and lightning fast, and about as black as you could get, and even Mr Callan treated him as an equal. Duff you with one finger the darkie could, thought Lonely, and reacted yet again. Callan hustled him into the hired Buick, and turned the air-conditioning on full while FitzMaurice coped with the luggage, then drove them into New York.

They had a suite at the Plaza, and Hunter had squawked about that too, but Callan had been firm. Geezers who own vintage Rolls-Royces don't inhabit Broadway fleapits. Callan gave Lonely dollars, told him what beer to drink and sent him out to explore before opening the box FitzMaurice had ready for him, extracting the woven holster and .357 Magnum.

He put them where they belonged, practicing the lunging draw until its swiftness satisfied him. He sat down then, and realised how tired he was. Plane trips, and planning, and fear waiting at the end.

"So now you've got all your clothes on," FitzMaurice said, "maybe we can talk." He poured whisky for them both. "We got a nibble. A reporter wrote your Rolls up for Vintage Car Magazine, just like you said. Valence wrote the day it came out."

He handed Callan a letter. *"Honoured guest ... rally of classic automobiles ... spirit of the 'twenties revived ... Naturally the chauffeur too would be accommodated....*

"Yeah," said FitzMaurice. "They got real good stabling for the niggers. Clean straw even."

"For God's sake don't start," said Callan wearily. "I'll be the chauffeur if you want."

"No sir," said FitzMaurice. "No sir, boss. This ain't no spade kill. No way." Then the jeering note left his voice. "You can do this job, David," he said. "And I can't. All I can do is cover for you."

"Maybe you could pray too," said Callan.

He fielded Lonely from the nearest bar and chivvied him off to bed. They both needed their rest, but Lonely had wonders to relate. Every man in the bar had talked like Kojak and some had even looked like him. It was better than the telly. But he went off at last and Callan could undress and shower, and lie down on the king-size bed and sleep.

Valence was impervious to bullets—what you had to do was throw cakes at him. Rock buns, sponge cakes, cherry tarts. Callan threw all kinds but Valence ducked and dodged and somebody switched a torch on so that Callan could see better, but the torch was in his eyes. Valence was escaping. Callan woke, his eyes still shut. Someone was in the room, using a pencil torch: someone who made about as much sound as grass does growing.

A pro. And the Magnum was under his pillow, and no matter how fast he moved the intruder would be there first. So he lay still instead, and waited until his visitor came for one last look, and lashed out with a fist strike.

It landed high, missing the target, the stomach, and jamming into the shoulder instead. Even so, the force of it was enough to send the opposition sprawling, giving Callan time enough to slide out of the bed, but only just enough time. The opposition came right back at him, and they fought in the dim light of the discarded torch.

Almost at once Callan knew that he was out-classed. His only hope, was to yell for FitzMaurice, asleep in the bedroom nearest his, but even so there was a drawing room between them. And how could he yell, and risk coppers and newspaper reports, when he didn't even know who'd sent the intruder, or whether it was just the geezer's own idea and he'd broken in to steal?

Callan managed a couple of good ones—a hip throw that should have ended it all, if the feller he was fighting hadn't floated down like a leaf from a tree, and a spear strike beneath the ribs that brought an acknowledging grunt of pain, but even as it landed the edge of a hand like an axe, hit the back of his neck. The light from the torch exploded into blackness.

He awoke to the pleasure of water, soothing, cool, pressed to his neck where an ache was pounding. FitzMaurice's massive fist was squeezing a wet towel to dribble on precisely where it hurt.

"You should have sent for me," FitzMaurice said. "Why get greedy?"

"Next-time I'll write," said Callan, and groaned his way back to the bed, lifted the pillow. The Magnum was still there.

"He must have been good." FitzMaurice said.

"Your class," said Callan. "The best."

"I wonder who sent him? Valence?"

"There's only, one way to find out." said Callan.

They'd had one piece of luck: Lonely had slept through it all and that meant that when they briefed him his mind was centred precisely on what they had to say.

They took him through it twice, using maps and plans and the zoom-lens photographs FitzMaurice had taken and after the second time Lonely got it.

Lonely, honest, was as thick as two planks, thought Callan, but get him on to thieving and he was a minor genius every time. They fuelled him in the dining room, where Lonely reduced the waiter to awe by eating two steaks, then left for Newport, Rhode Island.

There they left Lonely in a hotel with a beer and used his room to change, Callan into a suit with a double-breasted waistcoat and spats, and an old Etonian tie knotted tightly over a gold tie-pin, and two-tone shoes. FitzMaurice into chauffeur's uniform of the period—hussar jacket, breeches and riding boots. They looked at each other.

"'I won't laugh if you won't," FitzMaurice said, and went to fetch the Rolls from its garage.

South Point had never belonged to a Vanderbilt but it looked as if it bad. Thirty bedrooms, acre after acre of garden, a million flowers, and a gloriously awful mixture of architectural styles, from Tudor to Edwardian Gothic.

The Rolls whispered down the driveway after they had been frisked at the lodge, and Valence's men had done a thorough job there: everything from prying hands, to metal detectors, and a geezer with, an old-fashioned tommy-gun looking on while it happened. "All part of the fun sir," he explained. "Real 'twenties style." But old fashioned or not, the tommy-gun looked like one that worked.

They reached the lawn, which was about the size of the Oval, and joined the long line of cars that were all in period; everything from a Stutz Bearcat to a Model A Ford.

There Callan got out, to join about a hundred people who were listening to a Chicago-style band playing "Lady Be Good," and drinking gin. Men in dinner jackets, in Fairisle sweaters, in blazers, and everyone with a cigarette case, or holder, or both: and the women—party girls all, bobbed hair, long beads, short skirts. Even outdoors the row was tremendous.

A man in a boiled shirt, in need of a shave and with an all too obvious bulge near his left armpit conducted Callan to his host. Valence sat in a wicker-work chair, flanked by other men with bulges—and one with a tommy-gun there was no way of hiding.

Valence was small, dapper and lean, with eyes that reminded Callan of frozen peas. He was eating an enormous portion of strawberry shortcake: no man had a right to be so lean and eat so much cake, thought Callan, but then, no man as wicked as he had a right to the blonde seated by his feet; the ultimate blonde, fragile and beautiful, and dressed in white from cloche hat to kid shoes.

She looked at Callan, blue eyes as unwavering as a cat's, while a tall Chinese in a mess-jacket handed him a teacup filled with amber fluid.

The Chinese looked as tough as any man there, but his right shoulder seemed to-pain him. All those teacups to fill, thought Callan, and sipped. It was single malt whisky and the cup was full.

"Glad to see you Mr Tucker," Valence said.

"Good to be here," said Callan. "Thank you."

The cold eyes looked into his. "I like your car," Valence said unheeding. "I want it."

And that was the start of the party; Charleston and rye, Black Bottom and bourbon, on the lawn or in the ballroom with the revolving globe, and relay after relay of musicians, and a Victrola and old 78s when they were all too exhausted, or too drunk, to play.

At midnight they went on the lawn again and spotlights played on an enormous cake, and Valence pulled a ribbon and the blonde jumped out: birthday suit for the birthday boy.

Callan wandered off towards the stables, near a garage, and behind him the jazz pounded, the champagne corks popped, and girls shrieked merrily as they were flung into the pool. Before him FitzMaurice appeared, a part of the night's blackness.

"You all right?" asked Callan.

"It's not exactly the Ritz," said FitzMaurice, "but I'll live."

"I'd appreciate it," said Callan. "He's got himself a blonde. I don't think he'll be up and about much longer. My room, quick as you can."

He turned and left, and the flowers smelled good and the band still played—and then he paused, wary as a hunting animal is wary. By a tree a man was watching him. Callan went up to him.

"Looking for something?" he asked.

"I was wondering if you'd like a piece of cake, sir," said the Chinaman, and held out a plate. "Everybody else got some."

FitzMaurice reached Callan's room unobserved, but even so he wanted to call it off.

"It's the Chinaman," said Callan and FitzMaurice nodded. "I'm ashamed of you," said Callan. "Racial prejudice, from you."

"I'm always prejudiced against risk," said FitzMaurice. "I don't care what colour it is."

"It's one we'll have to take," said Callan. "We'll never get a better chance." And they waited for Lonely.

Lonely in the Valence livery of striped waistcoat and bootlace tie, with a cake on a silver salver. Smug Lonely, because he'd got in no trouble at all, and when he carried the cake no one even glanced at him. There was cake wherever you looked.

"Smashing party, Mr Callan," he said. "Can't I stay?"

"It might get a bit lively, old son" said Callan.

Lonely sighed. "Could I have a bit of cake then?"

"I shouldn't," said Callan. "You might get lead-poisoning." Lonely fled.

The cake was too small for a girl, even a midget, but the two Magnums and the silencers were a snug enough fit. The two men prepared, and Callan picked up a bottle, and they moved to Valence's suite. Outside the door, a man was sitting. He rose as Callan lurched up to him, supported by FitzMaurice, and his hand disappeared inside his coat. "You lost, sir?" he asked.

"I'm sorry," FitzMaurice said. "He just can't seem to remember his room. No way."

Callan raised the bottle, drank and then staggered, and FitzMaurice grabbed for him, but somehow the grab missed Callan, and the two hands struck, one at the man's forearm beneath the coat, and the other along the jaw-line where the nerve is exposed. The man crumbled, rubber-legged, and Callan caught him as he fell, relieved him of a Colt .38.

"That was the easy part," said FitzMaurice.

Callan took out the silenced Magnum. "Tell me something I don't know," he said. "Now you open that door and take cover."

FitzMaurice argued, but obeyed at last. Callan was leader after all, and, if he failed, somebody had to get Lonely out.

The door swung open and the man with the tommy-gun grabbed for it too late The Magnum made a soft popping sound, like a wet bag bursting, and Callan grabbed for the sub-machine gun left-handed, as its owner thudded down, then kicked open the bedroom door.

The blonde was wearing a white kimono and Valence a black one. He was also eating cake. He put down his fork and glared at Callan.

"Out," he said. "How many times—" then the anger died and fear replaced it. This wasn't a bodyguard. His hand slid to the pocket of his kimono.

"Scusi," said Callan and the Magnum plopped, once, then again; head and heart, and Valence went down like a fly swatted. The blonde winced: no more than that.

""What is this?" she said. "The Saint Valentine's Day Massacre? Not frightfully British, old top."

Behind Callan a voice said "Not British at all. Put the arsenal on the floor, please." Callan did so, and turned to face the Chinaman, who held a gun that worried him not at all, for behind the Chinaman was FitzMaurice. FitzMaurice leaped, and the fight that followed was epic. Callan retrieved his arsenal in case the blonde got nervous, then settled with her to watch.

"Oh boy, oh boy," the blonde said. "If only we'd sold tickets The Chinaman went down at last, but FitzMaurice looked far from well.

"You boys are wasting your time." said the blonde.

"Not really," said Callan.

“Not really,” she mocked. “He was already dead, my friend. That cake was just about to disagree with him.”
“I suppose you baked, it yourself?” said - Callan. She nodded, her blue eyes unwavering. Callan looked from her to the Chinaman.
“C.I.A.?” he asked.
“Hunter’s Section?” asked the blonde. “I think we’d better go, chaps.”
She went to a cupboard and took out her clothes—fringed dress, cloche hat then changed. Her body matched her face...
FitzMaurice got to work on the Chinaman and he came to at last.

They got to the stables and a Cadillac vintage 1976 but at the lodge their luck ran out. It seemed that they weren’t supposed to leave without permission and the guards brought their guns from the lodge to prove it.
Callan dropped the Thomson and reached for the silenced Magnum, but the blonde picked up the submachine gun, unleashed a blast of sound that shattered the night. Bullets whined over the heads of the security guards, and they fled in panic.
Callan looked at the blonde: cloche hat still in place, tommy gun held just right: the ’twenties personified. All she needed was a cigar clenched in her teeth. He waited for the party to coalesce into a single scream. But the party roared on regardless.
“Relax” said the blonde. “It’s all part of the Roaring Twenties, isn’t - it? There’s always a little action at a Valence party—and anyway, it’s ’twenties tradition. Loose off a Thomson and all that happens is the band plays louder. Now let’s pick up your little friend and get you out of our territory.”

“The C.I.A. got on to us because of the car” said Callan. “Once they’d seen it they thought it might be bait for Valence. So they sent the Chinaman to check up on me.”
“But they let you continue,” said Hunter.
“That’s right,” Callan said. “For two reasons: we were the back up team if they failed, and if they needed a scapegoat we were it.”
“But they didn’t make you the scapegoats?”
“Two reasons,” Callan said again. “One I had a Magnum and the tommy gun’s magazine was empty. And two, Lorelei fancied me.”
“Lorelei?” said Hunter. “Preposterous.”
“All right,” said Callan. “So I don’t know her name. But I’d know her again, believe me.”
“And she’ll know you,” said Hunter. “Why on earth did they do it?”
“Valence had sweetened his Chinese deal with a C.I.A. man too,” said Callan. “So they went after him as well. We had what you might call a dead heat.”
But Hunter was impervious to irony not his own. “I’m not happy about this at all,” he said.
“You should be,” said Callan. “Valence bought that Rolls. He paid fifty thousand dollars for it. Cash.”

File on a Tired Traitor

"Somebody seems to think he's seen Alfred Dawes," said Hunter.

"Dawes? He must be clocking on a bit now," said Callan.

"Nonsense." Hunter's voice was testy. "He can't be a day over 60. A man in his prime."

Oh dear, oh. dear, thought Callan. When will I learn to be tactful?

"Dawes," Hunter said again. "The first of the great defectors. Sell all thou hast and give it to the Russians."

"He sold for cash then?" Hunter glared, and Callan added gently, "It was a little before my time."

"How you do harp on age," said Hunter. "But it was a cash deal. The KGB gave him a quarter of a million, and he gave them all he knew about the H-bomb we were trying to make. . . he knew rather a lot."

"Where was he spotted?" Callan asked.

"Cordoba," said Hunter.

"Where?"

"It's in Spain," said Hunter kindly. "More precisely in Andalucia. Moorish city. You'll like it."

"I'm going then?"

"Indeed you are," said Hunter. "You're going to bring him back."

Hunter swivelled, to the drinks table, measured precise amounts of ice, Chivas Regal and water into a Waterford tumbler, his hands as sure as a pharmacist's. Callan took a healthy swig. He hated defector jobs, so often they invoked heart rending grief.

"Who spotted him?" he asked.

"Keith." said Hunter.

"Sandy Keith?"

"Mr Alexander Keith to you," said Hunter, "He's only addressed as Sandy when he appears on that squalid little box."

Sandy Keith, thought Callan. Telly pundit. King of the highbrow chat-shows. Whimsically intellectual, diffidently progressive and with a dash, no more, of Scottish feyness.

"He would recognise Dawes after all these tears?"

"Twenty-seven," said Hunter. "Indeed he would. They were at Cambridge together—as undergraduates and dons. He served as secretary, to the H-bomb group Dawes worked with—as a civil servant, that is. Keith's not a scientist." He waited until Callan had taken another sip of his whisky.

"You won't like him," he said. "That doesn't matter. Just talk to him—then, go and fetch Dawes for me."

His hands scooped up the file from the Sheraton table, and. handed it to Callan: yellow cover, surveillance only.
"You don't want Dawes knocked off then?" Callan asked as he took it.
"Certainly not, just bring him to me, as I said."
Good dog, thought Callan. Fetch it—Good boy. He finished the whisky and rose, "Suppose he won't come?"
"I have every confidence in your powers of persuasion." said Hunter.
Once Callan would have argued that one, but not any more. Hunter wanted Dawes, and all Callan could do about it was the best he could, and he wouldn't know what that would be till he got to Cordoba. Best to save his breath.
He walked to the' door then turned, one question still unasked.
"Why won't I like Sandy Keith?"
"He's not likeable," said Hunter.

Callan spent the rest of the day with Dawes's file, and mulled over it as he drove to Keith's house in Hampstead. Alfred Dawes, M.A.(Cantab.), Ph.D., a whizz-kid grammar school boy who had won a physics scholarship to his college, and gone on to achieve fantastic things by the time he was thirty—and then, when he was thirty-three, betrayed his country, took the money and ran.
It took all sorts, Callan thought, but the ones who took the money sooner or later had to talk to Hunter, even if Hunter had to wait years and Callan had to bring them back from Spain. Good dog. Fetch. Fetch.
He parked the car by a neat little Georgian box a stroll away from the Vale of Health. Gleaming maroon doors, gleaming brass knocker; very nice. Callan walked up a path of worn brick between two manicured lawns, and a girl looked up from the flowerbed she was weeding: a long-legged brunette with a pouting mouth and eyes that deplored his suit.
"Yes?" she said.
"Mr Keith," said Callan. "I have an appointment."
She didn't believe it; she wouldn't have believed it if he'd told her what two and two made.
"Mr Hunter sent me," Callan said. "My name's Callan."
"I see." She stood up then, taking off her gardening gloves. Her legs were admirable, but her mouth still pouted. Somehow we hadn't, expected anyone quite, so—" Her voice tailed off, and Callan wished desperately to know quite so what, and hated her for not telling him, as she preceded him to the front door.
"You'd better come in. I suppose," she said, then, as he did so, "You didn't bring a briefcase—I mean for tape-recorders and things?"
"No briefcase," said Callan. No .357 Magnum either, he thought, but then I didn't expect I'd have to shoot my way in. She waited while he wiped his feet.

Down a corridor, then a room that held a Persian carpet, an oil by Derain and a water-colour by Turner, and a Sheraton sofa table almost as good as Hunter's; a room that would be insured for scores of thousands of pounds. Chat shows, it seemed, paid well.

The man behind the desk seemed smaller than he looked on the box—small, spry and enormously fit for a man of 60.

"It's the man from Security," the girl said. "He says his name's Callan."

"Then he's probably lying," said Keith. "All Security men do." He smiled to show that there were no hard feelings. "Get him a drink, Kirsty."

The girl poured from a bottle as if it contained her life's blood, and handed it to Callan.

"I'd like water with it," he said.

"It's fifteen year old single malt." said the girl,

"I'd still like water."

She picked up a carafe and drowned his drink.

"I take it you're not a Scot, Mr Callan," said Keith.

"No," said Callan. "I'm not." He sipped his whisky-flavoured water. "But then I'm a liar; so when l say 'No' I probably mean 'Yes' and I'm an undercover man for the Scottish Nationalists." He smiled to show that there were no hard feelings.

The girl, Kirsty, looked furious, but Keith merely nodded as one acknowledging a point scored by an opponent on a chat show.

"You've come about Dawes," he said. "What will you do to him?"

Sandy Keith's eyes were expectant, anticipating a treat.

"What I'm told," said Callan, and Keith's mouth pouted as the girl's had done. Callan looked from him to Kirsty.

"This is very confidential stuff." he said. "I think it would be better if we talked alone."

"But we are alone," said Keith. "Kirsty knows all my secrets."

She isn't going to know mine, thought Callan.

"Besides, she was there when I saw Dawes."

"Perjhaps you'd explain where you come into this. Miss—?" Callan said.

"Miss Lomax," said the girl. "Christine Lomax. I'm Sandy's—Mr Keith's—P.A. - personal assistant. We'd been researching a programme on cities in decay, that's why we were in Cordoba, and—"

"And we saw Alfred Dawes," said Keith.

"Could you tell us exactly where? "Callan asked.

Keith said at once, "I don't remember. Neither does Kirsty." He settled himself into his telly pundit's pose and reached for his pipe—a gesture Callan had seen him make a dozen times, just before he switched off the set.

"A funny thing about memory." said Keith. "It almost always needs what is called a trigger. I knew Dawes for almost 15 years—I knew him, observed him, was concerned with him. I still am concerned."

Callan nodded, as if in agreement. "That's why you shopped him," he said.

Again it was Miss Lomax who displayed anger.

"No indeed," said Keith, "it was why I did my duty as a citizen. Why I'm trying to do it now, if only you could supply that trigger I requested."

And there it was: unless you tell me what you'll do to Dawes, I won't tell you a damn thing. Callan told Keith what he wanted to hear: "I can't give you details," he began.

"It would be improper of me to request them." said Keith.

"But Dawes is accountable for his actions," said Callan. "He will be brought to account."

"By you?"

"That's not decided yet."

"I hope it's you," said Keith. "I've dealt-with your sort before—during my days at the Ministry. You look as if you'd be more than adequate at that sort of accounting."

The nastiest, compliment I ever received, thought Callan.

"Cordoba the beautiful," said Keith. "The most exquisite of mosques, the loveliest of balconied streets where Christian and Arab and Jew lived together and were content under the benign rule of Moorish kings. And then, alas, Cordoba fell."

Stop writing your script, thought Callan. Just tell me where Dawes is and let me get back to sanity.

"Cordoba, one of the three great jewels in the Moslem crown. The equal of Damascus, or what John Milton calls the great Alcairo—"

"Whereabouts is Dawes?" said Callan.

"I'll take you to him," said Keith.

"That won't be necessary."

"Oh but it will," Keith said. "Kirsty and I are going back there to do some work on the programme and anyway, I insist."

And Callan knew he meant it: if there was to be a death, Keith wanted to be in on it, otherwise his memory would go again, and so would Kirsty's.

Callan put down his glass of whisky'd water, and said "I'll pass on what you've told me."

"Please do." said Keith and Callan rose.

"That Milton you mentioned; does he write your scripts for you?" he asked. Keith nodded again—he could afford to. He was well ahead on points. Kirsty Lomax led Callan to the door. When they reached it she said "You're damn rude."

"I know." said Callan. "I worry about it. Do you think it could be because of the company I keep?"

The door slammed behind him and he got into the car, drove off towards the Heath.

He'd heard there had been foxes sighted there, and sure enough he saw one that dashed across the road in front of him with a pigeon in its mouth; It was a charming beast, flaring russet pelt, jaunty movements, and so he swerved to avoid it—and the fox repaid him by saving his life. For as he swerved the bullet, entered the windscreen to his left, thudded into the passenger seat and kept on going.

The windscreen's safety glass instantly became a jellied mass of fragments, clinging together opaquely, but even so Callan out his foot down and kept going on into a deserted by-road, braked and leaped from the car, right hard instantly reaching for a .357 Magnum he wasn't carrying.

He hadn't thought he'd need one just to drive across Hampstead Heath.

"Unoccupied house with a balcony," said Hunter. "Ideal for a sniper. No fingerprints or anything else of that sort. No cartridge shell. One wouldn't expect that if it was a pro. But we have identified the bullet. Russian—or so the boffins think. High velocity. That probably means a Kalashnikov rifle with a telescopic sight. You were lucky. Who knew you'd be going that way?"

"Keith," said Callan. "And the girl saw me drive off."

"But why on earth should he?" said Hunter.

Callan shrugged. "You were right about one thing." he said. "He really is not likeable."

"But Mr Callan, it doesn't make sense," said Lonely.

"I'm whimsical," said Callan. "I always was. Even in the Scrubs."

Lonely sighed. He could never understand Mr Callan's passion for breaking into posh gaffs and then not nicking anything.

"All I want you to do," said Callan, "is open up the place and accept a modest fee."

"How modest?" said Lonely.

"A hundred nicker."

"Blimey," said Lonely, "it must be a tough one."

"Manson alarm system," added Callan. "I saw it."

The smell came then, but the merest whiff, the first hint of a breeze that could yet become a gale force wind.

"Mansons is murder," said Lonely. "It could take hours."

"Take as long as you like," said Callan. "The owner's away."

"You're, sure?"

Solemnly Callan licked his finger. "Cross my heart and hope to die. And I'll be your minder, won't I?"

"Oh well, in that case," said Lonely, and suddenly there, was no hint of a smell. "You're on, Mr Callan. Always happy to oblige a friend. Could I have it in oncers?"

He got it in oncers, and opened up Keith's gaff in a manner that was an education just to watch, first waiting in cover for the Panda car to drive by, then a quick nip round the back to immobilise the alarm-system by the kitchen window, then slowly, painstakingly cutting a hole in the window, reaching through to unscrew a second alarm, before he swung the window wide, climbed in without a sound, and opened the back door to admit Callan.

They went to the drawing room and Lonely opened up the filing cabinet for Callan to browse through. Lonely wandered restlessly and finished up by a glass display case that held a collection of snuff boxes. Callan looked up then. Lonely loved snuff boxes.

"See if you can find a safe," said Callan. "Open it up. It'll be a bit of practice for you."

The safe, a combination job, was behind the Turner water-colour, and Lonely twirled busily away as if he was dialling telephone numbers thought Callan, as he carried on with his reading. The filing cabinets were filled with evidence that Keith was to be seen on the telly and nothing more. But Lonely went on twirling and found the right combination at last, and Callan wandered over to see what he'd found.

Keith's interest in whisky was more than just national pride, it seemed. He owned a third of a distillery and there were the share certificates to prove it, which explained why he was rich. And that was about all that there was—except the scrapbook.

Keith, it seemed, was fascinated by Keith. The book was crammed with clippings, cuttings, photographs, all about Keith. And going back in time from the present to his childhood—the first was one of Keith in his pram. Callan flicked through it impatiently; so impatiently that he very nearly missed the only one worth having.

It was a menu from some long-forgotten, dinner, and it was too thick. He took a knife from his pocket and prised delicately, while Lonely went back to the snuff-boxes. Behind the menu was a photograph. A young man, tall, athletic, poling a punt, and written across it. "With all my love, A.D."

Lonely watched moodily as Callan produced a camera, and photographed a photograph. Barmy. The whole job was barmy. Callan replaced the menu, put the scrapbook back in the safe, locked it and replaced the Turner water-colour.

"Want to take a look upstairs?" said Lonely.

"Yes," said Callan. "I do. As soon as you've put that snuff box back."

Miss Lomax slept there too, it seemed, but by the look of it chastely enough. She had a lot of clothes, and she read a lot of books, and in one of them she had hidden a photograph—or used it as a bookmark. A young man tall, athletic, on horseback, riding across a landscape that was not English.'

On it too was written: "With all my love." But that was not in English either. Callan photographed that one too, and it was time to go.

Meres enjoyed the flight to Malaga. Their hostess was pretty, and served the kind of Scotch he preferred. Besides, there was the prospect of Spanish food—and of action. If he was sent as back-up man for Callan there had to be the chance of action.

They arrived on time, and a hired Ford was waiting for them, and in its glove compartment two .357 Magnums.

Action. They drove to Cordoba, skirting Cadiz, then, leaving the sea, past orange groves and vineyards to where the high Sierras provided the frame for Keith's city in decay.

That it was beautiful they had no doubt, but they had not come for beauty. The mosque with a cathedral inside it, the great houses with their walled gardens; for these there was no time. They were hunters in pursuit of the ultimate prey and for them beauty was meaningless. They went to keep their rendezvous with Keith. Like two leopards, thought Callan, relying on a jackal.

But Keith and Miss Lomax, it seemed, were dining with some geezer from Spanish television, and so they could do nothing but wait, so they ate changuetes and callos a la Madrileau, drank Rioja wine, and went back to their rooms. Waiting was something they knew all about; all you could do was endure it.

Meres went into his room and ducked without knowing why. All he knew was that there was danger. So he ducked and threw up his arm and the knife sliced open the sleeve of the best light-weight jacket he'd ever owned.

Its owner struck again and Meres swerved, the knife slammed into the door. Meres lashed out then, but his attacker was already moving away with a dancer's grace, letting the impetus of Meres's blow bring Meres close enough for the assailant to hit back, and hit hard. It was over in seconds: when Callan came in Meres was on the floor and groaning the only signs of his attacker, a butcher's knife stuck in a door and an open window.

Callan fetched water, but Meres took whisky. The violation of his jacket had upset him. He looked suspiciously at Callan: "You're trying not to laugh," he said. "What's so funny?"

"A tall feller?" said Callan. "Athletic?" Meres nodded. "He must have got our rooms mixed up," Callan said, and laughed aloud. "He was after me."

Keith and Kirsty Lomax got back at 11.30, which made it an early dinner in Andalucia, and came at once to Callan's room where Callan and Meres waited.

The girl looked haggard, but Keith was bouncing with energy; couldn't wait. He gave them Dawes's address.

Callan left, and Meres stood up, and made a languid, graceful gesture that finished up inside his second best lightweight coat, took out the Magnum, "How about a little three-handed bridge until our leader gets back?" he said. At first Keith couldn't believe it. But in the end he believed the Magnum.

The house Callan broke into was old and cool, and, apparently, deserted except for a sleeping servant, but it had a garden that was mostly flowers, and in the courtyard Alfred Dawes sat reading by the light of an oil-lamp. It had to be Dawes, thought Callan, had to be the older version of the man whose picture he'd found in Keith's scrap-book, but his face was a monument to enduring pain. He looked eighty, at least.

Dawes looked at the-intruder without any visible sign of fear. The pain made fear of death irrelevant. He began to speak in Spanish.

Callan said: "I haven't come to steal, Mr Dawes."

The old man sighed to hear his real name mentioned. "British Intelligence?" he asked and Callan nodded. "I've been expecting you for twenty-seven years. You've come to take me back?"

"That's right."

"I have osteo-arthritis," Dawes said. "It's at the terminal stage. What's the point of putting me in a prison hospital?"

"What's the point of betraying your country?" said Callan.

"There were two actually," Dawes said at once. "The first was that I thought it right to do so."

"You took money," said Callan.

"Oh indeed. My second point, I had just been told that I had this affliction. Suddenly I longed for sunlight. I could no longer work, but I wanted my rest to be comfortable."

"There's no word about your illness in your file," said Callan.

"How could there be? It was diagnosed in California just three weeks before I went back to England and defected."

"You came straight here ?"

"Russia first", said Dawes. "I had so much to tell them that needed a lab."

"But they let you go?"

"Quite happily," said Dawes. "Once the diagnosis was confirmed I could no longer work, you see. So they arranged a cover-story for me: a new name, a new identity, and I came here and was happy between bouts of pain."

"But why Spain?"

"Can you think of a country less likely to harbour a Communist sympathiser? And I love this city." He talked of it then, rhapsodising as Keith had done, but with a real affection. On and on he talked, until Callan interrupted, and said, "I must warn you, Mr Dawes, if anybody should come in on us—I'm armed."

The old man said, "No one will do so. Not tonight, you have my word." He laughed then, harshly, "If a traitor's word is acceptable. Who betrayed me?"

"Alexander Keith," said Callan. "He saw you here when he was setting up a TV show."

"Poor old Sandy," said Dawes. "I loved him once, and he loved me—in so far as he was capable of loving. It took a woman to show me what a fool I'd been."

"If he loved you—why would he betray you?"

"Because I left him" said Dawes. "I wonder—could you pour me some water? My pains have started again."

Callan poured water from a jug on a table by the old man's side, and took it to him, waited, impassive, as Dawes fumbled a little bottle from his pocket, and shook tablets from it, swallowed them, and sipped the water.

"Twenty-seven years," he said at last. "It's time enough to be prepared."

"How long will the tablets take?" Callan asked.

"You knew then?" Callan nodded. "And you didn't stop me? I'm obliged to you. It won't be long." Callan sat and waited.

Dawes said: "I insisted that if this happened I must accept the consequences, but he doesn't always listen." The eyes dropped; the voice sounded faintly once more: "There are so many things one regrets. But there was happiness too."

His head dropped forward: it was as if he were asleep.

Callan went back to where Meres waited, with only Keith and Kirsty Lomax and the Magnum for company. At once Keith started yelling about his friends in high places. Callan said to Meres, "If he doesn't shut up belt him"—and Meres smiled, no more. But it was enough: Keith was still.

Callan turned to the girl. "Where is he, love?" he asked.

"I don't know what you're talking about," she said.

"Dawes's son," said Callan. "Where is he? Come on darling. He loves you. He wrote it in. Spanish on the photograph he sent you. He's probably waiting for you now to tell you how he sliced Meres's sleeve with a knife. Where is he?"

"He wouldn't," she said. "He promised me—"

"His word's not as good as his father's," said Callan. "You tipped him off I was coming to see you in Hampstead."

"I told him," the girl said. "But it wasn't a tip off. I just told him . . . He had to know."

"He shot at me with a rifle," said Callan. "Only I was lucky. A fox saved my life."

"Good God," said Keith.

"Keep on saying that," said Callan. "You're on the list too." He swung back to the girl. "Where is he? Look Miss Lomax, I only want to tell him it's no use. Not any more. His father's dead."

She wept then, and told them where he was.

It was a room above a cafe where flamenco blared, their own secret room, hidden from his father, from Keith, where they, could be happy. But it was Callan and Meres who went there and kicked in the door to face the tall, athletic man with guns in their hands to hold him still as Callan told him Dawes was dead. It was over. But the tall man didn't think so, and grabbed for a pistol, and Meres shot him while flamenco blared.

Callan cursed and ran to where the tall man lay, not quite dead. "My father," the tall man said, "My father." He said it in Spanish.

"He told me his mother was Spanish," said Callan. "But she was a Red too. Dawes met her in Moscow. By the time she died six years ago, she was paymaster for the Red network in Andalucia and she had her son trained at Lumumba University all ready to take over, which he did. It's the best foreign agent school the KGB's got."

"So Meres was justified in killing him," said Hunter. "In a way," said Callan, "But even so, the feller loved his father."

"Very proper," said Hunter. "But he didn't love us. Did Dawes know what his wife and son were up to, do you think?"

"I think he did," said Callan, "but he was a Red too, remember. And the only big thing in his life was pain."

"And so you let him die," said Hunter. "You acted humanely and for once you were justified. We should not persecute the dying. It would be bad for what Keith would call our image."

He paused, then continued: "This girl, this Lomax person. I've had a chat with her. She seems innocent enough—of everything except her own emotions—though of course we'll open a file on her now.

"That hardly seems an adequate penalty for the trouble she's made. She met young Dawes and they had an affair in Cordoba and then in London, and she told him things—" he scowled "- as women will.

And young Dawes took action. Violent action. Why didn't he just send his father away?"

"Where could he go and be happy?" said Callan. "And anyway, a journey would have killed him. Besides—"

"Go on," said Hunter.

"He must have told his KGB controller what was happening," said Callan, "and I think they saw this operation as a chance to kill me. They didn't give a damn about Dawes. His use was over years ago. But it was a chance to have a go at me. I hope I don't sound big-headed."

"Not at all." said Hunter. "The KGB has wanted you dead for years."

And one of these days they'll get what they want, thought Callan. Aloud he said, "What happens to the girl?"

Hunter looked it his watch and turned on the TV set. "What do you suggest?" he asked.

A picture of Keith appeared.

"Give her back to him," said Callan. "That should be punishment enough—even for you".

File on a Harassed Hunter

The Lear executive jet began its descent, and Callan fastened his seat-belt.

"This is going to be a hell of an expensive night out in the theatre," he said, and looked down at the landscape that rushed to meet him: moorland for a background, limitless and vast, but a foreground of old, neat stone houses, and then the strip of concrete that the Lear's tyres softly kissed in making the smooth, unflustered landing of a pilot who worked for Hunter for one reason only: he was the best.

"You like the play?" said Hunter.

"*Hamlet*? I always have," said Callan, "but couldn't we have waited till it came to London?"

"Unfortunately that may never happen," said Hunter.

His voice was sour, and Callan knew why. There was no Bentley waiting at the airport, because a Bentley would have been far too conspicuous in that grimy Northern town.

Hunter loved his Bentley—not least its bullet-proof coachwork and windows of specially toughened glass. And here he was reduced to riding in a hired Daimler, with the local Section operator for a chauffeur and nothing but Callan to protect him from a shot from the right. For a shot from the left there was no protection but the car door and a bullet from a Magnum revolver could go right through a car that hadn't been specially treated, all the way from the boot to the engine block.

It had to be a big one to get Hunter out like this. Standing orders were that he was to take maximum security precautions at all times, and here he was without even the statutory two bodyguards. Not just a big one, thought Callan; a very, very secret one as well.

They travelled in silence; there was a dividing panel between passengers and driver, but no written guarantee that the Daimler wasn't bugged.

They reached the hotel at last. Hunter looked at it and sighed.

All right, thought Callan, it isn't the Ritz. But did you *have* to come here? By the look on Hunter's face Callan decided that he'd had to do just that.

They went up to their rooms, and Hunter waited as Callan went over them both for bugs and booby traps, waited and sipped at sherry that was pale and dry enough even for him. Thank God, thought

Callan, as he worked. If the hotel had sent up Oloroso, Hunter would have burst into tears. Callan went on searching. No bugs. No bombs under the bed.

"Well?" Hunter said.

"I don't like it here," said Callan,

Hunter looked disgustedly round him: wallpaper that for some reason reminded him of the soup at his school, and a carpet that recalled the cabbage.

"Who would?" he said.

"I mean I don't like the set-up," said Callan. "The locks aren't even a joke—and there are too many ways up: stairs, lift, fire-escape. . ."

There was a knock at the door, and the Magnum came into Callan's hand as if he'd willed it there. He moved Hunter from the line of the window then went to the angle of the door. "Yes?" he called.

"You ordered beer and sandwiches sir," said a voice.

Callan transferred the gun to his pocket; kept his hand on it, and opened the door. A waiter with a tray, chicken sandwiches, two bottles of beer . . . And that was all. Callan gave the man money, and watched him leave and Hunter's hand reached out for a sandwich. Callan reached out to stop him. His hand closed on Hunter's forcing the fingers open so that the sandwich fell and parted: chicken that by the look of it hadn't died without a struggle.

"David, what the devil?" Hunter began.

"I think we're at risk," Callan said. "You are at risk. My orders say that should never happen. Never. But it is happening and if you die I'm to blame."

Hunter jerked his hand, trying to pull away, and found he couldn't; not any more.

"Don't you think you'd better tell me what I'm mixed up in?" Callan asked, and Hunter nodded at last. Callan released him, and Hunter looked at the livid-marks that Callan's fingers had made.

"You don't know your own strength," he said.

"Oh, but I do," said Callan. "Your experts taught me years ago. Why are we here?"

"To learn a man's address. And find the man—and kill him."

"And you broke cover for that? Why not just send Meres with me—or FitzMaurice?"

"I have to know this man is dead."

"My word wouldn't be good enough for you?"

Hunter looked towards the table.

"I'm hungry," he said, "thirsty too."

"Me an' all," said Callan. "But first I've got to know" His voice altered. "Sir, please," he said. "For God's sake tell me."

Rare indeed to hear Callan beg, thought Hunter.

"The man I'm after is KGB," Hunter said. "His code name is Lubov. That's all I know. He's a wet-job expert. Grade Four."

And that was all it needed. Wet-job was KGB jargon for assassination and Grade Four was the highest there was.

"There's an actor at the theatre here who knows who Lubov is—and I want Lubov."

Hunter paused, and for the briefest of moments. Callan thought he saw a human emotion on Hunter's face, and the emotion, was grief. Then Hunter became impassive again.

"I want him for one of the first jobs he ever did," said Hunter. "A wet-job in Budapest, just before the Hungarian uprising."

"But that was years ago".

"Twenty," said Hunter. "I wasn't the head of the section in those days and this was the first big job I was responsible for. Lubov killed one of my operatives. A good one."

Callan thought: But this is craziness. Blokes like Hunter expect operatives to get killed. It's a risk they take, and they know it. And Hunter knows it. And if he loses one, he sends another. He doesn't start yelling for revenge like Hamlet's father.

Aloud he said: "You want Lubov knocked off because he killed some geezer twenty years ago?"

"Not a geezer," said Hunter, "A woman. A young, brave, intelligent woman."

"Yes but even so—"

"She was my daughter."

The only sane thing would have been to get him out of the hotel, now and over to the airport, and back to London—except by the look of him he wouldn't ruddy go. It would have to be sweet reason, after all.

"You've got to be joking," said Callan. "You of all people setting up a hate killing. And how could it be a daughter of yours anyway? That's dead against orders. No relatives. It gives the Ivans too much leverage."

Hunter said impassively "I didn't know it was my daughter. Not then. I'd met her mother in Budapest before the war when I'd just got in to this...this game." He spat out the word. "It wasn't until the girl was dead that I even knew I had a daughter and then her mother got word to me, just before she died too."

"Lubov again?"

"A tank shell," said Hunter. "A Russian tank. Now may I have a sandwich?"

"Why not?" said Callan. "It we're going to behave like amateurs let's go all the way,"

But the sandwiches contained nothing more lethal than the chicken.

"Who's the actor?" asked Callan.

"Evan Lang," said Hunter. "I doubt if you've heard of him but he's good. He did a job for me. Just one. He was on some kind of cultural tour in East Europe—which is how he met Lubov. He has a quite remarkable memory."

"He has luck too," said Callan, "if he met a Grade Four and survived it."

The performance of the play was less than memorable. True, the actor who played the prince was one of the five fully paid up members of the Trotskyite Workers Party, and the actress who played Ophelia performed her mad scene naked, which occasioned some novel use for her wild flowers, but the only actor worth twopence was Polonius.

Polonius was Evan Lang. A big man who could look old, comic, crumbling, an actor with the range and ability and power to play Othello, or Lear, with any company in the world. And here he was shoring up this shambles: a lion among baboons.

During the interval Callan said, "He really is good." Hunter nodded. "Then what's he doing in this disaster?"

"He gets drunk," said Hunter. "At every available opportunity."

Evan Lang died beautifully behind the arras, but wasn't on stage for the curtain call.

When it ended, Callan said: "Do we go back?"

"No," said Hunter. "You pick him up and we talk at the hotel."

Callan went round to the stage-door. That meant Hunter was alone in the Daimler, but what else could he do?

It was worse than an amateur job, but he was stuck with it. The best he could manage was to tell their driver to cruise around at random, but to pass the street-corner by the stage-door at three-minute intervals. The driver had very properly looked incredulous at such idiocy but he'd known for long enough that they were all loonies at Hunter's H.Q. and dangerous loonies at that. So he did as he was told, and Callan waited for Evan Lang.

They jumped him efficiently enough; three young men in street-fighters gear: crash helmets and motor-bike overalls and steel-shod boots, one with a knife and two with coshes; three lads with a job to do, lads in a hurry. They must have been: they even left their car engine running, as they fanned out in a line across the street and moved in on Callan.

They were a problem, no doubt about it. He had the Magnum, of course, and even by the rather dodgy light of a street lamp he could shoot them with no trouble at all but was it right to start gun-play in this fair, if grimy city?

Was it even wise? Suppose a copper came? I'll shoot only if I must, thought Callan. I'm not taking a leathering from these three and proceeded to do the unexpected.

Instead of shrinking hack, he charged at the central figure of the three, the one with the knife, and swerved as the knife blade lunged, got two hands to the knife-man's wrist, pulled him sideways so that he cannoned into one geezer with a cosh, then pulled again so that the knifeman hit the other and in the process found that his arm was broken, and began to scream. But the scream died as a hand like an axe blade smashed against his jaw and he fell and Callan leaped him, to kick one cosh-man in the gut, took a blow from the other cosh-man across the ribs but, even so kept going, threw a fist strike at the throat and knew at once that it had connected, that there was a good chance that the second cosh-man might be dead, though there was no time to find out.

He wanted to know things, and for that he needed the living. He went to the man he'd kicked, who was on his knees, groaning, but even so looked up appalled as Callan-stood over him.

"Who sent you?" said Callan.

The young man groaned out a blasphemy, and Callan stooped, his thumbs pressed into the young man's armpits, found the pressure points even through the overalls. The young man's next groan became a scream, and he shot upright.

"Who sent you?" said Callan again. He was in a hurry too. "Look," he said, "you'd better tell me otherwise I might get rough." The pain beneath the armpits flicked, just once, needle-sharp.

"Plastic Mac," the young man said at once.

"Who?"

"Joe MacNamara," the young man said. "We call him Plastic."

"Have you been to my hotel too?" asked Callan.

"Not us." the young man said.

"Who then?"

But the young man was slow in answering, and Callan was impatient, and pressed again, and pressed too hard. The young man fainted. Amateur night.

The stage door opened, and Evan Lang appeared. Evan Lang, who'd missed his curtain call and had been loose for an hour or more. He moved into the dodgy lamplight and stooped to peer at the unconscious knife-man.

"What bloody man is that?" he said.

"Wrong play," said Callan, "That's Macbeth."

Lang seemed to be having difficulty in getting himself upright and when Calian went to him he found out why. Lang was monumentally drunk. Callan didn't find the fact surprising, not that night.

He steered Lang away up the street and waited for Hunter. The fight had taken a couple of minutes, no more, and Callan stood in a fury of impatience until the Daimler appeared and he hustled Lang into the seat by the offside door and ran round to the near-side. A little more protection for Hunter. Lang had once worked for Hunter, too. He must learn to take his chances. The driver's voice came over the speaking tube.

"Where to?" he asked.

"The hotel," said Hunter, but, Callan vetoed that.

"Just drive around for a bit," he said.

Evan Lang spoke then—his voice resonant and unslurred. "I must have a drink," he said, then added, to make his point clear: "An alcoholic drink." And Callan knew he spoke the truth. The trouble was the pubs were shut, all part of the night's disaster.

He tried the driver. "Where can we get a drink?" he asked.

"Your best bet is MacNamara's," the driver said. "That's a club out by the airport."

Callan asked more questions, and found they'd got a bit of luck. They were about due for some. Callan listened as the driver talked, then asked: "If it's a club we'll need a member to sign us in."

"I'm a member," the driver said, and Callan sighed. He put down the speaking tube, and Hunter said: "I'd like your report." Callan looked at Evan Lang. He was sitting bolt upright and by the look of him, sound asleep.

"There were three young fellers by the stage door who wanted to

give me martial arts lessons," said Callan. "It was very educational."
"No doubt," said Hunter. "Are they dead?"
"One of them may be," said Callan. "But there's more."
He told it, and Hunter listened.
"You can handle it," he said at last.
"I could if I had a back up man," said Callan.
"You've got one," said Hunter. "Me."
The craziest night of the year. . . . Suddenly Lang opened his eyes and said: "Murder most foul, as in the best it is. But this most foul, strange and unnatural—!" then instantly went back to sleep.
"*Hamlet* again," said Hunter. "I take it he saw the men you dealt with. The sooner we get a drink into him the better."
"Drink'll be the death of him" said Callan.
"Perhaps," said Hunter. "In our business we die as we must."
Hunter philosophic was more than Callan could take. He sought refuge in practicalities.
"You can't be my back-up man," he said. "You need a gun."
"I've got a gun," said Hunter.
Hunter never carried a gun; generals never do. Callan wished he were as drunk as Evan Lang.

MacNamara's was brash and opulent, and served by barmaids who thought that night's Ophelia had had a good idea. Or perhaps it was the heat, thought Callan. But at least it helped to get rid of their driver: he went straight to the bar. Skin and tonic. And let's get him out of here while he can still drive, thought Callan.
Now it was time to talk while they could still hear. The blare of disco music was deafening, but at least Lang had been able to walk. All Hunter had said was, "There's a drink waiting," and Evan Lang had moved. Like Frankenstein's monster—but he'd moved.
They poured whisky into him and his speech, though slurred came at last. And he knew what Hunter wanted.
"Lubov," he said. "Somebody sent me on a job in Budapest." Callan flicked a glance at Hunter. "And I met Lubov."
Evan Lang too turned to Hunter. "Was it you who sent me?"
"Just tell it, old son," said Callan. "You know it's rude to be nosey."
"Lubov," Lang said again. "He killed Ophelia. Only mine had all her clothes on. But I saw. I was there. He killed her. With his hands. All that vitality, that loveliness—just switched off. Put out the light."
"Why didn't he kill you?" said Callan.
"He thought I was on his side," Lang said. "Funny thing—I never used to drink much before I saw Ophelia die." He smiled, then drank. "I played Hamlet in those days. I was going to be good."
"Where Lubov now?" asked Hunter.
"Notting Hill," said Lang. "Hamlet Street. Funny, that. Number 43. Top floor." He brooded for a moment. "Another funny thing. It was 20 years later—and I knew him at once. He didn't know me. I was going to take the flat below—but not after I saw him. Not where Lubov...keeps Death his court! That's Richard II." He turned to Hunter. "I played Richard on that tour too. And then I started drinking. You owe me my career."

He went back to sleep, still sitting bolt upright. Callan sipped cautiously at his Scotch.

"You've kept an eye on that for 20 years?" he asked.

"I had no choice," said Hunter. "He was once engaged to my daughter. Shall we deal with MacNamara?"

"What about him?" Callan nodded at Evan Lang: a man who should have been in his prime, but was already so sunk in decay that—

"Leave him," said Hunter. "Even we can't hurt him now."

To get to Joe "Plastic Mac" MacNamara it was necessary to eliminate two bodyguards first, two muscular gentlemen who lurked behind a door marked "Private" in scarlet letters three inches high, where the disco music was still all too audible.

Callan found he couldn't take them both, and was relieved to find he didn't have to. Hunter still knew how to use a revolver's barrel as a club. The two bodyguards fell softly to the thickly-carpeted floor, and Callan and Hunter moved to the door marked "Director" and pushed it open—still as deft as Meres or FitzMaurice—and Callan leaped inside. The man behind the desk looked into the Magnum's barrel and was still.

"You're making a mistake," he said.

"The story of my life," said Callan. "Only it's the other geezer who dies when I do."

"No protection money, not ever." MacNamara said.

Callan shook his head. "Just a little information," he said. "That's not much to ask in exchange for your life."

And in the end he got it, even if MacNamara resented bitterly that for once he should be obliged to give rather than receive. And when he'd got what he came for Callan thanked him nicely and turned as if to leave and MacNamara grabbed for the Llama 33 Super he kept in his desk drawer, because you never knew when such a thing might come in handy. And Callan shot him twice, head and heart, the shots echoing the beat of a bass guitar.

He came out to where Hunter waited, and they walked down the corridor together. The bodyguard Hunter had hit pushed up on his hands, groaning, as they approached and Hunter tapped him again. He went back to oblivion.

"I take it that MacNamara is dead," Hunter said.

"He talked first," said Calian. "We've got all we need. Let's go home."

"To the hotel you mean?"

"No," said Callan, "I mean home. Where you're safe."

"Very well," said Hunter, "If you insist. But I think we should take Evan Lang with us."

"I thought you would," said Callan.

So they tore their driver away from the topless barmaid, and their pilot from a poker game, and poured Lang into the Lear and put him back to sleep with more whisky, and the jet climbed, and the lights of the grimy town twinkled below them, tiny as diamond chips. And then suddenly there was a big one too, a real Koh-I-Noor of a diamond, that erupted and shimmered as the Lear continued to climb.

"Your hotel room," Callan said to Hunter. "They didn't call him Plastic Mac for nothing."

The Lear sailed on into darkness. "No more irony," said Hunter. "Just tell it."

"A man came to see him," said Callan. "Gave him five thousand pounds to have us both killed and promised five thousand more when he'd done it. So he set his three rough boys on me, fifty quid apiece and petrol money." He grinned. "It seems they used to enjoy their work. For you he put a plastic bomb under the bed while we were at the theatre. We were blown before we even started, and you could be dead. They'd have loved that in Dzherzhinsky Street."

"Who hired him?"

"A bloke with a briefcase full of fivers. Bloke in his forties. No scars, no accent. But MacNamara didn't think he was English."

Evan Lang opened his eyes again.

"Lubov," he said.

Callan looked at him. "You back with us?"

"Lubov has grey hair and grey eyes," said Lang, then added as if it were part of the same sentence, "I need a drink."

Callan reached out to a locker and grimaced as his ribs reminded him of the blow they had received, produced whisky and glasses.

"You and me both mate," he said, and poured and sipped as Lang drained his glass.

"You'll kill him tonight?" Lang asked. "Lubov. Hamlet Street. He'll die tonight?" Callan said nothing, and Lang turned to Hunter. "It's got to be tonight," he said. "I've got a show tomorrow." Then he went back to sleep.

Hunter said: "I think it would be best if you did kill Lubov tonight." Then he caught the look in Callan's eye, and added testily: "I'm not thinking about revenge."

"Aren't you?" said Callan. "Sir?"

Hunter forced himself to speak honestly with this man whose life he had so irresponsibly put at risk. "Not exclusively. Lubov has manifestly been sent here to kill me, quite possibly you too. That's why he allowed Lang to see him. He knew that Lang would contact us. How fortunate for Lubov that to see Lang I had to leave London. It made his job so much easier."

"You're saying that he was on to Lang, then?" asked Callan. "That he knew Lang had done a job for you all those years ago. Lubov must have done — otherwise he wouldn't have used Lang as bait to get you." Hunter nodded. "Then why wait 20 years?"

"I told you." said Hunter. "Twenty years ago I wasn't the head of the Section—and you hadn't even joined. I suppose in a way Lubov being sent to kill us both is rather a compliment." He settled back in his seat. "All the same, I want you to get rid of him."

This time there was the Bentley waiting, and a couple of bodyguards to help decant Evan Lang, and Callan made his own way to Hamlet Street, to look at the flat where a KGB operator lived, an operator who owed five thousand pounds to a dead man.

No lights on in the flat, or in the whole house, but the locks on the door would be too much for him even if Lubov slept. For locks like that he'd need the help of a friend, and the friend would need a gallon of aftershave if he ever found out what Callan was up to. But it had to be quick, before Lubov had time to read his morning paper and turn on the news and learn that the wrong, man had died.

"At this time of night?" said Lonely.

"At this time of night," said Callan.

"You get me out of a nice hot bed just so I can open up some geezer's drum and then scarper?"

"That's right," said Callan.

"Why?" said Lonely, putting his finger on the problem, then added, to make himself clear, "What for?"

"A hundred quid," said Callan.

Lonely sighed, and reached for his trousers.

Deft, thought Callan. That was the word. Deft. Lonely and his magic fingers. Just that, and some skeleton keys, and a few twirls. Plus an oil can, judiciously applied in order that the door wouldn't squeak. And at the end of it all Lubov's drum was open to him and Lonely hunched down into his raincoat and prepared to go back to bed.

"A hundred nicker you said." His voice was a whisper.

"Tomorrow," said Callan. "You know I'll pay you."

For some reason Lonely looked up then. All those years thought Callan. All those jobs. The little man knew him like a greasy, well-thumbed book.

"You take care of yourself Mr Callan," he said, then although he was niffing, he added, "Want me to come with you?"

"No," said Callan, "I'll manage." I've got to, he thought.

"See you down the boozer then," said Lonely, and tiptoed away as if from a grave.

Come, come, Callan admonished himself: this will not do, and took out the Magnum he had so carefully cleaned and reloaded. He entered Number 43 Hamlet Street, screwed on the silencer, and climbed the stairs.

Lubov woke up and his hand went at once towards his pillow, the Magnum gave two soft thuds, like boots slammed down on a carpet, and Lubov, whose business was death, was dead.

Callan looked at him: grey hair, grey eyes. Even as a corpse he looked ten years younger than his age. Would his loved ones mourn him? he wondered. He went back to his own flat, and brewed coffee, and meditated on Hunter's madness, and in the middle of it all answered his own question: No one would ever mourn Lubov, any more than anyone would mourn him, Callan, when his turn came to die. Not even Lonely would mourn him, because nobody would tell the little man that Callan was dead.

File on a Beautiful Boxer

"You ever heard of Rod Mercer?" asked Hunter.
Callan did his best: "Pop singer?" he asked.
Hunter snorted. "He's even richer than that. He designs engines, makes them, sells them. A vulgarian, but remarkably wealthy for this day and age."
"You don't like him?"
Hunter snorted once more: first a wrong answer, then an irrelevance. Not my day, thought Callan.
"He's a nuisance," said Hunter, then gestured to the drinks table to show Callan he was forgiven, went on as Callan mixed Chivas Regal, ice and water. "Clever people so often are. He designed an engine for a motor boat, a very large, very fast motor boat, the sort that can carry rockets and cannon. The Admiralty were quite keen for a while then somebody else came up with something better, or so they thought."
"Too bad for Mercer."
"Not immediately," said Hunter. "Mercer went elsewhere—Israel to be precise. The Israelis liked it very much. Just the sort of thing they need. They ordered several million dollars' worth."
"So British know-how triumphed once more?"
"Not exactly, no," said Hunter His hands went out to the yellow file—surveillance only—on the sofa table in front of him, and moved it so that it was exactly parallel to the table's edge.
"You mean he didn't deliver?" asked Callan.
"Oh he delivered," said Hunter. "He was pleased—he'd been paid in dollars after all—and they were pleased, they had their engines. Only they're not pleased any more. The engines don't work."
"They'll sue him?"
"They'll do rather more than that;" said Hunter. "They'll kill him."
"A bit drastic," said Callan. "If we all started that every time an engine broke down there wouldn't be a car dealer left alive."
"Shin B'eth have looked into it," said Hunter. "In fact one of their people was killed on a test-run. They say it's a particularly clever kind of sabotage and that one of the Palestinian groups put Mercer up to it. That's why he's going to die."
"And what am I supposed to do?" said Callan. "Send a wreath?"
"You're supposed to keep him alive," said Hunter.
Against Shin B'eth. Pros as good as any in the world: tough,

dedicated, deadly with small arms. For them to kill Mercer was as easy as blowing out a match, for Callan to keep Mercer alive was about as difficult as picking up that same match and making it light a second time.

"Why don't you give me an easy one for a change?" said Callan. "Just to relieve the monotony."

"You're too good for the easy ones," said Hunter, "and we both know it." He pushed the file towards Callan. "The Admiralty have changed their minds about Mercer's engine," he continued. "They've now decided it's better than the one they opted for."

"But how can it be?" said Callan. "You say the Israelis have tested it and it doesn't work."

Hunter said expressionlessly "The Admiralty says the Israelis tested it wrong." In the same, expressionless voice he continued: "I've never met a sailor yet who wasn't certifiable. All the same, they want Mercer. His corpse would not be an acceptable substitute." He pushed the file closer to Callan. "Most urgent, David," he said,

"How long before the Israelis move?"

"Two days, perhaps three," said Hunter. "An execution needs very high authorization, but they'll get it."

"That's a hell of a good bug you've planted in Tel Aviv," said Callan.

Hunter looked complacent, "The best." he said, then the complacency vanished, "But fiendishly expensive."

Rodney Albert Mercer—call me Rod. Aged 43. Educated at a secondary modern and a long list of technical colleges. Married twice; divorced twice. But still fond of women . . . and wine. Estimated net worth, three million. House in Berkshire, flat in Mayfair, house in Jamaica, but had a nasty tendency to bob up in other-places too. It wasn't just unfair, it was downright impossible to keep this disappearing jet-setter alive if Shin B'eth wanted to kill him.

Callan called Mercer's design office and got a secretary; the house in Berkshire yielded a caretaker, the Mayfair flat nothing at all. The house in Jamaica produced a very Caribbean mixture of static and incomprehension. Well at least his first job was obvious. First he had to find Rod Mercer, it wasn't easy.

To begin with Mercer didn't have a factory, just the design office Callan bad phoned, and Callan sent Meres there as a prospective customer to talk to the secretary, and Meres when he was trying could get anything out of a secretary.

The trouble was that there was nothing to get. All she knew was that Rod was away somewhere and that was a good thing, because when Rod came to the design office he went raving mad—working day and night, even sleeping in the place and the phone never stopped and the secretary's mum didn't like her coming in so late. Though, mind you, Rod was a lovely feller. He got his stuff made under licence, it seemed. Holland, West Germany. Once it had even been Japan. You never knew, with Rod.

Spencer Percival FitzMaurice drew the house in Berkshire, and the caretaker instantly assumed he was an oil sheik, which annoyed

FitzMaurice, who was proud of the fact that he was about nine times as black as any oil Sheik could ever hope to be.

Nevertheless he listened politely as the caretaker told him that the house wasn't for sale and he'd no idea where Rod was—no idea at all.

Never told you a thing, Rod didn't. Never a sign of him from one month to the next, then up he'd pop in a white Rolls-Royce full of birds and champagne, all set for a weekend rave up. Old Rod was a bit of a sheik himself, if you asked the caretaker.

That left the flat in Farm Street. It was a conversion, and its front, door would have taken Lonely a minute, no more, even under the uncertain light of the street lamp.

It took Callan five, but he was in at last, and climbed the stairs. Pop music from Flat A, Moussorgsky from Flat B, but from Flat C, Mercer's flat, no sound at all. No light either.

Callan took a set of keys from his pockets, and set to work. He made no more noise than Lonely would have done, but the little man was lightning fast. A hell of a time for him to go out on an honest night's thieving, thought Callan, and went on probing, twisting, until at last the door's locks yielded: he slipped inside.

A hallway that was mostly parquet, and one exquisite painting on silk that Mercer must have picked up in Japan, and to the right of it a mahogany door that led into a living-room with a desk. Callan took a pencil-slim torch from his pocket and examined the lock, and sighed: another long job. He reached for the keys once more, and as he did so the lights went on.

"You'll ruin your eyesight, working in the dark like that," said a voice, it was a woman's voice, mocking: low-pitched. Callan spun round.

She was a sight to see all right and there was a lot of her visible. A tall and rounded redhead wearing nothing but a towel, and a Purdey shotgun that aimed straight at Callan's midriff.

Worth a couple of thousand at least. An expensive way to die.

"I suppose you're going to tell me you've come about the drains," said the girl.

"No," said Callan, "I've come about Rod Mercer."

"He's not here," said' the girl. "And you knew he wasn't here, you've come to steal."

She lifted the shotgun very slightly.

"The phone's on that table over there. Pick it up and call the police." Callan made no move.

"Listen," said the girl. "We're living times of equality — or hadn't you heard? Women drive airplanes now, and dig ditches—and pull triggers." And to save his life Callan couldn't be sure whether she would or she wouldn't...to save his life. He shrugged, and moved towards the phone, a move that brought him a little closer to her.

"Your towel's slipping," he said, and she looked down because the way he said it she believed it: the smug male chauvinist pig way when the pig is in for a treat. . . By the time she looked up again Callan had leaped, and the flat of his hand had slapped the shotgun's barrels, knocking it from her hands.

It lay on the floor beside them, still at full-cock, and she bent for it and he grabbed her and this time the towel really did slip, but all he could think as she struggled was how strong she was, then her right hand became a fist that slammed into the side of his neck, and Callan grunted with the pain and paid his tribute to women's lib, caught the fist as it aimed a second blow, twisted and threw her.

The carpet was thick, but even so the fight was over. He had all the time he needed to pick up the Purdey and extract the shells as she got up, already aware of bruises.

"I told you your towel was slipping," said Callan, and this time it was. Her fingers leaped to adjust it.

"What now?" she said. "Rape?"

"How your mind does run on assault," said Callan. "First shooting, then a punch-up, then rape."

"You forgot theft," said the girl.

I didn't come to steal."

"You couldn't anyway. Rod doesn't keep drawings here."

"He keeps you here."

"Only when I want to come," said the girl.

"Where is he?"

She shrugged, and the towel only just survived the strain.

"He didn't leave a forwarding address," she said, "and even if he had—"

"Now it's your manners that's slipping," said Callan. "Give him a message, love. Tell him a man came about his life insurance."

"What about it?"

"Tell him to increase it."

He got out quick then, and found a 'phone booth that hadn't been vandalised, dialled the long familiar number.

"Yes?" Hunter's secretary said.

"Let me speak to Charlie, please."

Hunter came through at once. Didn't he ever sleep?

"You've got something?" he asked.

"Yeah," said Callan. "A clip round the ear. Can you get an exchange tap on Mercer's phone in Farm Street?"

Hunter sighed. The G.P.O. were never happy about tapping phones.

"If I must," he said.

"You must," said Callan, and told him why.

"Who is she?" Hunter asked.

"According to the file she's Mercer's business consultant," said Callan.

"Her name's Angela Wain. She's got a mole on her right thigh."

"That isn't on Mercer's file." Hunter memorised files.

"I deduced it," said Callan. "I also deduced she'd been taking a shower."

"You'll stay with her of course," said. Hunter.

Callan looked out of the phone box: rain was falling, dreary and persistent.

"Oh, of course," he said. "Why should I want to go to bed when I can stand about outside and get wet?"

"Precisely," said Hunter, and hung up, and Callan passed the time by phoning Lonely. It took eleven calls: a great night for thieving, thought Callan, and hoped the little man had done better than he had.

By the time Lonely came to relieve him the rain had stopped, but even so the little man was sunk in gloom. He and his partner of the moment had not had a successful night.

"Four houses we done, Mr Callan," he said, "and three flats. And we hardly made petrol money. I tell you straight—this old country of ours is in a mess."

Callan rubbed the spot where Angela Wain had hit him and agreed, then told Lonely what he must do, and at once the little man was happy. He didn't even haggle about money, because following posh birds was his hobby anyway. Callan went home to bed, and slept, but not for long.

Lonely, rang him at 9:30. The subject was at a travel agent's, buying a ticket for Malaga. She'd also inquired about a hire-car from there to a place that sounded like Puerto Sanchez.

"Just one ticket?" Callan asked.

"Yeah," said Lonely. "Iberia. Afternoon flight. It was the first she could get." His voice hoarsened a little.

"You really see her with nothing but a towel on?"

"I did," said Callan. "Stay with her."

"Be a pleasure." said Lonely, and hung up, awed by Mr Callan's achievement. Most geezers would have to pay good money to see the subject in a towel and Mr Callan goes and does it for nothing—and gets to wrestle with her 'an all.

Hunter said, "Puerto Sanchez? I think better you'd better go there."

"She's on the first available flight." said Callan.

"That may be, but you'll be there before her," said Hunter. "Heathrow. You'll be met."

"If it's Shin B'eth, I'll need equipment."

"You shall have it." said Hunter.

"Angela Wain make any phone calls?"

"None," said Hunter. "I find that interesting."

And so did Callan. It would seem that Miss Wain had a damn good idea who Callan was—and what he could do.

Meres met him at Heathrow, and handed over the airline tickets reluctantly. Meres loved Spanish food. Near them an indignant citizen denounced the morals of British Airways. They had no right to over-book. He had business in Malaga—export business. Callan thought that Hunter must reallv want him in Puerto Sanchez in a hurry.

On the plane he drank one cautious whisky, and read the notes Meres had brought for him. Puerto Sanchez was a yacht harbour for yachts that cost a thousand pounds a foot or more. It wasn't St. Tropez yet, but it was on its way. Callan looked at the wad of pesetas Hunter had sent him. Puerto Sanchez really must be on its way, if that was the kind of money it took. He read on. Rod Mercer didn't own a yacht, but he quite frequently hired one. And he liked them big. The way he likes his women, thought Callan. A reminder that the Admiralty, though sailors and therefore certifiable, still had a right to demand that Rod Mercer be delivered, breathing, to the Admiralty.

There followed a P.S. in Hunter's own hand. "Try not to overspend," it said.

The hire car waiting for him was a BMW, and in its glove compartment, to which he already had the key was a .357 Magnum and a box of ammunition. This was droll. Shin B'eth would send two hit men, three at most: not an infantry battalion, in the ammo box was a note: Miss Wain's hire car was a Seat 120. It even gave him the licence number.

He drove along the Marbella road to a restaurant with a car-park, and yawned his way over lunch, then went to sit in the car until a white Seat 120 went by, and noted that Miss Wain looked almost as good in a green linen sheath of a dress as she did in a towel.

He dawdled along behind her, and the BMW growled unhappily: it was not a car designed for dawdling—until they reached a sign that said *Puerto Sanchez* and turned, off into a different world: a world where the trees gave more shade, where even in the height of summer there were roses, and grass that was as green as Angela Wain's dress, and sprinklers at two yard intervals to keep it that wav.

She turned into a car park that contained everything from a Rolls-Royce Carmargue to a beach-buggy, and Callan kept on going to where the shopping streets began, parked in the first space out of the sun, and went back to wait.

She didn't waste any time. All she had with her was an overnight case and a small procession of admiring Spaniards. Callan followed them all to the yacht basin — several million pounds worth of white paint, glowing mahogany, gleaming brass.

Miss Wain went aboard a floating pleasure dome called *La Joya* - The Jewel - but Callan reckoned it would take a fist-full of diamonds to pay, for it.

She was greeted by a squat and muscular man in a yachting cap who was not Rod Mercer, then stared at her followers until they scattered to other humbler yachts, and Callan went back to his BMW, and drove to the hotel Hunter had Telexed for him, weeping, thought Callan, as he read its daily rates.

A nice hotel, with a dark cool bar that served dark, cool drinks; the sort of bar that should have appealed to Mercer, if he were around, but all Callan drew were two Germans, blonde and sun-tanned and with that air of arrogant assurance in the Deutschmark that makes even old American money look vulgar.

Callan gave up, went to his room and showered and took his time about it. He couldn't think of anything else to do. As he left the shower his bath-towel slipped from his hands into the shower-stall and came out sopping wet, which was par for the day.

He came back dabbing himself with a wet towel and found he had a visitor: a squat and muscular man who had discarded his yachting cap and was wearing a knife instead. He wasted no time on preliminaries, just moved in and lunged.

He held the knife point upwards, the pro's way, and the lunge was professional too, and Callan only just got out of his way, and the squat man spun, elegant as a dancer, and moved in again, and as he did so Callan flipped the wet towel at him.

The sound it made as it hit his face was quite audible, and the squat man raised his arm, and Callan lunged for the knife-wrist with the axe-blade of his hand. The squat man dropped his knife and gasped with pain, then moved to the door and left, not even hurrying, because Callan was naked and very British, and there was nothing in the world he could do except check his locked case for the Magnum and find to his relief that it was still there.

He dressed fast and raced downstairs, and bumped into one of the Germans, who stared at him in Teutonic hauteur, then raced to the yacht-basin, and was even more relieved to find that *La Joya* was still there too.

From the well-deck there came sounds of merriment and a cork popped. Callan adjusted the lightweight jacket that was far too hot—but what else would you expect if you carried a Magnum?—and walked aboard, and at once a sailor appeared and blocked his path to the companion way. If Mercer was there it would take more than one sailor to stop him.

"*Senor?*"

Callan said in English "Rod Mercer's expecting me," saying it the way Mercer would have said it, at once bored and angry; bored because *La Joya* was just another boat and he owned a whole fleet, angry because a menial was keeping him standing about in the heat. The sailor stood aside, and Callan went down the companion-way to the well-deck and Miss Wain in something white and shimmering and Rod Mercer in a pair of trunks and a great deal of sweat, pouring champagne. He looked once at Callan and shifted his grip on the bottle, turning it into a club.

"I don't think I know you, squire." he said.

"My name's Callan. I advised Miss Wain about your insurance," said Callan.

Mercer turned to Angela Wain. "You know him?"

"We've met," she said. "Briefly. I think he works for Shin B'eth."

Mercer moved forward then and Callan's hand made a short, abrupt gesture: the Magnum appeared.

"If I did you'd be dead," he said and looked at the bottle. "That champagne's French. Pity to waste it."

"You're cool," said Mercer. "I like that. Sit down and have a drink."

"Thank you, Mr Mercer."

"Call me Rod," said Mercer, automatically, and poured Dom Perignon. "You really need that thing?"

Callan put the gun away, and accepted champagne.

"What's the score about Shin B'eth?" Mercer asked and Callan told him.

"But that's impossible," said Mercer. "Those engines are perfect."

That's what the Admiralty say, thought Callan, but the Admiralty would have to wait.

"Your engines blow up," he said aloud. "They kill people. The Israelis call it sabotage— they think you take money from the Palestinians."

"I'm not a spy," said Mercer. "I make engines."

"No," said Callan. "You design them. Somebody makes them for you. Who?"

"It's impossible," Mercer said again. "Jorge wouldn't."

"Wait," Angela said. "We can't, be sure..."

"Who, Rod?" Callan asked.

"Jorge Pascal," Mercer said. "He owns a nice little yard near here. Angela found him for me. Angela sort of lends me a hand now and again."

"She does indeed," said Callan. The girl sat, impassive, and Callan wondered whether the Shin B'eth men were already on their way. At least he now knew how the Admiralty and the Israelis could come to diametrically opposed conclusions and both be right. But knowledge was no use to a dead man and a dead man was no use to the Admiralty. He put down his glass. "I think we should go for a little cruise," he said, but Mercer shook his head.

"This is Jorge's boat," he said, and Callan remembered the yachting cap. "He had to go to take care of something, said he wouldn't be back till dinner time."

So they drank more champagne and Callan idly waited and watched the crowd go by, including the two Germans, loaded with snorkel equipment, who got into a power-boat and roared off. Fishing in the dark, thought Callan. Maybe they use radar now. At last Mercer said "Jorge. Well, well."

Angela Wain said, "It could be me."

"That's right," said Mercer. "Or you and him together." He turned to Callan. "What do you think?"

Callan thought of towels, of shotguns, of knives. "It depends on whether she's the sort of girl who learns by her mistakes," he said.

"If I were, I wouldn't be sitting here waiting for two men to see sense," said Angela Wain.

"Women's Lib at a time like, this," said Mercer. "That's all we need." He turned to Callan. "You got any ideas, chum?"

"How many does it take to run this boat?"

"You and me could do it."

"Get rid of the crew then."

It took the girl to do that; but in the end she succeeded, blasting them ashore with a burst of Spanish like machine-gun fire. When they'd gone, she said, "I think, I honestly think, I've gone off you, Rod. You can't prove it's Jorge."

"I can't prove it's you, either," said Mercer. "But I can't prove it isn't."

Callan loved him like a brother.

When Jorge appeared, Callan showed him the Magnum and he put to sea; reluctantly, but he went, sliding past all that white sleekness, silvered by moonlight.

"But I am your friend, Rod," he said, more in sorrow than in anger. "Your partner."

"You're not my friend," said Callan. "I had to slap you with a wet towel"

Angela Wain looked up then. "I see," she said. "Perhaps I should learn by my mistakes."

Jorge said, "Angela told me to do it."

Mercer was only Just in time to catch her as she leaped.

"I said I thought Callan was Shin B'eth," she said, still struggling. "I said I spotted him following me. But if I wanted him killed, I'd do it myself. In fact I very nearly did."

To starboard Callan could see the lights of fishing boats, chugging on slowly as their nets dragged—and then suddenly he knew.

"Belt up, will you?" he said, and the girl's yelling died. He turned to Jorge "I don't trust you," he said. "I don't trust you at all. Stop engines." Jorge looked at the Magnum and obeyed. Callan turned to Mercer. "We'll be safer on our own. Get the power-boat over the side."

Mercer hesitated. It was the girl who said, "Do it."

They lowered it, and one by one stepped into her. "I hope Shin B'eth does get you," said Jorge from the deck of the yacht. "You are not my friend."

"Too true," said Mercer, and ripped at the starting-cord, the outboard roared, and they steered in towards the lights of Puerto Sanchez, remote as fairyland.

"You going to tell us what you're playing at?" Mercer asked.

"Two Germans," said Callan, "only they looked like actors playing Germans. And they took snorkel gear out just before dark. And five minute's later they came back. Ah, well, if I'm wrong I'll look a fool. It's happened before."

The explosion came then and a millionaire's toy became a single sheet of flame that the sea fought to quell.

"It hasn't happened often," said Mercer. "Limpet mine."

Callan nodded.

"How very appropriate," said Angela Wain.

Callan went to the hotel bar. In his hand he carried a floppy and ridiculous straw hat. He walked over to the two Germans and sat beside them. They too were drinking champagne: it seemed it was a night to celebrate.

The taller German said. "*Was wollen sie*?"

Callan said in Hebrew: "All I seek is peace and love."

Once it had been a Shin B'eth code signal. The two men froze. Callan added in English, "And if I don't get it I'll blow your heads off. There's a Magnum under this hat."

He talked on, and they listened, and then he produced Mercer and

Angela Wain, and they listened some more, and in the end Mercer bought more champagne.

"So now the Admiralty's got him," said Hunter. "He's not exactly ecstatic, but they've got him."

"Why isn't he ecstatic?" Callan asked.

"They won't pay him in dollars." He sipped his coffee. "Shin B'eth are satisfied they blew up the right man?"

"They were after they broke into Jorge Pascal's office," said Callan. "They found some correspondence from the Palestinians."

"Oh dear, these amateurs," said Hunter.

"That's what they said," said Callan.

"But why send men supposed to be Germans?" said Hunter.

"Why not?" said Callan. "They'd hardly send a couple of rabbis. Their idea of a joke, I suppose. A bit black for me."

"And why send them so early? They can't have got permission for the kill until they were actually in Spain."

"Quicker that way," said Callan. "Better cover, too."

"But how did they know where to be?"

He's full of questions today, thought Callan. Too bad he had to ask this one.

"They got on to your bloke in Malaga," said Callan, "and now he's working for them too. He tipped them off where Mercer was."

Hunter's face turned an unpleasing puce, and Callan rose.

"Sit down." Hunter snarled. "I want a full report."

"Sorry," said Callan, "it's my rest day. And I've promised to give a lady a boxing lesson."

The Script
GOODBYE MARY LEE

{Originally titled: *The Senator's Daughter*}

A 'Callan' Episode

(unfilmed)

CAST:

CALLAN

LONELY

HUNTER

SECRETARY

CHARLOTTE RIGBY

MARY LEE TOWNSEND

ROBERT HACKER

DETECTIVE INSPECTOR (D.D.I.)*

BARMEN

CYPRIAN (Host at Party)

POET

Guests at party.
People in cocktail bar.
Police.

Technical notes: **INT – interior setting; EXT – exterior scene; SOV – Sound of Voice only, character not seen on screen; POV – from the Point of View of the character; (Beat) – dramatic pause; FILM – pre-shot location footage filmed outside television studios.**

*D.D.I. – the rank of Divisional Detective Inspector in the Criminal Investigation Department of (in this case) the Metropolitan Police, which is no longer used. The modern equivalent would be Detective Superintendent

ACT I

INT. V.I.P. LOUNGE. LONDON AIRPORT. DAY.

HUNTER watches from window.
International Lounge.

INT. LONDON AIRPORT. DAY. (FILM)

CHARLOTTE RIGBY crosses
lounge towards V.I.P. door.

INT. V.I.P. LOUNGE. DAY.

CHARLOTTE enters.
HUNTER stays by window.

CHARLOTTE:	Good afternoon, sir.
HUNTER:	Good afternoon. (Beat) Well?
CHARLOTTE:	She had these, sir. (Hands HUNTER papers)
HUNTER:	Where?
CHARLOTTE:	In her handbag.
	(HUNTER looks at the papers.)
HUNTER:	You know what they are?
CHARLOTTE:	I don't read Czech, sir.
HUNTER:	This is Polish.
CHARLOTTE:	Serious, sir?
HUNTER:	Not yet...but it will be. Tell me about her.
CHARLOTTE:	She's very nervous, sir. Very antagonistic. Towards men especially. It seems a pity.
HUNTER:	Why?
CHARLOTTE:	She's very beautiful, sir. I think she had a big paternal fixation, but it went sour.
HUNTER:	A big what?

CHARLOTTE:	She was in love with her father, sir.
HUNTER:	You're not my analyst, Rigby. Or anybody else's.
CHARLOTTE:	It's relevant, sir. She hates her father.
HUNTER:	A lot of people do.
CHARLOTTE:	He's not their father, sir. She's reacted against him. Violently. That's why she supports North Vietnam.
HUNTER:	She on to you?
CHARLOTTE:	No, sir. There was an American on the plane. I think he was C.I.A. She's on to him.
HUNTER:	That's nice, Rigby. I like it.
CHARLOTTE:	Thank you, sir.

INT. LONDON AIRPORT. DAY. FILM.

MARY LEE TOWNSEND walks across lounge. She wears air-hostess uniform. American Airlines.

INT. V.I.P. LOUNGE. DAY.

HUNTER:	I see what you mean. (CHARLOTTE joins him, and sighs.) You're not fond of her by any chance?
CHARLOTTE:	No sir. Just envious.

INT. LONDON AIRPORT. DAY. FILM.

An American walks across lounge. He carries a zip-bag.

INT. VIP LOUNGE. DAY.

CHARLOTTE:	That's the American, sir. His name's Hacker. Robert Hacker. I can call him Bobby.
HUNTER:	Do you?
CHARLOTTE:	I will tonight, sir.
HUNTER:	Splendid. Anything else?
CHARLOTTE:	She has a boy-friend, sir.
HUNTER:	I thought you said she hated men?
CHARLOTTE:	Not this one, sir.
HUNTER:	Who is he?

CHARLOTTE: I don't know sir.
HUNTER: Then find out, Rigby. Find out at once.

INT. CALLAN'S FLAT. DAY.

CALLAN busy with toy soldiers. Ring at bell. CALLAN opens door on chain, sees MARY LEE, unobtrusively removes chain.

CALLAN: (Southern accent) Well hi you all.
MARY LEE: (As she enters) Now you just stop that.
CALLAN: You all just come inside honey, and Uncle Tom will fix you the finest mint julep you all ever did see.

(He locks and chains door.)

MARY LEE: You're still worried?
CALLAN: I'm always worried.
MARY LEE: But why, David?
CALLAN: You don't ask me and I won't tell you.

(She shrugs, then stands, facing him.)

MARY LEE: Well?

(CALLAN kisses her.)

MARY LEE: I shouldn't always have to ask.
CALLAN: I like it when you ask.

(HE goes into kitchen. MARY LEE looks at battle laid out on table. (Model soldiers.) CALLAN comes back, carrying glasses.)

MARY LEE: What's this one?
CALLAN: Second Bull Run. Lee's still going to win.
MARY LEE: He always does. People have got Robert E. Lee all wrong.
CALLAN: You don't tell me.
MARY LEE: The original White Anglo-Saxon Protestant bastard. Because he was a gentleman people don't notice the rest.
CALLAN: Such as?
MARY LEE: He fought for slavery. And he fought to win.

(She turns. CALLAN hands her a glass. She sips.)

MARY LEE: Mint julep. (She sips again.) It's good.
CALLAN: Of course.
MARY LEE: Where on earth did you –
CALLAN: I did a job there once. Richmond, Virginia.
MARY LEE: What sort of job?

CALLAN:	I was a kind of executive.
MARY LEE:	Business?
CALLAN:	Yes. Business.
MARY LEE:	You might have met my father.
CALLAN:	I didn't.
MARY LEE:	I mean, Richmond isn't all that far from Washington. (Beat) Do you know how long my father's been a Senator?
CALLAN:	How long?
MARY LEE:	Twenty seven years. For twenty seven years my father has blocked every attempt at progress in the United States. I guess that must be a record. He hasn't made one decent, liberal gesture in his life.
CALLAN:	So you're making up for him?
MARY LEE:	He's what they call a hawk. You know what that means? He's for the war in Vietnam all the way, right up to the bomb. He'll do anything for a vote. He used to show my mother around as if she was Miss America – and then he tried the same thing on me. Only I wouldn't let him. I started to think for myself – go to protest meetings. I even went on a Freedom March in Alabama and I wound up in goal. You know what he did? He disowned me. On TV coast-to-coast hook up. He's my father. And I hate his guts. I wish he was –

(CALLAN covers her mouth.)

CALLAN:	That's enough.
MARY LEE:	I'm sorry.
CALLAN:	Don't start that either. (Beat) You were supposed to cook my dinner tonight...shall I do it?
MARY LEE:	No. I'll be all right in a minute. Just hold me, David. Just hold me.

(CALLAN embraces her.)

INT. HUNTER'S H.Q. DAY.

CHARLOTTE with HUNTER.

CHARLOTTE:	I'm afraid I missed her sir.
HUNTER:	You know where to reach her?
CHARLOTTE:	She's at a hotel in Victoria.
HUNTER:	Get on to her. Find out about her boy-friend.
CHARLOTTE:	Very good, sir.

(Buzzer rings. HUNTER presses button.)

SECRETARY:	(on screen) Mr Hacker sir.

(HUNTER looks at screen. HACKER being searched.)

HUNTER: Show him in.

(He turns button off)

HUNTER: (to CHARLOTTE) Wait next door, will you? Watch this on the monitor. We might learn something useful.

(CHARLOTTE goes out. HUNTER waits as HACKER enters.)

HACKER: Colonel Hunter.
HUNTER: How do you do, Mr Hacker?

(HACKER buttons his jacket)

HACKER: You guys are pretty thorough.
HUNTER: That's the way we stay alive. Your identification, please.
HACKER: But I already showed it to –

(HUNTER holds out his hand. HACKER shrugs, hands over papers. HUNTER reads, sits back.)

HUNTER: What can we do for you, Mr Hacker?
HACKER: It's kind of a long story.
HUNTER: I'm rarely bored, Mr Hacker.
HACKER: Back in the States we have a Senator called Townsend. He's pretty big stuff. On a lot of committees. A hawk we call him. You know what that means?
HUNTER: He wants to drop H-bombs on Vietnam. (Beat) He's a damn nuisance, Mr Hacker.
HACKER: I envy you, Colonel. You're allowed to say what you think about Senator Townsend. I'm not.
HUNTER: You want me to get rid of him?
HACKER: Oh brother! (Beat) He's got a daughter, Mary Lee. Her mother died three years back. Her mother was from Savannah Georgia. A very beautiful woman. So's the daughter. Unfortunately the mother was the only one who could control her. Since her death, Mary Lee's run pretty wild.

(HUNTER goes to cupboard, takes out a file.)

HUNTER: She's joined some protest organisation. Done a Freedom March. Some Ban the Bomb stuff.
HACKER: You're pretty thorough, Colonel.
HUNTER: She did some of her protesting over here.
HACKER: The worthy senator's disowned her. It's like something out of Dickens.
HUNTER: Cast out into the snow.
HACKER: Only she didn't starve. She got herself a job.

HUNTER: Air hostess. American Airlines.

HACKER: That's right. She does a trip from Panama to the West Indies, then London. We figure she may be –

HUNTER: Acting as a courier for Cuba. And so she is, Mr Hacker.

HACKER: You're sure of this?

(HUNTER hands over papers from file.)

HUNTER: This is stuff she brought from the Polish trade mission there.

HACKER: How did you get hold of it?

HUNTER: Mr Hacker, please. The translation is there too.

HACKER: O.K. (Reads)

HUNTER: As you can see, it's relatively harmless.

HACKER: Yeah. So far. (He puts down papers) What do you propose to do about it?

HUNTER: I? Nothing. She'll know by now that the papers have gone. That's her warning. It should be enough. Her Majesty's Government has no wish to embarrass the daughter of an - er - eminent Senator.

HACKER: That's not quite the way we read it, Colonel.

HUNTER: No?

HACKER: The way we read it, she'll do anything to hit back at the Senator. This courier stuff's just a beginning. Once the Commies get their hooks on her, they'll use her for something big – then blow her. We'll have to put her on trial. The headlines will look great, won't they: 'Senator's Daughter Spies For Reds'.

HUNTER: That's quite possible, of course. But hardly my business.

HACKER: We want you to make it your business.

HUNTER: To do what, Mr Hacker?

HACKER: Get rid of her.

HUNTER: My dear fellow –

HACKER: Hell. Don't get me wrong. I don't mean we want her killed.

HUNTER: What then?

HACKER: (shrugs) A few years in prison. For something non-political. Five would be about right. Townsend won't run again after his next term.

HUNTER: But why don't you do it?

HACKER: In the States? Townsend couldn't take the publicity. If it happened here - he could just about get away with it.

HUNTER: The Senator mightn't like us for this. He could be a bad enemy to my people...

HACKER: Colonel - it was his idea.

(HUNTER looks at him.)

HACKER: Of course I'm authorised to offer a certain amount of information in return.

HUNTER: What?

HACKER: A new escape route from East Berlin.

HUNTER: No, thank you. We have our own arrangements.

HACKER: Red China? Their first strike plans for Hong Kong?

HUNTER: We have them, Mr Hacker. But it might be useful to check them against yours.

HACKER: It's a deal then?

HUNTER: It's a deal. Where can I reach you?

HACKER: I'm in Belgravia. I've got a service flat there.

HUNTER: How grand you Americans are.

HACKER: You can reach me here.

(Hands over card.)

HACKER: How soon will it be?

HUNTER: You're in a hurry I take it? (HACKER nods: yes.) We'll get on to it at once. (Beat) You free for dinner tonight?

HACKER: No, thank you, Colonel. Unless it's business, I've got a date for tonight.

(Shot of CHARLOTTE, watching monitor. She grins, and goes to work on her makeup.)

INT. CALLAN'S FLAT. DAY.

MARY LEE in front of mirror. She wears Callan's robe. On table are remains of meal. CALLAN lies on bed, pours wine.

CALLAN: Having a good time?

MARY LEE: It'll cost me a quid just to have my hair put right...Quid's what you say, isn't it?

CALLAN: Sometimes. Sometimes I say a nicker, but not when I take you out. Nicker's vulgar.

MARY LEE: So are you. I like you a lot.

CALLAN: (sprawls on bed) If you don't you're a hell of a good actress.

(She goes to him, lies beside him.)

MARY LEE: Swine.

(They kiss. She eases away, imitates his voice.)

MARY LEE: Having a good time?

CALLAN: The best.

(He kisses her again.)

MARY LEE: I'm sorry David, I've got to go.

CALLAN: You off again already?

MARY LEE: No. I've got this business date. (Beat) I'm free all day tomorrow.

CALLAN: Tomorrow I'm not all that expensive myself.

(She gets up, goes to mirror.)

MARY LEE: You're the nicest swine I ever met. (Beat) Oh - look at my hair.

(She opens handbag, takes out comb. As she does so, she sees an envelope, flap out. She takes it out, pulls out folded newspaper. CALLAN lies watching her. She turns to him.)

MARY LEE: I want my papers, please.

CALLAN: I don't get it love.

MARY LEE: My papers. I want them back.

CALLAN: What papers?

MARY LEE: Look David, if this is some kind of a joke -

CALLAN: I don't play that kind of joke on anybody. Least of all on girls who look like you.

MARY LEE: Do you want money then? I haven't got any right now - but I can get –

CALLAN: Mary Lee, don't be stupid.

MARY LEE: Oh, my God. I should have known if I met a guy like you it wouldn't be for anything but –

CALLAN: Finish it, love –

MARY LEE: Trouble. That's all I ever got from any man.

(CALLAN gets up, goes to her, takes her by the shoulders. She tries to break away, but can't. He holds her chin, turns her so that her eyes look into his.)

CALLAN: You think I'm an actor too? You think what we had from each other was just a big act? Do you?

MARY LEE: I don't know any more. I just don't know. Maybe I needed you too much. So I fooled myself –

CALLAN: You're not very flattering to me, are you?

MARY LEE: You took my papers?

CALLAN: When? When did I take them?

(She hesitates.)

CALLAN: Let's see what you've got.

(She holds out newspaper and envelope.)

CALLAN: Wait...what are you mixed up in, love?

MARY LEE: Are you trying to tell me you don't know?

CALLAN: Do the coppers want you?

MARY LEE: They might. But it isn't – wrong. I swear it isn't.

(CALLAN sighs, puts on gloves from drawer, then handles blank sheets and envelope.)

CALLAN: Somebody slit this envelope with a sharp knife - right? (She nods.) A knife like a razor. See how carefully it's done. You can hardly see the cut. Then they cut the newspaper exactly to size. This newspaper. (Reads name.) The New York Times. Look at it. Now you can search this flat all day and all night if you want to - and I'll give you a million for every page of the New York Times you find. (She looks away.) And look at this envelope. It's out, just like the newspaper. How long would it take to do that? Two minutes? Three maybe. We haven't been a minute out of one another's sight since you got here.

MARY LEE: David, I'm sorry.

CALLAN: You're at it again.

MARY LEE: I have to say it. I have to. I had no right to doubt you like that.

CALLAN: Forget it. Rule Number One is Doubt Everybody. You better start remembering that. (Beat) What are you up to anyway?

MARY LEE: No. I can't tell anybody - even you.

CALLAN: You said the rozzers might be after you.

MARY LEE: Rozzers?

CALLAN: Fuzz. Cops.

MARY LEE: I'm not a criminal. David.

(CALLAN smiles.)

CALLAN: No, love. I didn't think you were.

MARY LEE: I'm just trying to do some good for people.

CALLAN: You want me to help you?

MARY LEE: Oh, please. But I can't tell you anything.

CALLAN: (quickly) I don't want to know. (Beat) They must have made the switch on the plane. (As she starts to question.) Where did you get the papers?

MARY LEE: Kingston, Jamaica.

CALLAN: You had the bag with you all the time, till you got on the plane. Right?

MARY LEE: Of course. Then I put it down.

CALLAN: Where?

MARY LEE: On a shelf near the john.

CALLAN: So anybody going to the toilet could have lifted it. Right?

MARY LEE: I guess so.

CALLAN: And one of them did. I don't suppose you noticed if anybody had a New York Times?

MARY LEE: We give them out to read. We had 53 passengers. I guess half of them took one.

CALLAN: You notice anybody special on the plane?

MARY LEE: No...there was Charlotte, of course.

CALLAN: Who's Charlotte?

MARY LEE: Charlotte Rigby.

CALLAN: You known her long?

MARY LEE: A couple of weeks. We met in Kingston. (Beat) Charlotte wouldn't do that.

CALLAN: You're forgetting Rule Number One.

MARY LEE: Her grandfather's an Earl or something.

CALLAN: We've had some pretty dodgy Earls, love ...

MARY LEE: But there was a man with her. An American. He tried to pick her up.

CALLAN: Blokes on business don't usually do that –

MARY LEE: And he looked at me. When he first came aboard. As if he'd seen me before. It's just - oh, it's hard to explain. I didn't like it.

CALLAN: Suppose it's him? What then?

MARY LEE: I don't know.

CALLAN: You think your friends here might want their papers back? They might play it rough?

MARY LEE: No. They promised me. No violence. Ever. Anyway - I don't know where he lives.

CALLAN: Charlotte might. (He waits.) You going to ask her?

MARY LEE: Maybe. (Beat) You know an awful lot about - all this.

CALLAN: I used to be a crook, love.

MARY LEE: You're joshing me –

CALLAN: No. I've done porridge - that's prison. Two years. And that was it. When I came out I went legit. It pays better. That's how I could go to Jamaica for a holiday and pick myself an air-hostess.

MARY LEE: Yeah, right off the trees. I never seem to bring anything but trouble.

CALLAN: Maybe you go looking for it. Look Mary Lee, when I was in the nick we had a couple of politicals inside as well. Communists. Blokes who gave stuff to the Russians. Now I'm not asking what you're up to, but I'm going to tell you something. Those people are trouble. You know why? Because they're fanatics. They don't care who gets hurt if it makes the world go their way. Now you remember that.

MARY LEE: I will.

CALLAN: And get out of here. Now, while you still can.

MARY LEE: It's too late, David. I brought the papers.

CALLAN: In a bloody great envelope. You poor little fool, don't you know anything? If those papers had been important they'd have been on microfilm. It's you they want.

MARY LEE: Why should they?

CALLAN: Because of your father. (She covers her face.) You've got to get out, love. Now.

INT. CHARLOTTE'S FLAT. NIGHT.

CHARLOTTE enters hall, switches on light. HACKER lurches in after her. Drunk. She opens living-room door. Enters. HACKER follows.

INT. LIVING ROOM. NIGHT.

HACKER: Just a nightcap, huh? What d'you say?
CHARLOTTE: Coffee?
HACKER: Ah, come on.
CHARLOTTE: Coffee.

(She goes into kitchen, sound of running water. HACKER sprawls on sofa. His head drops. CHARLOTTE comes back in, lifts his feet on to sofa. Takes off his shoes.)

CHARLOTTE: Might as well be cosy.
HACKER: That's right. (His head falls back.)
CHARLOTTE: Mr Hacker. (No answer) Bobby darling. (No answer. CHARLOTTE begins to search him.)

INT. CALLAN'S FLAT. NIGHT.

(CALLAN alone, reads London Telephone Directory.)

CALLAN: Rigby. Charlotte. Chelsea. Where else?

(He picks up phone. Dials a number.)

LONELY: (SOV) Yes?
CALLAN: Lonely, old son, you're in luck. I got two birds for you to follow.

INT. CHARLOTTE'S LIVING ROOM. NIGHT.

(CHARLOTTE replaces the sleeping HACKER's wallet. The phone rings.)

CHARLOTTE: Damn.

(She goes out to hall, picks up phone.)

CHARLOTTE: Yes? Oh hello, Charlie.
HUNTER: He's with you?

CHARLOTTE:	Yes. That's right.
HUNTER:	You searched him?
CHARLOTTE:	Not a thing. Not a single, solitary thing.
HUNTER:	It isn't in his room either. Why do the CIA have to practise being cautious on us?
CHARLOTTE:	I'm awfully sorry –
HUNTER:	Not your fault. We'll just have to give him what he wants.
CHARLOTTE:	Just as soon as I see her.
HUNTER:	You haven't found her yet?
CHARLOTTE:	No. I have been rather busy –
HUNTER:	So have I. Try the hotel.
CHARLOTTE:	I have.
HUNTER:	And?
CHARLOTTE:	Not yet. Later maybe.
HUNTER:	This is most urgent, Rigby.
CHARLOTTE:	I'll remember.
HUNTER:	Good. Find out about her boyfriend, too. And don't underestimate friend Hacker.
CHARLOTTE:	I won't.
	(She tilts mirror with her foot. Shot of HACKER searching her handbag.)
CHARLOTTE:	Not any more.
HUNTER:	Quick as you can, Rigby.
CHARLOTTE:	Sweet of you to ask me. Goodbye Charlie.
	(She hangs up, loudly. Enters living room.)

INT. LIVING ROOM. NIGHT.

	(HACKER on sofa, exactly as he was.)
CHARLOTTE:	Colonel Hunter says I shouldn't under-estimate you.
	(HACKER sits up.)
HACKER:	Well I'll be damned.
	(He puts on his shoes.)
HACKER:	I had you tagged for the opposition.
CHARLOTTE:	No. I'm the one who's going to put your little girl away for you, Bobby darling.
HACKER:	Great. Only you get the Hong Kong information afterwards, baby. Remember that.
CHARLOTTE:	A girl has to try, Bobby darling.
HACKER:	A girl has tried. So knock it off, huh? You deliver - and I'll deliver.
	(Bell rings. CHARLOTTE goes to Speak-Phone system.)

CHARLOTTE:	Yes?
MARY LEE:	(SOV) It's Mary Lee, honey. Can I come up?
CHARLOTTE:	Darling, of course. Just give me a minute to slip something on. (She turns to HACKER) You'll have to go, Mr Hacker. That's my old chum. Mary Lee Townsend. Don't you think that's nice?
HACKER:	I think that's wonderful, baby. I think you are too. (Beat) You'd better be.

END OF ACT ONE

ACT II

INT. CHARLOTTE'S FLAT. NIGHT.

MARY LEE alone. CHARLOTTE, wearing dressing-gown, enters from kitchen. She carries coffee. Pours as they talk.

CHARLOTTE: You really think this fellow Hacker robbed you?
MARY LEE: Yes, I do.
CHARLOTTE: But darling –
MARY LEE: I'm not saying he was a thief or anything.
CHARLOTTE: But that's exactly what you are doing.
MARY LEE: No. This is a personal thing.
CHARLOTTE: You mean it has something to do with your father?
MARY LEE: My father. Yes. Where can I reach him, Charlotte?
CHARLOTTE: Darling, I don't know. (MARY LEE looks at her.) If I did I'd take you there myself. Honestly.
MARY LEE: I don't know where to start looking –
CHARLOTTE: Wait a minute. I almost forgot. He asked me to a party. Tomorrow night. He's supposed to give me a ring, tomorrow, to find out if I can go. Why don't we both go darling?
MARY LEE: I don't feel much like a party.
CHARLOTTE: It'll give you a chance to talk to him. Find out what he's like. He didn't look like a sneak-thief to me.
MARY LEE: He wouldn't.
CHARLOTTE: I quite liked him actually. (Beat) You ought to give him a chance, Mary Lee. You haven't got an awful lot to go on, have you?
MARY LEE: Maybe not, but –
CHARLOTTE: And you want to meet him anyway.
MARY LEE: All right.
CHARLOTTE: Good. I'd just as soon take a chum along. (As MARY LEE looks.) It could be pretty wild, darling. One of these psychelelic do's. L.S.D. and all that, I can't say I'm madly fond of it myself, but it makes people do the most extraordinary things.
MARY LEE: I don't want to take that stuff.

CHARLOTTE: Darling, of course not, if you did you'd miss all the fun.

MARY LEE: This Hacker - is he hooked on it?

CHARLOTTE: I shouldn't think so for a moment. Rather dreary, I thought. He's just got a couple of arty friends. (She laughs) Don't worry, darling, everybody will be so blocked, they won't know a word you're saying. (Beat) Bring your boy-friend along if you're worried.

MARY LEE: David? I don't think he'd go for that sort of party.

CHARLOTTE: Tell him you want protection.

MARY LEE: But how can we go? We don't know anybody. We haven't even been invited.

CHARLOTTE: Darling, nobody else will, either. It isn't that sort of party.

MARY LEE: Well. O.K., I'll ask him.

CHARLOTTE: I hope he's a big, strong man.

MARY LEE: Big enough.

CHARLOTTE: And good-looking?

MARY LEE: Yes.

CHARLOTTE: You don't sound very sure.

MARY LEE: He's very gentle. He makes me laugh. And yet sometimes - I'm scared of him.

CHARLOTTE: Scared he might hurt you?

MARY LEE: He's the kind of man - if you got him mad, really mad, he wouldn't stop till he killed you.

CHARLOTTE: I adore men like that. Where on earth do you find them?

MARY LEE: There's only one.

CHARLOTTE: Darling, I'm not trying to steal him from you. At least I don't think so. It's just that if I'm taking him to a party, I've got to know his name.

MARY LEE: It's Callan. David Callan.

INT. HUNTER'S H.Q. MORNING.

HUNTER sits, watching film. The film is not very good – 8mm. stuff - shots of men in cars, walking etc. Buzzer sounds. HUNTER flips switch.

HUNTER: Yes?

SECRETARY: (SOV) Rigby's here, sir.

HUNTER: Send her in.

(He continues to watch as CHARLOTTE enters.)

HUNTER: Sit down, Rigby. Watch.

(She sits. Shot of short, burly man.)

HUNTER: Who is he?
CHARLOTTE: Dimitri Mihailov, sir. KGB executive.
HUNTER: And this?

(Shot of another man.)

CHARLOTTE: Luka Mimonnian, sir. Another KGB executive. He often works with Mihailov.

(HUNTER turns off film.)

HUNTER: What do they do?
CHARLOTTE: They're executioners, sir.
HUNTER: One day they might be yours. Do you ever think of that?
CHARLOTTE: Yes, sir.
HUNTER: And?
CHARLOTTE: It frightens me - but I couldn't give this up.
HUNTER: You're doing very well.
CHARLOTTE: Thank you, sir.
HUNTER: Just keep watching the pictures. Know your enemies. Know them the minute you see them. (Beat) How is Miss Townsend?
CHARLOTTE: She's going to a party tonight. A psychedelic party.
HUNTER: Drugs?
CHARLOTTE: It's mostly nonsense, sir. Rather pathetic people trying to show off. Some of them will take L.S.D. - some won't. But a pusher might go there. (HUNTER smiles.) Mary Lee's father has a lot of money - and she's had to start to live on her salary. She might try to augment it a little. (Beat) I understand it's easy to get heroin in some of the places she visits.
HUNTER: How much will you need?
CHARLOTTE: Quite a lot. A pusher would go to a party like that to sell, sir.

(HUNTER makes a note.)

HUNTER: You'll get it by this afternoon...what's the punishment for selling drugs, Rigby?
CHARLOTTE: For a first offence they usually get five years, sir.
HUNTER: What very tidy minds women have. (Beat) Did you find out about her boy-friend?
CHARLOTTE: Yes, sir. He might be a difficulty.
HUNTER: Indeed?
CHARLOTTE: It seems he's the violent type, sir.
HUNTER: He's going to the party?
CHARLOTTE: Yes, sir. I thought I'd better have a look at him.
HUNTER: Hacker going too?
CHARLOTTE: Yes sir.
HUNTER: He ought to be there. See the goods delivered. He can keep an eye on this violent feller too. What's his name?

CHARLOTTE: Callan, sir. David Callan.
HUNTER: Oh, good God!
CHARLOTTE: You know him, sir?
HUNTER: He used to work for me, Rigby. He's very, very good.
CHARLOTTE: Too good for Mr Hacker sir?
HUNTER: Callan could eat Mr Hacker and then go out to lunch.
CHARLOTTE: I could plant some on him, too.
HUNTER: No, Rigby. Leave that to me. I don't think you're quite ready for Callan yet.

INT. EXPENSIVE BAR. DAY.

Bar is ante-room to restaurant. CALLAN sits on bar-stool. He looks at home in these surroundings. LONELY enters, crosses to him.

CALLAN: (without looking round) Blimey - who d'you think you are - Rockerfeller? This isn't you at all, mate.
(He subsides as barman comes over.)

BARMAN: Yes sir?
LONELY: Half of bitter.
BARMAN: We don't sell draught beer.
CALLAN: Give him a lager then. Imported. And call him sir. He likes it. Makes him feel he's back at Eton.
BARMAN: Yes sir. I'm sorry sir.
LONELY: And give my friend a large Scotch.
BARMAN: Yes sir.

(He goes.)

LONELY: Thanks, Mr Callan. Geezers like that get right up my nose. My money's as good as anybody elses.
CALLAN: It smells more, that's all.
(Barman brings drinks. LONELY pays with note. BARMAN goes.)

CALLAN: What the hell are you doing here anyway?
LONELY: I lost her, Mr Callan.
(BARMAN brings change. LONELY looks at it. Picks it up.)

LONELY: Here, my man.

(Gives tip.)

BARMAN: Thank you sir, it'll come in useful if I want to make a phone call.
LONELY: Sarcastic git.
CALLAN: What do you mean you lost her?

LONELY: She went in the 'Ladies' at Waterloo Station, Mr Callan. There's three entrances. I couldn't follow her could I? I'd get myself arrested. So I waited in the station. She'd just bought a ticket to Richmond. Only she didn't use it.

CALLAN: Did she rumble you?

LONELY: I don't think so. I always do my best work for you, Mr Callan. But she's wide, that Rigby bird is, very wide. (Beat) She's not on the batter, is she?

CALLAN: Language, Lonely.

LONELY: Didn't look like it to me, anyway. But she's bent, I know she is.

CALLAN: How?

LONELY: I got a feeling. You know how we are, Mr Callan. Always on the look-out for trouble –

CALLAN: Yes. I know.

LONELY: This bird's like that. Wide.

CALLAN: Is she now?

LONELY: I'd sooner follow the other one, Mr Callan.

CALLAN: You're a nasty, lecherous little man.

LONELY: Just a hobby, Mr Callan.

CALLAN: Here. (Takes out key) Go back to my place. There's some beer in the cupboard.

LONELY: Thanks, Mr Callan.

CALLAN: If anybody phones me, say I've gone away for a few days.

LONELY: Where to, Mr Callan?

CALLAN: You don't know. Tell them you're a poor destitute waif I brought in off the streets and gave a temporary home to - and don't touch anything.

LONELY: You can trust me, Mr Callan.

CALLAN: I can do more than that, mate.

LONELY: Mr Callan, I swear to you.

CALLAN: That's all right, Lonely. Off you go.

(LONELY leaves. The BARMAN approaches, sniffs, then comes round and removes LONELY's stool.)

CALLAN: It takes all kinds, doesn't it?

BARMAN: I suppose so, sir.

(MARY LEE enters, comes up to CALLAN and kisses him.)

MARY LEE: I'm not late, am I?

CALLAN: You're never late. Very unfeminine.

MARY LEE: Really?

CALLAN: The rest of you makes up for it. What would you like?

MARY LEE: Whisky sour, please.

(The BARMAN prepares drink.)

MARY LEE: David, I -

(She breaks off as BARMAN comes up with her drink, then leaves.)

CALLAN: Yes?

MARY LEE: I have to go to a party tonight. Hacker's going to be there.

CALLAN: You going on your own?

MARY LEE: No, Charlotte's going. It was her idea...it sounds like a pretty wild party. L.S.D. and all that.

CALLAN: You want to get mixed up with drugs?

MARY LEE: I can't help it. I've got to see Hacker.

CALLAN: You've got to get out of here. Believe me, love. I told you that last night and I meant every word.

MARY LEE: If it was just for myself - of course I'd get out. But there are others. Poor people. Good people. They depend on me. The least I can do is try to get my papers back.

CALLAN: If you get nicked you haven't got a chance.

MARY LEE: I know it. But the people I'm working for - they've never had a chance.

(CALLAN sighs)

CALLAN: All right. Go on.

MARY LEE: I don't know what –

CALLAN: Haven't you got a job lined up for me?

MARY LEE: I want you to take me to the party.

CALLAN: I'm the heavy, is that it? (She looks be-wildered.) The minder, darling. The bodyguard.

MARY LEE: I know it sounds silly.

CALLAN: No. Not silly at all.

MARY LEE: What then?

CALLAN: Dodgy. Very, very dodgy.

MARY LEE: If you can't do it, of course. I'll understand -

CALLAN: I can do it. (Beat.) But there's only one way... my way.

MARY LEE: (hesitates) All right.

CALLAN: Don't you see what you're getting into?

MARY LEE: It's only this one time.

CALLAN: They should set that to music. It would sell a million.

MARY LEE: If you'd seen the people I've seen. In the Caribbean, where the tourists go. The slums. They're like a nightmare. People like me are the only chance they've got.

CALLAN: All right. I'll come with you. This time.

MARY LEE: Thank you.

CALLAN: You always going to put the world right?

MARY LEE: I'm going to try.

CALLAN: (sighs) What on earth started you off on it?

MARY LEE:	College, I guess. I loved it there. It was the first time in my life I felt I'd got away from my father.
CALLAN:	Bryn Mawr?
MARY LEE:	Vassar. With all the other poor little rich girls.
CALLAN:	I knew a girl who went to Vassar.
MARY LEE:	I hate her already. What happened?
CALLAN:	It was very sad. She took ill. Very ill. In fact she was dying.
MARY LEE:	Oh.
CALLAN:	I went to see her. She had something to ask me. Very important, she said.
MARY LEE:	What was it?
CALLAN:	She wanted to know if poor people went to the same heaven as rich people, and I told her they did...so she went to Bermuda instead.
MARY LEE:	You bastard. Just for that I won't invite you back for lunch.
CALLAN:	If you don't, I'll stay here and get drunk...And a heavy's no good with a hangover.
MARY LEE:	I don't want to think about tonight.
CALLAN:	I want you to think about it. It's your life. What do you want to wreck it for?
MARY LEE:	O.K. Let's go and eat, and maybe I'll tell you.

INT. CALLAN'S FLAT. DAY.

LONELY at ease, with beer. He is playing patience - and cheating. Phone rings. LONELY picks it up.

LONELY:	Hallo?
WOMAN:	(SOV) Mr Callan please.
LONELY:	(posh) Who's calling?
WOMAN:	Tell him Charley wants to speak to him.
LONELY:	Mr Callan's away for a few days. He said –
WOMAN:	One moment please.
	(LONELY scowls at phone.)
HUNTER:	(SOV) Hallo?
LONELY:	Hallo.
	(INTERCUT with HUNTER at HQ. CHARLOTTE listens on earpiece.)
HUNTER:	I'm an old friend of Callan's I'd like to speak to him now. It's rather urgent.
LONELY:	Sorry guv. He's had to go away for a few days. I'm just looking after the place for him.
HUNTER:	I see. When will he be back?

LONELY: He didn't say. He's like that, Mr Callan is.

HUNTER: Yes indeed. If he should contact you, ask him to give me a ring will you?

LONELY: Right you are guv. What name shall I say?

HUNTER: Just tell him to call Charley. He knows the number.

(LONELY hangs up, resumes cheating at patience.)

INT. H.Q. DAY.

HUNTER with CHARLOTTE.

HUNTER: He'll be there at the party, Rigby.

CHARLOTTE: That man may be telling the truth, sir.

HUNTER: That man is an inveterate liar. That's one reason Callan uses him. He also has the most disagreeable smell I've ever encountered on another human being.

(CHARLOTTE reacts.)

HUNTER: Well?

CHARLOTTE: There was a man like that on the tube this morning.

HUNTER: Was there indeed? Do be careful, Rigby.

CHARLOTTE: I will sir.

(HUNTER takes from drawer some small, white packets.)

HUNTER: Heroin. (He hands them to her.) Do you ever find our trade disgusting?

CHARLOTTE: No, sir. Just necessary.

INT. HOTEL ROOM. DAY.

MARY LEE putting on dress. CALLAN zips her up.

MARY LEE: Thanks...I hope this is right for a psychedelic party. I don't know what you're supposed to wear.

CALLAN: Everything. Or nothing. (Beat) This feller Hacker. Did you ever get close to him?

MARY LEE: I served him dinner.

CALLAN: Was he carrying a gun?

MARY LEE: Of course not!

CALLAN: You sure? Because I'm not, love.

(She turns to him. CALLAN embraces her.)

CALLAN: Just take it easy. We'll be all right.

(He goes to phone. Dials.)

LONELY: (SOV) Hallo?

CALLAN: Callan.

LONELY: Just one call, Mr Callan. Bloke called Charlie. You're to call him. Urgent, he said.

CALLAN: O.K.

LONELY: Can I go now?

CALLAN: No.

LONELY: Don't you want me to follow any more birds, Mr Callan?

CALLAN: When I say you can go, you follow your own birds. (He looks at MARY LEE.) It won't do you any good.

(He hangs up.)

MARY LEE: I'm all set.

CALLAN: You look marvellous.

MARY LEE: Say my name as well.

CALLAN: You look marvellous, Mary Lee.

MARY LEE: That was nice. But I'm still scared. (Beat) Let's go.

INT. FLAT. EVENING.

The flat is in an expensive part of London. It is spacious, wildly decorated, full of way-out people. Music in background (e.g. Thigpen Psychedelic movie projected as a poet recites through megaphone).

POET: As the mushroom expands into a disaster
That negatives the sky
And the skin dissolves
The bones melt into steam,
And all flesh is a barbecue
Roasted on politics spit
Then it is too late,
Even for the flower.
Because without a man
Any man
There can be no symbol.
Even a flower.

(The POET subsides. HOST hands him L.S.D. on sugar-lump.)

HOST: You want to make a trip?
POET: Want to? Have to.
HOST: Go man.

(POET takes sugar. CALLAN and MARY LEE enter. HOST ignores them. It is CHARLOTTE who goes to them.)

CHARLOTTE: Darling.

(She goes to them, kisses MARY LEE.)

MARY LEE: This is David Callan.
CHARLOTTE: Mary Lee's told me so much about you.
CALLAN: It was nice of you to ask me.
CHARLOTTE: Well I didn't. Not really. It was Bobby's idea. (Calls) Bobby darling!

(HACKER comes over.)

CHARLOTTE: This is David Callan.
HACKER: Hallo David.
CHARLOTTE: Bobby Hacker.
CALLAN: How d'you do?
CHARLOTTE: You remember Mary Lee, of course?
HACKER: Indeed I do. That was a very pleasant flight we had together.
MARY LEE: Why, thank you.
CHARLOTTE: Cyprian! Cyprian darling! (The HOST comes over.)
CHARLOTTE: Cyprian, these are two very special friends of ours, Mary Lee Townsend and David Callan.
CYPRIAN: Welcome darlings. Any friend of these good people I know I can trust.
CALLAN: You can indeed.
CYPRIAN: Dear boy, one has to be so careful. Now what can I get you - or have you brought your own?
CALLAN: Scotch please.
MARY LEE: Me too.
CYPRIAN: Sweet old-fashioned things.

(He goes away)

CHARLOTTE: Isn't he scrumptious? (To MARY LEE) Come and hang your coat up. I'll show you where.

(They go)

HACKER: You like this sort of party?
CALLAN: (watching the women leave) I like any sort of party.

(CYPRIAN brings drinks.)

CYPRIAN: We must be kindred souls my dear. Do tell me - do you do something creative?
CALLAN: Not any more.
CYPRIAN: But you did once. I'm sure you did once.
CALLAN: I used to be a kind of critic once, but that was a long time ago.

CYPRIAN: Critics terrify me. So objective. (Sees another man enter) Roger!

(CYPRIAN swoops.)

HACKER: Who did you do your criticism for?

CALLAN: Oh - it was all local stuff. Nothing you're supposed to have heard of.

HACKER: You'd be surprised what I'm supposed to have heard of.

CALLAN: Are you a critic too?

HACKER: No. I'm more of a promoter when I work.

CALLAN: And you're working now?

HACKER: I'm still in business. You're not.

(A girl at far end of room on sofa moans, then writhes, gasping. The rest of the party kneels beside her.)

HACKER: Looks like she's having a bad trip.

(The girl screams. CYPRIAN takes her hands, whispers to her.)

HACKER: Freak-out. I hope she makes it back.

(CALLAN watches. He is unobserved. He hits HACKER hard, then catches him, lowers him into chair. As he does so, MARY LEE enters, sees him.)

MARY LEE: What are you doing?

CALLAN: He's having a bad trip too.

MARY LEE: Is he -

CALLAN: He's the man who wants to destroy you. (He moves back. She follows.) Stay with him. Tell Charlotte I've gone for a doctor. Say you asked me to. (She hesitates.)

MARY LEE: You're leaving me?

CALLAN: No. (She is still uncertain.) Do what I tell you love. Or take your own chances.

(She goes back to HACKER. CALLAN moves behind curtains. Shot of CYPRIAN calming the girl. CHARLOTTE enters, comes up to MARY LEE.)

CHARLOTTE: What happened?

MARY LEE: I don't know. He just seemed to collapse...like that girl...

CHARLOTTE: Where's David?

MARY LEE: I sent him for a doctor.

CHARLOTTE: You fool. (Beat) I'm sorry. But you should have asked me first.

(As they talk, CALLAN eases out from curtains, to bedroom.)

INT. BEDROOM. NIGHT.

(Coats piled on beds. CALLAN goes to MARY LEE'S coat, searches it, and her handbag. Finds white packets, opens one, tastes it carefully.)

CALLAN: (SOV) You know your stuff, Charlotte. You really do.

(He finds CHARLOTTE's coat. Puts packets in lining.)

CALLAN: (SOV) It couldn't happen to a nicer girl.

(He goes out.)

INT. LIVING ROOM. NIGHT.

(CYPRIAN kneels by HACKER.)

CYPRIAN: I really think he's unwell.

(CALLAN comes up with towel and bowl of water.)

CALLAN: I think you're right.
CYPRIAN: I mean, it isn't a freak-out at all.

(CALLAN goes to HACKER, loosens his collar, drops one white packet into his breast-pocket, then bathes his forehead. As he does so, loud ring on door-bell.

CYPRIAN: Oh my God! What next?

(He goes. CALLAN still attends to HACKER.)

CHARLOTTE: Did you fetch a doctor?
CALLAN: No. I didn't think it was a good idea.

(CHARLOTTE looks to bedroom, moves away.)

CALLAN: No love. (He takes her arm. She can't move.) Just look after your boyfriend and you won't get hurt.

(He puts the towel in her hands. She attends to HACKER. He groans. CYPRIAN comes in with police including a D.D.I. and a Det. Sergeant.)

CYPRIAN: But I assure you Inspector –
D.D.I.: Later, sir. (To Det.Serg.) Take a look at that one. (Indicates girl.)

(He comes over to HACKER.)

CYPRIAN: I promise you there's nothing –
D.D.I.: It's all in the warrant, sir. Where's your cloakroom?

CYPRIAN: Over there.

(D.D.I. nods his head at door. Two police go to bedroom. D.D.I. crosses to HACKER, whose eyes are open.)

CALLAN: Feeling better, old chap?
D.D.I.: Is one of you Miss Townsend?
MARY LEE: I am.
D.D.I.: Who's this?
CALLAN: This is Mr Hacker.
D.D.I.: You been on a trip, Mr Hacker?
HACKER: I have not. I passed out.
D.D.I.: Stand up sir.

(CALLAN helps him up. D.D.I. searches him. Finds packet, opens it. Tastes.)

D.D.I.: Well sir?
HACKER: I want to talk to a lawyer.

(Policeman comes in with coat.)

D.D.I.: Well?

(Policeman shows him the rest of the packets.)

D.D.I.: Is this yours, Miss Townsend (Indicates coat.)
MARY LEE: No.
D.D.I.: Are you telling the truth Miss?
CALLAN: Of course she is. (To CHARLOTTE) That's your coat, isn't it Charlotte?

END OF ACT II

ACT III

EXT. CALLAN'S FLAT. DAWN.

CALLAN walks to door. Opens it. Chain holds door.

CALLAN: Lonely! (Beat) Open up old son.

(LONELY unhooks chain.)

LONELY: You had me worried, Mr Callan.

(He steps aside. CALLAN enters. Inside, HUNTER sits at table. He and LONELY have been playing cards. He drinks whisky, LONELY, beer.)

CALLAN: Make yourselves at home.

LONELY: This is Charley, Mr Callan.

CALLAN: I know.

LONELY: He said it would be all right to wait here.

CALLAN: Yeah. He would.

(He looks at LONELY's hand - four queens. Then at HUNTER's four aces.)

CALLAN: How much you lose?

LONELY: It wasn't no good playing for money Mr Callan. He cheats more than I do.

CALLAN: A lot worse. (Beat) You better scarper. I'll square up with you tomorrow.

LONELY: Right you are. (He yawns) Goodnight, Charlie. (He goes to door. CALLAN follows.)

LONELY: You want to watch out for that geezer. The posh ones is always the worst.

CALLAN: (Looks at his suit) I was posh myself tonight.

LONELY: Ah. But you was pretending, wasn't you?

(He goes. CALLAN shuts door.)

HUNTER: You should have done what you said. Gone away. Right away.

CALLAN: I couldn't let you do it, Hunter. Not to her.

HUNTER: You did it to my girl. She'll get five years.

CALLAN:	She deserved it.
HUNTER:	Do I deserve it too?
CALLAN:	God alone knows what you deserve mate. (Beat) What happened to Hacker?
HUNTER:	They're deporting him.
CALLAN:	He's lucky.
HUNTER:	Unlike me. The Americans were paying me for this job.
CALLAN:	Information?
HUNTER:	The best. I won't get it now.
CALLAN:	You shouldn't have started on my girl.
HUNTER:	Your girl? I see. Supposing she'd been plain - and not your girl at all. Could I have had her then? Or do I have to ask your permission every time the woman's pretty?
CALLAN:	It's late, Hunter. And you've lost. Go home.
HUNTER:	I never lose, Callan. I can't afford to. (He rises) You're good at your work. Very good. I admit it. Tonight you were masterly. (CALLAN bows) But find yourself another girl. (Beat) This one's ours.
	(He goes out. CALLAN chains the door, sits down, pours drink. Phone rings.)
CALLAN:	Yes?
MARY LEE:	Darling - how are you?
CALLAN:	Fine.
MARY LEE:	Is it all right to come over now?
CALLAN:	Wait
	(He goes to window. Looks out.)
CALLAN:	All right. But make it quick.
	(He hangs up, picks up drink, puts it down. Go to kitchen, takes Noguchi Magnum from behind knife-drawer, straps on shoulder holster.)
	FILM SHOT - MARY LEE leave phone-booth by CALLAN's flat.

INT. CALLAN'S FLAT. DAWN.

	(CALLAN cleans pistol. Knock at door. He goes door.)
CALLAN:	Yes?
MARY LEE:	(SOV) Honey, it's me.
	(CALLAN opens door. Pulls her in. Shuts, chains door.)

CALLAN: Come in.

(He goes back to cleaning pistol.)

MARY LEE: David - what's happening?

CALLAN: We're down to the final argument, love. This one.

(He lifts the pistol.)

MARY LEE: What's happened? Was there someone here?

CALLAN: Yeah. I told you there would he. (Beat) Look - it was you they came for tonight, wasn't it?

MARY LEE: The police asked for me, for sure –

CALLAN: Because you were the one who was supposed to have the heroin

MARY LEE: But –

CALLAN: I found it in your coat.

MARY LEE: And put it in Charlotte's.

CALLAN: She was the operator.

MARY LEE: She was my friend –

CALLAN: Operators don't have friends, love. Just assignments. (Beat) A man came to see me tonight. I'm to lay off you, he said.

MARY LEE: What man? Who sent him?

CALLAN: These jokers never tell you. They don't need to...to me he's the bloke who can have me beaten-up - or even killed - if he thinks it's worth it. Now you get out of here and don't come back. Because there's going to be a next time, believe me. And when it comes, I'm going to need this.

(He lifts the gun again.)

CALLAN: You're lucky I can use it.

MARY LEE: I can't let my friends down now. I can't.

CALLAN: You want to see me kill somebody?

MARY LEE: No, David. I'm going to leave you, too. (He makes no answer.) Please my darling - don't you see - I have to?

CALLAN: It's your life, love.

MARY LEE: David, please. This is the hardest thing I've done in my whole life...I love you.

(He puts down gun.)

MARY LEE: Can I - stay a while?

(He unbuckles holster.)

INT. H.Q. MORNING.

HUNTER with scrambler phone

HUNTER: Yes. Yes. I know. I'm terribly sorry about it.

AMERICAN VOICE:	(distort) Colonel, I'm sorry - but if I don't get action soon, it's no deal. I mean it. I got to get the Senator off my back.
HUNTER:	I'm attending to it now.
VOICE:	I hope so Colonel. For both our sakes.

(Click as AMERICAN hangs up. HUNTER replaces receiver, presses intercom, button.)

SECRETARY:	Yes, sir?
HUNTER:	What time is Meres due back from Geneva?
SECRETARY:	5.30, sir.
HUNTER:	Tell him to see me straightaway.
SECRETARY:	Very good, sir.

(HUNTER releases switch. Yawns. Suddenly he looks weary.)

INT. CALLAN'S FLAT. MORNING.

(CALLAN and MARY LEE in bed. MARY LEE smoking.)

MARY LEE:	What I said to you...I meant it.
CALLAN:	What did you say?
MARY LEE:	Greedy!...I love you...I never thought I'd be able to say that to anybody. (Beat) You going to miss me?
CALLAN:	Yes.
MARY LEE:	How much?
CALLAN:	All the way.

(She turns to look at him.)

MARY LEE:	Yes...you really mean it, don't you?
CALLAN:	Please get out, Mary Lee.
MARY LEE:	Don't spoil it. Let me be happy. It won't last very long.

(She clings to him, then lies back.)

CALLAN:	Want some coffee?
MARY LEE:	I would adore some coffee.

(CALLAN gets out of bed, goes to kitchen, puts on kettle, takes out cups and coffee.)

CALLAN:	(SOV) She deserves the best that one. The very best. (Looks in mirror) And that isn't you, mate. I'm sorry my darling, but you've got to get out of here. And I'm the one who's going to make you. There isn't anybody else.

(He goes from kitchen, looks at her. She lies back, half-asleep, very vulnerable, very beautiful.)

CALLAN: Sorry love, I've got to go out for a bit.
MARY LEE: Must you?
CALLAN: Business. It's important.
MARY LEE: It better be.
CALLAN: I promise you it is. (Beat) Look, you take it easy for a while then I'll come back for you and take you out to lunch.
MARY LEE: And afterwards?
CALLAN: Whatever you say.
MARY LEE: I've got a marvelous idea.

(She yawns, her eyes closes CALLAN picks up phone (soft) takes it to kitchen, looks again at girl asleep.)

CALLAN: Goodbye, Mary Lee.

(He dials number)

LONELY: (SOV) Hallo?

PHONE BOOTH. DAY.

LONELY making a call. CALLAN opens booth door.

CALLAN: You going to be long?
LONELY: Nearly through, guv.

(A woman walks past.)

LONELY: I got it, Mr Callan. Cost you a fiver. (Hands over a phial of liquid.) Nasty stuff that is. Makes you drunk like.
CALLAN: Makes you vicious. Lets you say all the things you keep bottled up. Latent aggression release.
LONELY: I don't get it, Mr Callan.
CALLAN: It means the nicer you are, the worse this stuff makes you. (Beat) You go, home and put your best suit on. I've got another job for you - up West.

INT. WEST END BAR. DAY.

BARMAN fairly busy. City gents and the odd couple with aperitifs. LONELY at bar, drinking lager. CALLAN and MARY LEE enter. CALLAN ignores LONELY, sits MARY LEE between LONELY and himself.

BARMAN: Yes sir?

CALLAN: Whisky sour and a double whisky - straight.

(BARMAN goes.)

CALLAN: We might as well have lunch later - we've got time.

MARY LEE: All the time in the world.

(He gives her a cigarette and a light.)

MARY LEE: Still off them?

CALLAN: Still off them. So don't tempt me.

MARY LEE: I'll remember that, when we get back to your place.

(The drinks arrive. CALLAN pays. LONELY knocks Mary Lee's bag to floor. She looks down.)

LONELY: I'm sorry, Miss.

MARY LEE: That's all right.

(LONELY fusses, picking up bag. As he does so, CALLAN empties phial in Mary Lee's drink. He hands her the bag, she turns to CALLAN.)

CALLAN: Cheers.

MARY LEE: Good luck. (She sips.)

CALLAN: Come on. This is to us.

(She takes a long drink.)

MARY LEE: Wow. What do they put in this stuff? (Louder) Wow - whee. Hey. This is all right. What d'you say, David?

CALLAN: It's marvellous. (To BARMAN) Give her another.

BARMAN: Sir?

CALLAN: I said give her another.

MARY LEE: You heard the man. Give me another.

BARMAN: Sir - I don't think –

MARY LEE: Give me another or he'll pull your ears off. That right, David?

CALLAN: One at a time or both together. You can choose.

BARMAN: Just one drink sir.

CALLAN: Make it straight Scotch.

(BARMAN shrugs. MARY LEE sips again. BARMAN brings Scotch. CALLAN pays, pours it into the whisky-sour glass.)

MARY LEE: It's about time. (She drinks again.) I think you should pull his ears off anyway. They stick out. (To BARMAN - loudly.) Your ears stick out.

BARMAN: (to CALLAN) Sir - don't you think - ?

MARY LEE: David thinks I'm right. That's what David thinks. Your ears stick out and that guy there is ugly and that one needs a shave and that one's been looking at my legs ever since I came in here.

(She indicates each one. Her voice is very loud. She turns to Lonely.) And as for you my friend, you stink! You know that? You stink like a skunk farm. (She leans forward. CALLAN hooks her stool away. She crashes into LONELY who hits a waiter. The waiter staggers back, pours drinks over a group at a table.) Hey. That was great. Let's do it again.

(She advances on LONELY.)

LONELY: You keep off me. This suit cost forty quid.

MARY LEE: Ah, come on –

(She advances on him. LONELY lifts his hands to protect himself.)

LONELY: Keep off.

CALLAN: You touch her and I'll flatten you.

LONELY: Look what she's done to my suit.

(The waiter and other customers start to complain - louder - louder.)

MARY LEE: Shut up, will you? Shut up.

(She opens her mouth and screams over the noise of the customers, who, seen from her POV, look more and more distorted.)

INT. CHARGE ROOM. DAY.

MARY LEE with D.D.I. She looks ill, weak.

D.D.I.: Drunk and disorderly, disturbing the peace, assault, damage to property - you could go inside for this.

MARY LEE: But I only had two drinks.

D.D.I.: That's not what your friend said miss.

MARY LEE: David?

D.D.I.: You'd been drinking all night, hadn't you miss?

MARY LEE: David Callan said that?

D.D.I.: I tell you straight, I don't like you or your kind. You were lucky last night - but I bet you're up to your neck in drugs too.

MARY LEE: I hate drugs.

D.D.I.: Of course you do, just like you hate drink. Now, I know who you are and what you are and I'm going to give you a choice. You can get out of this country now – voluntarily; or I'll have you deported. And if you come back here again I'll see you land up inside. All right, which is it to be?

MARY LEE:	O.K. I'll leave.
D.D.I.:	I'll send a policewoman to help you pack - and you get the first plane I can find.
MARY LEE:	Back to the States?
D.D.I.:	They're welcome to you. (He rises) Mr Callan's still here. You can have five minutes with him.
MARY LEE:	No –
D.D.I.:	Suit yourself - but he's the only friend you've got.
MARY LEE:	I'll see him.

(He goes. CALLAN enters.)

MARY LEE:	That man says you're the only friend I've got.
CALLAN:	You need more than one, Mary Lee.
MARY LEE:	Not like you, I don't. You bastard. You rotten bastard. You put something in my drink, didn't you?
CALLAN:	Yes.
MARY LEE:	You're just like my father, d'you know that Callan? You get me and use me - and then you betray me.
CALLAN:	I did it for you.
MARY LEE:	My father always says that too. What shall I do now, David darling? Go back to him and betray my friends?
CALLAN:	Go away by yourself. Think. Find out who your friends are.
MARY LEE:	I know who they are and I'm going back to them, now. You'll be seeing me again, Callan - and next time, I'll be ready for you.
CALLAN:	Goodbye then. (He goes)
MARY LEE:	I hate you, Callan. I hate you.

INT. V.I.P. LOUNGE. DAY.

HUNTER watches from window. SECRETARY hurries in.

SECRETARY:	I'm awfully sorry, sir. Mr Meres' plane was delayed taking off. He won't be in till later.
HUNTER:	That's all right.
SECRETARY:	You have another job for him, sir?
HUNTER:	I thought I had. Yes. It seems I was wrong.

(He watches as MARY LEE comes into airport lounge. FILM: escorted by policewoman. SECRETARY joins him. HUNTER looks further into lounge (FILM) where CALLAN stands.)

SECRETARY:	Callan sir?

HUNTER: Yes, Callan. He fouled it up.

SECRETARY: You going to take any action against him, sir?

HUNTER: No. Not this time. It's already been done.

(He watches as MARY LEE and POLICEWOMAN reach CALLAN. CALLAN steps forward. MARY LEE walks past him without a glance.)